They *were*
the beautiful people

From Washington's halls of power to New York's glitzy discos, they clawed their way to the gilded top of the turbulent seventies. Five friends bound by passion, ambition...and the scandalous secret that nearly destroyed them.

MERITT DU NORD. The promise of fame on Broadway lured darkly exotic Meritt to New York. Pounding pavements did not deter her; vain and selfish lovers did.

LISA DUNNING. Rich, beautiful, and emotionally bankrupt, ruthless Lisa played in the fast lane. "Adore me" was her motto, lovers were her playthings, and "comeuppance" was a word she would learn the hard way.

LAUREL WILLIAMS. The driven daughter of a political legend, she seemed destined for a brilliant future—until the shocking past threatened to destroy her life.

SAM ROSS. Picture-perfect and super-sexy, he was much too nice for the nightmare fate had in store for him.

MARTIN VANDERZIEL. Vengeance and destruction were second nature to Martin. A psychotic millionaire father and a Vietnam prison commandant had seen to that.

Also by Ann Miller

NOTORIOUS
WILD NIGHTS

Published by
POPULAR LIBRARY

GUILTY PLEASURES

ANN MILLER

POPULAR LIBRARY

An Imprint of Warner Books, Inc.

A Warner Communications Company

POPULAR LIBRARY EDITION

Popular Library® and the fanciful P design are registered trade-marks of Warner Books, Inc.

Cover photo by Pat Hill

Popular Library books are published by
Warner Books, Inc.
666 Fifth Avenue
New York, N.Y. 10103

 A Warner Communications Company

Printed in the United States of America

First Printing: September, 1988

10 9 8 7 6 5 4 3 2 1

• *One* •

Fifteen-year-old Meritt du Nord huddled in a closet and waited for her father to come kill her. Her fist was jammed in her mouth to stifle her jagged breathing; her arms gripped her legs tightly together. Her mother's best dress, fragrant with lingering perfume, hung against Meritt's face. The scent of lavender combined with the shadowy blackness and her fear and fixed inside her memory forever.

Downstairs, Philip du Nord tore from room to room in full froth, bellowing like a madman. "Meritt! Where are you, you little sow? When I find you I'm going to smash this board right through your skull!" Meritt heard a two-by-four crack against a wall. "You hear that? You'd better hide good, girl, 'cause when I find you I'm gonna split your face wide open. I'm gonna teach you a lesson you'll never forget."

The daughter-beating monster was a side of Philip du Nord people would never have recognized. A solid citizen of Tangipahoa Parish, he was darkly handsome, with an aristocratic Creole face and a Clark Gable smile. He moved through crowds like a force of nature, briskly winning everyone in his path. Men strove not to wince as he aggressively shook their hands. Little old ladies made him pitchers of lemonade as he repaired their roofs and fixed their plumbing; and when they pretended they wanted to pay him, he always said, "No charge. Just tell all your friends to come on out to the Park."

The kids at Meritt's school wished that roguish, down-to-earth, uncomplicated Philip du Nord was *their* dad. They envied Meritt quadruply, for she was older-looking and beautiful, she was smart, and on top of everything else, she got to live at the Louisiana Wildlife Park.

The Louisiana Wildlife Park was the kind of entertainment that is so uniquely American, the roadside mom-and-pop amusement park. It was located on a particularly scenic mist-shrouded stretch of bayou that drew in tourists headed for New Orleans. Meritt's family owned and operated the attraction, a large petting zoo where visitors could feed and photograph tame deer, elk, buffalo, game birds, and small bear, as well as animals indigenous to Louisiana —armadillo, wart hogs, wild turkeys. The Wildlife Park endowed the four du Nord children with idyllic childhoods, since they got to care for and play with the animals on exhibit. Their mother ran the souvenir shop, where you could buy dried Spanish moss, cotton balls, and sea monkeys—microscopic powdered shrimp that came to wormy life when dumped in water.

Philip had built an adjoining "Mystery Vortex," a large shed in which gravity appeared to play bizarre tricks. Compasses didn't work inside it. Balls rolled uphill. People in the building found themselves leaning toward its middle at a ten-degree angle. Their cigarette smoke made spirals, and a thirty-pound ball hung at an angle from a chain. There were no supernatural forces at work in the Vortex, though the du Nords swore there was. It was an optical illusion Philip had built using a compass, a plumb bob, a light meter and a carpenter's level.

Philip du Nord could do anything, Meritt believed when she was little. He had grown up a swamp rat in the bayou, and he was on intimate terms with the murky bogs and their teeming abundance of wildlife. He taught her how to identify birds by their calls and mammals by the tracks they left in the rich Mississippi mud. Philip taught her jokes and songs and the constellations by night. Her father was her hero.

Then she changed and he changed, along with his business. In the mid-sixties, the intersection of Highways 55 and 12 were upgraded and moved several miles south and west of the Louisiana Wildlife Park. New freeways all over the country were diverting traffic from the tourist attractions that had flourished on two-lane highways like U.S. Route 66. The wonders of California's Disneyland were imitated in smaller regional complexes like Worlds of Fun and Six Flags over Texas. Vacationing families headed for the slick, high-tech theme parks, which were quickly driving roadside tourist traps to extinction. To better support his family and business, Philip got a machinist job in a factory forty miles away. When he was home nights and weekends, he took care of the Wildlife Park business that his wife and four children couldn't handle.

About the same time he started working away from home, Meritt's body started to ripen under a child's clothes. Meritt didn't pay much attention to the fullness of her figure until she overheard a tourist lady snap at her mother, "*Dress that girl properly!*" Her breasts were no longer small, and her jeans were too tight in the hips and too big around the waist. At age eleven her ivory flesh had the lush radiance of a sexually mature woman's.

The first time Philip struck her was an evening when she wasn't bringing food to the table fast enough. He was hot and exhausted after a day at the factory, and Meritt was dawdling, talking on the phone to her best friend. All of a sudden, the receiver was yanked out of her hand. Her father picked her up and body-slammed her to the floor, then started punching her. She felt the shock of his closed fists more than she felt the pain. It seemed he would never stop. When he finished, Philip snarled, "I'll get supper myself, dammit. I have to do everything around here." Slowly un-curling from her fetal position on the floor, Meritt saw her older brother and her younger brother and sister regarding her in stupefaction. Behind them stood her mother, who averted her eyes and turned away.

Cecile du Nord never contradicted her husband, so she wasn't about to come to the defense of her daughter. Meritt could read clearly the guilty expression on her face: *Better her than me*. Nor did she offer any aid during the attacks to come. Cecile looked away when Philip would toss Meritt across the living room, pin her to the wall, punch her and spit in her face. Increasingly, when Meritt's siblings sassed Philip, he'd strike them, too. But Meritt was singled out for unprovoked attacks, and her brothers and sister joined in the entertainment by ridiculing her.

Ironically, the pain and hurt Meritt sustained made her even lovelier by etching character into her face prematur-ely. By the time she was thirteen, her expression was fully, regally adult, the chin held high above the delicate stem of her neck. Both her parents were descended from the Creole, the caste of refined, French-speaking quadroons of old New Orleans. An offspring of mixed marriages, Philip and Cecile both had endured childhood taunts like, "*You* been touched by the *tarbrush!*" They had European fea-tures but skin that was slightly darker than most whites'. Their child Meritt had an exotic, almost Hispanic look. Her nose was delicately pointed up, with small, flaring nostrils, and her lips were as plump as a tulip. She had knowing amber eyes set deeply behind a sweep of eyelashes and a high, broad forehead that came to a widow's peak from which her hair tumbled thickly in masses of waves. Though she looked absolutely Caucasian, Meritt was proud of her mixed blood.

Meritt's sultry hothouse beauty provoked Philip du Nord

to concoct scenarios that didn't exist. He was sure that all men viewed her as he did, as a provocative vixen whose hips moved in oiled undulations as she walked. He imagined that every man and boy alive who saw Meritt wanted her, and many did. Philip had seen for himself how men could not turn away from her seductive eyes, framed by her creamy face and thick raven hair. Before she reached her teens she had real breasts like a woman, and Philip envisioned her as an antebellum octoroon courtesan decked in silks with fiery diamonds lying cold against her décolletage, where the skin was the color of wax candles.

That a father should hold such depraved thoughts was deeply shaming to Philip. He couldn't bring himself to tell his priest that he was frightened by the emergence of his daughter's womanhood. The only relief open to him was to blame Meritt for arousing him and making him unhappy. On the slightest excuse he'd yell, "You think you're some kind of princess sashaying around here, don't you?" or, "Trying to sneak off again to your boyfriends, you little slut?" He'd flog her as though trying to beat the demons out of himself, and for short periods, it worked. By punishing her he could punish himself.

Meritt could only whimper in emotional anguish, for if her father heard her cry aloud, he'd thrash her all over again. The physical pain was bearable; the tortured bewilderment was not. Why did he hate her so much? Her friends thought she was faultless, yet Philip treated her as if she were a criminal. He never had a kind word for her anymore. He was never contrite. Why did the rest of the family back him up? She could not endure her mother's complicity by silence. And what had she done to lose the sibling loyalty she'd known throughout childhood?

At school Meritt could keep her home existence a secret. She was a top student, and much admired. The other girls tried to copy her special saunter, her husky laugh, her one-line cracks. Actually, there was no need for Philip du Nord to pretend to be the guardian of her virtue; level-headed

Meritt did a good job at cooling young men's fires all by herself. If a boy of any age tried to get close to her, she'd quell his lust by making a funny face at him.

When Meritt was in the ninth grade, a high school teacher thought he recognized a certain star quality in her and suggested that she join the drama club. Meritt initially enjoyed the drama club because it was one more extracurricular activity that kept her after school. She found herself able to get away from reality for a while. The drama coach gave her the female lead in "The Little Foxes," and she displayed surprising depth and potential.

Life was fine for Meritt while she was at school, where she had all the popularity and respect a teenager could wish for. She also enjoyed the nightly task of cleaning out the exhibit pens of all the animals at Louisiana Wildlife Park, because the time alone allowed her to daydream recklessly about future stardom on Broadway, on television, in movies, about glowing reviews and rewards to come. Once she went back to the house, Meritt had to listen for her father's tread and divine whether he was in a relaxed mood, or if he was tired after a hard day at work. At such times a blow might strike her from out of nowhere, then her father would pound her body till she was bruised or bleeding. By her sixteenth birthday she was certain that he planned on killing her. She had to get out of the house before he succeeded, but there was no place for her to go.

One day in civics class, Meritt learned a way the government could help her out of her predicament. She applied to the program, but she knew her chances of being selected were so remote that she forgot all about it.

Meritt tracked her father's footfalls as he raced from room to room downstairs. She tried fiercely to remember anything she'd done recently that might have triggered today's attack. Had she done all her chores this morning? The closet's lavender scent was cloying in her nostrils. She could feel the floor under her vibrate as he pounded up the stairs. The footsteps came into the room, and Meritt was so scared that she lost a second's control over her bladder. The closet door flew open and a sickly yellow light assaulted her eyes. Philip shouted triumphantly. "Thought you could get away, huh? You can't outsmart me!"

"Dad, I'm sorry—" Meritt said automatically, but then her arm felt as if it were being ripped from the socket as Philip used it to haul her from the closet floor. He lifted his doubled-over belt and brought it down on her back so forcefully that her T-shirt ripped. Meritt saw how his face was flushed with the passion of his fury. She twisted and writhed in the grasp of his arm as he wielded the belt in his other hand. It went up again, then it came down on Meritt's forehead. She stared up at him over the warm blood that began to trickle over her eyes. The words choked out of her. "Why me?"

"Don't you look at me," Philip roared. Meritt threw her free arm up to take the next blow. He brought the belt down against the side of her face, and she felt herself losing consciousness.

After some time she opened her eyes and saw flecks of her blood on the rug. Philip was gone, and Meritt's only thought was that she had to run away, before the next unprovoked onslaught ended her life.

Meritt lurched upward to get on her feet. Slowly she made her way down the stairs to the bathroom to wash herself. The house seemed empty. She passed through the kitchen and noticed the Saturday mail tossed on the kitchen table. The envelope on top was addressed to her. The return address was the blue-and-gold seal of the U.S. Congress.

With shaking fingers she took out the parchment letter, which was signed by one of the U.S. senators from Louisiana. It was dated the previous Tuesday of August 1970. The letter began, "I am very happy to tell you—". The

U.S. Congress wanted her in Washington, D.C., to work as a Capitol page!

She wasn't needed until *January* of 1971. That was six months away! Then a smile touched her lips, and she was imbued with a strange self-assurance. She'd survive till then. She'd make damn sure of it.

A haze of lethargy hung over the high school study hall at Lubbock Senior High. Some of the students whispered and passed notes across the aisles; most sat propped up on their arms, pretending to be awake. Samuel A. Ross sat with a book spread open before him. His firm chin rested on a fist. Outside the window Sam could see dust blow through the streets. The airborne dirt turned every building an exhausted pumpkin color. It was only March, and already the annual dust storms were visiting Lubbock, the tornadoes right behind them. There were 179,000 people in Lubbock, and most of them grew cotton. At night they listened to Wolfman Jack on the radio, along with Brother Al selling autographed pictures of Jesus. The last notable event in Lubbock had occurred ten years ago, when flying saucers flew over the city in squadrons. They came to be known as the "Lubbock Lights." Buddy Holly had managed to escape Lubbock at an early age. Why couldn't Sam do the same thing?

His gaze went to the clock that trapped him at his desk. The dismal reality was that he was only seventeen, near the end of his junior year. School was a chalk-smelling prison in which he was forced to do time, and he felt he didn't have much in common anymore with the other inmates. Would his friends like him so much if they knew what he thought of them: that they'd never make it out of town?

Sam knew something was wrong with his life. A certain discontent sat heavily on him, but there was nothing specific he could put a finger on, but one thing was sure: this town, this state had nothing more to offer him.

Sam was a shining example of the American Dream, the man who triumphs at every venture he undertakes. He excelled at every sport he played and had been captain of the state championship football team of 1968. Sam was tall, intelligent, and, because he loved to read, well-educated. His teachers respected him, for he voiced his opinions confidently but softly. He was always happy when he could assist a friend, and for a seventeen-year-old he was amazingly thoughtful and considerate. And he was incredibly handsome. His eyes were a brilliant green; his bright white teeth were as even as the rest of his features, and his untidy thatch of sun-kissed, dark honey hair fell over his eyes in a way that made girls want to reach out and brush it back.

If he'd been aware of how dazzling his exterior was, he would have been uncomfortable with his looks.

Sam had not always been so attractive. He was born with a cleft palate and ears that stuck out like car doors. "Promise me you'll have plastic surgery performed on him as soon as he's old enough," Arva Ross begged her husband, Marvin Ross. It was a deathbed wish, for she died from complications resulting from her pregnancy's interaction with her crippling asthma. Marvin saw to it that his infant son went under the knife, and he became a beautiful little boy with only a tiny scar above his upper lip.

Marvin Ross never married again, and Sam was his only child. Marvin was a tax attorney. To him there was only one way of life, that of self-discipline and moderation. He was so proper that he did his gardening in his vest and watch chain. He never dated after Arva's death, but he gave Sam a pleasant childhood. Marvin had a midwestern accent, and Sam picked it up, so no trace of Texas marked' him. Both Rosses were so indifferent to Texas style that neither one of them even owned a pair of cowboy boots.

The foundation of Sam's upbringing was Catholicism. As a child he had even felt a passing interest in becoming a priest. He didn't attend parochial school but had had never dated a girl who wasn't Catholic. His girlfriend, Theresa

Mayhen, was president of Saint Perpetua's youth group.
Though Sam was free of the self-righteousness that charac-
terizes the ultra-pious, his faith shaped the way he saw the
world.

Sam had broken nearly every one of the commandments at
one time or another, but the church forgave. He committed
adultery at age sixteen by sleeping with the lonely twenty-
two-year-old wife of a traveling oil worker. Audrey Lopper
had been new to the neighborhood when she first eyed Sam
fixing steak for supper on an outdoor grill. "What a hunk o'
lettuce," she murmured in awe. The next day she asked
Marvin if his son ever mowed lawns. "Sure, I'll send him
right over," Marvin replied guilelessly.

When Sam had finished her yard, Audrey told him, "Step
into the kitchen a second." He entered the house. Sweat
gleamed seductively over his torso, which was as muscular
as that of a high-relief Grecian athlete statue. As Audrey
fished through her purse, she asked shyly, "Do you like me?"

Sam knew exactly what she wanted. "Sure, I like you
fine." With a silent "Why not?" he wrapped his arms
around her to deliver a powerful wet soul kiss that led to an
uncommonly fine consummation. He didn't get paid for
the lawn work, not in money.

Sam went back to Audrey twice before he decided to be
a man and tell her, "This is no good. Ask your husband to
come home more often." He didn't feel guilty about his
introduction to lovemaking; he viewed it as a rite of passage. He knew enough of the wonderful pleasure to want to
save it to share with a special woman.

Recently, his girlfriend Theresa had been demanding that
they have sex. "I want to go to bed with you, like we're
married." With infallible logic, she'd point out, "Your dad's
at work all day. We could do it right, at your house, while he's
gone." Underlying her insistent pleas was the solid assump-
tion that they would marry. "We're the ideal couple, Sam.
Everyone says so—you tall and fair and me smaller and
dark-haired." Sam knew that to touch Theresa was to obli-

gate himself for life. One touch of a virginal breast and he'd be bound to her by guilt. Making love was the way to make shackles, to make babies. Theresa was fun to spend time with, but not a lifetime. With every kiss Sam felt Theresa was adding a link to an iron chain that would hold him in bondage. Sam had to unload her before she mentioned anything more about china, silver and crystal patterns. He wanted to shed it all like a snake's skin and disappear from Lubbock.

Even his father sympathized with Sam's small-town blues. Marvin had put in the good word to Texas Representative Clayton Thormond when Sam had applied to the U.S. Senate to become a page. Pages were the teenage "go-fers" who ran errands, answered phones and shuttled messages for U.S. congressmen. The job was a front-row seat to history in action, and the pay was excellent. And when the day was done, the young pages were done with all adult supervision. Their lives were their own.

Sam stared at a portrait of Andrew Smith I in his book and brooded. In Washington he could research the life of "Smitty" Smith, who really interested him. The Republican senator from Michigan had run against Franklin Roosevelt in the presidential election of 1936.* Though thousands of Americans had regarded Smitty as a shining ideal of statesmanship, he had left the public arena after the 1936 campaign. As the decades slipped past, Smitty drifted into oblivion. Sam knew he hadn't died yet, and he was rumored to be a recluse in some Virginia suburb.

Shaking off his reverie, Sam glanced around at the other students in study hall. One girl was giggling, another whistling, another eating Twinkies. Some kid was making rude noises and jabbing the student ahead of him. Of three girls in a row, the first was ripping paper out of a notebook and

*Author's note: Alf Landon was the candidate who actually ran against Franklin Roosevelt in 1936. "Smitty" Smith is a fictional character and no resemblance to the real candidate is intended.

crumpling it, the next was snapping gum, and the one behind
her was snapping a cigarette lighter open and shut. The boy
across the aisle from Sam started to sing "Yankee Doodle"
while belching. Then the bell rang. Sam slipped shut the
book and rose to join the elbowing crush toward the door.

When Sam got home that evening, his father greeted him
with a bemused smile. He held up an envelope. The return
address was Clayton Thormond's at the U.S. Capitol.
"Lookee here," Mr. Ross teased, "What do you suppose
Representative Thormond wants with you?"

"Exedent. E-X-E-D-E-N-T. Exedent," the Alaskan girl
spelled briskly. A large audience of parents, teachers and
children clapped dutifully for her. They were at the forty-
third annual National Spelling Bee, sponsored by newspapers throughout the United States. This year, eight million
children had participated at the local level. At the end of May
1970, 185 state champs showed up in Washington, D.C., for
the national contest. This afternoon, nine girls and six boys
had survived the cut going into the ninth and final round of
competition. Of those fifteen, the process of elimination had
left three finalists standing on the stage of a Mayflower Hotel
ballroom. The crowded air reeked of nervous tension, and
the audience's muted voices provided a steady level of noise.

"Macerate," was the word the judges hurled at the sole
boy left, a sallow-faced fifteen-year-old from What Cheer,
Oklahoma. Sweat ran down either side of his beaky nose.
"Macerate," he repeated. "M-A-S-E-R-." The judges
flagged him down, and the boy turned away with a stran-
gled sob. That left only the Alaskan contender and Laurel
Williams of Omaha, Nebraska.

Laurel looked like an airline stewardess in a navy blazer,
white shirt and grey skirt. She smoothed an invisible wrin-
kle on her skirt, took a deep breath and successfully spelled
"elucubrate." There was fear in the other finalist's face;
then she spelled "vouchsafe" correctly. The Alaskan girl

was of Eskimo descent, Laurel thought. Or she was an Inuit, rather—wasn't that what Eskimos preferred to be called nowadays?

She wondered if her rival had as much stake in the spelling contest as Laurel did. If the Alaskan placed second in the bee, she'd get one thousand dollars instead of the fifteen-hundred-dollar first prize. If Laurel won only second place, her mother wouldn't love her anymore.

Laurel's mother was the formidable Congresswoman Mavis Williams, one of Nebraska's three members elected to the U.S. House of Representatives. After ten years in Congress, Mavis had emerged a major force on the foreign relations and budget committees. She was known as the sharp-witted, spirited conservative with a gift for instant, penetrating analysis. As a right-wing Republican, she'd participated in moral crusades on the House floor; and though she'd been divorced and was on her own, she opposed the Equal Rights Amendment and legalized abortion. "Women's issues aren't necessarily the whole country's issues," she insisted.

Mavis had been in the national spotlight since her election in 1960, and so had her children. In an Omaha newspaper story Laurel had been called "an exceptionally bright girl who has it all together at an amazingly young age." Laurel *was* penetratingly bright, but after fifteen years as her mother's personal experiment, she was an emotional wreck.

Mavis had been determined to have a child in her own image, a child of accomplishment, so when her first child, a son, was born retarded, she was severely disappointed. Her next child, a girl, proved to be very intelligent, but she was handicapped by complete deafness. When Laurel came along as an "ordinary" baby, Mavis went right to work on her. Soon her time was devoted exclusively to her pet project and to politics, and when her husband left she scarcely noticed.

Laurel lived in Washington with her mother most of the year, where she attended the American School for children of

diplomats, congressmen and other government officials who
lived away from home states. She struggled, usually successfully, to meet her mother's unrealistic standards of con-
duct and scholarship. In grade school she founded a chess
club and a school newspaper, and she became the top performer in her gymnastics group. Laurel shone at her piano
and ballet recitals. She won most children's contests she
entered, such as essay writing, speechmaking and short-
story writing. People constantly congratulated Representative Williams on her intelligent, well-rounded daughter.

Laurel hated all of it. She simply wanted to love her
mother, but Mavis returned love in the form of a carrot that
was rewarded to Laurel or yanked away, depending on
whether her performance met strict standards. When Laurel
did anything Mavis didn't like, she expressed her attitude
with icy silence.

Laurel was totally incapable of resisting her mother's
will. She always played to Mavis's approval; she actually
had to woo her own mother. No matter how perfect she
tried to be, it seemed she could never quite do anything the
way Mavis wanted her to. Perfect wasn't good enough for
Representative Williams: she expected the *extraordinary*.

Though Mavis intended Laurel to mirror herself, mother
and daughter looked nothing alike. Approaching her mid-
fifties, Mavis's face was a tapestry of lines and wrinkles
that made her look wise and statesmanlike. Her hair and
eyes were matching battleship gray. Laurel was unremark-
able-looking for a fourteen-year-old, but she was getting
prettier. Her straight blade of a nose and finely arched eyebrows were patrician, while her high cheekbones, hollow
cheeks and wide lips added some drama and sensuality to
her face. Her hair was shiny dark brown, very dark brown,
with strands that burned auburn in sunlight. It was straight
and hung a little past her shoulders. She had vivid lapis
blue eyes, ringed with spiky long eyelashes.

Those eyes were as sharp as they were beautiful, and
Laurel's memory was virtually photographic. She shrewdly

scanned whatever came into view, and her brain stored away the data for future use. Teachers were amazed, and, sometimes, her friends were a little afraid, when Laurel instantly recalled the name of Kookie's restaurant on "77 Sunset Strip" (Dino's), or the year that Henry II ascended the throne of England (1154). There was no real trick to it; she only had to look. Such a memory was invaluable when it came to remembering the state capitals or spelling words. Words she remembered by pairing their syllables. Yet as gimmicky and unfailing as her memory was, Laurel had met her match in the Alaskan girl, who'd just managed "gelid."

"Lekvar," a judge called to Laurel. "A prune filling for Danish pastry. Lekvar."

She licked her dry lips. "Lekvar. L-E-K-V-A-R. Lekvar." As her opponent spelled the next word, "incisor," Laurel looked blankly into the dark crowd beyond the stage. Her mother wasn't out there. Mavis was in Nebraska this weekend, pressing the flesh and helping her son move into a group home for mentally disabled people. A retarded brother, a driven mother, a deaf sister, and the absence of a father made for complex family relationships.

"Shalloon," was Laurel's next challenge. She spelled it correctly, then automatically smiled widely, the way she'd been coached by her mother: "Learn how to smile right and people will forgive you anything."

In public, before her future constituency, Laurel could behave as if she'd been tutored in charm by ten Miss Americas. But away from strangers, Laurel disintegrated into a closet neurotic mess. The drive for perfection had taken its toll. She had started smoking heavily in junior high. She quit any school activity that demanded physical exertion. Her intellect twisted and acquired a cynical edge. Over time Laurel's speaking voice turned rusty and ragged, as though its trip through her larynx was a treacherous one. She drank gallons of coffee and skipped meals because of a nervous stomach, till her wrists were no thicker than a bundle of twigs.

Laurel held up to the spelling of "staphylococci," and the other girl onstage gasped. Then she took on "deification," and the ball was back in Laurel's court.

"'Maculature.' An impression made from an engraved plate to remove ink from recessed areas. 'Maculature.'" The word echoed hollowly at Laurel. Her mind blanked out. She felt panic and she tried to keep hopelessness out of her voice.

"'Maculature,'" she said. "M-A-C-H-A—"

The crowd went wild, and the opponent's flat golden face lit up. Laurel had given her a chance at first place. Now was the moment of truth. "Hydrophyte," was the next word at bat, and the girl spelled it without hesitation. Laurel felt as though she had been slugged above the heart. Dazed, she turned to hug the winner. She made a tremendous effort to collect herself as people swarmed up onto the stage. Mechanically she accepted the congratulations from strangers and her teachers. She collected a silver trophy cup, and an envelope was pressed into her fingers. It contained the thousand dollars she'd earned as first runner-up.

As soon as she could exit gracefully, Laurel went out a side door of the hotel into the May sunshine and lit a Camel. The first inhalation was a blessing to her lungs, though the familiar feeling of disappointing her mother had turned her body leaden. Slowly she began walking west toward the Watergate Hotel, where she shared an apartment with Mavis. First runner-up. It wasn't good enough. It just wasn't good enough.

Laurel was sure she was the only spelling-bee contestant who could walk home instead of taking a plane. Awash in self-pity, she muttered, "I'm so tired I wish I was dead. I'm so tired I wish I'd never been born."

After forty-five minutes of trudging and chain-smoking, Laurel walked into the lobby of the C-shaped Watergate. The doorman nodded at her. Using a multitude of keys, she unlocked her door. A pile of mail lay on the black-and-white tiled floor of the foyer. On an hickory end table sat the phone

and an answering machine, whose red light was on, signify-
ing messages. Laurel hit the rewind, and Representative
Williams's voice streamed out of the speaker at her: "I've
been told you didn't win the spelling bee. That's not any
daughter of mine," she chided in a singsong. Laurel shook
her head, marveling over her mother's network of contacts.
Mavis always knew the news the moment it happened. She
had more sources of information than the KGB.

"And another thing," the voice went on. "Bert Nowacki
—the representative from Kansas, you'll recall—says you
can work as a page on the Hill under his sponsorship, if
you want."

Lisa Dunning slid off the rumpled hotel bed and reached
for her purse. She took out a hairbrush and slowly, luxuriously, began to brush her silver-gilt blond hair. Aloofly she
posed herself before the mirror so the image of her hair and
body would be doubled for best effect. Her high school
trigonometry teacher lay back on the pillows, replete, sated
and gloating, his face twisted with lustful appreciation. Her
body was the sweet, slender form of a Botticelli virgin with
the smoothness of ivory, her face was exquisite and she
hadn't reached her full growth yet!

If anyone had ever told Mike Litton that someday he
would bed down with a seventeen-year-old student, he
would have reacted as if he'd been called a child molester.
Mike was fortyish, a staunch, double-chinned family man,
and one of the better instructors at Sumter Day School in
Charleston, South Carolina. Till recently he'd lived a mor-
ally correct life of full fidelity to his spouse. The teenage
boys and girls he taught were nothing more to him than
sexless, pimply children from well-heeled families. Outside the classroom, he didn't give a thought to his students,
what they were like, what they did with their precarious
adolescences.

Lisa Dunning, daughter of a trucking magnate, stood out

from the crowd because of her rare and classical pulchritude. Her face was luminous with a young child's innocence, yet Lisa carried herself with the sophisticated poise of a woman in her thirties. The combination was highly provocative. Mike had never seen a young person exhibit such self-assurance. Her bearing was that of someone who would never stumble, never fall. So when she'd entered his trigonometry class last year, in autumn of 1969, Mike was surprised to discover that she was a math illiterate. She dutifully attended class, but she never turned in homework, and she only pretended to take the tests, handing in blank test forms. Litton got the idea she assumed he'd silently assented to join her in some sort of conspiracy.

In October, Mike had finally asked Lisa to stay after class. Before he could bring up the problem at hand, Lisa bent over his desk and propositioned. "Mistah Litton, couldn't we discuss this better . . . somewhere else . . . like at a hotel?" He froze, unsure of what he'd heard. The manipulative magnolia in her voice bloomed and she leaned forward suggestively. "Mistah Litton, a southern gentleman *nevah* refuses the request of a lady."

Mike Litton didn't think twice; in fact, he didn't think at all. He followed Lisa to his car, and they made haste to a chain motel outside of town, where her troubles with trigonometry went unmentioned. They continued to meet about once a week, to Mike's ongoing delight. Lisa Dunning's face and body inflamed his senses. He spent pleasurable hours speculating which quality of Lisa's was the more sexually enticing, the unparalleled beauty, or her air of guileless innocence. He found himself excited about breaking the traditional taboos against consorting with jailbait.

During sex she never exhibited arousal, much less erotic skill. She'd drape her arms around Mike and make some noises, but basically, she only had to be there. Her teacher enjoyed her just the way she was, and didn't make attempts at schooling her in sexual techniques—arts he didn't possess in abundance himself.

During one Saturday afternoon's interlude in December, Mike slid himself off Lisa's supine form and sighed with the deepest content. His partner was staring at the ceiling. She put on a smile for him as soon as she realized he was looking at her.

Mike indicated their hotel room with a gesture that managed to take in their entire affair. "Lisa, what are you getting out of all this?"

The marble-sized azure-blue eyes widened. "Whah, Mistah Litton—Ah'm getting an 'A' in your class, you know that!"

Litton was only momentarily astounded as he understood how Lisa earned some of her superior school marks: she paid for them with sex. Then he felt moronic for believing that she'd been attracted to his animal magnetism rather than his grading power. When she had propositioned him, she'd seemed just like eighteen-year-old Cleopatra tumbling out of a rolled carpet to offer herself to Caesar. He'd allowed himself to believe she was his!

He'd wrecked his honor to enter an affair with Lisa; now, by giving her "A's" for a class she'd stopped attending, he'd thrown away his integrity as well. Now, in May 1970, he watched Lisa dress and wondered if it had all been worth it. He watched with regret as she fastened a pristine white bra over her tender, babyfat breasts and pulled underpants up over the sweet blond pubic hair, concealing her body parts from his sight.

"Mistah Litton, when were the fourth term report cards mailed out?" Lisa asked lazily, sliding a yellow cotton skirt up her legs.

He reached for his watch. "I believe they're going out today."

"And did you give me a final 'A' for the year?"

"Of course! You deserve it," Mike said with laughing sarcasm.

Lisa was checking the back of her outfit in the big mirror over the standard motel dresser. "Too bad this will be the last time we see each other."

"What?" Litton sat up straight in bed. Blood rushed to his face.

"I want to thank you for giving me the grade I wanted all four quarters." Lisa's southern accent evaporated when she wanted to be assertive.

"And today you damn well made sure I couldn't alter your *final* grade." He was beginning to feel that he'd been used like a laboratory rat. "You're one of those who goes for grades instead of an education. Good Christ, if at college you throw as much energy into studying as you do into your little performances, you'll make Phi Beta Kappa!"

"We've served our purposes. The agreement is concluded."

"What about my feelings?" Mike was surprised to hear himself protest. He began to slide out of bed, then sat back, pulling the sheet up over his torso so his out-of-shape, middle-aged body couldn't be viewed. She'd never seen his full body at one time. "We had something more going here than a goddam *agreement!*" The loss of illicit trysts with Lisa abruptly seemed unendurable. He tried blackmail. "What if the principal of Sumter Day School finds out you're well known around Charleston's 'no-tell motels'?"

Lisa gave a short, dry laugh. "Now, *who* is that you're going to complain to? The principal? The administration? Your wife?" Litton's double chin sagged. Fully dressed, Lisa walked to the door. She turned the knob, then turned to look directly at her teacher. "I gave you more than sexual favors, Litton. *I supplied your fantasy when reality had denied you.*"

The door closed. Mike stared at the mirror in which Lisa had just been primping. He had no idea she could be so articulate. Dammit all, she was right.

Lisa had to cut the speed of her powerful Corvette Sting-ray convertible as she neared the area of Charleston known as the old city. She loved to tear along the local freeways with her gleaming mane streaming horizontally behind her as if levitated. The passengers of every car she passed smiled admiringly at the spectacle of the blonde racing at the speed of sound in the low-slung, fire-engine-red sports car.

She drove by Market Street's tile-roofed antebellum arcades without seeing them. Lisa coasted down Broad Street, the street that was so important to "live below," according to distinguished Charlestonians. The colors of old and elegant great houses, swishing palmettos and black wrought iron, elaborately worked, blinked at her in shades of light and dark as she passed them. The air of her neighborhood was scented with Cape jessamine, oleander, and coral vine. She zipped into the alleyway that led to the Dunning courtyard. Without bothering to garage the Corvette, she stopped and leaped out of the car, leaving the key in the ignition. Like most other spoiled children, Lisa didn't take care of her playthings.

The brick three-story home she entered was famous for its splendid architecture. Her father and mother had moved here from Toledo, Ohio, when she was five and had purchased the house from the descendants of its builder. As crassly industrial, northern outsiders, the Dunnings had never been invited to join the Hibernian or St. Cecelia Societies or attend their balls. The artistic and historic merit of the house meant nothing to the Dunnings except as a reflection of their rise. It symbolized old money, which was the only distinction they cared about. Ken Dunning had inherited the trucking wealth from his father and grandfather. He let others run the business while he traveled the country, slapping the backs and signing contracts, passing out bribes and "protection" funds to the mob.

Lisa was just about to ascend the impressive two-story-high circular stairway when she heard Ken Dunning's golf cleats clatter noisily on the black-marble main floor corridors. "Hold on there, moonpie," he said.

"What's up, Pop?" she asked blandly.

Dunnings's perpetual tan was the kind acquired through years spent on the greens of the world's championship golf courses. "I've got a surprise for you," he said, beaming with the joy of a giftgiver who was about to bestow an imaginative, well-thought-out present.

"What is it, Daddy?" Lisa squealed, her eyes sparkling with the expectation of one who had learned to only expect the best from the giftgiver.

"Six months in Washington, D.C. You're going to serve as a Senate page, same as your older brothers did."

"What!" Lisa wailed just as Mr. Litton had an hour before.

"Yup. Old Senator Lovett called to tell me so this morning," Mr. Dunning said. "It's a prestigious appointment, and you'll actually be earning a salary for the first time. They've even got their own little high school up there."

"But, Daddy, I wanna finish high school here. Next year I'm gonna graduate one of the top ten at Sumter Day School! I could be salutatorian or something! I don't wanna miss out on the graduation ceremonies!"

"You should be honored. Only senior members of Congress get to pick pages. It's one of their most cherished forms of patronage."

"But I'll be away from my friends! They'll forget me!"

"The kind of friends you hang out with are best forgotten—all those over-pampered rich thugs. You'll make better friends in Washington. Nineteen seventy-one is going to be the first year girls are allowed to work as pages. You'll be part of history." Mr. Dunning's voice was forcefully stern. "It did your two older brothers good to spend some time in our nation's Capitol, and my daughter's going to do it, too."

"But Bud and Bill said that you've gotta run errands all day, acting like you're every pea-brained congressman's slave nigger!"

"That's enough. You're going to Washington and you know it," Mr. Dunning said with dark finality. His expression lifted again as he withdrew a tiny velvet box from an inside pocket. "Here, this might make you feel better. It's a little gewgaw I picked up on impulse this morning."

Lisa snatched it out of his hand but didn't bother to open it as she ran up the stairs, sobbing dramatically. She slammed the door when she reached her moss-green damask bedroom. Its windows faced east, toward the Cooper River and Fort Sumter, where the first shot of the Civil War had been fired. Cracking open the jewelry box, she glanced just long enough to see that it held a pendant that was a mass of precious stones. With a face of extreme irritation she flung it onto the dresser, where her jewelry box was filled with similar pricey baubles. Why wouldn't her dad ever learn that her set didn't wear real jewelry! It was just so damn stodgy and grown-up.

Lisa petulantly tossed herself face down on the bed and wept loudly, uncaring that mascara was being smeared into the satin damask bedspread. God, she was going to be on the senior honor roll at Sumter Day School next year, and he didn't even care! Didn't every father want to see his kids honored for academic excellence! She had had all those gross, sweaty screwing sessions with teachers in whose subjects she was deficient, all for nothing! Didn't ambition count for anything to her dad? All that hard, hot work for nothing! *Nothing!*

• *Two* •

Lisa Dunning and Meritt du Nord leaned over the visitors' balcony that overlooked the ornate congressional chamber, trying to one-up each other by putting down the House pages who sat at the base of the speaker's huge multilevel podium.

"Look at him." Meritt pointed at a pomaded boy. "He looks like he combs his hair with buttered toast."

"Ah bet he's from Ah-owa," Lisa replied. During her first week in Washington, she'd quickly found that while folks back home were not fooled by her exaggerated southern accent, people here were easily duped, and charmed. "Jesus H. Christ on a popsicle stick. That femmy boy there—limping down the aisle—has got to be gay. Which rep brought *him* to Washington?"

"You know, I've always wondered . . . if a guy is gay and I'm attracted to him, does that mean *I'm* gay?"

"Not necessarily, but you'd be having problems."

Lisa and Meritt were pages for the Senate, the "upper body," and they didn't know many House pages yet. The Ninety-second Congress, under President Richard Nixon, had commenced on the third Tuesday of January, and they'd been working only three days. Just one of the House pages was a girl, and Meritt pointed her out. "That must be Mavis Williams's daughter." Lisa gave a grunt of recognition. "She looks like she came here straight from a reformatory." Sitting at a small mahogany table, Laurel Williams was biting her fingernails, eyes skittering around nervously. Her humped-over posture managed to make the page's uniform of blue jacket and skirt look even more ill-fitting that it was. "Isn't it unethical for a rep to appoint her own kid?" Meritt asked.

"Her mom took care of that. She got some other congressional stooge to let her daughter in here." Lisa's mind was already elsewhere. "Ah wonder who that prime slice of beef talking to her is. Sex *ahoy!*" Meritt blinked at the distance and saw the man—not a boy at all—a young man whose relaxed, old-fashioned masculinity was evident even from afar. Something Mavis Williams's daughter whispered back at him made him smile, and Meritt felt a pinch of envy, wishing she were the one who'd made him flash that open I-have-no-secrets grin.

Meritt said, "Well, you know who that is, the page leaning against the wall on the right?" Framed by the white marble wall was an unrealistically handsome young man with a forelock of black hair, an iron jaw, and an indistinct gaze. "That's Martin Vanderziel."

"You mean of *the* Vanderziels?" Lisa said disbelievingly.

"You're kidding me," Laurel whispered to Sam Ross.

"Of course not," Sam murmured. "And what's more incredible is that he's kind of a friend of mine. He asked me to room with him at the Vanderziels' Washington house. He says there's plenty of room there—he's the only person living in a twenty-room townhouse, besides the caretaker couple."

"Why were you lucky enough to be asked?"

"I don't know. He just seemed to take to me. He's not very talkative."

"You know, I hate to admit this, but I don't know all that much about the Vanderziels. I know that Old Man Vanderziel is a land developer..."

"Yes, with six billion dollars of projects in the ground, and four billion more in blueprints," Sam answered.

"T. Wayne Vanderziel is one of the richest men in the world. He's over seventy, and doesn't show any sign of kicking the bucket. Martin is his fourth son and sixth child, out of four different wives."

"What does Martin think of his father?"

"All the biographies of T. Wayne say he's eccentric. Martin says his elevator doesn't go all the way to the top floor. One of Martin's sisters committed suicide last year, and she was T. Wayne's favorite kid. He couldn't be bothered to attend her funeral, though it was held just a mile away from his office.

"He loves to haul people and corporations into court. He protested World War Two, the Korean War, and the Vietnam War—but one of his companies is a defense manufacturer that provided arms for all three wars. He's a vicious anti-Semite, yet most of the top executives of his companies are Jewish!" Laurel and Sam's whisperings were more than drowned out by the floor leader speaking into a microphone on his desk and the general hubbub of hundreds of people moving around and talking to each other. Behind them, arrayed on three tiers, the journal, tally, and reading clerks, the parliamentarian, and the other staff toiled.

"Martin started here Tuesday, when you did," Sam told Laurel. Sam had a nine-month appointment, so he'd been running House errands since September, four months ago.

Laurel looked back at Martin. He had a steel mask for a face, and his half-lidded eyes were surrounded by a sooty smudging, almost as if he'd gone three nights without sleeping. He didn't return Laurel's eye contact but kept staring out at the rows of 435 congressmen's desks, which ascended in elevated tiers to the rear of the room, overlooked by the visitors' gallery.

A congressman stumbled by them on his way to the retirement room, sloshing coffee on the blue-and-gold medallion-patterned carpet. He looked as if he'd just stepped off the tour bus. His face was like a cartoon character's and several political cartoonists had discovered they could draw him as two round eyes surrounded by wire glasses below a receding hairline and above a tightly pursed mouth.

"Andy Smith sure stands out in a crowd," Laurel said as he passed. Newly elected Representative Andrew "Andy" Smith III was from Michigan. His father had been Andrew Smith II, a respected federal judge, and his grandfather was Andrew "Smitty" Smith, the sacrificial Republican who'd run against Franklin Roosevelt in the presidential election of 1936. Andy had been almost incompetent as a state official back home, and he wasn't at all talented, but his background and amiable personality were sufficient to get him elected to the U.S. House.

Sam commented, "I think Andy Smith's a discredit to his grandpa, Smitty Smith. Smitty's one of my personal interests, unfortunately. He's still alive, you know, in his nineties."

"Where is Smitty now?"

"Hardly anyone knows this, but the old man is supposed to live right outside Washington, in Virginia." Sam compressed his lips in mild frustration. "I would love to see that old place, see if he's really there. But I can't track down the address."

"Why not just ask his grandson, Representative Andy?"

"I plan to." Sam's green gaze roved the rows of Democrats and Republicans, swiftly picking out Barry Goldwater, Jr., Morris Udall, Tip O'Neill, and Pierre du Pont IV. With a burst of boyish exhilaration, Sam exclaimed, "Isn't it exciting to be in Washington and see close up how policy and federal laws are made? To work with such powerful people? God, the names here! The history!"

Laurel found herself smiling instead of gagging. He was sincere. "You're part of it now, sport," she teased. A light flashed on the congressmen's seating chart in the back of the chamber, indicating that a rep needed an errand run. It was Laurel's turn in line, and she leaped up.

Sam straightened his posture, squaring his jaw. He felt silly. He'd forgotten that Laurel was Mavis Williams's

daughter and that Laurel spent most of the year living in
Washington with her mother. She was used to brushing
shoulders with the famous and powerful.

Something up in the visitors' gallery distracted Sam.
Two young women in page blazers. They had to be Senate
pages, since Laurel was the only female page in the House.
Both of them were very attractive. One girl had raven hair
tumbling to her shoulders, and she had a full figure, with
breasts that pressed against her severe uniform. The
slightly taller one looked more delicate with long blonde
hair worn pulled back. The girls seemed to be gazing
steadily at him; then the blonde turned and walked to the
exit. The dark girl looked a moment longer at Sam before
following her.

It was Friday night, and the first floor of the vice-president's house was crowded with all forty-eight House
pages, plus the thirty pages from the Senate. Spiro Agnew
and his wife were hosting a mixer for the teenagers, "to
celebrate nearly two hundred years of the congressional
page system."

Standing next to Meritt in the middle of the living room,
Lisa remarked, "Ah haven't been stared at so much since
the day Ah was two, when Ah shed all my clothes and took
a walk down the street." Her comment would have been
monstrously conceited, except that it was the truth. Many
of the pages were staring gauchely at Lisa, not bothering to
hide their fascination. She was totally at ease in a velvet
peasant dress in dark jewel colors, her burnished gilt hair
spilling halfway down her back. When boys came up to
her, she exhibited the southern belle's ability to manage
men without seeming to do so. One teenager had already
asked her for a date. Lisa wiggled out of the invitation,
then muttered to Meritt, "Ah'd rather date an open *grave.*"

"I've been meaning to tell you that I love your necklace," Meritt said to Lisa. "Are those rocks real?"

"Oh, this? Of course it's all real. My daddy gave it to me to celebrate my appointment as a page." The pendant was made of large purple amethysts that formed the blossoms of a magnolia flower. Several emeralds served as leaves, and a teardrop diamond shimmered on the flower like a drop of dew.

Meritt tried to keep the plaintiveness out of her voice. "I don't know a lot about jewelry and clothes... quality things. I haven't been around money very much."

"Then Ah've got to take you shopping soon. To look, not buy."

A curly-headed boy approached them and told Lisa, "I came to this party specifically to meet you."

"Really? Why?"

"Because you're the prettiest woman in the world."

"Good!"

Meritt left them. As she headed for the punchbowl, she was oblivious of the boys who were looking shyly at her. The house was decorated in elegant reproductions of Federal Early American furniture, with antiques mounted in places where maladroit guests could not tip them over. The house itself, of Victorian design, was surrounded by a graceful veranda. She saw the vice-president deeply engrossed in conversation with several boys. Others were flirting with Mrs. Agnew. Quite a few of the boys were smoking. And so was Laurel Williams, who stood by a large window, gazing at the snow slowly falling outside. The house sat on a small hill overlooking Massachusetts Avenue, and the city lights made the sky glow lilac. Laurel turned to Meritt and gave a faint smile.

"Look at the borders of these windows," she said pointing at the thickness of the glass and the fat caulking around it. "They can't ever open them. Secret Service says so."

"Then that means we're sealed in here like ants in an ant farm." Laurel and Meritt chuckled, then introduced themselves. Laurel offered, "I'm from Nebraska."

"I know who you are. What's it like to be the daughter of a congresswoman?"

Meritt's question was so blunt that Laurel instantly trusted her and told the truth matter-of-factly. "Kind of what it's like to be the daughter of a minister, I guess. Preachers' kids are usually the wildest in town. I do as I please most of the time. I drink a lot, and I've done some drugs. No sex to speak of, unfortunately. In public I'm fairly antiseptic, but the real me slips out sometimes. One time when Mom and I were campaigning in the middle of nowhere, I told a guy that his pet bulldog was 'slobbering like a politician near money.' Some Podunk reporter happened to hear, and the little item ran nationwide."

"Oh, no!"

"Ironically, it added luster to my mom's image of straight-talkin' honesty, so I lucked out that time. Anyhow, when reporters or voters are around, I'm a hypocrite for Representative Williams's sake. And I've got to pretend some respectability, in case *I* run for office someday."

"Respectability? What's that?" Meritt asked, and when Laurel chuckled Meritt added in a quieter voice, "I can't imagine the pressure there must be in growing up as Mavis Williams's daughter."

"I don't know. I'm sure there's pressure living in a small town in Louisiana, too." At that moment Laurel's dark blue eyes looked so intensely into Meritt's own it was as if she knew about Meritt's abusive father. *She knows. She understands,* Meritt thought. Something within her relaxed.

Laurel gestured toward the semicircle of young men caught up in the sparkle of Lisa's iridescent personality. "That must be Lisa Dunning. You're friends with her?"

"We live in the same rooming house. She's so rich she's never cleaned house in her life. I had to teach her how to make her bed and run a washing machine. She can be really funny when she wants."

"I'm intimidated by her."

"Whatever for?"

"You know, all that southern charm... 'hush mah mouth!' and 'the darkies on the l'il ol' plantation drinkin' mint juleps.' And that toothpaste smile is so bright it hurts my eyes. I feel I'm not qualified to stand in the same room with such a demigoddess... like I'm the cat who doesn't dare look at the queen."

Hardly believing Laurel's sincerity, Meritt stared at her melancholy, delicately wan features and thought how attractive she could be—if she'd just straighten up and push some of that hair away from her face. "Does it help to know that Lisa's accent goes away when she's not careful?"

Laurel smiled just as Sam Ross came over to them. "I see you've met my new best friend," he told Meritt. He slung a possessive arm over Laurel's shoulders, but kept his gaze locked to Meritt's immense amber eyes. They had the effect of making him want to write out a check for starving Biafran children.

Meritt returned, "She's now my new best friend."

Sam said to her, "And I want *you* to be my new-new best friend."

As the three of them started talking, the Very Important Couple, the vice-president and his wife, retired to their private living quarters upstairs in time to see the news (the eleven o'clock news was an addiction unique to Washington). Several boys promptly poured flasks of liquor into the punch bowl, and somebody started dealing cards on a table. Someone else found the stereo controls and turned the FM radio to a funk station. The atmosphere was considerably looser and louder.

Watching while Sam talked, Meritt realized what Sam had that puzzled her so. It was a lack of sexuality. While he *looked* appetizingly sexy, there was no sex appeal to him, at least not as far as Meritt could see. There was no erotic physical presence to him that would make her want to push back his golden hair and stroke his face. There was no hint of voluptuousness in his full lower lip to provoke a desire to kiss him. He was safe. Glancing at Laurel, Meritt was sure she felt the same way around Sam, too. He would introduce them to his friends; he would safeguard them, admire them, and give them a hard time when they deserved it. It was a relief, then, to find out that they could be on equal terms as friends. It was harder to find a friend than it was to find a boyfriend.

That Martin Vanderziel was another kind of guy entirely, Meritt thought. She'd never seen any person look so cold and aloof. His ice-blue eyes were truer than steel. He stood alone, and he had probably always stood alone. Beneath the billionaire boy's forbidding appearance was a man who needed an arm around him, she decided.

Lisa had taken it upon herself to approach Martin, who was watching the fire burn down in the fireplace. She'd been wanting to speak with him all night, but abruptly he turned, went to collect his coat and walked out into the night. Lisa blinked once, and found herself intrigued.

She'd learned that Martin Vanderziel was nineteen years old, when pages were supposed to be only fourteen to eighteen years. Another Senate page had told her that Martin had been educated by tutors all his life but couldn't say if Martin had even finished the equivalent of high school. Academic excellence weighed heavily in the page selection process. "Then how did he make the final cut here?" Lisa had asked.

In return the page asked, "You're not that naive, are you? He's got strings, contacts, pull, influence. On top of that, he's got the Vanderziel name. My guess is that someone in the family thought that a stint here would give Martin some leadership qualities."

That was one of the reasons her dad had forced her to become a page. To enhance the building of her character, he'd made sure that she lived in a quaint all-woman boarding house, where she had to spend time among the plebes. To Lisa it was a very spartan living situation, and she hated the place, except that she liked living with Meritt, who didn't have a dime to her name and couldn't afford anything else. Surprisingly, Meritt was about the only female peer Lisa had ever liked. She knew they looked striking when they walked together. Their good looks contrasted with and complemented each other: Meritt was dark and full-bodied, while Lisa was fair and slender as a fashion model.

Lisa knew Meritt was intensely conscious of her lack of money, especially in a town where dollars equalled power. Genuinely curious about what it was like to live in reduced circumstances, Lisa asked, "How do you keep yourself from envying all the other pages? Most of their daddies have bucks."

"I can't envy anyone, because I know how lucky I am to be here. While everyone else here is building up their résumés, I'm escaping from my family." Meritt's honesty about her upbringing was refreshing to Lisa, since she dealt so much in artifice.

Lisa came up to the group of three by the window. They were talking about the TV show "Star Trek," which was in its second season of syndication. "I like it because it offers hope for the future," Laurel said. "After all, it's based on the earth's making it to the twenty-third century, right? And that aliens are just like us, only different looking."

"It's innocent and idealistic."

"What I like is the way it shows regular people carrying on their lives in science-fiction settings." Sam shook his head. "Too bad the whole show was so low-budget and cheesy."

"Sleazy."

"Greasy," Lisa interjected. "Let's get out of here. I'm bored," she said to Meritt in a way that included Sam and Laurel. She had assumed the instant intimacy of pagehood.

Laurel stabbed her cigarette on a china plate. "Pizza, everyone?" Agreeing on pizza by silent consensus, the four of them piled into their coats and gloves, and left behind them a party that was getting increasingly louder and smokier.

Outside, the city was absolutely silent. The cottony snow was falling so heavily that it had softened the hard angles of buildings and fences and transformed trash cans and automobiles into pillowy igloos. Laurel spread out her arms and started singing, "It's lovely weather for a gay ride in leather with you."

They came upon a corner where a travel agency was situated. It was dark inside the plate windows, where shadowy airline posters begged pedestrians to become tourists. An electric billboard was on. It conveyed a message, which emerged, letter by letter, and went around and around: THE WORLD IS YOURS... THE WORLD IS YOURS... THE WORLD IS YOURS.

Meritt, Sam, Lisa and Laurel found themselves irresistibly drawn forward, closer to the glass, as though the phrase had a special meaning for each of them. Rapt, they followed the pinpoint lights that spelled out, again and again, THE WORLD IS YOURS. Meritt glanced around and saw the wispy frost they made with each breath. Each of them shoved hands deep into coat pockets and gazed intensely at the words as if there was something to be learned from it. The snowy night air hummed with a complex of harmonies. The future seemed so close, as if it were concealed just behind a veil, so tangible was the magic of the moment, so fine and clear.

Abruptly Lisa broke the spell of the moment by spinning away from the sidewalk, her long crimson cape whirling around her. She lifted her face and yelled with sarcasm, "The world is ours! The world is ours!" The others laughed, then started walking again, slowly, as if coming out of a trance.

That night as they ate their pizza, they talked seriously, in dead earnest, revealing themselves to one another till two in the morning. They continued talking at Laurel's apartment inside the Watergate, where the view encompassed the Virginia lights, spangling the black water of the Potomac River. Over popcorn and soda pop, they talked about life, politics, and "Star Trek," pouring themselves out for each other until the first pale light of dawn. They argued about which of the "Little Rascals" were still alive, and how old Chuck Berry was. Disparate as they were, from far-flung regions of the country, the four of them discovered they vibrated to the same frequency. It was the only thing they had in common, but it was enough to glue them together as friends, to form a mystical, powerful alliance between people who till that night had been strangers.

• *Three* •

Martin sat on the edge of his bed, watching a basketball game on television. His blue eyes reflected the picture so well you could watch TV in them. He had just stepped out of a shower and wore only a bath towel around his waist, and he held a lit joint in his hand.

Lisa stood in the doorway regarding him, her arms crossed, her attitude impatient. "Are you just going to sit there watching those pituitary cases?" Martin took another hit off the joint, then set it aside, and sat with his hands behind his back. She took a few steps closer to the bed, then hiked up the hem of her garnet wool miniskirt. Keeping her eyes pinned on Martin, Lisa slowly pulled her white lace panties down over her bare legs and stepped out of them.

She went over to the bed and playfully tied the panties loosely around his wrists. "Stop watching TV!" she yelled, pushing Martin back on the bed. She straddled his hips with her back facing him.

"Don't, Lisa. Get off me," Martin said mildly.

Lisa undid his towel so he was fully exposed to her. "But you don't want me to get off, do you?" She gradually curled her fingers around his penis, and giggled as it responded to her ministrations.

"Let go," Martin growled. When she didn't stop, he reached up with his right arm and pulled back on her neck, practically flipping her over on top of him.

"Okay!" Lisa yelped. She stood up and pushed masses of blond hair away from her face. "You should have said so in the first place. You should have been more of a gentleman."

Totally naked, Martin stood up and started digging through a dresser for clean underwear. Lisa's eyes roamed over him, lasciviously taking stock of his powerful, well-muscled body. As he pulled jock shorts on, he said, "You know, if you want to impress people, you should get rid of the cracker accent."

Automatically Lisa pouted. "Ah'm from the south. Ah can't help the way Ah talk."

"Too bad, because you sound really feebleminded." With his eyes constantly on the basketball game, Martin pulled on a sweater and jeans.

Lisa felt unjustly chastised. "You're adding insult to injury, Martin!" She paused. "Why won't you go to bed with me?"

He reached for the marijuana and inhaled. "Because I know you."

"Not that well."

"I know the kind of person you are. I've met lots of girls just like you. You don't enjoy sex, but you like to think it gives you power over people, as if they owe you something. Every guy who goes to bed with you is just feeding your ego. Am I right?"

"You're weird." Lisa was flustered. "You're nasty."

"And you're a fraud." Martin looked over at her. He had strange, piercing, ice-blue eyes that unnerved people when he looked at them too long. "Am I right?"

Lisa came over and took the joint from him. "In some ways. Maybe."

"Yeah, you want to be desired. Endlessly desired. The best compliment any dork could give you would be to kill himself over you. Every time a man desires you, you think you've got control over him. Well, I don't desire you. And when I want sex, I choose when."

Lisa's chin went up. "Then why did you ask me to come home with you after work if you didn't want to—"

"I asked if you wanted to smoke some dope while I took a shower." Martin pulled on the shriveled remains of the joint, then reached for an alligator clip on the bedstand. He extended the roach to Lisa. "Now do you want to be friends or not?"

"Fine, we'll be friends," Lisa answered belligerently.

They'd been working in the Capitol building for nearly four weeks. Lisa had been feeling victorious since earlier in the day when Martin extended an invitation to come to his house after work. The Vanderziels' Washington residence was three townhouses on Dumbarton Street that had been combined into a mansion. Lisa was struck by the lavish display of naked wealth inside. The lofty center hallway led off to other hallways, to interiors rich with color and pattern. The main corridor was of marble, and other floors were highly polished parquet, covered by monochromatic Persian carpets. Fresh cut flowers were everywhere, in bouquets and in bowls. Everywhere she turned her eyes, she saw expenditure without inhibition. Lisa had never seen any house like this before. No one in South Carolina had a museum for a house. The Dunnings were rich, but this was wealth she'd never dreamed of.

Martin's bedroom was furnished in futuristic designs straight out of a Pace International showroom, furniture of a scale Lisa could be comfortable with. She took the roach clip and toked on it, then scooted up the king-sized bed till she could lean back on the smoked Plexiglas headboard. It featured an alarm button Martin could press in case of a midnight kidnapping. Her eyes went to a flower arrangement on a lucite pedestal in the hall. Petulantly she asked, "Martin, why are these flowers in the house? It's the dead of winter. You're the only Vanderziel here, and you're just a boy. They're wasted on you."

Martin turned his head so Lisa could see only his profile. "It doesn't matter who's here or who sees the flowers. It keeps people employed, doesn't it?"

"What does your dad do again?"

"He builds skyscrapers." Martin pressed the remote control to turn up the volume of the basketball game.

"Representative Smith!" Sam called. "Representative Smith."

The freshman lawmaker from Michigan blinked his eyes and turned around slowly, as if awakened from sleep. His weak chin bobbed as he saw Sam in his page uniform with navy blue blazer, pants, and tie, rushing toward him. His glasses flashed in the fluorescent hallway lights in the Longworth Office Building, where the representatives' offices were housed.

"Yes, uh—" Andy peered at Sam's brass nameplate. "Uh, Samuel Ross?"

Respectfully, Sam started, "Representative Smith, I'm a big fan of Smitty Smith, your grandfather, and I've devoted some time to studying him."

"A lot of people are his fans, huh?"

Though Andy's face was pointed at Sam, his muddy brown eyes darted back and forth, up and down the hallway, as though he was afraid he'd miss something. Sam thought Smith's attention span must be pathetically abbreviated, but he plunged on earnestly, "I've heard rumors that Smitty is living in Virginia, not far from here. Is that true?"

"Not any more." Andy's little red mouth was permanently puckered, like that of an infant about to suck a bottle.

"Did you ever go to that house in Virginia to visit him when you were young?"

"Heck, no. That place was sold before I was born. Never saw it."

Sam tried once again. "Well, Smitty's all right, isn't he? Do you know where he is?"

"Grandpa is very old. He's living, if it can be called that, in a nursing home in a small town in Michigan." Andy's tone became very put-upon. "My family *respects* his privacy."

"Then I respect it, too," Sam lied. He doubled the lie. "I'm sure you're going to follow in his footsteps, Congressman."

"Call me Andy." The representative coughed into his hand, and put the other on Sam's shoulder. "Say, champ," he said quietly, "have you been paying attention to what-all's going on, on the House floor?" Sam nodded. "Could you jog my memory—yesterday, how much did the administration request Congress to increase the debt limit to?"

"Forty billion dollars, sir."

"No, I'm *Andy*," he stressed. "And what's the interest figure on government bonds they want to repeal?"

"A four-and-a-half-percent-interest ceiling, uh, Andy."

Andy clapped him on the shoulder. "Thanks, lad, there's some people in my office I'm supposed to talk to on that matter. I can't seem to keep hard numbers in my head, can you?"

Sam stood and watched in mild disbelief as the congressman scurried away, his shoulders stooped, his trousers fitting too snugly around the buttocks. He had to remind himself that Andy was only thirty-five, though he had the posture and look of premature middle age.

It was six o'clock at night when Sam left the Capitol building, carrying schoolbooks and homework under one arm. All pages attended a high school that met on the third floor of the Library of Congress. The classes started at 6:45 A.M., and the work day started three hours later and often continued into the early evening, leaving pages little time for mischief.

Sam stopped for a moment on the Capitol's western terrace to look at the imposing, brightly illuminated monuments that cast light into the sky. In his mind, he saw the view sweeping out over the city, over Virginia, stretching west across the entire nation. The buildings were deceptively peaceful, as if nothing urgent ever took place inside, as if the decisions made in them did not affect the entire country. At the end of the wide, flat space of the Mall, a weary, pensive statue of Abraham Lincoln sat inside the Lincoln Memorial, reverently spotlit. The first time he'd seen it, Sam had picked it out as his special monument, the one that said it all for him.

He began walking north, headed for the Vanderziel house, where he'd moved his belongings a month ago at Martin's invitation. Though Sam wasn't sure if he even liked Martin, he couldn't turn down the chance to live in one of T. Wayne Vanderziel's residences. The Vanderziel name was emblazoned on cranes wherever you saw skyscrapers under construction. The curmudgeonly founder of the empire, old T. Wayne, lived most of the time in a monstrous, sprawling chateau outside Paris, France. He hadn't visited the Washington house in eight years, yet the residence was always kept in readiness in case he should desire to walk in the door any instant. Martin hadn't seen his father in five years and hadn't talked to him on the phone for a good eighteen months.

Sam knew Martin had been boarded at a military academy since he'd been six and that he'd seen his father about once a year since babyhood. He seemed a little in awe of the old man, calling him, "Mr. Vanderziel." T. Wayne was preoccupied with his current wife, his mistress, and money; his children were low-priority projects. "I think it was perfectly logical that my father didn't attend my sister's funeral," Martin had commented. "There was nothing he could do for her. Business was more important than attending an empty ceremony. Don't you agree?" Martin told Sam that he'd been in the same room together with all five siblings only twice. He scarcely knew his half-brothers and half-sister, most of whom lived in Europe. T. Wayne treated all his children in the same way, coldly and often sadistically, extending trust money to them, then withdrawing it, promising to visit, then refusing to see them when they were in France; yet he told the world that he planned to establish a construction dynasty with his sons. Hearing about T. Wayne made Sam glad that hs father was ordinary Marvin Ross of Lubbock, Texas.

There was much about Martin that wasn't quite right, and Sam attributed Martin's strangeness to his unusual upbringing. He had a secretive manner; sometimes he was gone all night, and he never said where he'd been. He seemed to have little need for humor. His smile was practiced and empty.

Sam would bet anything that Martin hadn't known many friends because his social interaction was so superficial. Sam wondered if Lisa, Meritt, Laurel, and he had been the first peers to accept Martin unquestioningly. All of them had been outsiders in their home towns, and perhaps that's why they were drawn together. They almost felt obliged to accept the isolated Martin, but actually, they were merely nice to him. He was very interesting, but he was just too weird.

The son of one of the richest men in the world was a shoplifter. Sam had seen the stuff that Martin regularly dumped into wastebaskets, new items with the price tags still attached: notepaper, a box of Band-Aids, clothes, candy, cheap Washington, D.C., souvenirs, a wrench, a radio. "Where do you get this junk?" he'd asked Martin.

"Oh, I steal it when I'm in a store downtown to keep things from getting boring."

Sam didn't know how to react to the apathetic confession. "Are you a kleptomaniac?"

"No, just a cheap thrill-seeker."

Sam suspected that he also stole things from people's homes. Once in the kitchen he found a silver pitcher he was sure he'd seen in a cabinet at the vice-president's house, and often he found things in the Vanderziel house that didn't look as though they belonged there. Martin seemed to drift into brief trance states at times. Sam recognized Martin was spaced out by the blank shield his handsome face sometimes acquired, or when he couldn't immediately respond to a question. But his icy eyes never changed color and always retained the same expression—a slash of cold blue steel. His corruption went deeper than the simple equation of too much time and too much money. Sam was fascinated by the fact that the billionaire's son was part of a world he'd never known, yet he felt neutral, uninvolved with Martin as a person.

Sam continued walking northwest through the February coolness until he was in the elegant back streets of Georgetown, where each refined Federal-style house was graced with a shining brass door knocker. He turned in at the wrought-iron gate of the pieced-together Vanderziel mansion, which had retained the facades of three townhouses.

Inside he followed the trail of TV noise and the faint reek of marijuana till he came to Martin's bedroom. There he found Lisa Dunning lying full length on the bed, watching a basketball game, her slender, dainty form carelessly stretched out, her silky blond hair fanned behind her, her wide blue eyes clouded over. Stoned to the gills. "Hi, Sam," she said. "Have you ever wondered what TV would look like if the screen was vertical instead of horizontal?"

Sam didn't respond. The South had left her voice completely, he noted.

Martin was sitting on a chair, expertly rolling a fresh joint held over a record album cover. It was impossible to tell whether he was under its effect. Using the tip of his tongue, he sealed the paper tube around the marijuana. "Want some?"

Sam shook his head. "I hate that shit." He went downstairs again. On the main floor he entered a high-ceilinged room where the wall displayed a sixteenth-century Brussels tapestry in gold, red, and blue. On the opposite wall was a large, tarnished mirror, its frame gilded in fourteen-carat gold. He knew it had to be an authentic Venetian mirror—that was the only kind of antique mirror he'd ever heard of. Next to it was a forbiddingly chilly, recent oil portrait of T. Wayne Vanderziel, accurately depicting the effects of a bad facelift. This was the den. Sam opened a cherrywood cabinet that hid a large TV screen. He hit a button on the remote control, and "Star Trek" came on. Immediately, he recognized the episode, "Amok Time," the one in which Spock shifted into mating season and went berserk. Sam had seen it eight times already, but he sat down and soon was engrossed.

At the end of March, Martin said to Sam, "You're from Texas—you must ride horses. Let's go riding." On a Saturday morning they took a car from an agency where he had an account. They drove for an hour till they were in deepest hunt country in northern Virginia. Martin located a stable he knew of where he matched a gelding for Sam and an athletic mare for himself. Then he carefully measured the properly fitting tack for each horse. Sam found himself surprised at how gently Martin handled the creatures, stroking and petting them tenderly, making sure that the bridles didn't scrape their eyes as he slipped them on. His apparent affection and concern for the horses was touching; it was the only emotion Sam had even seen him display.

Martin rode English style, but Sam could use only a western saddle. As his comfortable cow pony trotted behind Martin over the green, rolling countryside, Sam was struck by the ease with which Martin rode a classical dressage seat. His talent at this style of English equitation, with its almost imperceptible commands and many fine points, was very difficult even for advanced horsemen, but Martin made the fancy riding look effortless. He seemed to communicate to the horse the feat he wanted a split second *before* he actually asked her to do it. He led the pretty chestnut mare through a series of equitation exercises, and led her over some jumps. Martin sat his horse with such perfectly weighted balance that he looked heroic, shoulders squared, his thick, shining black hair bouncing in rhythm with every step of his mount's gait. He was a naturally aristocratic horseman.

At one point in the afternoon, Martin's and Sam's mounts were walking peaceably side by side on a gravel road. Far to the east a train whistle sounded, and shortly thereafter a freight train came into view, the locomotive's steel shell glittering under the bright sun. Martin clucked to his horse. "C'mon, Sam, let's beat the train."

"What!" The train was soon to cross the railroad tracks that awaited them a quarter of a mile away. Before Sam could yell, "You've got to be kidding," Martin had forced the mare into an all-out gallop and was pounding down the road. He would never make the tracks before the train got there. Sam followed helplessly, certain that Martin was going to kill himself. The train engineer leaned on the whistle in warning.

At the tracks the horse abruptly stopped, just as the locomotive hurled itself over the crossing. The cars passed a foot away from her nose. The mare was so frightened that she reared high into the air. Martin began kicking her in the belly, as if to force the thoroughbred to run straight into the side of the train. Her eyes rolled back, terrified. "Go, you stupid bastard, *GO!*" he roared. His face was stretched by fury. The horse screamed and kept rearing as Martin brought down his crop on her neck. Martin's boots made bloody rips in the belly where he was kicking her. Sam shouted at Martin to stop, but he didn't seem to hear. It was one of the most horrible things Sam had ever seen. The cars seemed to go on forever, hopper cars after flat cars and tank cars after stock cars.

Finally the caboose clanged past. Martin's horse simultaneously bolted for the open road, racing full out as if Beelzebub were chasing him into hell. Sam watched horse and rider till they were nearly out of sight, then wearily pointed his horse back in the direction they had come from. He was sickened and appalled by the animal abuse he'd seen and didn't feel like riding anymore. At the stable, he steered his horse around the outdoor arena, practicing basic skills such as backing up and walking sideways until Martin rode back. His chestnut mare responded as sensitively to him as she had all day, but her belly showed the bloodied tracks where Martin had kicked her.

Martin smiled and greeted Sam as though nothing untoward had happened. "Good ride, eh?" After dismounting, he removed the saddles and bridles and groomed the horses with the same gentle fondness he'd shown earlier. Sam couldn't quite believe that Martin had done what he'd done. If Martin had a soul, there was a dark wound in it, a filthy, malignant evil that he kept hidden. Whatever it was, Sam had caught a glimpse of that unnameable section of his soul.

• *Four* •

In a little over a year, the Watergate complex would attain notoriety as the site of an attempted break-in at the Democratic National Committee's headquarters. In April of 1971, it was known mostly as the posh, expensive address of many congressmen.

Laurel Williams was sprawled on the living room floor inside her mother's apartment, propping up her dark brown head with one hand. She had on only a worn T-shirt, panties, and George Harrison's *All Things Must Pass* album, and she was critically regarding the length of her lanky body. Did she still have a chance of developing a lithe figure like Lisa's, with small breasts and a neatly delineated waist? Though Laurel was sixteen years old, her form remained stuck at the beginning of adolescence, all harsh angles. Her long, gardenia-white legs were skinny and shapeless, like a child's.

She stood up before an oval Ricardo mirror and regarded her face with the objective intensity of a surgeon about to operate. Her straight nose and slack dark brown hair looked so ordinary. Her blue eyes weren't the incomparable, changeable blue of Lisa's, which sparkled with shifting stars. Every room Lisa walked into became an ally in making her look beautiful; wherever she was, she stood out in bold relief against the surroundings. Laurel faded into the background, as was the wont of studious, dull brown girls.

Laurel's attitude toward Lisa was wildly ambivalent.

Just when you thought you couldn't take one more dose of that sickly, troweled-on, ersatz southern charm, Lisa would suddenly win you completely, clearing the air with a friendly, frothy, cheerful, or tartly clever remark.

The standard greeting in Washington was "Where are you from?" Early this morning their high-school class had been assigned a substitute teacher, an imposing woman whose expression made her look as if she was smelling something bad. "Where y'all from?" Lisa had asked her politely.

"From a place where we don't end our sentences with prepositions," the teacher responded in a subzero tone.

"Oh. Then where y'all from, *bitch?*"

Laurel's physical inventory was interrupted as Mavis Williams's bright loud voice hit out at her: "Put some clothes on, for God's sake! What if I'd brought someone in here with me?"

She turned to face her mother, who had just stepped into the apartment. "He would have been pleasantly surprised."

Mavis, who looked like Barry Goldwater with long gray hair, started pulling off her coat, shaking her head simultaneously. "I saw you spill water on Scott Jankowicz today." Laurel had indeed dropped a glass of water on a congressman during the House session. He'd laughed when she tried to mop it from his lap. Laurel also had laughed it off, but now she was shamefaced. Her mother had the ability to make her feel that way. "It was an accident." She moved over to a pseudo-Chippendale console that held liquor bottles and glasses. She turned off the stereo and poured herself a whiskey. "Would you like a drink, Mom?"

"Yeah, a scotch." Mavis sat down on the couch, whose fabric was dotted with American eagles and Liberty Bells. Her outfit, nautically flavored in blue and white, had taken her through the day and a dinner with a subcommittee chairman and three chemical concerns' lobbyists.

Laurel brought her mother the drink in a large shot glass, folded her legs and collapsed onto the olive carpeting. She reached for her cigarettes on the Sheraton coffee table, and, hacking like a tuberculosis patient, lit one. "Give me one of those." Mavis compressed her mouth in a lipless grimace. "I don't know why I allow you to keep up your unhealthy, illegal, little addictions. What if my constituents saw you?"

"They'd congratulate you for not being a hypocrite."

"True hypocrisy is pretending to be bad when you're actually good." Mavis leaned forward and uninterestedly sifted through the mail thrown on the coffee table. She held up the new *National Enquirer* a moment and roved over the headlines about UFOs and an ice cream diet, then let it drop. Her eyes narrowed on Laurel through the cigarette smoke. It had been a good month since the overworked mother and daughter had had a chance to exchange more than greetings. "How do you think your page experience is going to benefit you?"

"I think it's the best way to be exposed to the political process without actually being an elected official." Mavis's chin went up in the manner that always signaled "I expect something better from you." Laurel amended her answer, in a fast, sarcastic sing-song: "My exposure to Congress at a time of debate over the Vietnam War is causing me to temper my youthful enthusiasms."

"That's better." Mavis's tone, to her daughter's ears, was that of a prison camp commandant. "When the time comes you have to present yourself impeccably. It's all for your own good, Laurie. I want you to outdo me in the political arena."

I will, Laurel thought fiercely. *And I'm going to be ten times better at it than you.* The reason Laurel felt she was going to be a more distinguished lawmaker than her mother was that she saw things more clearly. In Washington, all around her at every moment, Laurel knew she was witnessing history being created—not the dross of politics. Politics was a game, a profession, a science. History was biography, perspective on the past, a chart for the future.

History almost made up for the shortness of life. Someday Laurel would accept the shoddy title of politician, but she was going to bring scholarship to the job, and an ability to explain complex issues in ways that everyone could understand. She lit a fresh cigarette from the one in her mouth.

"Don't hunch your shoulders so much, Laurie. It makes you look anemic." Using her special tutorial voice, Mavis asked, "Are you making contacts with the other pages?"

"Huh?"

"For the future. You're with the cream of American high school students right now, and they're going to be influential people some day. All of you should be working on developing a network."

"You mean like spiders weaving a web?"

"Though you've always been around influential and quality people, I don't think you've had a chance before to associate all that much with privileged youth. I'm pleased that you've taken up with T. Wayne Vanderziel's son."

Laurel's head whipped up. "Martin Vanderziel! You think someone's last name makes him a good person to know? Or is it that I'm supposed to tap him for the campaign coffers further down the line?"

"No, he's just a very exemplary young man—"

She'd seen that "very exemplary young man" sizzle a fly to death with a match today. Cynically Laurel offered, "How about Lisa Dunning? All that Dunning trucking money—"

Mavis's voice went impressively dark, accusatory, truth-seeking. "Has your friend Lisa mentioned anything about Abner Scoville?"

Abner Scoville. A vision came to Laurel's mind of a "preppy" congressman from Massachusetts, his brown hair sun-streaked by summers at Martha's Vineyard; he looked like a drawing in a magazine romance story. Representative Scoville came straight at you with a strong handshake and unflinching eye contact, and his athletically built body carried shoulders that marked him as an ex-footballer at some not-quite Ivy League school. His open smile made him look guileless and unsoiled even though he'd been in Congress three terms. When the Ninety-second Congress commenced in January, the pages had chosen him as "Most Kennedyesque Guy Serving in the House."

"Why would Lisa say anything to me about Abner Scoville?" Laurel's face assumed a dewy innocence. "Did you know Papa Doc died today? That means Baby Doc will be dictator of Haiti."

Mavis ignored her attempt to change of subject. "Your friend Lisa is hanging around Abner too much. I'm not the only one to notice. She's going to create trouble."

"You're imagining things. And he's not even married. I don't see what the scandal would be." Evasively, Laurel's eyes slid away, and her head dipped. Lisa had made no secret of her crush on handsome Representative Scoville, and Lisa always got what she wanted. Last week, when Laurel had attended a party at the Iranian embassy with her mother, Lisa had entered the room right behind Scoville. The couple had left at the same time. Laurel was half-revolted by the age difference and half-envious of Lisa for getting whatever she set her sights on. Laurel wondered if they kissed. She wondered what it would be like to kiss a man who was pushing forty.

"I don't want you associating with that Dunning girl anymore. The silly way she behaves around some of those representatives and pages is a disgrace to all women."

"She simply can't stop herself. She's a hard-core flirt. And you've got to realize how exciting it is for her to be here. Lisa's always been around money. She's been around some important people. But for the first time she's learning what power is, and where it's at. She wants a little of it to rub off her. And—"

Leaning forward, Mavis pointed aggressively at her daughter. "Lisa Dunning is merely one of a flock of pretty young things who roll into town every year, who think they're going to sink their claws into some VIP. They hop into bed with any man with the semblance of power, never knowing that'll be as far as they get. I don't want *you* to be seen with one of those mealy-mouthed sluts."

Laurel took a deep drag from her cigarette. Her hands were shaking like those of an elderly woman with Parkinson's disease. No matter how companiable her conversations with her mother might be, under the veneer of filial badinage, Mavis ruled with an iron hand. Her steely tone demanded obedience. Laurel knew exactly how far she could defy her mother before she ended up doing what her mother demanded.

"I *have* to be around Lisa, it's the job. Today the Doorkeeper assigned the two of us a great honor. Prince Charles is in town, and tomorrow he's going to address a joint session of Congress, which means the representatives and senators will get together in the House chamber."

"I know that."

"Well, the Doorkeeper asked Lisa and me to open the front chamber doors for the prince. We're not supposed to do anything so gauche as to actually speak to, or touch, the royal guest." Laurel stopped as she suddenly realized something. "Oh, God!" She thumped her forehead. "If Lisa is power-hungry, the Prince of Wales should send her into mad-dog delirium!"

Mavis laughed. They talked about Nixon's relaxation of trade restrictions with China, then the congresswoman went to bed. Laurel went into the kitchen to warm up a can of chicken noodle soup. As she idly stirred the saucepan, she thought of how little she actually ran into her mother within the limited acreage of Washington. Laurel was free to continue seeing Lisa as much as she ever had.

On Tuesday morning of the following week, Lisa painfully limped out to raise the Capitol flag, which was to be hoisted half an hour before Congress convened. Because pages spent so much time running messages, they could easily cover between fifty and seventy-five miles a week, and most of them suffered from swollen feet and blisters. Early in the session, Meritt and Laurel had given up their high heels for comfortable, and uglier, walking shoes. Lisa never gave up her high heels, since she considered them part of her feminine person, as essential as her delicately floral L'Air du Temps perfume.

Lisa anchored the halyard rope to the base of the flagpole, then stepped back to see the stars and stripes flutter and snap in the spring breeze.

"'And the rocket's red glare, the bombs bursting in air...'"

She pivoted quickly and nearly bumped into Representative Abner Scovill. He laughed, flashing his strong white teeth toward the sun. "Whah, Representative Scoville! Ah never knew you possessed such a charmin' singin' voice."

Scoville's arm slid around her waist, as they headed toward a Capitol entrance. Suggestively he muttered into her ear, "You should take some time to learn *all* my talents, my southern lady." He took his arm away as he saw a senator some twenty yards distant, posing with a constituent's family for a photo on the terrace steps.

"Ah keep asking y'all when we're goin' to spend some time getting to know each other better."

"Soon, my dear Lisa, soon. We've got to be careful. We don't want anyone to suspect we're involved in an affair."

"Nosiree. It would be the biggest scandal since President Warren Harding fathered a child on his office couch."

As yet there was no romantic relationship between the congressman and the page—it was all a private joke. They'd started the banter as soon as Lisa had introduced herself to the congressman and had made a big show of their flirtation since. Many people suspected them of having a fling, but their relations were completely innocent— though not for lack of trying on Lisa's part. Abner Scoville had never so much as kissed her, and the omission was starting to make Lisa feel unwanted and insulted.

"Do you have any free nights later in the week?" Lisa asked, trying to sound as if she didn't care whether he was free or not.

"I'll see, and send you a note about it." Scoville's answer was so sincere that Lisa's heart turned a little flip. Sounding the slightest bit jealous, he said, "I saw the way Prince Charles looked at you when you opened the door for him. Doesn't he know about us?"

They were back on track. Lisa smirked. Come to think of it, Prince Charles had actually made eye contact with her. "He begged me to break it off later, over dinner." Coyly she added, "He *is* closer in age to me, you know."

"Don't forget—the Prince of Wales is just an inbred chinless wonder, while I'm a duly elected member of the United States House of Representatives!" Scoville said self-mockingly. They entered a side door of the Capitol, and after a discreet good-bye, Lisa headed for the stairway that would take her to the Senate. Triumph filtered through every vein. No man had ever refused her, and it looked as though Abner Scoville, the most distinguished man she'd yet turned her sights on, was not about to break her record. Scoring with the most eligible bachelor in Congress was crucial to her already inflated self-esteem.

Though Meritt looked Caucasian and was accepted as a white girl, she was highly aware, and proud, of her black blood, and chafed with resentment every time she heard a racial slur. She couldn't believe that in 1971 racial prejudice was still part of many people's makeups.

That's why Meritt was unable to keep back a gasp when she heard Representative Andy Smith tell a "nigger" joke. She was in Andy's office inserting newly introduced bills into an expandable binder when Andy said to a squat administration official sitting opposite him, "What's the definition of 'renege'? . . . To change a shift at the car wash!"

Both Andy and his visitor horselaughed, but Meritt's

abrupt loud, sharp intake of breath surprised them. For a
second all three people were paralyzed, then Meritt continued lacing the bills into the binder as though she hadn't
made a sound.

Until she heard him make that rancid joke, she'd considered Andy to be just another elected buffoon in an arena of
535 jolly clowns. Now she knew he was a viciously stupid
buffoon. She couldn't believe that Andy Smith was the
descendent of such a great man as Smitty Smith. In attitude, intelligence and looks, there seemed to be no connection.

Meritt had read up on Smitty, Andy's antecedent, and
found his life absorbing. He was a "legend in liberalism"
who'd come out of Michigan to serve in the Senate during
the 1920s. He was a Republican in a Democratic Congress,
and by assenting to the economic measures the Democrats
introduced, he held on to his seat while other Republicans
lost theirs. Despite his Republican association, Andrew
"Smitty" Smith the First became a champion of liberalism
and isolationism. His soaring idealism troubled some and
inspired others because he spoke of building a world where
war and want were ended forever. Smitty was even inspir-
ing in appearance because he resembled Thomas Jefferson
as portrayed on every nickel.

Smitty's greatest test came when his party asked him to
be their presidential candidate for 1936. It was taken for
granted by most Republicans that Franklin Delano Roosevelt would be reelected as president, and it was taken for
granted that Smitty was serving as a sacrificial lamb. Yet
he'd won congressional elections before against towering
odds, and he actually believed he might be able to win this
one against FDR.

When Smitty inevitably lost the 1936 election, he turned
bitter, and a career that had known triumph ended as one of
tragedy. He gave up on his political party and refused to try
for any elected office again. He moved out of Michigan to
a Virginia suburb, where he became something of a re-

cluse. When asked to help administer the Marshall Plan in Europe after World War II, he refused to respond. Ironically, his foresighted opposition to monopolies and unjust taxes proved to be uncannily correct as the decades went on. Smitty wouldn't respond to any requests for media interviews; he wanted to keep away from the title of elder statesman.

Gradually the world forgot about Smitty Smith, just as he'd wanted back in November of 1936. His son, Andrew Smith II, went on to some prominence as a federal judge. He'd died of leukemia in 1965, but Smitty was still alive.

Meritt was becoming as curious about the old man's whereabouts as Sam was. He'd told her, "I'd love to find out why Smitty suddenly gave up on the causes he'd championed and disappeared from public life. And where did he go?"

Grandson Andy Smith had descended from two great men. No wonder he'd gone so far and so fast, despite his incompetence. He had a solid gold name that would take him anywhere, plus a winning hail-fellow-well-met personality that engaged most people when they met him.

When Meritt finished the chore of inserting bills in each congressman's office binder, she checked her appearance in a ladies' room mirror. She'd pulled back her wealth of black hair into a neat French plait, and her amber eyes were outlined in black, which made them glisten as if large tears were ready to fall. She straightened her shoulders and brushed an invisible lint speck off her dapper navy blazer. It was time to go to the Senate chambers, where today she was to operate the quorum and roll-call lights and buzzers that summoned senators to vote.

As she crossed north over Independence Avenue, Meritt looked over the flat, richly green spaces of the Mall. It was hard to believe that five months ago she'd been living like an animal trapped in a cage from which no one would help her escape. Now, at the end of April, walking through the soft spring air, Meritt felt she had reinvented herself.

During her time in the nation's capital, she'd made her final commitment to devote herself to acting. In Washington there were so many theaters that she had been able to immerse herself in drama for the first time. She'd been childishly enthralled by each performance—by the lighting, the costumes, the props and makeup, the artistry of it all. Now she couldn't wait to get before the footlights to take her chances.

What would her new friends say when she told them that she was planning to join the ranks of high-school dropouts? After the freedom and independence she'd been given as a page, Meritt simply couldn't go back to Louisiana to finish her junior and senior years in high school and live again with people who hated her. She was going to take the money she'd earned as a page and move to New York. Although she was only sixteen, she was sure she was tough enough to meet any challenges the city would present.

Inside the Capitol building, Meritt ran into a gaggle of tourists who blocked her passage through Statuary Hall. A few of them gave her a penetrating once-over, and she felt a small swell of pride at being one of the "in" crowd on the Hill. The Statuary Hall had served as the original House of Representatives till 1857. Each state was asked to contribute statues of its two most famous citizens, but it turned out that that many statues would be far too heavy for any floor to support, so there were only twenty-five statues.

The Capitol tour guide, distinctive in her red blazer, instructed her group to gather around the spot where John Quincy Adams's congressional desk once sat. Meritt crowded into the group to listen. The guide crossed the room and whispered, "John Quincy Adams was the only president to serve as a representative *after* his presidency. Our sixth president was always a step ahead of the opposition, because the ceiling of the Statuary Hall bounced their conversations right to his seat!"

The tour group ooh-ed and ah-ed, because they'd heard the guide's every syllable and inflection perfectly. Freak acoustics! Meritt was delighted—this acoustical trick belonged in the "Mystery Vortex" back at the Louisiana Wildlife Park. If any room of the Capitol were haunted by ghosts, it would be the Statuary Hall, with its population of shadowy likenesses ranging from Will Rogers to the inventor of the ice machine.

Meritt glanced at her watch, then began hurrying to the Senate wing. She entered the door to the Doorkeeper's office, and followed the small maze into the chamber. Behind the desk of the president of the Senate was a chandelier with two lightbulbs below it. The red one indicated an executive session; she switched on the white bulb, which meant a regular session was meeting. Showily, she pivoted to face the rows of empty leather seats and she threw out her arms like a minstrel. To the echoing chamber she exclaimed, "It's showtime, folks!"

• *Five* •

For a rare moment, the Capitol's marble-and-brocade hallways seemed deserted. It was five o'clock, and anyone who didn't work in the building had to be out by four-thirty; and both houses were in session. After completing an errand, Sam Ross walked from the main doors of the House chamber to the corridor that led to Statuary Hall.

As he strolled from statue to statue, he studied the nameplates on the pedestals. In the watery half-light that poured in from ceiling windows, each figure shone as though it were polished. The only name he recognized, besides Will Rogers's, was that of Charles Russell, Montana's famous painter and recorder of gritty scenes of the Old West. As he lingered in front of the copper figure, the clack of hard shoes on stone sounded at Sam's back. Swift as a lizard, he moved in back of the statue to see who was coming. Sam was supposed to be serving in the House chamber, not loitering outside it.

Behind Charles Russell, Sam looked up at King Kamehameha of Hawaii, the only likeness of a king in the Capitol. The gargantuan king was everyone's favorite figure in the Statuary Hall. He was ebony-colored all over, except for his elaborate headdress and skirt, which were covered with resplendent gilt.

Suddenly Sam heard a quiet, disembodied male voice. It sounded vaguely familiar. Obeying an immature instinct, he flattened up against King Kamehameha, then peeked out into the middle of Statuary Hall, where he saw a side view of Representative Andy Smith. A man of medium height, his hair and suit a matching black, stood next to Andy with his back to Sam. From Sam's corner, it appeared as though they were regarding the same statue.

"What about this?"

When Sam's eyes dropped to the men's heels, he suddenly knew why he could hear their hushed tones with headphonelike clarity. They were standing on the brass disk that marked John Quincy Adams's desk site, and the freak acoustics of the curved marble ceiling were faithfully delivering all their words straight to him. It was about the poorest place one could ever choose for a private conversation.

Andy's creaky voice was soft but clear. "We sure can't talk anywhere in the perimeter of D.C., that's for sure. This entire town is infested with bugs where you'd least expect 'em. Tell you what. Why don't we meet at my Grandpa Smitty's old house in Virginia?"

So Andy *did* know where Smitty's last dwelling was! He had told Sam a bald lie, but Sam had not really expected the truth. Andy was no Honest Abe.

"I'd be very interested in seeing the home of Andrew Smith the First," the stranger said. Sam craned his head to see if he could get a better look at him, but he could see nothing more than a complete rear view. "Your grandfather was a great man, wasn't he?"

"Depends at which end of the political spectrum you stand when you look at him. He's a pinko. A New Deal liberal, even if he did run against FDR. Smitty's a real nutcase. Always talked Eugene V. Debs socialist bullshit, but then, you'd probably go for that lefto kind of line, huh?"

The rhetorical question met with hard silence. "Tell me how to get to your grandfather's house." Andy related some road directions that were blessedly uncomplicated; Sam squeezed his eyes tight shut in the effort to burn the directions onto his memory. "May I be confident that you'll be there, Andrew?"

"Yeah. I'll be there. And call me Andy."

"Ahn-dee," the other man uttered unsurely. What was that accent—Mexican? Middle Eastern? East European? The men began to move and Sam squeezed farther behind King Kamehameha. He tried to control his breathing. From the men's brief dialogue, he could tell they hadn't meant to be overheard.

The two pairs of feet beat a loud tattoo on the stone floor and faded as the men headed toward the Rotunda, the central portion of the Capitol. Sam peeked from around the base of Kamehameha, leaned against the cool back wall, and yanked open the knot of his tie and top shirt button. His torso was coated with sweat. Somewhere, he knew, John Quincy Adams's ghost was smiling.

"What are you so excited about?" Laurel asked when he came to sit by her on the pages' bench. There was hectic color in his face and his clear green eyes sparkled.

Sam told her everything he'd heard in Statuary Hall. "I've got to get there. I want to see the house, and I want to see if Smitty is living there! I didn't hear Andy discuss a time or date to meet there, so I think it'd be best to go as soon as possible. Like tonight. Want to come?"

"Sure! But how are we going to get there?"

"We can get Martin to take us. He can get a car from a rental chain where Vanderziel companies have an account."

"You've got to take Meritt, too, now that you've got her interested in Smitty. Lisa will probably come, too, if Martin's driving. Wherever Martin goes, Lisa follows."

"Because they're a matched set of decadent rich kids, like Leopold and Loeb."

"Come on, Laurel," Sam said with some disgust, "they're both our friends."

"Or so they keep saying!" Laurel rolled her eyes. Sometimes Sam was so much of a nice guy she could swear he was campaigning for sainthood.

Martin rented a Lincoln Continental Mark IV that could accommodate the five of them easily. When they climbed into the car, the sun was low on the western horizon. Before the Lincoln left the borders of the capital, they passed the travel agency where the sign blinked at them: THE WORLD IS YOURS . . . THE WORLD IS YOURS. . . . and Merritt could keep her secret no longer. When her appointment as a page was over, she was going to New York instead of returning to high school. The others couldn't understand why she wanted to be a dropout, so she told them about her abusive family, from whom she hadn't heard since December, when she'd moved to Washington.

Her four friends fell into silence. For the first time, they fully knew her. Sam and Laurel silently agreed that from Meritt's limited range of options for post-page life, perhaps staying away from her father was best. Under the deadening effect of a Quaalude, Martin's gaze followed the white tunnel the Mark IV's large headlights bored into the glowing dusk. Lisa watched as the city gave way to suburban Virginia, to Virginia countryside, where she could spot some of the great old houses of the planters. Damn! She wished that she'd come from one of the older families down South, instead of coming from ordinary Ohioans. She ached to belong to the right kind of people, whose background would afford her a *position* in society. Abner Scoville might just be her ticket out of Charleston.

On Sam's instructions, Martin steered to the right off the highway, which took them a mile over a gravel road that passed two farms. He took another right, carrying them even farther from civilization. Sam said to turn left at a deserted plow, and they drove a mile over a one-lane road overgrown with grass, and then through crumbling brick pillars. The twilight revealed the looming shape of a huge Victorian house, its mansard roofs and chimney flues outlined in sunset orange. A phantom skulked at every blackened window. Behind the house stood a small barn, a water pump, and some outbuildings, all of which were covered by invasive creeper plants. A large patch of earth on the side was choked with tangled brambles and corn stalks that suggested it had once been a garden. The lot was forested with sycamore trees.

"This must be it!" Sam was as happy-eyed as if he'd made the summit of Mount Everest. "Kind of puts the 'u' in ugly, doesn't it?"

"Uh, it looks like the house the Addams Family lived in," Lisa said.

"I wonder if Cousin Itt is home?"

"Nobody lives here," Martin asserted. "Nobody could possibly live here." He parked the car behind a dense, wildly overgrown thicket. The pages climbed out of the Lincoln. They were all wearing blue jeans, old shirts, and tennis shoes or boat shoes. Sam and Laurel switched on the heavy flashlights they'd brought along. Lisa warned, "Ah hope there are no wood ticks out here, Samuel Ross." *Ah hope your frail constitution can bear the saht of rats and spiders,* Laurel thought maliciously. She personally couldn't bear the wide-eyed southern belle pose Lisa assumed when she wanted to appear too weak to undertake any challenge.

Meritt plunged into the deep grass ahead of Sam. "Hey gang, let's break all the trespassing laws!" From behind he noted how snugly her jeans fit her hips, yet her middle was so tiny she'd had to tie in the waist with rope. She tripped She over an abandoned tire that seemed the right size for a Model T, and sprawled headlong on her face. In a second she was up and running again. *For all her beauty,* Sam thought, *she's as tough as an old bayou alligator.* She vaulted onto the veranda, avoiding the rotting front steps, and threw herself at the peeling front door. Meritt slapped her palms on it, yelling, "Is anybody home?" The bay windows that looked onto the veranda were cracked, but not broken. Sam guided the beam of his flashlight onto the rusty doorknob. Meritt yanked it, but it was locked. Out of control with venturesomeness, she lifted her foot to kick in the arched door, and it splintered open with her first jab.

Lisa picked up one of the cats that was wandering in the yard. "What are you doing out here, kitty?"

"Watch it, Lisa," Laurel said. "Way out here in the farmland, cats can be carrying rabies."

They gathered inside the Smith vestibule. A hall with a stairway was directly in front of them. So many of the steps were broken, it was unclimbable. Laurel and Sam trained their flashlights on a large room that appeared to have been the parlor, then on another room, which may have been a library. There was no furniture. The flashlights picked out a vast draping of cobwebs, so many of them they seemed to pull down the stained ceiling. Powdery plaster lay everywhere, and every painted surface was covered with cracks, like roadmaps without destination. The floorboards were perforated with treacherous-looking holes. "God, this place is just like Miss Havisham's," Lisa exclaimed, "straight out of *Great Expectations*."

"Except Miss Havisham didn't have any cats," Martin said.

Everywhere cats walked in and out of the spotlights, mewing and blinking. They picked their way carefully around the gaps in the floor. Several of the wild cats hissed at the invaders like cobras and arched their backs. In a corner, a black cat and an orange cat fought savagely, clawing at each other's eyes. "I'll bet anything this place doesn't have a mouse problem," Meritt said.

"I wonder why all these cats have congregated here. Someone must have been feeding them."

The stale odor in the air seemed to coat the lungs like fungus. Lisa identified it. "This place smells like old news-papers and cat turds. Ah wonder how often anyone comes out here to look at this place."

"Some dump Andy's picked for a clandestine meeting," Meritt said.

"Why in hell did he want to meet that guy out here? And what for?"

"Maybe they were daring each other to sleep one whole night in a haunted house," Laurel said lightheartedly. Walking into the library, she swung the cone of light above an unkempt fireplace. It caught on a ripped campaign banner. Two surprised spiders scurried over its face. "Here's your proof this was Smitty's house."

Sam approached it and read the block letters: SMITTY FOR PRESIDENT IN THIRTY-SIX. He hunched his shoulders with guilt as he sneaked a look back at Laurel. "Would it be criminal if I took this?"

"For anyone else, yes. For a scholar like you, not at all."

From the library they raggedly trailed into a morning room in back of the house, which had French doors leading out to a veranda. The glass in the doors was missing, and they were boarded up. The doorway led to a huge, out-moded kitchen, where a wood-fed stove and the remains of an icebox were coated with dust. Sam's light shone onto a counter. He gagged. It was scattered with the remains of packets of luncheon meat and bread bags, and peanut butter, pickle, mustard, and jam jars.

"Don't get sick," Martin said. "Whatever hasn't been dragged away by cats has petrified." He went up to the counter for closer inspection. "God! I wonder who bought and ate this shit?"

"Smitty."

"It couldn't have been too long ago," Laurel said, coming up from behind. "See the Morton salt box? It's got the latest incarnation of the Morton salt girl on it. Last time she changed was 1968."

"*Where* do you *come up* with that stuff?" Lisa eyed Laurel with venom. Bewildered and slightly hurt, Laurel began fumbling in her jeans pockets for her cigarettes. Lisa added, "And don't you dare light up in here unless you want us all to go up in flames!"

The kitchen had a separate, empty pantry, and the pantry opened onto the back stairs. A set of swinging doors led to a vast dining room lined with pilasters and a fireplace so big one could stand in it. Cats prowled around the room's perimeter, staring at the humans with glassy taxidermal eyes. There were some nondescript, fragile-looking dining room chairs here but no table. The walls had been papered in a faded, rain-stained chintz floral. Next to the base of the fireplace, Martin saw a tabby squeeze itself out of a hole in the wall. Curious about what was behind the wall, he squatted down and ripped at the hole's right edge. Wallpaper and particle board crumbled off in his hand. Sam bent next to him. Pointing the flashlight up a narrow flight of dusty stairs, he started laughing. "I don't believe it. A *secret passage!*"

"And this . . . is a secret panel," Martin said, forcefully tearing away more of the flimsy wall. There was a grin on his face. It signified he was genuinely experiencing fun.

"Who wants to try to see if those steps hold up?" Laurel asked.

"Me!" Meritt snatched Laurel's flashlight and charged up the secret stairway. There were more cracking, splintering sounds as she bashed in another panel at the top stair. After a pause she made a loud sound: "*Sheeesh!*" The violence of her proclamation sent the four others rushing up the stairs. They arrived in a large, high-ceilinged room. It was thick with cats and kittens, who regarded the strangers serenely. Meritt's flashlight beam was pointed at the bed that dominated the rancid-smelling room. It was king-size and covered in grubby gray sheets. The top sheet was rolled back as if someone had just climbed out of the bed and would be back in a moment. A calico with feeding kittens lay in the middle of the bed.

"That solves it," Laurel said. "Smitty fed the cats, and several generations of them have made their home here." The shadowy light bounced off her cheekbones eerily.

Lisa said, "He must have lived here till a few years ago. It looks as if he was removed from here one night, and that no one bothered to come back here to clean it up."

"Maybe Smitty *is* in a nursing home in Michigan, just like Andy said."

Sam trained his light on the nightstands at either side of the wide bed. Each table was littered with glasses, medicine bottles, spoons, and plates of food that had been cat-nibbled. Wheeling the flashlight around the ruin of the room, he saw broken-down chairs, remnants of magazines, and a chest of drawers that had collapsed upon itself. There were two closet doors, and an interior door, the "unsecret door," leading to the main upstairs hallway. Sam looked up at the ceiling and saw several gaps where rain had trickled through the attic and through the ceiling, to wet the furniture underneath, making the wood swell and allowing mold to grow over it. The dormer windows looked to the back of the house, where the sky was turning black as shoe polish.

Sam concluded that the last years Smitty had lived here,

he had been an eccentric hermit, as wicky-wacky crazy and superstitious as Howard Hughes. There was no aura to the room that signified that a great man had once existed here. The only mark he'd left was the tattered campaign banner in the library. The cats, the wretched stench, the secret passage, the rotted food—somehow they all added up to mental illness. The strain of a presidential campaign and being the target of so many political attacks had finished him. Smitty had felt forced to leave his life of public service and retreat from a society he'd helped lead. He'd given up on the world and retired to this spacious, cat-infested wreck.

"Wow, this place is a real head trip," Martin commented, his smudgy eyes lit with bizarre enthusiasm. Lisa opened up her glossy-lipped mouth to say something, but she was stopped by a loud creak downstairs that echoed through the empty rooms. Swift as a gasp, Sam and Meritt snapped off the flashlights. A car door slammed.

"It's gotta be Andy," Sam whispered under his breath. "Don't move or the floor will creak." He didn't have to say it; everyone had frozen in his tracks. Startled, several cats fled up the stairs while several others squawked and ran downstairs, their paws thumping on the hollow wooden steps.

It *was* Andy. They heard the congressman's creaky, rachety voice welcome another person, "Well, here we are! Not too hard to find it, was it? You wanted to see how my communist grandpa lived. What do you think? I hope you like cats."

The other person's response was muffled, but the voice was male and soft. Sam was sure it belonged to the dark-haired man he'd seen from the back in Statuary Hall today. He felt like a nincompoop, because he'd taken for granted that the assignation would be set for a more distant date than tonight.

The two of them were in the dining room. A bright light emanated up through the passage, then swung away. From

the lowering and rising sound of their voices Sam figured
they had circled back through the kitchen area and around
to the library. The pages stood fixed in their places in the
blackness, each one of them concentrating on willing the
two men to stay downstairs. When she heard Andy say
deprecatingly, "The dungeon's in the basement 'n' the torture chambers are upstairs!" Meritt thought she was going
to lose her bladder control. She exhaled when the men
returned to the dining room. There was the scraping of
chair legs on the floor. One of the chairs was dragged
within full view of the pages and a Coleman gas lantern
was set down on the floor. The man Sam had described,
with black hair and black suit, also had a black mustache.
He was elegantly slender and smallboned. He sat down
gracefully and remained sitting rigidly upright, so that they
could see his right profile. He looked quite young. His
inky black eyes were emphasized by olive skin pulled taut
over the elegant ridge of his cheekbones. The delicately
handsome features had no trace of humor to them.

Andy's voice boomed up the secret passage. "I'd offer
you some coffee or a glass of wine, Oliver, but as you can
see—we're all out!" He snickered for a while at his own
wit.

"Why haven't you used your grandfather's house as a
suburban home?" Oliver's voice drifted upstairs with clarity.

"It'd be too expensive to fix up," Andy responded, his
voice a little fainter. A chair groaned in protest as he sat
down on it. "My dad said this house was pretty far gone
when Grandpa Smitty moved into it."

"He lived here all alone after he lost his campaign?"
Oliver's tone was reserved. His accent was strongly British
and Middle Eastern at once. He could have been Semitic or
East Indian.

"I guess there were some hired hands for a while who
kept up the crops. But Smitty's wife, my grandma, was
long dead, and his kids were all grown up. My dad didn't

want to leave Michigan. But there were a couple of times he brought us kids here to visit." Andy paused. "See that fallen-in wall over there? That's a secret staircase going up to grandpa's room, don't know why it was built. But we kids had a lot of fun playing in there."

Oliver bent at the waist to glimpse up the dark hole of the passage. He could see only blackness, while the five pages standing in Smitty's room got a clear look at him, expensively dressed, big black eyes gleaming with sharp intelligence. He sat back up.

"Grandpa hated us. He sure was a crackpot. Each visit ended with a big blowout between him and my dad. Smitty was a cranky old fart—get the hell out of here!" A tomcat yowled as Andy kicked it away. "By 1960, he was living in his room all by himself, coming down every once in a while to get some food and open cans for all the cats who lived up there with him. Just think—he wouldn't leave his bed, even when John Kennedy sent him an invitation to the inauguration. Even when this haunted house was condemned, he wouldn't go."

In polite tones Oliver asked, "When did your grandfather finally decide to leave?"

"Ha ha! Smitty *didn't* decide—we had the funny farm boys drag him out of here not long ago! Carted him off to a nursing home in my home state. The wife and I took some of the old junk out of here for firewood, and I haven't been back since. Thank Christ the rest of the world never found out how senile Smitty got."

"And he's alive, Mr. Smith?"

"Call me Andy. Yeah, he's a living vegetable, but at least he's in a *clean* bed now." Angry frustration entered Andy's expression. "Reason I've never been able to sell off this place is that no court will give me power of attorney. Smitty's name still means something to a lot of people."

Oliver pushed a cat off his knees. Andy said, "Want some gum?"

"No, thank you."

After a pause, Andy assumed a firmer let's-get-down-to-business tone. "So, your older brother Mohammed, the one I went to the University of Michigan with, has done a lot of talking to me already. I can't turn down the money. I mean, I've never been a guy of closely held scruples, I think any of my friends would tell you that. But why do you need me? I mean, what's the story?"

"Simply put, I am a representative of the world's non-aligned nations. You've already been briefed about our organization. Poor as we are, we've managed to pool our resources to form an alliance. Jointly, we have constructed an intelligence plot that is designed to bring the United States down to its capitalistic knees."

Upstairs, none of the pages stirred. Andy said, "That's kinda what I figured from what Mohammed told me. Why?"

"It will be an easy way to prove that we, too, are a major power on a global scale. Our list of grievances is long. So-called Third World countries resent being forced to provide cheap labor in exchange for the occasional carton of infant formula. Our caucus of nonaligned nations, to paraphrase your own president, will show that we will not be kicked around anymore."

"How?"

When, Where, What? What are you talking about? Laurel thought impatiently.

"Our operatives are gathering a list of men and women in this country who have no apparent relationship with one another. They're in key positions in the directorates of major corporations, banks, the Federal Reserve, the government, and the military. Just a hundred people, inconspicuous but crucial decision-makers, acting individually and unaware of the others, will bring down the U.S. economy. All they have to do is take certain actions, make decisions that may go against the grain of their conscience."

"Why would these folks do this for you?"

"If these well-placed people don't do what we ask, we can destroy them through blackmail." Oliver's words were simple and precise. "You see—you see, Ahn-dee—all of us are susceptible to blackmail. Every American has done something deeply wrong that he's tried to cover up—legal misrepresentation, business malpractice, insider trading, illicit sex, tax evasion. No one is wholly honest, even those who consider themselves uncorruptible."

"I don't believe that many people can be exploited."

"No? We all have our little secrets. Your wife, for instance—your 'Honeypie', as you call her." The nickname "Honeypie" was so pervasive people forgot the congressman's wife was named Ann Smith. Oliver continued, "Remember long ago when you tried to break off your engagement to Ann, and she told you that she'd been pregnant and gotten an illegal abortion?"

Andy's response was layered with shock. "Yes, I felt so guilty that I ended up marrying her. Who told you that? No one knows about it but me!"

"That was Ann manipulating you. She was never pregnant, Ahn-dee. She never had an abortion. She knew how to get at you. And think of what would happen if her secret were made public, since you're well known for your opposition to abortion."

"Who told you that?" Andy repeated, stricken.

"That is immaterial. Sorry to give you second thoughts about your marriage, my friend. Just proving a point. But that story is nothing—a trifle—compared to the information we have on other people. And if our 'Trojan Horse' finds a key person whose past is pristine, we will try to tempt him into a vulnerable position."

"Trojan Horse?"

"Isn't that a perfect name for our project? We have insinuated ourselves into high places in the United States without anyone being aware of it. Our Trojan Horse List of key decision-makers has taken a long time to build, and it

will take years before it's ready for implementation. But
you have been selected to be the kingpin in our plans! You
will be the highest-placed U.S. government official on the
list. You will be the guardian of the project, and your actions will light the fuse leading to an explosion of chaos.
My associates are convinced that your name identification
will carry you straight to the top. Nothing will stop your
career climb except death."

With a gullible eagerness that made the pages gasp,
Andy asked, "You really think I can make president or
vice-president?"

Oliver chuckled tactfully. "If not president, you can certainly maneuver your way into his cabinet. We have the
utmost confidence in you." He reached for something
beyond the eavesdroppers' view, then brought forth a
briefcase. "To cement our agreement, I am leaving you
with this gift."

"Cash, I assume?" Andy guffawed. "Tell me, Ollie, how
come you've got a name like Oliver Remick when your
brother is Mohammed? I never could figure that one out."

"We are Muslim. My brother earned the name Mohammed by making the pilgrimage to Mecca. I have not."

"When will I hear from you again?"

"Within the year. I will contact you. We will never meet
face to face again."

There was silence after this declaration, a dramatic silence. Then a chair tipped over with a crash, and the house
became dark again as Oliver and Andy left with the lantern. Upstairs, the pages didn't move a muscle. They heard
the faint sound of a car engine starting. After a minute
another car revved its motor. Meritt was the first to move.
She ran through the door across the hallway into a room on
the front side of the house. The others followed.

In the distance they could see the lights of two cars
moving out to the gravel road. One car turned right, the
other left.

Sam and Laurel turned the flashlights back on. In the eery light each face except Martin's was drawn in fear. Laurel spoke.

"We've got to talk."

• *Six* •

"There's no such thing as a 'Trojan Horse Project.' It doesn't make sense that anybody would choose Andy Smith to be a 'kingpin'! That was all a bunch of cheap bullshit," Martin said, opening a beer. "A steaming heap of compost."

Meritt agreed. "Yeah—a plot in a very poorly conceived espionage thriller. More ludicrous than the worst episode of 'The Girl from U.N.C.L.E.' I wonder what that guy Oliver is really up to. His story couldn't be real."

"Real or not, don't you think we ought to talk to the police? Or the FBI?" Laurel suggested.

"Or the CIA? Or Interpol? Or Smersh? Or THRUSH?" Lisa said. "You expect them to believe us?" Her Southern accent, for the moment, had left her.

"Maybe one of 'em was wearing a tape recorder. Entrapment."

Meritt wrapped her arms around her knees and rocked slightly. "How are we going to prove the existence of a conspiracy to topple the U.S. economy? Will the cops go talk to Andy? Or Oliver Remick? We have no concrete evidence that would warrant any investigation." She held a low opinion of authority figures. The two times police had come to her house to arrest her father for family abuse,

Philip du Nord had charmed them into going away. "Even though we're congressional pages, the pigs are bound to call us drug-addicted juvenile delinquents."

Two hours after overhearing about the Trojan Horse Project, they were finding it hard to believe, and equally hard not to believe. Sam, Meritt, Lisa, Laurel and Martin sat on the floor of the Vanderziel drawing room, smoking cigarettes and drinking beer. The tufts in the carpet under their ashtrays and cans had been hand-tied by Persians long ago; authentic Louis Quatorze and Quinze chairs stood around the room; but Martin's guests were too absorbed to notice.

Sam said, "Look—if this conspiracy thing was real, do you think it could really be pulled off? A decade-long plot sounds absolutely implausible."

"It's not implausible at all," Laurel said fervently. "Remember the case of the eight-eyed spy? It was a family of four spies in Honolulu, who helped bring America into World War Two. They conspired with the Japanese and Germans for *six years,* till they were arrested for their part in Pearl Harbor." With shaking fingers she stubbed out a Camel.

"I just hope someone is playing an elaborate practical joke on Andy," Meritt declared. "He'd be an easy mark."

"If this is an elaborate practical joke, what about that suitcase full of real money?" Laurel asked.

Lisa said, "If we told the police, do you think there's any way they could pin something on Oliver Remick? There's gotta be some headquarters for this Trojan Horse —if it exists—and they could trace it through him."

"Who the hell is Oliver Remick?" Martin said reasonably. "We don't know if that's the guy's real name, or where he's from. We don't even know which of the nonaligned nations he represents." He got up to freshen the ashtrays. Martin was being the perfect host for this postmortem party. He provided the ice-cold beer and had called out for pizza. His manners were so impeccable and incongruous, as if this were a social gathering.

For another hour the pages dissected what they'd seen and heard. Maybe Remick and Andy were goofing around, talking about something that possibly could be. Yet Remick had been all business. Perhaps they were concocting a scenario for a spy thriller they were collaborating on—plenty of lawmakers had been novelists. Maybe the pages had experienced one of those moments of "crowd psychology," building a scene together that had never actually happened.

As they talked, they became irritated with one another, angry with themselves and everyone else. Each was feeling guilty, and wanted to blame another for making him or her feel that way. They were doing something wrong by not going to the authorities with their information, and deep down they knew it. Yet each had reasons for the decision.

Profoundly agitated, Laurel puffed away at cigarette after cigarette. Andy Smith was a Republican congressional representative. So was her mother. God, if she caused any trouble with one of Mavis's colleagues—especially trouble over a situation that might prove to be nothing at all—Laurel was in for a handcart of hell. Besides, she intended to launch her own political career within the decade, and couldn't allow her plans to be tampered with in any way. Her eyes flickered over her friends. Could they see the guilt on her face? Would they judge her to be a rank opportunist who'd do anything to serve her greedy ambition?

Are they going to judge me to be a rank opportunist who'd do anything to serve his greedy ambition? Sam wondered, anxiously chewing his bottom lip. His green eyes were clouded over with thought. Always conservative and conformist, Sam concluded that running off to the police would be rash. If he caused any sort of scandal with a federal representative, his reputation would be shot even before he entered Northwestern University. Trying to think of a comparable situation, Sam remembered that Roy Cohn survived the McCarthyism mess and went on to be an all-powerful lawyer, despite his homosexuality. But Roy Cohn's character was that of the toughest bully on the block, and Sam could never be aggressive enough to overcome a blot on his past. Besides, the Trojan Horse Project was a joke. It had to be.

I wonder if these guys think I don't have a conscience, Meritt thought, biting her thumb. Don't they know that if we brought what little we know of a Trojan Horse List to the law, they'd just laugh at us—or even file a libel suit? And where would I end up? Back with my loving father.

After finishing his share of pizza, Martin leaned back against a white brocade couch and tuned out, oblivious to his friends' distress. Before this discussion, he'd assumed it was common knowledge that blackmail and scandal were a tradition in corporate finance. His father had put the squeeze play on quite a few of his enemies. And if there truly was a Trojan Horse Project, and if the U.S. economy came crumbling down again after a crash like the one in 1929, old T. Wayne Vanderziel would flourish again, just as he did during the depression.

When other investors ran for cover from the stock market crash, T. Wayne had had the guts and foresight to use the depression to his benefit. While others were selling, he was buying oil stock at a fraction of its earlier value. Observers thought he was making a fatal mistake, but the risk paid off when the stocks tripled and quadrupled in value as the economy slowly grew healthier. The profits T. Wayne Vanderziel made during the early years of the depression formed the foundation of his fortune.

Martin's icy blue eyes traveled over the other four pages. He'd carefully cultivated his lack of emotion for so long that anger frightened him. They argued with such malice that he didn't know how they could stay friends. This was the first clique Martin had ever felt a part of. The emotional connection between them was stronger than any he

had with a member of his family. He didn't want them to
break up!

All his life people had sought him out solely for his
surface qualities, his wealth and good looks. They wanted
to use him for what he could do for them. Lisa, Sam,
Laurel, and Meritt accepted him for what he was. They
affirmed rather than criticized.

Close friends could help so much, but friendship gave
them an equal power to hurt, Martin was learning. A grim
smile quirked a corner of his well-chiseled mouth. Even if
these four someday came to hate each other, their knowledge of the Trojan Horse Project would bind them together
inescapably.

Lisa gloried in the length of her incomparable blond
hair, the color of a ray of sun. Standing before a wall mirror, she swung her head to watch the dazzling sheet swing
back and forth in a thousand shades of pale blond, all the
way down to the small of her back. Naked, she climbed
into bed and reclined, the back of her head on the pillow,
and slowly began to spread out the shining tresses so they
formed a circle like golden petals around her face, the
center focal point, the flower.

She looked up at the ceiling and thought about the Trojan Horse List. It had been two weeks since her friends had
overheard Andy at Smitty's house, and since then they'd
viewed one another with repulsion. Thank God, she was
just about at the end of her page appointment, as were
Laurel and Sam, so she could stop avoiding them. Meritt
and Martin were supposed to continue work until the end
of August.

It was kind of funny how a mutual secret had dispersed
their little group, instead of bringing them together. Lisa
didn't know what the big deal was. Didn't her friends
know how silly it was to be ashamed of one another? Sam,
Meritt, Laurel, and especially Martin had been the best

friends she'd known in her entire eighteen years. She was determined to hang on to them as she grew older, even if she had to shackle them together. In fact, if she had the proper opportunity and proof, her knowledge of a supposed Trojan Horse Project could make her a darling of the press for a while, a media sensation.

The front door was being unlocked. Lisa was perfectly still until Abner Scoville came to the door of his bedroom.

"*Aiiiii!*" he yelled in astonishment. His eyes were wide with shock. "Lisa!"

"You were expectin' maybe someone else?" Lisa sat up slowly so the cover slid down, revealing her waist-up nudity. Her hair fell into place like a curtain.

"Actually, I am." Representative Scoville's jawline, as strong as a leopard's chin, began to quiver. He'd always seen this southern child fully dressed in a page uniform, on page territory. He'd never extended her so much as a peck on the cheek. "How did you get into my apartment?" he demanded.

"Doorman let me in when Ah said Ah was your visiting sister." She slid out of his double bed and walked up to him with the hip grinds of a strip teaser. "Incest is best!"

Abner froze on the spot, fascinated by the moist satin of all that skin, accented by the silverish blond hair. All that innocently asinine repartee they'd shared—she wanted to make it all come true. Her body, with small, uplifted breasts and curved hips, was so dainty, her skin was like rose-tinted cream.

Lisa's delicate hand slid up Abner's suit jacket, then inside a lapel to the warmth of his shirt. "We could share some time together, then ... Ah'd love to go to that White House dinner and meet Richard Nixon. Isn't that where you're headin' tonight—to his dinner for the Foreign Relations subcommittee you serve on?" Lisa pressed her pelvis against his upper thighs. His manhood stiffened, just as it was supposed to. She looked closely up at Abner. "Did you know that, a long time ago, one of President

Nixon's campaign slogans was 'They Can't Lick Our Dick'? Isn't that amusin'?"

She didn't understand. He was showing all the right responses, but he hadn't put a hand on her. She slid a hand inside his trousers and sighed, "Ah bet you think Ah'm still a virgin. You don't have to worry about anything—"

"Get away from me!" Abner screeched. He pulled her hand out of his pants and used her wrist to push her. "Don't you know breaking and entering is a crime?"

"But—you wanted me. You always said so—"

"You always knew I had a fiancée. You really took me *that* seriously? My God, do you really think I'd betray her for a quick roll in the hay with some little political groupie?"

Lisa's brows came down and her lower lip slid out. "All politicians love to play around. It's part of the game." She truly believed what she said.

Abner was stalking around his bedroom, removing one tie, grabbing a new one and sliding it around his neck. "You're one of those southerners who grows up with junked cars on the front lawn, aren't you?"

"I'm from a good antebellum family in Charleston, South Carolina!" Lisa snapped. "Many of my ancestors *died* in the Civil War!"

"Funny about that accent of yours. How it seems to come and go." Anger singed the corners of Lisa's self-control. Abner calmly brushed his hair. "There's something I've got to know, Lisa. Do you really believe that the sight of your naked body has the power to cloud men's minds so they'll take you to dinner at the White House?"

She didn't answer. As Abner tightened his tie in the reflection of the mirror in which Lisa had been appreciating herself earlier, she came up behind him and locked her arms around his waist. "You don't know what you're missing."

He eyed Lisa coldly. "Yes, I do. Nothing."

She dropped her arms. Her naked body was taut with

fury. "You may think those boyish looks of yours are an asset, but at age forty you're beginning to look pretty weird. Kind of like a grownup with a toddler's head." Lisa threw her chin up. "Why have you remained a bachelor all these years? You're really a fag, aren't you? You say you've got a fiancée as a cover-up, don't you?"

As Abner knotted his tie, he acquired the appearance of indifference. "I'm going to the airport now to pick up my fiancée. I'm bringing her back here to dress for the White House dinner tonight. And when we come back here in an hour, you'd better be gone."

Lisa remained standing in the middle of Scoville's bedroom, legs wide apart, her fists clenched at her sides. After the front door shut, her rage congealed hotly in her blood. She lifted her face to the ceiling and screamed. How *dare* that middle-aged turd from Massachusetts treat her so disrespectfully! Every man wanted her. How dare he pretend he was any different?

"You led me on for months!" she hissed through her teeth. Her eyes were squeezed together tightly. "You've spoiled all my plans!" Now she had no idea of where she'd go or what she'd do after she graduated from the page high school.

Lisa opened her eyes wide, and for a moment she literally saw red. She'd squished her baby blues so tightly that mascara had smeared around her eyelids. For the first time she really saw Scoville's apartment, all bachelor-bare of decoration. The very fact that the place was sitting there, just waiting for a wife's hand to provide homey touches, fed Lisa's madness.

Determinedly, she stalked the apartment hunting for a scissors. She found one in a kitchen drawer. If anyone was going to provide a woman's touch, Lisa would do it first. Quickly she started snipping at her hair. Some cuts were made half the way down, some right close to her neck. Lisa kept walking round and round the apartment as she hacked away, and the platinum locks cascaded down her naked body like silken threads. She made sure she got a lot in the bathroom, the kitchen, some in the living room. Much of her prized hair landed in the bedroom, some right on the bed. Wherever the hair came to rest like scattered wheat, it sparkled as beautifully as it had while still attached to Lisa.

Lisa's handiwork was finished within thirty minutes. She put back on her sedate page uniform and in the mirror studied the effect of the navy blue with her new, shaggy mop of hair. It was not displeasing. As she went through the door of Scoville's hair-strewn apartment, she paused to yell back into it, "Try explaining *that* to your wife-to-be!" She slammed the door behind her.

Memorial Day, 1971, coincided with the end of their terms as pages for Lisa, Laurel, and Sam. They chatted with overbright politeness with Meritt in the Capitol Rotunda, directly under the cast-iron, nine-million-pound dome. Lisa delivered the news about Martin: three months before his page appointment was over, he'd run away, in effect, and enlisted in the army. The billionaire's son currently was on his way to grunt camp.

The news would have been stunning, except they all knew how secretive Martin was, how strange his behavior could be.

"He must have believed those posters that say 'Today's army wants to join you'," Laurel said. "What about you, Sam? Do you have a game plan set for the military?"

"I'd never enlist, but if I'm drafted, I'll serve my country," Sam said gravely. "My father served during the Second World War; he was wounded, as a matter of fact."

Meritt told them she planned to stay in Washington till the end of August; after that, she'd didn't know where she'd be living. She intended to be working on the "Great White Way."

Lisa's short hair caused comment, and she explained that she'd cut it on impulse. "It's flatterin', don't ya think?"

After giving one another their parents' addresses, Sam, Lisa and Laurel parted from Meritt with toothy smiles and secret relief. Keeping quiet about what they'd witnessed two weeks ago was to all of them a cowardly, disgraceful cop-out. None of them never wanted to be reminded of it.

• *Seven* •

Meritt du Nord stood outside the Times Square subway station, looking up at the yellow street sign indicating BROADWAY.

Dangling from her hands were two cardboard suitcases that held everything she owned in the world. Up and down the street she could see marquees and billboards for current hits: *Lenny, Follies, Jesus Christ Superstar*. Though it was bright daylight and though the commercial theater was in decline, Meritt couldn't help but be dazzled by the marquees and flashing signs that set the show business style for all of Manhattan.

As she stood on the sidewalk craning her neck back, she heard a click over the street noise. Meritt snapped her face forward and saw that a small, balding man had just taken her photo. "What was that for?" she demanded.

"I'm a street artist," he responded as he wound the film. He reached into his stained photographer's bag and flipped out a green sheet of photocopied paper. "Here." He shuffled off.

A taxicab stopped right in front of Meritt to discharge a

passenger. She stuffed the green paper into a pants pocket
and swiftly flung her suitcases inside the open door. She
threw herself inside just as another person tried to claim the
cab. "Avenue C and Eleventh Street East," she ordered the
Nigerian driver, and he stepped on the gas. She felt like a
prisoner en route to jail behind the grille divider and yellow
stickers announcing that the driver couldn't change more
than five dollars.

Meritt was straight off the train from Washington. She'd
been in New York City just once before, on July 4, when a
former New York page had invited her to watch the fire-
works over the Hudson River. Now it was September, and
she was in the big town for good, eager to start a new life
but armed only with the savings she'd made from nine
months as a page.

The triangular prow of the Flatiron Building plowed
through the traffic as Meritt's cab drove south to the East
Village. She was headed for a place she'd never seen to
share an apartment with a woman she'd never met. Heloise
Kiedrowski was the sister of an older page who had heard
that Meritt planned to move to New York. He told her he
had a sister studying film at New York University who
needed a new roommate. Heloise's previous roomie had
been a Buddhist vegetarian who'd suddenly wigged out
and taken a job as a librarian in Ohio.

"The apartment is halfway between Avenue B and Avenue C," Heloise had explained over long-distance phone,
"or as we Villagers call them, Fire Base Baker and Fire
Base Charlie." Meritt grew apprehensive as the city's des-
sicated brown buildings gave way to a bleak landscape.
The apartment buildings reminded her of photos of bombed
out Hiroshima, except that people actually lived among the
ruins. When the cab stopped on a deserted street, she paid
the taxi driver and went in the tiny entry of 633 Eleventh
Street. Meritt had been instructed to buzz Apartment
Twelve, since Heloise didn't keep her name on the intercom. She stood nervously at the front door until a smiling,

black-haired girl in a black leotard and skirt came to admit her. Deep dimples made parentheses to either side of her mouth.

"Hi, Meritt, I'm Heloise, Heloise as in Heloise and Abelard, not the Heloise of household hints." She lifted one of Meritt's suitcases. "Come on back."

They set down the suitcase in a small, windowless room containing a stove, a refrigerator, a sink, and a bathtub. "Welcome to our imitation apartment," Heloise said cheerfully. There were doors on either side of the room. The north room was Heloise's. It was eight by ten feet, and counterculture gewgaws hung from every available space. Her clothes, which appeared to all be black, were stuffed under a small sleeping loft, accessible by ladder. The south room was Meritt's. It was identical to Heloise's, except there was a door on the wall opposite.

"Where's the bathroom in this place?"

"Uh, we don't have a *bathroom*, exactly. Open that door and you'll see." Heloise held her breath, as though afraid her new roommate would bolt, once she saw what was behind the door. There were several wooden steps leading to a toilet stool. There was no sink in the tiny, unventilated closet. You had to wash your hands in the same sink used for washing dishes. Apologetically Heloise explained, "See those little steps? It's literally a throne." Her grin twisted as she said sarcastically, "Gosh, did you ever dream someday you'd get a room with your very own toilet?"

"I'm going to choke to death from the air freshener fumes."

"You'll live through it. Besides, nobody really *lives* in a New York apartment. You spend time at home mostly to sleep."

Meritt tried to keep the disappointment off her face. She'd been warned in advance that the neighborhood wasn't the greatest, but when she was told the place was a two-bedroom apartment, she'd hoped for something out of a Rock Hudson–Doris Day movie, with a uniformed doorman and modern, sleek furniture, and a sweeping view looking out over the sparkling city. Heloise laid a kind hand on her shoulder. "I was afraid you'd expect something better than this. But when you see a few other places, you'll realize what a bargain we're getting here. Besides, we don't have any cockroaches or mice. . . . What's this?" She bent over to pick up a crumpled piece of green paper from the ugly tile floor.

"That must have fallen out of my pocket. Some weird guy shoved it at me in the street. Said he was a street artist."

"Some people call themselves street artists to excuse their psychotic behavior. Hmmm . . . looks like an invitation to a party, for *tonight*. 'His most loyal fans invite you to a gathering in honor of Oscar Moore Travis.' This address is in the Tribeca area."

"Who's Oscar Moore Travis?"

"You don't know? He's this interior decorator for high society, who's supposed to be kind of an Andy Warhol—"

"How can a society interior decorator be an Andy Warhol?"

"It's in the people he attracts, the parties he goes to."

"I don't know. I didn't like the look of the guy who gave me this. He took my picture and ran."

"My God, Meritt, you've got to go! And take me along, too, of course. Just think about it." Heloise glanced at an old clock on the wall that said HAVE A PEPSI DAY. "Look, I've got to run to my dance class. You get settled in. You may want to look at that issue of *New York* in my room, 'cause there's a long story about Oscar Moore Travis in there. Nice meeting you!—'Bye!" Heloise was gone like a whirling dervish.

Meritt shrugged at her surroundings. Lethargically, she opened her suitcases and began putting her clothes on hangers. She was pleased to see that her clothes didn't take much space on the pole suspended under her sleeping loft. If she were careful to keep her room uncluttered, it could look cleaner, larger, and well-ordered. She checked out Heloise's room, and saw that her roommate had a thin mattress atop her sleeping loft. Meritt would sleep on her sheets tonight, and tomorrow go buy a small mattress for herself.

During one late night in Washington this summer, Meritt and six of her page friends had sat in a restaurant in Chinatown, debating whether a person's personality could be safely judged by perusal of his book or record collection. Meritt argued against the theory: "I don't own any books or records, and y'all have never called me a moron!" Yet she wondered if her new roommate's quarters were indicative of the real Heloise. Heloise's tiny corner of New York turf looked as if Hurricane Alice had visited. Face powder and blush lay on everything like a thin coat of dust. On the wall there was a poster of Golda Meir that asked, "But can she type?" As befitted a film student, the rest of the wall space was plastered with movie stills. Every cranny from which something could be suspended had cheap jewelry dangling from it. Soft surfaces were stabbed with message buttons. Heloise seemed to collect tiny toys, like plastic fish and frogs, and minute kissing dolls and chattering teeth, which were strewn in the confusion like chocolate chips in cookie dough. Ticket stubs and theater programs were scattered over every space, including the floor.

The refrigerator was full-size, and Heloise had it stocked with the four basic food groups—plenty of milk, frozen meats, and fresh fruit. Such solid nutritional sense didn't seem to belong to a woman who lived in the hurricane-blasted room Meritt had just seen. She took out a Granny Smith apple and sat down on the floor with the issue of *New York* magazine recommended by Heloise.

The story on Oscar Moore Travis was titled "Oscar Wilde? Oscar *Tame*." There was a photo of a tall, thick-set man of pale coloring. His great eyes were light blue and heavily lidded, and there was sensuality in his loose lower lip. Unfortunately, under his mouth his chin sank into several chins. In the photograph he wore a striped, pastel blue shirt under an ecru-colored coat and vest, and a hat to match.

The article pointed out that there was more resemblance between Oscar Moore Travis and Oscar Wilde than just their names and appearances: Travis was becoming legendary for his slashing wit. A box toward the end of the story featured a few of his epigrams:

Love is like pantyhose, or so I'm told. It expands as far as it can and then it runs.

If the Gods had seen you, they wouldn't have created the universe.

She makes Bella Abzug look like an airline stewardess.

Cats are merely effeminate dogs.

Love is two people being stupid together.

The piece reported that Oscar Moore Travis circulated in Manhattan's low life and its high society. Now forty-three years old, Travis had started out a painter at age twenty-two in the downtown's vivid art community. He'd started making decorative objects a few years later, then started telling people how to best use his and others' decorative objects in a room. By age thirty he'd gravitated to advising people on how to decorate their houses.

Travis specialized in creating the ambiance of past eras. His biggest triumphs were in Art Deco or Depression Moderne design. When he'd started decorating rooms for a couple of New York bluebloods during the sixties, the lady of the house often would ask him to lunch with her and a few friends at Le Cirque or La Côte Basque. The lucky ladies at the table were so won over by Travis's wicked gossip and bon mots that he was accepted into New York's Rich and Beautiful set without having to climb the usual

ladder. "Anyone can pal around with the rich and mighty,"
Travis had told the interviewer from *New York*. "Just as
long as you remember to say 'curtains' instead of
'drapes'."

Oscar never bothered to write down and remember his
maxims, but plenty of other people did. Oscar's detractors
—and victims—said his true calling was writing situation
comedy for TV. He said his true calling was being a party
monster. He loved going to parties and he loved giving
them.

When Heloise returned home a couple of hours later,
she found her new roommate in a festive mood. "I think
I'm ready to go to that Oscar Moore Travis party," Meritt
said. She wore a crimson body stocking that put her lush
curves on full display. Over the body stocking she'd
draped a chain link belt and a heavy gold coin necklace.
She'd topped all this with a satin baseball jacket! Her
raven hair was pulled to the back so that her shoulder-
length bangle earrings and sculptured cheekbones were
fully revealed.

Heloise was stunned by Meritt's appearance. Irv, her
younger brother, had written her that Meritt was excep-
tional-looking, and Heloise had agreed that Meritt was
pretty when she'd shown up, but tonight she was remarkable! Her lips looked wider and fuller, and with that shining hair pulled back she looked high-fashion haughty. The
body stocking outlined a form many men described as their
fantasy: swinging hips and luxurious, deep breasts that
stopped a millimeter short of too big. The gold chain belt
around her waist defined its smallness. It made Heloise
glad that her dancer's body, slender and reedlike, was
formed in an entirely different way. No competition.

Embarrassed at being so dumbstruck by her roommate's
appearance, she playfully recited, "She walks in beauty
like the night. . . ."

Meritt gave her husky laugh. "Come on, Heloise. Get

dressed and then I'll take you out for a housewarming dinner."

At midnight the two young women stood outside a corner building several blocks from Chinatown. It was a five-story warehouse, and only the second floor was lit. Party sounds, the hubbub of music and talk, streamed out the open windows. Meritt found a door and knocked on it. In a gruff voice she answered herself, "Come in!" Giggling, they ran up the flight of stairs.

To Meritt's wondering eyes, this party was nothing like any she'd attended in Louisiana or even Washington, D.C. The brightly lit room was the size of a ballroom, and its dirty wooden floor was crowded with people wearing get-ups far more outrageous than her body stocking. Many wore black, just like Heloise: it was the color of rebellion. Others wore see-through shirts, ballgowns, antique clothing, and torrents of jewelry. To Meritt's right a disk jockey was working the sound system, tailoring the music to the party. To her left a messy row of card tables held beer kegs and sloppy bowls of potato chips and dip and Doritos, and big bottles of alcohol.

A redhaired man in a T-shirt that had a tuxedo screen-printed on it came toward the exit. "I love your body!" he exclaimed to Meritt in passing. She laughed and glanced at Heloise—but Heloise was no longer at her side. Quickly Meritt scanned around the party, looking for her new roommate's black tube dress. When she had counted four black tube dresses just like Heloise's, a small cloud of anxiety settled over her, the same kind of distress a child experiences when he's left off at summer camp.

Meritt stood on her toes in an attempt to look over the crowd. From across the room a dark-haired man stared directly back at her, directly *through* her, in fact. A lamp with a single bare bulb created a halo of light around his head.

Meritt bit her lip and looked away. The man's nonchalant gaze had unsettled her. Hoping to locate Heloise, she set off through the crowd, wading through a sea of hot bodies. She couldn't help overhearing threads of conversation shouted over the music as she pushed herself along.

"I got a letter today that's gonna solve all my problems. It came from the Publisher's Clearing House . . ."

"This entire My Lai business makes me want to up-chuck. It's society's fault that Lieutenant Calley killed all those village people. He is us! We're all responsible for this war's immorality. You and I are to blame for turning soldiers into slaughterers."

"I don't know what to say." "You could tell me to jump in the river." "I don't want you to jump in the river."

"I saw you looking at me from across the room."

Meritt's eyes snapped upward to see that the fluctuating tides of the party had placed her in front of the man she'd stared at. He was about half a head taller than she, and very young. Meritt, who was sixteen going on seventeen, looked several years more sophisticated than she was.

"I wasn't looking at you," she claimed. "You were looking at me."

He teased, "You seem to be suffering from a mild case of selective amnesia." Then he smiled, revealing teeth that were tobacco stained, but large and beautifully straight. Meritt's knees turned weak. His face was dazzlingly fine, with a strong mouth and sparkling grey eyes that shone with sardonic humor. The grey eyes underlined the deep brown of his tumbled hair. His pallor was that of a man who didn't go outside much, and he was dressed for the indoors in a simple white shirt, black jeans and work boots. This was most definitely an urban man, the ultimate insider who probably knew every secret to be found in the big city. "Do you know anyone at this party?" he asked.

"No! I was handed the invitation on the street today by a man who called himself a street artist."

"That'd be Pee Wee Eisenmann. He does moronic things, then calls them art. He doesn't want anyone to know he lives with his parents." He reached over to rest a hand on Meritt's shoulder, and the simple touch released an exciting turbulence of feeling in her. Her color rose as she fought to keep her face impassive. He added, "And I . . . I was invited by a friend of Oscar Moore Travis."

"What kind of people are here?"

"You honestly don't know?" He was looking at her keenly and curiously. "This is the East Village you see here—artists, writers, models, actors, transvestites—and some business executives, each one of them trying to project a downtown bohemia image. . . ."

"How do you know all these people?"

"They're my friends. I specialize in comforting artists in torment, which many of them are."

"What do you mean, artists in torment?"

"You know—a struggling artist is confused, full of rage and self-doubt, though he feels superior to others. You can easily identify the artists here. They're afflicted with baggy eyes and a fifties beatnik-junkie style. Their very favorite thing to do is to go to parties where they can act mysterious."

Meritt laughed with her head thrown back and mouth open, exposing her teeth and delicate pink tongue. There was something about the blasé, casually striking young man that charmed her.

Heloise's hand clapped onto her upper arm. "Hey, Meritt, I found Oscar Moore Travis. He's in the next room."

"Wait, I was talking to—"

"Come on!" her roommate said impatiently.

"I'll be back!" Meritt promised the young man as she was enveloped by the crowd. Cripes, she hadn't even gotten his name!

Meritt was completely overwhelmed when Heloise led

her down a hall into a beautiful room where the thick pile
of the carpet muffled the click of their heels. This room,
where Oscar Moore Travis was holding court, was the opposite of the large loft they'd just exited. This kind of
beautifully proportioned space, more of a library, was uni-
maginable south of Park Avenue. The reproductions of
nineteenth-century furniture were made of rare woods and
accented with gilded carvings and brass animal forms. The
walls were lacquered with aubergine and adorned with
original paintings, each lit by pin spotlights. A tall book-
case in one corner held leather volumes of books in four
different languages. A light film of cigarette smoke hung
suspended in the air. This room was nearly as impressive
as some of those in Martin Vanderziel's Washington house
and to Meritt's eye, a lot more tasteful. It was then that she
realized the party was being held in Oscar Moore Travis's
own *house*. That meant that *he* was throwing this party . . .
in honor of himself! She guessed that he rented the adjoining ballroom-sized space for storage and/or a place where
young, homeless men could crash—Oscar's own "Hustler
Hotel," where it was easy to check in, and sticky to check
out.

Like a generator, Oscar Moore Travis provided all the
electricity in the room. He stood in the geographical center,
surrounded by people sitting on fake French First Empire
chairs and scarlet Turkish couches, and by people sitting
literally at his feet. *This looks like Jesus with his disciples*,
Meritt thought.

"No, Oscar, I swear on my mother's grave!" a delicate
young man was protesting.

"But, Lambert, you never *had* a mother," Oscar replied
in a smooth yet sensual voice. To the room he announced,
"Lambert crawled out from under a rock."

As Meritt laughed, so did the entire room. Next to her
Heloise was giggling, too. Meritt's hands idly played with
a gold rhinoceros she'd picked up from a table. It was a

worthless trinket. With so many strangers around Oscar's house, she guessed that all his objets d'art were.

"Say, Rodney," Oscar said, puffing on a tiny brown cigar, "I saw the small exhibit of your sculpture on display at the Santiago Gallery. Judging from that, I'd say you've got the right stuff. Competent, quite competent." Oscar used his rich, resonant voice like a fine instrument.

Rodney, who stood close to Oscar, responded, "Thanks, Oscar. I'm still working on making a more definite statement. Those weren't as well done as I wanted them to be."

"Pipe down, Rod-nay. You're not talented enough to be *that* humble."

The entire room rocked with laughter. Oscar's delivery was so perfectly timed that his feeble remarks came out sounding like brilliant wit. The conversation went on to Mr. Santiago, the gallery owner. Meritt studied Oscar's appearance and decided he wasn't as physically pleasant as *New York*'s photographs had made him out to be. His body was tall, but his vested banker's suit couldn't hide how massive and disproportionate he was. His small head rested like a baseball atop his form, and his button nose was just a little dab on his face. His thick lips were as moist as if he'd just bitten into a tomato. Perhaps Oscar Moore Travis enjoyed dealing out Don Rickles-type insults because he was so homely. If he could triumph over his appearance to become so famous and popular, Travis deserved admiration not affection.

Meritt whispered to Heloise, "I'm going back to the party. I met a guy—"

As she maneuvered with her back against the wall, feeling for the door to the hallway, Oscar's smooth voice rang out: "Leaving so soon, my dear?" It took Meritt a moment to notice that all the heads had turned to look at her. She gave Oscar a shaky smile, and tried to move on. "You see what delicacies I offer to my friends?" Oscar said with his plump hands outstretched. "Regard my Nubian princess! Mother to generations of courtesans bred especially for the

white masters—exotic, sensual, dusky quadroons, octo-
roons—"

"You mean darkies!" a black man yelled.

Meritt couldn't identify the rage swelling within her. She
started to walk backward and her heavy necklace clanged
against her metal link belt.

"Look at the chains with which this nubile member of a
blackamoor tribe is bound." With his heavy-lidded eyes
Oscar looked as though he were sneering. "You should be
put in a cage and sent to Charleston to be sold in the slave
market." His pronouncement was met with nervous, eager-
to-please laughing from people who didn't know if he was
being funny or not.

He was a woman-hater, she realized. In a tight, cold
tone Meritt retorted, "I bet your family is *awfully* proud of
you."

She yanked open the door and retreated to the bright
lights of the other room, Heloise following her.

"Gosh, Meritt, I'm sorry, I never should have dragged
you in there."

"No, it's okay! I wanted to see what Oscar Moore Travis
was about. And I did—I learned that everybody is fair
game for him." They were back in the brightly lit loft.
Meritt stood on her toes, craning her neck. "Heloise, I met
this great guy, and now I don't see him." She sagged
against the wall. New York, the city of her dreams, was
starting to seem dirty and depressing.

"Wanna dance, honey?"

"No." Meritt looked up at an androgynous male in jeans
and a T-shirt. It took a second to realize that the slender
boy was actually a woman. *"No!"*

She went away. Heloise said, "You need a chaperon."
She paused. "Meritt, are you really black?"

"Yes. As black as you can be with fifteen-sixteenths of
your blood white as snow."

"Then you're free to be just about anything you choose,
huh?"

Before Meritt had a chance to respond, a middle-aged man with an eager face came up to her. His bald head gleamed. "Say, are you an actress by any chance? Or a model?"

Meritt eyed him warily. "I'm studying to be an actress."

"We're putting together an off-Broadway musical, and we'd be real pleased if you auditioned for us." He flipped her a business card that read SUNBRIGHT PRODUCTIONS over an address and phone number.

Turning instant chaperon, Heloise demanded skeptically, "Is this legit?"

"We've been in business for twenty years!" the man answered huffily. "Sunbright is always on the lookout for fresh faces, new talent." To Meritt he said, "Give us a call as soon as you can, huh?" and walked away.

"A musical!" Meritt held the business card in front of her. "I don't think I can sing."

"Don't worry, Meritt. You can fake it." Heloise was thinking that with Meritt's face and body, she didn't have to worry about singing.

The offices of Sunbright Productions were bright, sunny, attractively appointed, and next door to the offices of the American Ballet Theater. Meritt sat across from Seymour, the man she'd met the previous night. Last night he'd been bald; today he had on an auburn toupee. She sat without touching the back of her chair as if prepared to run, because she'd just been startled by Seymour's revelation that she had to strip for the audition.

"What! You want me to take my clothes off onstage? To orate in the nude?"

"Along with twenty other people, sure."

"But what about the acting! The songs! You need actors who can do more than look good naked, don't you?"

"No, we don't." Seymour spread his hands. "Look sweetheart, everybody does it nowadays. Look at the productions of *Hair; Oh! Calcutta; Let My People Come; Score.* Lots of nudity. Tourists don't care about the songs. You must have read about those shows."

"Yes I read about them, but I'll never go see them." Meritt tried to sound reasonable. "Look, I'll strip down to a bikini for any role, but that's as far as I go."

"Honey, don't you realize the chance I'm giving you? You were lucky that I discovered you at all. You're never gonna get another break."

Meritt couldn't help giggling. "If that line was any more lame it'd be on crutches."

"Get outta here."

Down on the street in the bright sunlight, Meritt berated herself for allowing herself to think that offer to audition hadn't any strings, and she vowed not to be so stupid again.

Walking north on Broadway, she thought about the grey-eyed, self-assured charmer she'd met at Oscar Moore Travis's loft the previous evening. She had a feeling he'd get a kick out of her experience. Meritt wasn't going to let herself be disheartened about everything that had happened since she'd arrived on Broadway twenty-four hours before. Resignedly she acknowledged that she had to face her new life like a mule in a hailstorm, hunkered down and braced against it.

"What do you think?" Meritt asked Heloise as she twirled around in a taffeta gown. The hem swept romantically from high in the front to low in the back. "Do I look tacky?"

"You look ravishing. But I'd keep the dress at the restaurant and change there if I were you. You don't want to ride the subway to work in a one-shoulder dress."

Smiling with satisfaction, Meritt started to remove the dusky lavender dress. It was provided free by the swanky midtown restaurant where she'd obtained a job several hours after she'd left Seymour and his nudie musical audition. The gown was the uniform she'd wear as a dining room hostess. The famous restaurant served nouveau French cuisine and was named Charolais, which amused Meritt. Didn't they know that Charolais was a breed of cow?

She was going to be working the evening shift, which would leave her free to attend casting calls and take acting classes during the day.

The phone in their little kitchen rang. "Could you get that?" Heloise called from her room. The small TV in her room was blaring out a rerun from "Star Trek," the "Arena" episode. In bra and underpants, Meritt dashed to pick up the phone. "Hello?"

"Is this Heloise Kiedrowski?"

Instantly Meritt recognized the voice. "It's you!"

"It's you!" he returned, sounding just as surprised.

Wait—don't sound too eager and overjoyed, she counseled herself. In a quieter voice she asked, "How *did* you get this number?"

"Simple. When Heloise pulled you away, someone at the party said, 'That's Heloise Kiedrowski. I go to film school with her.' So I tracked down Heloise's phone number . . . hoping I could get your number from her."

That offhand sexuality of his came straight over the phone line. Meritt answered, "Yes, we live together. What'd you want my number for?" Oh cripes, Meritt thought, don't be coy, that's not you!

"To get your name."

"It's Meritt du Nord." She paused. "And your name?"

"Jeremy Serkin."

"I know this is a pretty clichéd opening question, but what do you do for a living?"

"I direct plays. Plays that are off-Broadway. And *off* off-Broadway. What do you do? Are you a student?"

I'm a high school dropout, Meritt thought. She said, "I'm what's called an aspiring actress."

Jeremy chuckled. "We'd make a great team, huh?"

Every fiber of Meritt's body tingled with gladness, and her excitement for Manhattan was reborn. New York was going to be the kind of adventure that would make her feel at last she was living real life.

• *Eight* •

Dr. Ping Chung, a highly esteemed neuropsychiatrist from Red China, was being led through the Hanoi Hilton, the main prisoner-of-war camp in North Vietnam. The deferential but proud North Vietnamese prison commandant seemed determined to give Dr. Ping and his several assistants a tour of the place. It had been built in 1940 by the French. "We got rid of the French, and now we'll get rid of the Americans, no matter how long it takes," the prison commandant declared. "We North Vietnamese are a patient people." Dr. Ping ignored him; he had no interest in the politics of the small nation.

They went into the main yard, which was surrounded by twenty-foot walls topped with broken glass and electric wire. Four guard towers stood against a white-hot sky of shimmering haze. There were no POWs to be seen, except for five American prisoners sitting cross-legged against a wall, their gaunt necks all connected at the back by a long rope. They wore prison pajamas, and had very white skin since they weren't often allowed outside. Forbidden to speak, they stared at the dirt with blank eyes, trying to keep from thinking. A cloud of flies buzzed around them in the oppressive heat.

"The majority of POWs have been United States Air Force and Navy pilots and air crew members, shot down in North Vietnam starting back in 1965," the prison officer said. "These men were shot down in December of 1971." Today was January 7, 1972. Since the middle of 1971 there had been a vague feeling on both sides that the war was ending, so U.S. POWs were threatened more than tortured.

"My people told you I'm searching for an army infantryman who was with them," Dr. Ping Chung said.

"You mean the rich man's son. He was unlucky enough to be aboard an F-4 that was shot down while on a mission to check on movement of our army troops. The simpleton actually volunteered for the mission upon his arrival, fresh off the boat. He's staying in what the Americans call 'New Guy Village'." The prison commandant had the dark skin of a Vietnamese peasant, with large crooked teeth so big and crowded he couldn't close his lips over them. Dr. Ping, though squat and ugly, had the fair skin of a Chinese, as did his two assistants. "Why are you waiting?" he asked irritatedly. "Take me to him."

New Guy Village was a wing by the main gate, right behind a room used for questioning. The North Vietnamese called the process interrogation; Americans called it torture. Screaming seldom issued from a North Vietnamese horror chamber, because POWs who cried out were punished with more pain. Dr. Ping Chung and his assistants were led down a short, unlit hall. The prison commandant unlocked one of the steel doors along the corridor, and it squeaked loudly as it opened, since the hinges had never been lubricated.

Private Martin Vanderziel was inside. He wore the fatigues of an infantryman. His imposing last name was printed over his right breast pocket. He sat in one corner, blinking at the light like a rodent flushed out of hiding. Martin was caught in the process of throwing some bread crumbs in the opposite corner: some POWs used that tactic in hopes that the rats would confine their visits to that corner, eat their rations and go.

The crumbs fell from his fingers. Martin stood up until his posture was perfect. His handsome face had been savagely scratched two weeks earlier because the trajectory from his forced parachute landing had dropped him through the jungle's razor-sharp palm tree fronds. He looked out at the Oriental men, awaiting their whim. A lug wrench couldn't have changed his closed expression. Dr. Ping was surprised by the boy's monumental indifference. He appeared not to care what would happen to him next, no matter whether he were released to his country or executed on the spot.

"You father no send person to rescue you, animal," the commandant said in broken English, raising a baton threateningly. Martin didn't flinch.

He was much taller than the Chinese. Dr. Ping Chung wore a light brown jacket that enhanced his resemblance to a cockroach. He was elderly, hunched over, and he held his tiny hands up against his chest as a praying mantis does. His small skull was completely bald, and scattered with dark blotches. His black beetle eyes were very tiny under magnifying glass-type spectacles and magnificently woolly eyebrows.

Martin continued looking down at him, and his grave eyebrows shifted into a little frown, as though he half-recognized Dr. Ping Chung and was trying to place him. As Dr. Ping smiled, showing irregular yellow teeth, his eyes, nose and mouth scrunched into a knot of wrinkles.

Dr. Ping stepped forward. He stated, "You are for me."

He motioned his assistants into the cubicle. One savagely grabbed Martin's right arm, expecting him to resist, but the American was still. The other young Chinese, a woman who wore a lab coat, reached into a pocket and swabbed the inside of Martin's left arm. From the other pocket she produced a long hypodermic needle, and punctured the arm while Martin watched interestedly. Within seconds his body began to sag.

After he lost consciousness, Dr. Ping placed a tender hand in his thick black hair and gave a sweetly sympathetic smile. To his assistants he said sadly, "Poor Martin will never awake. From this moment, he is dreaming a nightmare that will never end."

When Martin regained consciousness several days later in Laos, he was not his own man. His lids retracted to reveal the ice-blue eyes glazed over and almost lifeless. Sweat dripped from every pore, glazing his face and torso. All he wore were North Vietnam Army pajamas that were too short for his tall American form. Reflexively, he twisted his limbs, to find his ankles and his wrists, stretched over his head, were shackled in irons. A catheter was connected from his bladder to the side of the concrete platform on which he lay. He was not uncomfortable.

The pungent odor of deep undergrowth and virgin greenery stung his nostrils. Through the top of a screened window, he saw only dense jungle foliage. A young woman sat in a chair in the corner of a small room, reading a book. When she saw that his eyes were open, she jumped up and ran out. "Doctor Ping! He is awake!"

Soon Dr. Ping Chung entered the room, and his expression as he regarded Martin akin to love. "Undo these things," he directed the girl, as she quickly released the irons holding Martin down. Then withdrew to the corner again. The infantryman slowly brought his arms to his sides, but remained supine.

"My child, do you know who you are?" Dr. Ping asked.

His patient whispered mechanically, "Martin Vanderziel."

"We are in a small hospital in northern Laos, hundreds of miles away from any American forces. It is a crude facility, but it serves my purpose. The Vietcong have been using this Laotian outpost as a base of operations. Do you realize, that all the time the Americans used their military might, our little guerrillas have been based from disorganized, scattered fortresses and outposts? It makes the American defeat all the more amazing."

Dr. Ping reached into his jacket pockets for Chinese cigarettes. His Mao jacket bore no sign of his rank, in keeping with China's egalitarian social order. "You do not know who I am, though I'm quite famous in my field. I am Dr. Ping Chung, the world's foremost expert on mind control." He sat on a stool so his large head was nearly level with Martin's on the platform. "You will be my greatest subject, though unfortunately no one will know about it for years.

"Martin have you ever heard about the mind conditioning that took place during the Korean War? When a handful of American military men announced that they wanted to remain in Communist Korea? That was my doing. In fact, I learned English only to communicate with those soldiers." Dr. Ping's eyes sparkled as he dragged on his cigarette and rocked his torso back and forth several times. "Americans called the process 'brainwashing.' The formal definition is an intense indoctrination aimed at changing one's basic convictions and attitudes and replacing them with a fixed and unquestioned set of beliefs. Most people want to deny that such a process is possible.

"They are wrong," he said proudly. "I invented it. I pioneered the study of mind control. Conditioning has almost been lost as a science, but I am determined to revive it."

The neuropsychiatrist went on to explain that he was an aristocrat among Communists, a member of the Communist People's Liberation Army long before the 1949 Red Chinese Revolution. "I have conducted medical experiments for the People's Republic since that time. Previous to that I studied in Soviet Russia, where I was trained in the reconstruction of personality.

"We've had few opportunities to work on humans after the Korean War. As a leading party official, I have been allowed to serve as an adviser in the younger nations under Communist domain. Here at our humble facility in Laos, we're free to work without restraint because we are unreachable, utterly remote from American forces. We've been given a free hand with prisoners of war since the world will never find out about our encampment."

Martin was in the state of posthypnotic alexia. His drugged consciousness, or what was left of it, drifted from the strange little man's monologue. The accented voice was foggy and muted to him. His mind was sealed away, leaving a blank slate waiting to be written on. The only feeling left to Martin was that something had *changed*. His eyes rolled back in his head from time to time. Dr. Ping's face shifted in and out of focus. Beyond him, flickering on the edge of his field of vision, was the young Chinese woman.

Keui-Lan listened intently and adoringly to every word that came from the master's mouth. Dr. Ping was a genius and slightly mad in a way that was alternately entertaining and scary. Yet the Caucasian had stirred her, awakening an old, dormant maternal instinct and romantic yearning. He was so handsome; it was a pity he was doomed.

"I have worked hard at perfecting my technique, Martin." Dr. Ping continued, "I have adapted some mind-alteration exercises that your Central Intelligence Agency financed during the nineteen-fifties and sixties at McGill University in Canada. In my hands, brainwashing has become an art."

Outside the screen window, a sunset glowed. The unseen life of the dark forest canopy was beginning its shrill nightly cacophony, starting with the insistent chorus of peeping tree frogs. Thousands of birds, mammals and insects slowly joined in with rasping, whistling and trilling noises. Sweat stood out on Dr. Ping's high forehead, misting his thickly lensed spectacles.

"And you, Martin, will be my masterpiece. When I was told that we had captured the son of a leading capitalist, I rejoiced. You are corrupt, like your father. When I first saw you, I knew you were a decadent young man already afflicted with a sickness of the soul. It will not be difficult to condition you to perform behaviors repellent to the nature of most human beings. My subjects usually are not easily induced to act against their conscience, yet you, Vanderziel, have no such qualms or scruples."

Unable to hold his excitement in any longer, Dr. Ping stood up and turned to his assistant. "What purpose shall we instill in this patient, Keui-Lan? Something to do with his father, surely." He rubbed his miniature hands together in anticipation as he moved toward the door, then turned back to fling one more comment at Martin.

"Even you must have read about Dr. Pavlov, the man who trained dogs to salivate at the dinner bell though no dinner was forthcoming. My techniques are considerably more complicated, but when I am finished with you, you will react to my commands automatically as those unfed *dogs*."

That night as he lay on the concrete sleeping platform, Martin's last real memory swept through his mind. Faces and bodies formed from the ghostly shapes that he saw moving about the room. The recollection came to him as a dream through a dream.

He was back in Saigon, the night his squad arrived in Vietnam. Hundreds of people scurried through the streets, most of them on errands related directly to the war. Martin and four of his acquaintances sat in a tiny, smoke-filled café dimly lit by the flicker of candles. A jukebox was playing the Rolling Stones's "Brown Sugar." Grouped around oilcloth-covered tables, the U.S. infantrymen drank Budweiser from the bottle. Relative strangers, they were feeling each other out as potential buddies. Within that somewhat cautious atmosphere, Martin was the most reticent soldier. Like the trainees in boot camp, his companions didn't realize that Martin Vanderziel was the son of *the* Vanderziel, T. Wayne.

A couple of guys were complaining about their bad luck in being shipped to Southeast Asia while other U.S. troops were already being sent home. They stopped their discussion when a pimply teenage boy, flanked by two prostitutes, came to their table. "You want good time?" he asked. "They love you long time. Make you very happy."

One of the diminutive, black-haired girls wore a miniskirt that stopped at her crotch; the other wore tight stretch pants. Their tank tops looked sprayed onto their small breasts. They had tight, closed faces and a petulant manner. The girl in the stretch pants rubbed her groin area in a circular motion. "Me horny," she said mechanically, looking over their heads.

"I love you long time," claimed the other girl in a robotic voice. "Fucky, sucky. What you want."

"Whoooo-eeeeeeee!" The soldiers laughed and stared: none of them had ever seen such bold soliciting before. "Where do we go?" asked a skinny Texan.

"You follow me," the teenage boy replied. Four of the Americans stood up. After a moment, Martin stood. Like a pack, they followed the adolescent pimp and the two whores down the street to a weather-beaten stucco building. Its walls were covered with peeling layers of propaganda posters and advertising. The night was hot and thick with humidity.

The front door appeared to be boarded up, but the boy pushed through it. The five soldiers entered a very dark room. The air was rancid. When their eyes adjusted to the dimness, they saw nine women, all Oriental, with heavily painted faces, sprawled over sagging couches and chairs. Some appeared desperate and forlorn, aged and grotesque; others seemed as guileless as if they'd never turned a trick in their lives. Most of them wore lingerie of a nylon that looked harsh as wire screening. It displayed their hard-used skin under hues of red and green and blue.

"It's okay if your dick is hard, fellas!" said one of the guys.

"Look at those garbanzas!"

"Wouldn't you like them spike heels to do a hoedown on your business?"

Presently a madam came in, a haggard concoction of perfume, teased concrete beehive, loud dangling jewelry, face paint and purple polyester lace. All the girls stood up as she entered and formed a straight line. The gawking infantrymen were immobile until a more experienced soldier muttered from the side of his mouth. "They're waiting for us to make a selection. Let's see if they have anything better to offer." In a louder voice he asked the madam, "Do you have anything besides this?" The woman's black tilted eyes glittered within layers of kohl, but she remained still. The soldier pressed some money at her, then she pointed down a dark hallway. Martin and his four colleagues felt their way to a heavy curtain.

Behind it was a small room where they stumbled their way into empty chairs. Other servicemen and some civilians, both American and Vietnamese, were seated already, watching the show in progress atop a broken daybed. Two young girls were dutifully performing oral sex on each other. Their exposed mouths and their private regions resembled fresh, ripe fruit. Some observers looked attentive or aroused; the others seemed bored.

Martin, who had not sat down, felt a tap on his shoulder. He swiveled his head to see the madam, who smiled at him suggestively through her red gash of a mouth. She had one hand locked onto the arm of a child, a girl approximately eleven years old. Even in the dark, he could see the smoothness of her yellow-brown face and the beauty of her black almond eyes. The madam, long experienced in judging which customer liked what speciality, had divined one of his sexual tastes.

"She for you."

Martin looked more closely at the girl, who wore only a

faded cotton shift. From another angle he could see that her lovely eyes were like those of an eighty-year-old. No doubt she'd been sexually trained at an early age. Like Martin, she'd been given little chance to grow up and be a human being.

Martin withdrew some paper money and slipped it to the madam while he continued studying the child. Instinct told her to fear him more than the other johns. She trembled slightly, but she took his hand and led him to a cubicle.

Deeply involved in his studies, Sam rarely caught any news that occurred outside the campus of Northwestern University. By chance, he picked up the New York *Times* on the second Sunday of January, 1972, and found the small item on a back page: "Vanderziel Son Missing in Action." The story reported that Martin had been aboard an F-4 shot down by the Vietcong. The entire crew had been taken prisoner.

The North Vietnamese POW camps were godforsaken pits of hell, where Americans were stuffed inside tiny "tiger cages," and chained in swamps with only their heads above water. They were driven to eat rats, insects, and small reptiles. Sam didn't care if Martin was a psychopathic creep—no soldier deserved that POW treatment.

Sam went into action. He persuaded Laurel's mother to call on the top brass, demanding a fact-finding mission. Within a week she reported that all that could be done for POWs was being done.

By phone Sam goose-chased around the country, trying to pin down a Vanderziel. For three days Meritt sat in the lobby of the Vanderziel offices, hoping in vain to speak to one of Martin's brothers. Just as Sam was running out of long-distance money, Lovell Vanderziel, a vice-president of Vanderziel International, called Sam from his office in Austin, Texas. "My father knows about Martin. He says nothing can be done for him."

Sam blurted into the phone, "Well, can't you hire some mercenaries to rescue Martin? Or a SWAT team? Did you think of that?" Immediately he was ashamed, feeling like a little boy who'd made up too many GI-Joe fantasies. But Lovell Vanderziel replied in wonder, "Hmm, mercenaries. We didn't think of that." In a brusque tone he snapped, "I'll talk to my brothers about it," and hung up.

With the aid of drugs, Dr. Ping began imprinting a precise psychological design on Martin's mind. There were seven other Chinese in the hospital-POW camp, all male except for Dr. Ping's personal assistant, Keui-Lan. They had been assigned Laotian servants, and the men guarding the compound were Vietcong. Though its remoteness kept it relatively safe, the fortress was heavily guarded. The compound was surrounded by crude concrete perimeter walls, with guard towers at each corner.

The seven Chinese, one North Vietnamese, and one Russian were there to study with the elderly doctor, and all were in such awe of the legendary Ping Chung that they hesitated timidly before speaking to him.

He explained the initial process of blanking Martin's mind before entering data that would restructure his personality. "We have a delightful dilemma before us," Ping told his students. "How shall we program Martin Vanderziel? What would you like him to do when he returns to the United States?"

"You spoke about his father." Keui-Lan recalled, and with the air of an apprentice anticipating her master's next thought, suggested, "It must be something to do with the father, surely."

"He is the essence of American capitalism and imperialism," said a Chinese intern, eager to reinforce the choice of an enemy. "Remember, T. Wayne Vanderziel was a strong supporter of Chiang Kai-shek, who led the Nationalists against the Communists during our revolution. He remains his friend even today."

"Yes, yes, I was hoping one of you would point that out," Dr. Ping said, his cheeks puffing as he smiled at his well-indoctrinated followers. "Martin gives us—I mean all of us here today—direct contact with one of the world's industrial emperors." Like a child making a choice in a toy store, he began delightedly to wonder aloud. "I'm curious what would happen if the elder Vanderziel were assassinated: Chaos on the stock exchange? Near collapse of the price of American oil? Devaluation of the dollar? Or, perhaps, nothing at all."

Keui-Lan gave voice to Dr. Ping's idea. "You want this man to commit patricide?"

Dr. Ping's eyes gleamed with amusement. "Yes. He shall slay his father. We will make Martin destroy what he loves, his fortune and his father. And because his psychological profile shows he is a man of little conscience, the exercise will be relatively easy to execute." In sheer delight, Dr. Ping began to giggle. "Imagine the impact we'll have had when the international press reports the death of the senior Vanderziel by his son's own hand."

At Dr. Ping's request, the North Vietnamese flew in film clips of T. Wayne Vanderziel. The films, grainy newsreels dating back to the thirties, showed the old man in all his guises: art collector, construction- and land-development magnate, hardbitten oilman, husband, womanizer, parent, unofficial cabinet member, unofficial diplomat, socialite. No matter what the role, T. Wayne looked the same: colorless and chilly. The movie unreeled constantly before Martin's eyes while he was under the effect of a nauseating drug. Within a week he began to get sick each time his wheelchair was pushed to the viewing room. Worse than his nausea was his inability to vomit; he could only heave without relief.

Martin's mind-alteration process included electroshock, sleep deprivation, and sensory deprivation. Each session was layered, laced, and underlined by a message: "You are to kill *that which you love the most.*" The subject's handsome features were immobile; the conditioning was being accepted without resistance. Over a month's time, Dr. Ping's instructions were engraved on Martin's brain.

At the end of the month, Dr. Ping Chung sat down, grunting with satisfaction, next to his favorite disciple, Keui-Lan. She was always so sanitary-looking in her white lab coats and her intelligence was so brisk she seemed almost antiseptic. As she poured him tea from a battered pot, she recited, "'Under certain circumstances, there are few hours in life more agreeable than the hour dedicated to the ceremony known as afternoon tea.' That is from *Portrait of a Lady* by the author Henry James."

"English or American?"

"American, but he fancied himself British." Keui-Lan blew on her tea to cool it. "You've completed indoctrinating the deep suggestions into the American. What still remains to be done?"

"We need to imprint on his mind a date and a method for liquidating his father. As he is now, our subject is a trained assassin, but one without a target. If he were unleashed upon the world now, he would be as dangerous as an unaimed torpedo." Dr. Ping squinted through his thick eyeglasses at the east, where a smoky curtain of hot afternoon haze hung over the browns and greens of a mountain range. "Before I go any further, I must let Martin's facilities rest for several days. If too much information is introduced too quickly—"

"Facilities? You mean faculties, don't you? His faculties?" Keui-Lan corrected.

"Ah, yes. Two entirely different words. Your English is

so much better than mine. A faculty is an intellect, and facility, a workplace, such as this compound."

With appropriate humility, Keui-Lan hurried to reassure him. "Doctor, you know how much I admire your entire body of work and all the technologies you've created. But most of all, I admire how you've managed to do so much with the limited facilities in this wilderness. With the very crudest of equipment, you've accomplished things that other great scientists could never achieve, even with the latest technology."

Dr. Ping accepted her praise. "Keui-Lan," he began, "this location—" Suddenly, he cut himself off in midsentence. *"Listen."*

After a moment, Keui-Len said, "Listen to what?"

"Someone's here."

"Where?" Panicked, the woman stood up halfway and looked around the yellow dust of the courtyard. "How do you know?"

Dr. Ping Chung whispered. "It's too quiet." Keui-Lan's ears strained. Silence hung in the air, as though the thousands of creatures of deep jungle life, all the unseen insects and birds, were holding their breath.

A guard cried out. A split second later, a whistling noise overhead made Dr. Ping and Keui-Lan duck instinctively. A shell exploded not twenty feet from their tea table. The detonation was accompanied by the sound of bullets being fired from heavy rifles and machine guns. Instantly, the camp swarmed with movement like a crushed anthill. The Vietcong guards ran around blindly, picking up weapons as they headed for their positions along the perimeter wall.

It was too late for defensive action. The guards in the four corner towers had been caught dozing in the afternoon sun, and the enemy's artillery was overwhelming. Screaming, Dr. Ping and Keui-Lan ran past a radio operator who was trying to call for reinforcements on a portable phone. They were midway across the parade ground when a grenade fell neatly between them. Its explosion killed them both instantly. The bodies of doctor and doctor-in-training lay feet to feet, thrown like rag dolls.

An Israeli counterterrorist squad wearing jungle camouflage broke through the main gate and charged, firing semi-automatic machine guns. They killed every Oriental person in their path, as they'd been ordered. Liberating this particular hospital-POW compound in Laos called for a take-no-prisoners assault. Though the heavy U.S. bombing was an open secret, officially there were supposed to be no American combat troops in Laos. The Royal Laotian Government and North Vietnam were unlikely to declare war on some Jewish soldiers of fortune.

Within fifteen minutes the gunfire ceased, and the special force started moving freely about. Dr. Ping's students —seven Chinese, a North Vietnamese, and a Russian—had been killed with their teacher. There were no American casualties.

A bullet-headed trooper freed all the American prisoners from their bamboo cages, twenty-six in all. He found Martin Vanderziel locked in a small, clean room inside the infirmary. Martin rose from his bed on unsteady legs and smiled tentatively at his rescuer. "Come on, chum, you're free, thanks to T. Wayne Vanderziel," the soldier said gruffly. He grinned at the welcome sight of one more American who'd survived the hell of Vietcong abuse. "He sent us here to retrieve his little boy and his friends. Have you seen Martin Vanderziel around here? Another guy told us he's here, alive 'n' kickin'."

"*I'm* Martin Vanderziel," Martin said vaguely, still in the edges of a drugged mental fog.

"You're Vanderziel?" The soldier's bushy eyebrows shot up. "But you're described as having black hair."

Martin ran his hand through his hair. He hadn't looked in a mirror in over a month. His hair felt as full-bodied as ever. He ran his hand through a second time, and pulled out several strands. In mild amazement he said, "Is all my hair this color?" The Israeli nodded in confirmation.

Six weeks of captivity and brainwashing had turned Martin's thick, jet-black hair completely white.

• *Nine* •

Dec. 8, 1971

Dear Laurel,

I'm in love with somebody, and it's a boy!

Remember on "Gidget" when Sally Field's highest praise was to call someone "ginchy"? Well, that's what Jeremy Serkin is—ginchy, ginchy as hell. Jeremy has James Dean eyes, just like Martin Vanderziel's, all smoky and half-squinting. He wears jeans and a leather jacket that make him look like a rebel, and he has that look —like he's got the blues, when actually he's really fun and nice.

He grew up in Brooklyn and he directs plays for a living. In fact, he's one of the few off-Broadway directors who make a living off it, and he's only twenty-three. He earns just enough to keep him going. He started by directing plays in his high school when he was only eighteen, but producers liked his work and asked him to work with them.

Jeremy and my roommate Heloise Kiedrowski,

age twenty-four, do not get along, probably
because they're too much alike. Heloise is sort of
imitation bohemian—all her clothes are black,
and she claims to be with the avante garde of the
New York University film department. She tries
hard to act like nothing impresses her, but Jeremy
is unimpressed for real. She knows what a hick I
am, so she's my seeing-eye dog in the big city.
Remember her brother, the Senate page Irv
Kiedrowski?

No flash bulletins on my career in the theatrical
arts. I don't think I'll be confident enough to go
to any tryouts until I spend some more time in
acting class. Besides, in order to get jobs, you
need an agent—and in order to get an agent, you
need experience. Then you have to get your
Screen Actors Guild and AFTRA cards. A few
people have asked me if I've ever modeled (who,
stumpy *me*?) but I know I'm too short to get
modeling work. At nights I work at a high-class
joint where I wear an evening gown and show
people to their tables. Fortunately I work while
Jeremy is rehearsing his plays, and I have the
days free to pursue my real calling. Right now
he's directing *The Iceman Cometh* for a theater
group in the oh-so-hip Village, where I live. If
you get to New York, please visit me. If you
don't come for a visit, a letter would do just fine.

> Your friend,
> Meritt du Nord

Laurel let the letter drop from her fingers and looked
unseeingly out the dormitory window. The overcute, too-
cheerful tone of the letter emphasized the alienation lingering between the ex-pages. Each ashamed by his or her lack

of action on the alleged "Trojan Horse List," Meritt, Lisa, Sam, and Laurel had all gone their separate ways from Washington. Between the lines of Meritt's letter Laurel sensed the unspoken gulf between them. She was glad Meritt had written and was glad that she was in love. She was sure Meritt had felt a bit apprehensive writing to her after their estrangement, but perhaps she didn't have anyone else to be happy for her besides her roommate.

What would Meritt say if Laurel told her all about *her* boyfriend? It was safe to say Harold Means was nowhere near "ginchy." He was twice her own age. The last thing she expected was that she'd end up on the casualty list of student-professor relationships in her first year at the University of Nebraska in Lincoln. Laurel wondered how much information she should give Meritt.

Laurel's affair hadn't been going on long, but she knew it would get physical soon. She flipped over onto her back on her narrow dorm bed and thought of the first time that the attraction had first pulsed between her and Hal.

Dr. Harold "Hal" Means was one of the better-known teachers at the U of N. She'd first spotted him on campus a couple of days before classes were to start; she'd heard enough about him to identify him immediately. He was supposed to be the best-looking teacher the college had, and young-looking for his age (he'd just turned forty). Though Hal taught an esthetic subject, he looked like a rock-'em-sock-'em rodeo cowboy with his deep tan and chiseled features. But Laurel hadn't signed up for "History of Western Art 101" because the instructor was handsome: she'd enrolled in the class because of its reputation. His classes were popular because Hal Means was so gifted a teacher that he inspired muscle-headed jocks to run to the nearest art museum to check out the old masters. While still in his thirties Means had been Assistant Curator of American Arts at the Carnegie Institute in Pittsburgh, and now he was content to teach and write books on art history.

At a school the size of the university, an in-demand class

like Western Art 101 had to be taught to a class of two hundred students in a cavernous auditorium. Means stood on a small stage before tiers of arena seating. Laurel couldn't see him well unless she sat down in front. She'd admired his trim figure as well as his virtuosity from the first day of class, when he gave a breathlessly quick tour of ancient art, skipping prehistoric art and going on to Egyptian, Greek, and Roman. "We've got to hurry if we're going to cover five thousand years of Western art," he'd said at the beginning of the next class. "We've still got twenty-five hundred years left!" And he launched into Early Christian and Byzantine art, from A.D. 100 to 1453. He wanted to devote more class time to art from the Renaissance to modern day, "where we can linger on favorites like Picasso and Renoir."

Since the start of school in September, Laurel had made friends in the dormitory, gone to parties, and lived like an average freshman—except that she was actually a seventeen-year-old sophomore. Over her mother's objections she'd taken and passed advanced placement tests so that she could skip her senior year at high school and her freshman year at college. Mavis acknowleged that her daughter had a precocious intellect, but argued that she was too emotionally immature to begin college. Laurel's aggressive campaign to move about at such speed was one of the few contests that she'd ever won against Representative Mavis Williams. Mavis had to be content that her daughter's double majors were political science and journalism.

Laurel found out right away that Mavis had been correct about her immaturity. At college Laurel was surrounded by girls who'd already had several sexual relationships while she hadn't even gone on a date. She was confused and confounded by the way her older friends behaved. At a noncostume Halloween party thrown at somebody's dilapidated house off campus, Laurel found herself pursued by a passably attractive freshman named Vic. He had come to the party as the date of Megan, a pale, plump senior with white eyelashes.

Vic was an instant, potent charmer. When he set eyes on Laurel's fine-boned features, he literally swept her into his arms and carried her out to the front porch. He made her lean up against the wall and planted his hands firmly on either side of her head. His nearness made her head spin. "Kiss me," he demanded, and he pressed his hard lips against her soft ones. She could taste the residue of cigarette smoke on his lips. Laurel's knees turned gelatinous. She was enjoying this!—the scent of his cologne, the melting away of their surroundings, and the tingling sensation that coursed through her. She made her lips touch his like a whisper. "Let's dump these losers and get out of here," Vic urged huskily. "Mmmm, I don't know," Laurel said, and immediately realized that she was playing the flirtatious tease. *Who, me?* she thought in delight, as though she'd never known herself before. Vic had just started opening his mouth against hers when Megan, his date, stepped out to the porch, followed by Jean, a friend of Laurel's. The clinch broke apart. Megan pulled Vic six feet away as Jean asked Laurel if she was getting a ride back to the dorm.

Laurel easily overheard what Megan was saying to Vic. In a little-girl whine that didn't belong to her, she asked, "Vic, when do we get to go?"

"Uh, I want to stay here awhile."

"Oh, Vic, please come home with me." Megan pleaded, kissing Vic's neck. Laurel was so shocked that Megan, who had clearly seen her date kissing another girl was so desperate for sex or affection that she didn't even care. Laurel realized that Megan, being plump and pale, was in no condition to pick and choose her lovers. Obviously, Megan had no pride.

Jean saw Laurel staring. "Oh, don't mind that Vic, he's just a jerk-ola." And Jean was correct, for after that night

Vic never called Laurel, though he'd presumably been hot for her on Halloween. In the space of minutes that night, she'd learned some hard facts about desire, need, and jealousy.

By the middle of November, Hal Means had reached art in the 1800s. As he went on blithely about Romanticism and Naturalism, Laurel sat in the third row, thinking about the public opinion class she'd attended the hour before. She didn't dream that the subject would be so stupefyingly wearisome compared to this class.

What was it that Means was saying? "To all intents and purposes, the Pre-Raphaelite Brotherhood died in 1882, when Dante Gabriel Rossetti died. The P.R.B. was finished. Their movement now seemed bland and had no further influence on art."

As if it had a will of its own, Laurel's arm shot up. Means pointed at her. Looking directly into his darkly intense eyes, she extemporized, "You're wrong! William Holman Hunt, and Ford Madox Brown, and Edward Burne-Jones kept Pre-Raphaelitism a force in art till the turn of the century at least. And the craft of the Pre-Raphaelite Brotherhood evolved into the worldwide Arts and Crafts Movement, followed by Art Nouveau, which evolved into the Modern Movement."

A few people in the auditorium snickered, while others kept quiet, irritated or aghast at her audacity. Laurel's cheeks colored as she realized the effect of her little speech. Means kept looking down at her from the platform without a change in his expression.

Laurel said, "I suppose you're going to say I should go away and teach my own class."

Means made a humorous face and waved his hand in a heck-with-it gesture. "No. I was going to thank you for pointing out some valuable facts." He continued lecturing as though he hadn't been interrupted. When the class bell sounded he asked Laurel to stay behind.

"Are the Pre-Raphaelites favorites of yours?"

Laurel gazed at Means from her seat, an inferior vantage point. His hair was reddish, actually curry-colored, and it fell into large curls that seemed to have been carved, lock by lock, around his head. Making conversation with an esteemed professor unnerved Laurel, and to hide her unease, she went about taking out a cigarette and lighting it.

"I don't know much about Pre-Raphaelite art."

"Obviously you know more than I do. If you haven't a class this hour, let me buy you a coffee so I can see how much knowledge I can gain from you."

"Okay."

Hal and Laurel walked the short distance to the student union, talking about Victorian Art all the way. Hal told her about the museums in London, his hazel eyes sparkling with enthusiasm as his hands made descriptive ellipses in the air.

They talked for three hours, stopping only when their stomachs began to growl because it was supper time. Laurel wondered if Hal was going to ask her to continue the discussion over dinner, but he merely told her he'd see her in class in two days. A week went by, then he asked Laurel after the art history session if she'd like to have supper with him.

At the table he started the conversation with, "So you're Mavis Williams's daughter."

Laurel stubbed out a cigarette. "Guilty as charged." She didn't like discussing her mother, especially when people used Representative Williams's name like an accusation.

"What's it like, being a congresswoman's daughter?"

Resentment pressed against Laurel's chest. She was so tired of answering questions about her mother. "Why don't you ask my sister, who's deaf? And my brother, who's retarded? Since I'm a child prodigy, we're all *freaks*. That's how it feels."

Instead of showing sympathy, Hal attacked her petulance. "I was only asking a conversational question. You didn't have to answer with a proclamation of self-pity." Behind a curtain of cigarette smoke, Laurel regarded him a moment over the table, and decided he'd been right to reproach her. "Tell me about your childhood, Laurel," Hal said.

Why should he care about my growing-up years? Laurel wondered, but she found herself talking on and on. He nodded his head attentively from time to time. He had a quick smile, and his expression was ever-changing. In Hal she saw a lot of the "golden boy" qualities Sam Ross had. She was beginning to think he was a very striking man for a forty-year-old. Was she attracted to him? From the way butterflies were fluttering in her stomach, she must be. But she'd never even been interested in a boy over the age of nineteen!

Laurel fought with her feelings for Hal over the next two weeks as they continued to stop for coffee and share a few dinners. Together they saw the movies *A Clockwork Orange* and *The Conformist*. She couldn't believe how well Hal's mind interacted with hers. There was never enough time to finish all they had to say. Finally she had found someone who understood everything she was talking about, everything she felt, and liked everything she liked. Hal enjoyed "Star Trek" reruns as much as she did.

By the end of November she had fallen completely under his spell. When they were together, Laurel was fairly sure that he was stimulated by her presence. He wasn't buying all that coffee and all those dinners merely for the pleasure of her company. Or for her kisses, since there hadn't been any.

But was it a romance? Or was this merely an extra-friendly mentor-protégé relationship? She found herself studying her image in her mirror at night. Could he conceivably think she was sexy? Could people tell she was a virgin? Or did Hal *not* desire her simply *because* she was a frumpy virgin!

It was bad enough that Hal Means was an older man. He had to be a professor, too, and Laurel had always thought student-teacher affairs were sleazy. Her fear that her mother and her friends felt the same way kept her from discussing Hal with anybody.

Laurel folded Meritt's chatty letter and decided she could confide in her fellow ex-page. But not in a letter or by phone; this incendiary topic needed face-to-face discussion. The phone in her room rang, announcing that Hal was here to take her out.

While Hal waited in the lobby of Laurel's dormitory, he found himself shaken once again at the idea of dating someone so young and vulnerable as Laurel Williams. He'd been tantalized by the girl since the day she spoke up in class. Against his better judgment, he'd found himself asking Laurel to meet for innocent dinners, when he knew he wanted her. He loved the way her wild, thick, brown hair gleamed in light and shadow, the way it billowed and puffed around her shoulders and her long, graceful neck. Hal was excited by the willowy delicacy of her body. Laurel was as slender as a boy, with small breasts and an apple-hard, taut bottom in jeans worn tight as sausage casings.

Laurel had the coltishness of a teenager. Her self-esteem was low, but she was justly proud of her intellect. She had all the conversational skills and smarts of a much older woman but was so much less demanding. She accepted him as he was: she was the first woman he'd known who didn't want to change him in some way. Looking into those lapis blue eyes, Hal could relax and drop the lordly self-confidence and burden of his reputation.

In his darkest moments, he had to admit to himself that he was caught in the feverish grip of love. The feeling had

come to him only once before, when he'd first known his
wife.

After a lobster dinner, the two of them went walking
through campus in the cool nighttime air. The neat and
orderly patchwork of the university campus was iced with
scraps of early winter snow. The moonlight washed the
entire town with a pale blue light. When Hal asked her if
she'd like to come inside for a drink, Laurel recognized the
standard seduction ploy and she nodded eagerly. She was
thrilled that she'd waited for him to make the first move
but scared that the drink would be just that.

Dr. Hal Means's two-story house was similar to most
other teachers' homes she'd seen, with books piled so high
they were teetering; tatami mats on the floors; a sophisticated stereo system with records scattered; coffee tables
strewn with issues of *National Geographic*, *Mother Jones*,
In These Times, and *Art News*; American furniture of classic lines to give the place a back-to-the-earth feel. "I know
what you're thinking," Hal said mischievously as he
handed her a glass of a California Chardonnay from Son-
oma-Cutrer, "you're thinking that my house is just like that
of every teacher you've known." She nodded sheepishly.
He sat down opposite Laurel on one of the twin corduroy,
cornflower-blue couches. "I protest. See how all the walls
are pristine white? See all the artwork leaning against
them?"

"Yes. It looks like you moved in and never found time to
hang the pictures."

"No! It's a special way I can display ten times more
artwork than if I'd hung my paintings. Guests inevitably
flip through them." Hal lifted his wine to Laurel in a toast,
then he toasted to the small Greek bust sitting on the end
table. "Here's looking at Euclid."

"That's Plato's bust!" Laurel sipped at the wine, and

tucked her chin into her chest to ward off nervousness. She was trying to avoid looking at his lips and wondering what they felt like. "I have a question to ask of you." She paused. "How many girl students have you brought into your house like this?"

She thought he would be angry at her, but his expression was that of a little boy who'd just been accused. Quietly Hal said, "I've never taken out a student before."

"I've never gone out with a professor before, either." Laurel's chin was shivering with held-back agitation. "Uh —have you ever kissed a student before?"

"Never. But I'd like to see what's it's like." With that Hal stood up and put himself down again next to Laurel. He smiled, tenderly amused at her naive prompting, then slid his arms around her. Tilting his head slightly, he brought his mouth down on hers. A rush of triumphant excitement went through her—he had wanted her all along! Her waiting mouth returned his firm, demanding kiss with the urgency of pent-up expectation. She threw her arms around him and opened her mouth under his, tasting, sucking, feeding, exploring as her mind reeled giddily at the sheer joy of kissing.

"Would you like to go to bed?" he asked in a whisper-of-the-night voice. "We don't have to—"

"No, no, it's what I want more than anything on the earth, Hal! I love you!"

"I love you, too."

Laurel thought her ears had popped because she couldn't believe what he'd just said. She couldn't believe what *she'd* just said. Quickly she said, "Let's go to your bed."

Afterward she never could remember how they'd made it upstairs, so sexually hypnotized were they. When they reached the room, Hal barraged her with kisses, murmuring words of endearment into her ears as he nibbled at her tender lobes. He caressed her shoulders and bit her smooth, white neck delicately, tasting her. His fingers found the zipper on back of her dress, and it fell to the floor in a puddle around her ankles.

Laurel was so impatient that she took no time to savor his skilled lovemaking. As he paused to admire her naked body, she pulled open his double bed and slid between the cool linens. Hal pushed the top sheets away so he could draw her into his arms. Feeling his strong body against her soft one seemed so beautiful and natural. Hungrily Laurel sought his mouth; she couldn't kiss him deeply or searchingly enough. Her hands stroked his hairy, well-muscled body, but she was too inhibited to kiss him all over.

Slowly Hal caressed her, his warm hands lighting a fire everywhere he touched. She stopped thinking altogether, surrendering to sensation and the bliss of knowing Hal Means wanted her and cared about her. His hands explored her gently, then, intimately. And she responded instinctively, rotating and pressing against the body over hers. Then, Hal crossed his arms behind her back and pressed himself into her slowly. She clenched her teeth with pain as he broke through her maidenhead. It all was what she had expected. She hadn't counted on satisfaction during this initiation, but she reveled in the feeling of being so close to a man. When it was over, she lay in Hal's arms, listening to him breathe. Unwilling to separate, they remained attached until Laurel spoke. "I love you."

"I love you, but can you really love someone as old as I am?"

"You're not old, Hal. Any age you are is right for me."

"You've kept your age secret, Laurel. You can tell me now, love."

"I'm eleven. I've been eleven for seven years. They keep holding me back." Hal didn't laugh, and Laurel said in a small voice. "I'm seventeen. Does it really matter?"

"A seventeen-year-old. *Jesus Christ!* Me, Dr. Harold Means of the Carnegie Institute and the University of Nebraska, is involved with a girl who can't even enter a bar! A girl one year over the age of statutory rape—one step above *jail bait!*" Hal started chuckling boisterously, and Laurel joined in. They stopped laughing when Hal pulled Laurel down to cover him.

In the morning Laurel sat on the edge of the bathtub, wearing one of Hal's bathrobes, looking upward at him as he applied shaving foam to his jaw. He wore only a pair of shorts. "Whaddaya think, buttercup? Do you think this face could use a beard? A goatee? A 'blues patch'?"

"At most, it could stand a mustache. It's not a face meant for facial hair."

Hal chuckled and picked up his razor. Laurel watched closely as it scraped through his whiskers. It was so wonderful to be watching her partner the morning after she'd made love for the first time in her life. The very nonchalance of his grooming intensified their intimacy.

Laurel sighed luxuriously and left the bathroom to refill her coffee mug. As she moved down the stairs, she could see into the living room, now flooded with morning sunlight, and she walked in to explore. My god, twenty-four hours earlier she'd never even stepped into this place, and now she was nearly mistress of the manor! The stacks of books falling onto every flat surface intrigued her. Hal apparently owned a fortune in valuable art books, the kind you opened only after washing your hands. Some of the titles intrigued her; many of his books were in foreign languages. It'd never occurred to Laurel before that Hal must be multilingual. She knew where he'd attended college and studied, but she didn't know anything about his parents or even if he had siblings. He'd lived twice as long as she had, which meant that Hal had had twice as many experiences as she. Laurel's skin suddenly prickled with a feeling akin to fear: how much was there yet to learn about the man she was in love with?

· Ten ·

"Who are these people?" Laurel asked as she studied the expensively framed studio photograph in her hands.

"My wife and son," Harold said quietly.

"Who?"

Hal miserably whispered, "My wife and my little boy."

Laurel had chanced upon the picture while digging through Hal's closet in search of Christmas wrappings. The photograph had smiled down at her from a shelf, propped up as if waiting for Laurel to chance upon it. As she walked to the desk where Hal sat writing Christmas cards, he laid his pen down and rested his hands on the desk top.

"Are they gone, honey?" she asked tactfully. "Have they . . . died?" He shook his head very slowly. Why had he kept this secret from her? Hal took the portrait from her and laid it face down on his desk. "You mean you're divorced?"

Again the slow shake of the head. "No. We're separated. Maggie's living with Sheldon in an apartment across town."

The puzzle of his unexplained absences was solved. "How long have you been separated?"

"Since September."

Laurel's anger quickly spread in geometric proportions. "And you've been in touch with them all this time? Without even mentioning to me, *your coed cookie*," she said through clenched teeth, "that you're a married man, and a father? Why didn't you tell me?"

Hal fixed a look of calm rationality over his features. "I *am* telling you. I didn't want to tell you earlier because I was afraid you wouldn't want me if you knew."

"As far as I see it, pal, you're an *adulterer*. And you've turned *me* into a mistress of a married man." Hal didn't answer, and Laurel put her hands in front of her face as if to ward off the impact of her discovery. Venomous rage at Harold's silence over this crucial issue grasped her heart. It was as if he'd been lying to her from the very beginning. She was humiliated at being taken in and outraged at being involuntarily put in the role of "the other woman" in the triangle. She was so jealous of his wife that she could nearly taste the green bile of envy. The very worst feeling of all was her terror that he'd return to his cozy family group.

Hal felt paralyzed, unable to explain himself. Uneasily he waited for Laurel to continue with the accusations.

Half-sobbing, she demanded, "How often do you see— oh, I don't want to know anything more! I'm *splitting*." Without another word, she grabbed her coat from the living room couch and ran out into the cold mid-December air. Hal did not attempt to chase after her.

On Christmas Eve when Harold turned up with a present for her, Laurel let him explain his predicament to her. He had taken her back to his home where under an elaborately decorated Norway pine, they stretched out on the floor holding brandy bowls. "It's such a . . . sticky situation," he said, sighing. "Maggie and I have been married for nine years. Sheldon's five. In the past few years it seemed that the . . . magic had gone out of our marriage. We didn't seem to love each other any more." Laurel groaned inwardly at the tired excuse, wondering why Hal couldn't have come up with something more original. "So we're living apart to see what happens."

"I thought you said you loved me. If you're still figuring out what to do about your marriage, where do I fit in? Have you told your wife about me?

He shook his head slowly. "If Maggie saw us together, it'd kill her."

"What about me, Harold? Don't you care what would 'kill' me?"

He looked straight at her eyes. "I do care." He seemed so sincere that Laurel almost forgave his sin of omission. "Be patient a little while longer," he begged. "I'll get this all straightened out."

Laurel took Hal at his word, but cracks developed in their relationship. She tried to empathize with his various dilemmas, yet the fissures widened as the winter went on. Laurel sensed, correctly, that Hal's occasional spells of sullenness were triggered by visits or a phone talk with his wife. Jealousy tore at her insides.

"Why are you seeing her when you're supposed to be separated?" Laurel cried.

"I miss my son."

"Then bring him here more often!"

Hal complied and began to pick up Sheldon for twice-a-week visits. Unfortunately, Laurel and little Sheldon didn't mix. Laurel thought he was an okay kid for a five-year-old, but at age seventeen she still felt rather like a child herself, lacking the authority to discipline him. When Laurel tried to prepare snacks for Sheldon, he cried that she couldn't make an ice cream cone the way Mommy did. His very presence in his father's house made her feel like a home-wrecker who was destroying Sheldon's family.

Hal didn't hesitate to introduce Laurel to all his friends, most of whom were faculty of the Art Department. He felt free to take her to parties. He said, "I'm not worried that

Maggie will hear about it since she didn't have any friends inside the university."

"Worry about *me* for a change," Laurel snapped.

At these informal gatherings, she had to sit and listen to people discussing deans; chairmen; who was on the tenure-track, who wasn't and why; who would become a senior professor or associate professor, who would be the new assistant professor. They debated about the risks of flunking star college athletes who brought alumni and all their dollars to the stadium. Laurel was surprised that the school's most distinguished scholars were concerned about job security above all other issues. She found university politics trivial after being around *real* politicians all her life.

"Don't those people have any ambitions outside the ivy walls of this college?" Laurel asked Hal one night as they walked to his house after a reception for a new professor. "There's so much more to life."

Laurel's criticisms were starting to annoy Hal. "When you snipe at my friends, you're picking at me, too."

Perversely, the more critical Laurel became of Hal, the more possessive she got. She began to eavesdrop on his phone calls and skim through his mail. She did not want his wife, Maggie, or any other female corresponding with Hal. It was in his best interest. He didn't need any of those communications while he was still in flux about his marriage.

What bound Laurel to Harold was their lovemaking. It was more of a novelty to her than an act of passion. Sex was her new toy, and Hal seemed amused by her continual interest in the activity. By March, though, she sensed a joylessness in their couplings, and she wondered if Hal was just too old to keep up with her. She speculated that a boy her age might have more energy than Hal. He was very youthful-looking, yet she noticed that the harsh morning sunlight exaggerated the fine, wrinkled sagginess of his skin.

Laurel had started off with him completely fresh, endowing the older man with her heart, soul, and virginity, and now every day brought in a new piece of harsh reality to mock her girlish ardor. Harold was an adult, with many more years of emotional life than an eighteen-year-old adult. The issues of mature adult life seemed much more complicated than hers . . . and they were irritating!

By the start of spring, Laurel's opinion flip-flopped, and she began thinking herself superior to Hal. Laurel felt she was strong and forthright about her emotions, while he was a wishy-washy wimp who couldn't decide if he wanted to be a husband and father. She loved her handicapped siblings freely, whereas if Harold had a retarded brother and a deaf sister, he would have moped his life away over the misfortune as if it were a family curse. In many ways, she was more worldly than he, accustomed to sitting at the dinner table with diplomats, big businessmen, and senators. The only celebrities he felt comfortable with were museum curators. He and his friends were people steeped in middle-aged complacency, dedicating themselves to feeling safe and cuddled in academic cocoons. Laurel had never been impressed with herself before, but now she realized that in many ways she was more grown-up than some people twice her age.

In January, when she'd told Harold that her colleague Martin Vanderziel had been shot down, the professor commented, "That's too bad. Tragic."

Laurel was shocked by his passivity and declared, "It's not some tragic lost cause. Our POWs are worth fighting for!"

"Oh, you restless students are all the same," Harold remarked, "so idealistic, thinking you can change the world."

By late April, Laurel was turning Harold Means into a villain. She was too wearing, too intense for his nerves to bear. In mid-May she picked a fight with him, turning him spiteful and deliberately cruel. She came into his office in the Department of Art, wearing jeans and a tight T-shirt, flopped down on the chair opposite his desk, and lit a cigarette. "Hal, don't you think all art should be confiscated and displayed in museums so everyone can see everything? I mean, why do rich people get to own art so they can keep it from the rest of the world?"

A smile touched Hal's lips. "I thought that politically astute people in this country didn't advocate socialism." Laurel crossed her long legs and said nothing. "If art were for everybody, nobody would go see it. Besides, look at how prolific some artists have been. Picasso created enough art for everybody to pass around, in houses and in museums."

Laurel stretched back in the chair and sullenly blew smoke rings into the air. Harold got the distinct feeling that this student had come here for a reckoning that couldn't be postponed much longer. He spoke quickly, before she could bring it up. "Laurel . . . we've got to end this. We've both turned into disagreeable people."

Her mouth turned hard. "So your wife is moving back in with you," she accused.

"No. I'm still not sure what Maggie and I are going to do. But you and I aren't so great together anymore." Hal's countenance was still and serious. "Last fall I thought it was incredible that two people with so many years between them could have such like minds. Now I think it's incredible that two people with so many years between them had ever shared any opinions!"

Confronted with trouble, Laurel took her usual course of action: She stood up and grabbed her knapsack. "Why talk any more if all you want is to get rid of me?" She headed for the door leading to the hall. "Your wish is my command."

Hal called Laurel a week later, asking to see her. He wanted to start all over again. She pleasantly told him it would be a bad idea since she was going to work in Washington for the summer. In effect, it ended with her walking out on him.

When she returned to Lincoln campus in the fall, it would be unlikely that she'd be running into Dr. Means. The Art building was fortuitously distant from the Social Sciences classes. If she wanted, Laurel could avoid Harold Means for the rest of college; but she really didn't care if she saw him or not. She had distanced herself from the romance already.

As she packed her clothes for Washington, she was able to accept this lesson as the one that had turned her into a woman, a strong woman. Even though she had mental ability beyond her years, emotionally she had been a child, trapped in an adolescent beanpole body. *I'm experienced and I'm still very young,* Laurel told herself fiercely. *The next time I fall in love, I'll do it right.*

Her real education had just begun.

While working as an aide in Washington that summer, Laurel had happened upon the listing, Remick, Oliver, in the D.C. phone book. Her eyes popped open like morning glories when she spotted the name she'd never expected to see again. Before her courage could fail her, she quickly dialed his number. The phone rang and rang, and then a recorded voice said. "We're sorry. The number you dialed has been disconnected or is not in service."

• *Eleven* •

Every bright young hopeful artist or performer who moves to New York believes he will achieve overnight success. As inevitably as death, disillusionment sets in the first day performers make the rounds of agents' offices and open auditions. Two weeks of making the rounds can turn them into hardened criminals.

In Manhattan, there are two kinds of entertainment agents: high-flying show-business dynamos ensconced in midtown skyscrapers and flabby, aging, bleary-eyed old pros holed up in Hell's Kitchen. The former group won't take on beginners. When you're new in town, you court the old pros, because at least they'll try to get you started.

Invariably, their offices are run-down and in disrepair. A secretary presides in a dingy office anteroom, facing over her desk the unemployed, who sit on broken-down chairs awaiting an interview with a "talent representative." Most of the unrepresented are young; those who aren't have defeat imprinted on their faces for having spent too much of their lives chasing a dream. All of them are desperate.

Meritt du Nord told herself, *I'm not like these others*, when in her heart she knew she was just like them. She caught on to the game quickly, though. The person she wanted to impress wasn't the agent; it was his secretary, the tough, middle-aged gatekeeper who decided who would be allowed passage into the inner sanctum. They were tough, because they'd heard every hard-luck story a hundred times over. And they were minor talent agents themselves, because they were empowered to invite, "Let us know if you're in something." In Meritt's second week of job-hunting, she began to bribe these women with candy, flowers, greeting cards, and charm. Sometimes she gritted her teeth over the necessity of buttering up these mean-mouthed, self-superior beings, but she'd do anything to get an acting job.

Meritt's strategies paid off. She won interviews with twenty-five talent agents . . . but not one of them wanted to sign her. She was told that she was "too ethnic," "too tall," "too short," "too exotic," "too sexy," and "we represent character types, so we can't use you." Like all the other beginners in the business, Meritt needed an Equity card if she ever wanted to act on Broadway. The only way to get a card was by performing in a production—it was the catch-22 of acting.

Good luck is often the right combination of opportunity and timing. It came to Meritt in March of 1972, on a chilly afternoon during a visit to a dentist. She considered her teeth to be an asset which should constantly be maintained, but she hadn't given her asset a checkup since she'd been a page. Her roommate Heloise recommended a dentist, whose office was in the Chelsea district. Meritt found the address, but there was no dentist listed on the lobby directory in the small office building. She went to room 225, where he should have been, but saw through a long window there was a suite of offices in room 225. The door read Carrie Enright Talent. Meritt opened it.

Inside was an anteroom, but no receptionist sat at the desk. It was Friday, the day everyone in New York heads home early. Behind the desk were several office doors. One office was open and lighted. A pale-faced woman sitting behind a large desk looked up from a script as Meritt approached. The walls were nearly covered with framed glossies of all sizes. Almost all were autographed, "To Carrie with love." Meritt realized she'd stumbled into the domain of a talent agent. "Yes . . . ?" the woman asked.

"I was looking for a dentist, but I think I've found something better," Meritt said. She took off her heavy winter reefer coat. "I am an actress looking for an agent. I have no experience, but I've got a lot to offer."

"Is that right?" the woman said patronizingly. In her forties, she looked to be an alley cat that had won most of her catfights. She was smoking a brown cigarette. "I happen to be in a signing mood. I'm seeking a ravishing brunette. You'd be perfect, except the script requires . . . a ravishing *male* brunette." She stubbed the brown cigarette into an ashtray that said "Toots Shor's" and gave her mouth a squirt of Binaca. "Seriously, I just got a call you may be interested in. Woody Allen decided to shoot on Long Island tomorrow, and his casting director needs to round up extras. Woody's whims always come at the last minute. Of course, if they weren't last minute, they wouldn't be Woody's whims. Are you interested?"

Meritt shook her head. She had her pride. "It wouldn't pay enough."

The woman put her hands behind her neck and stared at the ceiling, thinking a moment. She looked back at Meritt and offered, "Okay, I'm desperate because I owe this casting director favors. If you go to Long Island for me tomorrow plus any additional days, I'll take you on as a client. We'll start little and go on to big. How does that sound?"

Meritt knew better than to pretend to bluff with this woman. She nodded eagerly, and the woman opened one of her desk drawers and handed Meritt a sheet of paper. It was a letter of agreement that would grant Carrie Enright of Enright Talent ten percent of Meritt's acting earnings. At this point Meritt would have been happy to give any agent ten percent of her firstborn son. Well, not *any* agent: some "talent representatives" were sleazy front men for brothels or were slippery with your earnings. Carrie Enright looked stalwart and well-grounded, and the Enright Talent agency apparently was doing well enough, since several other agents worked under its roof. Meritt had the feeling there wasn't a lot Carrie's brown eyes hadn't seen.

"In case you haven't figured it out, I'm *the* Carrie Enright." Carrie gave more documents for Meritt to sign. "What's your name, kid? It helps if I know your name."

"I'm Meritt du Nord. I'm from Louisiana."

"Is that your real name or your stage name?"

Meritt froze like a rabbit. "It's mine. What do you think, should I change it?"

"Oh no, I've got an absolute beginner on my hands!" Carrie said with mock despair. "Use a name you like. It's your choice."

Meritt was sitting on the edge of a chair, skimming the faces in all the photos on Carrie's walls. "Christopher Colacello . . . don't tell me you represent him!" Christopher Colacello was a magnificent ash blond Adonis. Within two years he'd moved from anonymity to fame. He was in the mainstream of American hero worship. "He's the only actor I've ever had a crush on. He's the only person I'd leave my boyfriend for."

There was an amused chuckle in Carrie's voice. "I represented Chris till a couple of years ago. He got too big for me—at Enright Agency we like to keep our client list at a medium size. We have no wish to work with the big stars because the bigger the name, the bigger their problems. When Chris got his first job in Los Angeles, we had to give him a few shoves till he signed on with William Morris. He thought changing agencies was disloyal. It's not."

"Please don't tell me Christopher's sexual preference . . . I like to keep my fantasies as they are."

"He's an arrow."

"What? An arrow?"

"As in 'as straight as an arrow.'"

"Oh."

Meritt told Jeremy the good news over a pay phone in Times Square. "And *I've* got good news," he said from his apartment in Brooklyn. "I've got a gig. A producer wants

me in charge of the book for a satiric revue about the
Nixon administration. The script is great. It says blaming
Nixon for this country's problems in like blaming Ronald
McDonald when you get a bad cheeseburger."

"What does 'in charge of the book' mean?"

"Unofficially I'll be stage manager, but I'll get a chance
to direct some of the skits. We'll open in Philadelphia before we stage it here." Jeremy was uncharacteristically excited. "You aren't working tonight, are you? Let's
celebrate."

They ate at an Upper West Side Japanese restaurant, then
took a cab to a disco downtown. Inside the loft the scene
was dance ecstasy. Men were dancing with other men;
bored-looking models in tight jeans and halters jiggled opposite shorter dates. The dance floor was checkerboard
tile, and the walls and ceiling were painted black. White
crepe paper dangled from the ceiling like no-pest strips.
Neon tubing flashed with the one-beat driven music, strobe
lights flashed intermittently, and whirling lights spun, all
shining on the dancers, who were the stars.

The sound system was mountainous. The room was hot,
and the music was pulsating and sexy. Meritt asked Jeremy
loudly, "Do you ever attract homosexuals?"

"Yes, because I'm not real preppy- or butch-looking. A
lot of guys have checked me out ever since I was a kid. But
I was always attracted to girls. *Very* attracted." He looked
straight at Meritt, and his gray eyes gleamed with odd excitement.

He surprised her by grabbing her wrist. "Where are you
going?" she asked.

"You'll see." He led her to an emergency exit and
pushed it open. The door slammed shut behind them, and
they were in an isolated, dim stairwell. He pushed her
against a wall and started kissing her hard on the mouth.
She tried to put her arms around him and kiss him back,
but he held her back with straight arms. She lunged, trying
to kiss him, but he kept his mouth away, teasing her. They

were both hot from the main room. The music was muffled but still loud. Meritt wanted desperately to kiss *him*. He nuzzled her neck, and she went weak in the knees. She tried to fall against him, but he wouldn't let her move.

Staring right into her eyes, Jeremy inserted his finger in his mouth, licked it wet, then used it to trace Meritt's curved mouth, wetting her lips. Then he frustrated her by kissing her eyes, her cheeks and ears, her neck, but not her mouth. He bit lightly on her earlobes, and she shivered. "I can't believe the way you make me feel," she gasped. Alternately touching her and resisting her, he was pushing her desire as far as it could go without climaxing.

Jeremy's body was hot and sweaty, and Meritt was hot and wet, panting as if at a high altitude, and yet he kept her firmly a foot away from him. With his right hand he gradually pushed up her skirt, his fingers sliding up the inside of her thigh. The hand slipped up the naked flesh into the wispy lace of her panties, and through her excitement she thought of how lucky it'd been that she hadn't put on panty hose. He lifted one of her hands and started kissing it and biting softly. Then, taking his time, he licked and sucked each finger all the way to the base. He withdrew his hand from her underpants and lightly placed it in her mouth, so she was forced to taste her own wetness. He put it back into her, making her wetter by moving it slowly, matching his hand's movements with long, savage kisses. Meritt kissed him again and again. With his other arm he pulled her to him, and he was hard against her stomach.

Meritt couldn't stand any more, and just as she started to climax, Jeremy suddenly unzipped his jeans and fell back against a step, at the same time pulling Meritt down over him. He entered her and immediately exploded.

For a moment afterward Jeremy held Meritt's dark head against his chest. They hugged as though they'd just survived a torrential storm, and they had. As Meritt listened to Jeremy's heartbeat slow down, she realized that she was completely under Jeremy's spell, and she didn't think she could live without him. She didn't want her love for him to stop.

When she looked up, Jeremy grinned and kissed her almost mischievously. They sighed with regret that their passion had subsided and stood up, Jeremy tugging her skirt back in place. "Now, let's dance," he said.

In September of 1972, Meritt had been in New York for a year. In that time, Carrie Enright had gotten her a handful of bit parts in plays and commercials. It was the year of "Shaft" and other "blaxploitation" movies, which meant a lot of location shoots in Harlem. Meritt had tiny roles in two "super-bad" epics. When Neil Simon's script for *The War between Men and Women* was shot, Meritt played a receptionist greeting Jack Lemmon. She donned a wig and worked as a "Mrs. Santa Claus" for a singing telegraph firm. There were two actors' workshops she attended regularly. One was a small group who met only to do cold readings from script and evaluate one another's performances. The other group was larger. Its members played theater games, rehearsed short, humorous sketches, and tested one another's skills at improvisation.

At night, Meritt went to her maître d' job at Charolais, the three-star restaurant. No one did a better job of pleasing the rich old men and their lacquered, glamorously gowned wives. Meritt knew how to vanish before the diner had made a request, and interrupt with nonintrusive tact. She was able to remember the diners' names. Her better-than-average tips kept her solvent.

Busy as she was, Meritt always found extra time for Jeremy Serkin. Since she'd met him, on her very first Manhattan night, he'd been her moon, her stars, and her inspiration. Jeremy Serkin, the fascinatingly brooding, disenchanted, sullenly poetic young director who was on the cutting edge of current theater. Jeremy Serkin, who introduced Meritt to lovemaking, and later had to tame the sex maniac he'd created. He unhesitantly told her he loved her, and called her "my diabolic Creole beauty." He played the slide guitar, and had nothing in his record collection except blues artists. When Meritt asked him why he wore sunglasses so much of the time, he'd joked, "I would rather not have my soul on constant display."

"You're so sarcastic!" Meritt teased. "Were you a sarcastic little baby, too?" Jeremy was so "cool" he could make fun of his coolness.

During the first month of their courtship both Meritt and Jeremy were a bit wary at having found each other and slipped into love so easily. By November they were enough at ease that they fell into a routine. Every day, during the hour before Meritt would dress to work at Charolais and Jeremy had to depart to direct a cast in some production, they would meet at her apartment on East Eleventh Street and make love. After work Meritt collapsed into bed and Jeremy was already at home in Brooklyn. Weekdays, Meritt attended her actors' workshops and went out to auditions or piecemeal work that her agent found her, and Jeremy went to interviews with artistic or casting directors of theater workshops, or worked on preproduction details of his upcoming plays. Both Meritt and Jeremy had much of their weekends free, and Meritt stayed at Jeremy's nonclaustrophobic apartment till Sunday night.

Their weekends were lazy, unexciting and romantic. Meritt and Jeremy spent most of their time in impassioned lovemaking; but when they were in public, Jeremy never touched her. It was part of his "cool" attitude. They stayed away from theaters, for that would be overdosing, and instead went to movies.

Their professions fit hand in glove, but Jeremy understood that Meritt would never audition for one of his off-off-Broadway projects, since his actors were willing to perform for nothing or for very little money.

"Though you're in the theater, I'm damn glad you're not an actor," Meritt told Jeremy over dinner. "I'd never want

to get involved with an actor, *never,* because *I* am one, and
I know what they're like."

"I know what you're talking about."

"Every actor I've met who's seemed interesting *at first*
turns out to be incredibly narcissistic or unstable ... or
gay."

Jeremy said, "You'll be the first one I'll tell if I ever
become narcissistic or unstable ... or gay."

Sometimes they got together during the day, meeting at
the Drama Bookshop, the Theater Arts Bookshop, or the
Library and Museum of the Performing Arts at Lincoln
Center. They were hangouts for actors, who'd stop in between audition rounds.

With Jeremy and on her own, Meritt discovered the
strong sense of community binding the artists. It was almost a private society, with unwritten rules and regula-
tions. For example, most artists and sculptors lived in huge
and illegal lofts instead of apartments. In the sixties, the
"artists' neighborhood" had been Greenwich Village; now
in the seventies it was SoHo. Every day Meritt met other
creative people at various levels of professional success:
musicians, ballet dancers, arts administrators, novelists,
graphic designers, playwrights, or film students like Heloise. Within that community, Jeremy was sort of a celebrity, since he'd worked with so many underground theater
companies. On the street he was always running into someone who wanted to talk to him.

Meritt had never known what it was like to talk shop.
Way back in the bayous of Louisiana and the wide green
spaces of Washington, she hadn't dreamed that such a vi-
brant spiritual fellowship existed, a neighborhood of
minds. Now she lived in the center of it, New York, which
was almost more of an idea than it was a place. It spurred
her on to follow her dream and try her best shot. She was
exhilarated by being in a city that was perpetually in a peak
moment.

Three years later nothing had changed for Meritt. She

was still in New York, still seeing the same people and living with Heloise. She was still enthralled with Jeremy, and she was still getting the same kinds of puny acting jobs and hosting five nights a week at Charolais, but in the summer of 1975, Carrie Enright called Meritt into the office. As Meritt sat twirling on her finger a mood ring she'd bought from a dubious street peddler, her agent said, "I've worked for you for three years, and your career has been stalled for the last two and a half. That means I've failed you." She told Meritt she should think about getting another agent, or she should think about getting out of show business.

After a while, Meritt looked down at her mood ring. It remained blue, the happy color. Typical street-scam merchandise—it was broken, or maybe it never had really worked. Just like her.

• *Twelve* •

Sam Ross stood on the southeast corner of Central Park, waiting for Lisa Dunning to show up. He looked at the placid horses lined up against the curb, draped with blankets against the snow, waiting for tourists or romantic Manhattanites to climb into their hansoms. This meeting would mark the first time he'd seen anyone he'd known during his Washington days since that May night when he and his page friends had stopped believing the world was waiting just for them. A month ago, Lisa had called Sam in Boston and asked if he intended to visit the Big Apple any day soon. He found himself pleased at hearing an alluring voice from the gloomy past, and he made instant plans to Christmas-shop in New York.

Lisa offered a special bonus. "I might be able to talk Martin Vanderziel into showing up, too." Although Martin had been returned to the United States in September of 1972, he hadn't called Sam. He wasn't surprised. Whether or not Martin knew of the ex-pages' efforts in his behalf, it was characteristic of the strange, isolated man not to thank anyone for anything.

The press had reported that T. Wayne Vanderziel paid an Israeli attack team to find and rescue Martin. The elder Vanderziel was unable to welcome his son in person. Throughout 1972, the newspapers and magazines had been filled with articles about the "poor little rich boy who was a prisoner of war," but in the three years since, Martin had stirred up so little news that the media forgot about him.

Lisa had asked Sam to meet her at the Plaza fountain, which was boarded up against winter. He leaned against the cold black wrought iron of the fountain in which Zelda Fitzgerald had once danced. Traffic was at a curdled standstill all around the Grand Army Plaza, horns honking uselessly. A light snow wafted down from the gray sky. It was a typical Friday in December, 1975. Sam had come down from Boston, where he was in his first year at Harvard Business School. After completing four industrious and gregarious years at Northwestern University, he'd gone on to Harvard to get his master's, because Harvard was the best B-school in the country, even above Stanford.

He heard the jaunty clip-clop of horses' hooves on hardtop and glanced toward a park path lined with bare trees, then did a double take. Enthroned in the middle of the seat of a horse and carriage was Lisa, giving him a big-screen smile. The ambivalence Sam had had about seeing her dissolved right into space. He struggled not to laugh. Lisa always had known how to make an entrance! She wore some kind of white fur coat with a huge shawl collar that framed her face. Her complexion was perfect as a bowl of fresh cream; her soft skin stretched tautly over high cheek-bones that Sam didn't remember her having before. She was hatless, and her short blond hair rose into a glamorous, gravity-defying sweep that resembled an ocean wave. The brilliant aquamarine eyes shimmered with the pleasure of seeing him. He walked up to the slowing carriage and extended his hand. Lisa took it in her gray kid gloves and stood up. She was wearing a dove-gray cashmere suit under the white fur. The flow of her ensemble was dramatic.

"Well, that was a lovely ride. Been waiting long, Sam?"

"All my life," he teased, giving her his open smile. He noticed how snowflakes had beaded on her eyelashes.

"We have reservations at the Plaza today." Lisa stepped down carefully, extending a well-shaped calf. "We'll be dining in the Palm Court."

Lisa kept a hand on Sam's arm—he wore an old but clean Army duffel coat—as they silently crossed the square to the Fifth Avenue entrance of the Plaza Hotel. Sam couldn't believe that this fantastic creature, as beautiful and high-glossed as a heroine in a James Bond novel, was the Lisa he had once known. He couldn't imagine why she'd wanted to keep in touch with a lowlife like himself.

The Plaza doorman welcomed them at the entrance. "I've never been here before," Sam confessed as they walked through the ornate lobby. Lisa laughed. "Neither have I. But I knew enough to get us a table." Martin would be showing up later, Lisa said, after a business appointment.

The Palm Court made Sam feel he was inside an impressionist's painting of an elegant European garden. Its colors were leaf green, cream and delicate pink, shades he had seen only on canvas. The ceiling was glass, and illuminated in such a way as to make the entire room look as if it were bathed in sunlight. The illusion made it hard to believe that winter was just outside. All around him mirrors shot off diamond-like sparkles. Fearing he'd tip over the crystal rose vase on the marble topped table, Sam sat down gingerly and put his feet firmly around the wrought iron pedestal.

Lisa smiled, touched by his exaggerated delicacy. Sam had always walked with the ease and swagger of a man of the great outdoors. He hadn't noticed the heads turning and the voices whispering when they'd strolled in to the restaurant: "Who is he? Who is she?" He had no idea people were talking about him, nor would he care. Lisa did.

"You like this place?" she asked, pulling off her gloves. "A lot of little old ladies hang out here, but so do celebrities."

"Would *you* want to be a celebrity?"

Lisa looked at him sharply, then remembered that Sam was too nice a person to be sarcastic. "We'll see," she said candidly. "I've been here only a couple of months."

They were approached by a mustached waiter in a white waistcoat, black trousers, and a green cummerbund. Lisa gave him drink orders in a half-dark honey, half-giggling voice with an all-purpose I-could-be-from-anywhere accent. When she turned back to Sam, he asked, "Am I right in thinking that the peach syrup is no longer in your voice?"

"There's no use lying to you, Sam. You know I spent my childhood in Ohio. Oh-hi-oh. I lived in Charleston for years, though, and I don't mind saying I'm from there, but South Carolina never really left its mark on me." Lisa's lips pouted appealingly. "I guess I never wanted to be a southern belle anyhow. The term reminds me of all those Tennessee Williams plays where the women sit around in front of fans, wearing only their underwear."

Sam laid his head back and laughed, showing his straight white teeth. "You already know what I've been doing for the past four years. What's happened to you since we left the Capitol?"

"What hasn't happened?" Their drinks arrived. Lisa took the first swallow of her double scotch and grimaced. "I spent a year at Villa Pierrefeu, above Lake Geneva in the

Swiss Alps. That's a finishing school. They still exist in Switzerland." She was about to tell Sam that it was the most expensive school of its type in the world, but she knew that talking money was vulgar. "I asked my dad to send me, because I wanted to attend a school that would teach me European culture and protocol. I badly needed the *savoir-vivre*. That means how to be at ease in any situation."

"I can't imagine you *uneasy* in any situation. What's a finishing school like? Do they really 'finish' a young woman?"

Lisa had been finished, polished, and burnished. The Villa Pierrefeu required fluency in French, something that Lisa failed at pitifully, so there was no use mentioning it to Sam. She also was chagrined when she recalled that students were expected to make their own beds, clean their bathrooms and iron their own clothes all year. They also had to prepare and serve meals for each other. "I learned how to make pastries," she allowed, "and we had a class on table decorations. For folding napkins, we studied blueprints. Can you believe it? For final exams, we had to prepare and host a banquet for two dozen people!" Lisa was trying to make a trying time for her sound droll. "On my night to host, I served shrimp sausages with some tasty Spanish wine. I'd neglected to remember that the Jewish girls and a couple of our Arab girls couldn't eat pork, and that Arabs can't touch alcohol. So I flunked my final exam but learned a lot about protocol."

"Why do parents pay so much to have their daughters work?"

"You'd be surprised at the ignorance of some of those pampered hothouse frauleins. A Belgian girl didn't know that a vacuum cleaner had to be plugged into a wall socket to make it work." Lisa adjusted her fur over her chair. "See, it's important for a girl to learn how to run an organized household, because it's likely that someday, as a rich man's wife, she'll supervise servants."

Sam made a funny face. "So the place teaches you how to be your own head housekeeper?"

"Let's say Villa Pierrefeu manufactures tomorrow's socialites today. Any ambassador or chairman of the board would love a wife with the skills I've got."

"And? Have you had many offers of marriage from potential diplomats?"

Lisa sighed ponderously. "Since I came back from Switzerland, I've broken off two engagements. I've been engaged once to Charleston's most eligible bachelor and once to Atlanta's most eligible bachelor."

The waiter interrupted to take their orders for lunch—fish quenelle for Sam, salad for Lisa. "If they were so eligible, why'd you dump them, Lisa?"

"Unlike you, Charlie and Harry had no destiny. Their faces were utterly vacant. They *lived* at their respective country clubs, keeping themselves constantly drunk. They were always running over people with their tiny sports cars. They'd go out hunting and shoot themselves in the foot. They wore Rolex watches that were always stopped. All the gentry forgives them, because they're rich and handsome." With the wave of a hand, Lisa summed up, "And because of Charlie and Harry, I am now a woman with a past."

"And you moved here, to take New York by storm."

"In effect, yes." Lisa told him how she'd persuaded her father to invest in her. He'd agreed to bankroll the social climbing she had planned, and he bought her an East Side apartment. "There are three ways into the international rich. You're born into it, you earn it, or you marry it."

It took Sam a little while to realize she was serious: Lisa had moved to New York City solely to find a rich husband. That was her job, her hobby, her vocation, her mission, and her higher calling. Her entire life was focused on finding a member of the opposite sex with big bucks. "Being from Ohio, Daddy is rather pleased at the notion of a daughter traveling in the upper crust. Sure, there's a high society in Charleston. But it's nothing compared to the international *aristocracy* based in New York."

Sam was smiling openly. For such a self-aggrandizing chatterbox, Lisa was sly and her energy was infectious. Her shocking, somewhat distasteful confidences were refreshingly honest. Her total self-centeredness had a magnetizing effect. He was enjoying her much more than he'd anticipated, yet he was relieved that he was much too small a prize for her engulfing net. He asked, "Why are you looking for a wealthy husband when your own family is so well off? Or at least, that's the impression I had."

"We're well-to-do, but nowhere near awesomely rich. Neither were Charlie nor Harry. To me, any man who can count his money is not a rich man." Lisa's salad arrived, and she picked up a silver fork that glinted like a weapon. "Sure, Daddy could afford to buy me a place, but it's puny. It's on East Sixty-first Street. Right where Marilyn Monroe's apartment is in the film *The Seven Year Itch*." Rapaciously, she plunged her fork into the salad.

Sam couldn't help suggesting, "What about going after Martin Vanderziel? He's 'awesomely rich'. Have you ever thought about Martin?"

Lisa gave a minimizing wave. "We're good pals. I've seen him about three times a year since he left Vietnam. He's never been attracted to me. Besides, ever since he got back from Vietnam, he's acted really creepy. I think the tiger cages and the Russian-roulette games affected him permanently."

"Martin wasn't forced to play Russian roulette! That's just a rumor."

"No matter how weirdly he behaves, I'm glad we're friends." *Because Martin is the only person with whom I can act myself,* she added silently. Lisa surreptitiously studied Sam's face as he ate his fish. His eyes were sea-green, as she remembered, with golden lights shining in the irises. The wheat-colored hair still fell rakishly over his high, tan forehead. The trustworthiness of his looks and his fine physique made Sam invincibly, nobly handsome. Here was a man who didn't parade his masculine beauty or even know he had it. He would never boast of a sexual triumph. Though he had a dominating quality, he would never be domineering. It was almost a pity that Sam's sexuality had to be reticent white bread instead of rawly aggressive red meat.

The fish eaten and gone, Sam relaxed and asked, "Since you're unknown in this town, how are you going to move into the circles of... rich people. High society? Is that what they're called?"

Lisa nodded. "I have stratagems. I'm armed with the lists of the right dog to buy, the right butchers and bakers, the correct florists and caterers, the right church to belong to. I've already taken the first bite of the Big Apple—I've been hired as an assistant by Oscar Moore Travis."

"Who's Oscar Moore Travis?"

"Don't you ever read magazines? He's an interior decorator who's invited to a lot of parties."

"Is *this* supposed to be an elite place?" Sam indicated the quiet grandeur of the Palm Court.

Endeared by Sam's naïveté, Lisa smiled. Sam was the only person in whom she'd forgive such lack of sophistication. "The Palm Court is nice, but it's not elite. You only need a reservation to gain entry."

"Have you seen Meritt's commercial?"

"For the diet soda? I recognized her face." Lisa caught the waiter's eye and ordered a fresh drink. "Meritt's in California right now, auditioning for a television pilot or something."

"Do you two go out much?"

"We... talk on the phone. We haven't gotten together since I moved here. But we will." She fixed a frank, sincere expression around her large blue eyes. "You see, the economic gap between us is so dramatic that I don't want Meritt to feel too... uncomfortable. I must find a... tactful meeting ground for us."

Sam laughed vigorously. *"You're* the one who doesn't want to feel uncomfortable!"

Lisa managed to look ashamed and amused at the same time. She retaliated, "I thought you always wanted to believe the best of people!" Sam started to come up with a retort, but Lisa looked over his head. "Martin's here."

Sam turned in his chair, and an electric shock traveled over his entire body. He would never have recognized the man walking toward him. Martin's unlined face and physique hadn't changed, but the startling thick, snowy white hair had altered his appearance to a degree none of the post-rescue newspaper photographs had conveyed.

Sam stood up so hurriedly to shake Martin's hand that he banged his knees on the marble tabletop. "Martin, hi, I'm glad to see you again."

"Glad to see you." Martin sat down. Their waiter approached them with a pastry tray. "None for me, thank you. Maybe some coffee." Sam abstained from indulging in dessert because of collegiate poverty; Lisa chose a cheesecake smothered in cherries and whipped cream. "People hate me. I can eat anything I like without gaining an ounce."

There was an awkward silence at the table until Martin spoke. "I'm sorry I never thanked you for persuading my brothers to send a special forces team to Laos. When someone saves your life, there is no way you can express gratitude."

"I understand." Sam cleared his throat. He was still disconcerted by Martin's appearance, the way his white hair contrasted with the ebony black of his vested suit. "I was so glad when you made it back alive I didn't need to be thanked!"

"I keep telling him he's got tangible proof his father is crazy about him," Lisa said, "arranging an incredible rescue like that."

Martin smiled. "And when I made it back to the States,

he gave me a job in the New York office of his Vanderziel Foundation."

Carefully Sam asked, "Do you still feel the effect of your days in Vietnam?"

"Of course, Sam. The U.S. didn't clear out of Vietnam till the end of April this year. I think Vietnam is still with everybody."

"No, I mean—your memories as a prisoner of war. Are you bothered by all that?"

Martin gave a light, cool, false laugh. "Sam, you forget —I was a prisoner for only two months. And it was almost fun. The camp personnel treated us better than they treated themselves. They fed us chicken and vegetables that tasted like they'd come from a Vietnamese restaurant. There was a small library of American books there, and card games, and horseshoes. I think they coddled us because they sensed the war was ending."

Martin's report, delivered in his emotionless, unvarying monotone, didn't ring true. Lisa interjected, "I had it tougher as a kid when we played World War Two! Since I was the littlest, I always had to play the POW. My brothers Bud and Bill tied me up to the cyclone fence and fed me dirt!"

Lisa's dismissive, trilling laughter irritated Sam. He heard a small boy at the next table ask in a piping voice, "Mama, what's a chocolate mousse?"

"It's pudding, darling."

Sam's eyes went to a table across the room, where he saw a blond, suntanned man looking intensely at Martin. Sam glanced at Martin and saw that he was returning the man's bullet-eyed gaze fully. Again the hair on the back of his neck prickled. Did this mean *Martin* was gay?

Martin's pale blue eyes flicked to him. "Have you been tracking Andy Smith since I saw you last?"

Sam had not discussed the none-too-bright congressman and his strange foreign friend, Oliver Remick, since that

May night in Virginia. Reluctantly, he said, "Yes I have. I'm surprised you'd think of my interest in him."

"Because out of the five of us, you were the one with the strongest sense of guilt. I figured you'd be the one of us most likely to worry about the existence of a Trojan Horse Project."

Sam felt defensive. "I'm concerned what could happen to the country if it was real, and if it were implemented. Laurel, Meritt and we three would have a lot to lose if it were made public."

Lisa couldn't control her burst of laughter. "But no one even knew we were there! Why worry about whether the Trojan Horse Project is real, or fake, or may come to life someday? You can't do a thing about the future, anyhow. I remember when you were eighteen, you had your life carefully arranged for years ahead in case you were in an accident or died that afternoon! Why don't you just live for each day?"

Perhaps Lisa was right. Sam thought of the precise roadmap he'd charted in his mind. His internal schedule had allowed four years for college and two years for Harvard Business School, followed by marriage, a move to New York, then children. All of those sunny things to come would be wiped out if it was discovered that Sam had failed to make the Trojan Horse Plan public when he'd had the chance.

Sam started to say, "Your future can be so much better if you start planning for it now—" but he found himself too annoyed by Martin's and Lisa's reckless "rich kid" indifference. What would Lisa say if she knew he'd already picked a potential bride? She might make fun of him for falling in love, especially when she learned Viola was a nurse. She'd say sarcastically, "How sweet—nursing is the most feminine profession in the world! Outside of babymaking."

Looking across the table, he sensed an affinity between Lisa and Martin that went beyond their monied backgrounds. Their intimacy was not friendship so much as an alliance.

He changed the subject. "Martin, what do you do at the Vanderziel Foundation?"

"Not much." His mouth spread in a thin-lipped smile. "My title is working trustee for the foundation. My job is to visit projects and see if we want to endow them. While my father's companies donate bucks, we also raise money from other sources. During the past twenty-five years, the Vanderziel Foundation has given away one hundred thirty million dollars."

"Martin works, he really does," Lisa said sincerely. "Often he works seven days a week."

Sam believed her. He was sure Martin didn't care at all whether he worked or relaxed or saw friends or had sex. He could visualize Martin working all day long, efficiently, adequately, and without imagination.

Sam stood up, signaling an end to their meeting. "I've got to get some Christmas shopping done before I catch the train back to Boston." He picked up the check, prepared to pay for their lunch. His eyes widened at the total.

"Let me get that," Lisa offered. "I'm the one who invited you here."

Stubbornly Sam held on to the check. His pride and etiquette were at stake.

Lisa shrugged. "I'm sorry you're going home so soon. If you ever need a place to stay in New York, call me."

The three of them exchanged pleasantries, and Sam walked away with the check in hand, fishing into his pants pockets for every cent he'd brought along. Just before he reached the darkly sumptuous Plaza lobby, he glanced back at Lisa leaning forward, talking earnestly to Martin.

When Lisa left the table, Martin remained another ten minutes, smoking mechanically. There was a painful fire burning in his head that needed to be brought under con-

trol. A red curtain had seeped into his eyes, making everything before him appear pink, and an awful roar in his ears
made it difficult to hear. He hoped he'd been able to hide
his state from Lisa and Sam.

After waiting five minutes, he went to the lobby to
make a phone call that lasted less than thirty seconds.
Outside, the Plaza doorman opened a taxicab door for
him. At a Murray Hill address, Martin paid the driver
and trotted up the snowy steps into a nondescript brownstone building.

A door on the second floor automatically opened when
Martin reached it. "Hello, Martin!" said an eager-looking
woman in her late forties. She was clad in turquoise lingerie. Her freckled face had seen better days, but her figure
was that of a twenty-year-old girl. "Come on in. Would
you like a drink, Martin?"

He gave no answer. Martin entered the living room of a
four-bedroom apartment that was being used as a brothel.
The living room served as the reception area, and the kitch-
enette behind it was the bar. There was one bedroom on
this level and three more bedrooms up the spiral staircase.
The entire place was decorated in hothouse colors accented
by black lacquer objets d'art. The furniture and pillows
were made of slippery, cool fabrics: leathers, vinyls, and
satins. Burning candles released a musky scent into the air.
The living room looked as if it had been picked out of a
Macy's floor display and plunked down here.

Martin didn't bother to sit down. Without looking at her,
he grabbed a Chicana girl with black pigtails and lacy car-
mine underwear and shoved her down the hallway into the
first bedroom. He slammed the bedroom door behind
them, then started to undo his tie. The girl, angered by
his harsh treatment, aggressively declared, "You pay me
first!"

Staring at the prostitute with his chilly blue eyes, he
fished in one of his front pockets and pulled out a handful

of twenty-dollar bills, then let them drop to the carpet in crumpled balls. When she looked down at them he slammed his palm on the left side of her face, and she fell on the floor beside the paper money. Martin kicked her in the pit of her stomach with his Vincent and Edgar shoes, custom-made from a cast of his foot. She began screaming, and he kicked her harder, pushing her across the floor next to the wall. Defensively she crossed her arms over her stomach, but he continued kicking at her arms. He stooped slightly to punch her face, and rip off her filmy undergarments, which tore with a hideous sound.

By the time the madam and her iron-jawed bouncer opened the door, Martin was pushing down on the girl's head with his foot, bearing down with all his weight as if he wanted to flatten her skull. When he felt hands grasping him, he cooled abruptly and stood back as if he'd never touched the girl. The Chicana groaned with the shock and pain of the attack. The freckle-faced madam stooped over her. She screeched at Martin, "My God, you broke at least two ribs. Call the ambulance, Artie, she has to go to the hospital!" As the bouncer left, the madam turned right into Martin's handsome face. "You're never coming back here. I don't give a shit what your last name is, I'm going to get the word out about you. You're the worst goddamn 'dumper' I've ever seen. If all you wanna do is beat up on defenseless girls, go attack one on the street."

Martin reached inside his coat pocket and withdrew a thousand dollars in hundred-dollar bills. The woman snatched them and shouted, "I don't care how many Benjies you wave around. I wish you'd never learned my address. You're sick! You didn't even take your clothes off! You're perverted. Rich daddy's little boy who's never worked a day in his life. You're sick, *sick*, you need psychiatric help bad. Piss off and don't come back."

The commotion didn't affect Martin in the least. He'd been thrown out of better places than this middle-class cathouse, much better. As he trotted out onto Thirty-second Street, he buttoned his coat. It was still snowing lightly. His face was twisted by a strange grimace resembling a smile. His head felt much better now, as if someone had eased the top off a pressure boiler.

• *Thirteen* •

Oscar Moore Travis had hired Lisa Dunning to serve primarily as bait for young men. It was an old, decadent homosexual gambit: Use a dazzling beauty as your escort, and some of the men attracted to her may be willing to accommodate you. He exploited her drawing power.

She was called a "personal assistant," and her duties involved acting as a human pet. Lisa kept silent at Oscar's bulky side while out in public. Whenever he had a hard day of interior decorating, when his creativity dragged and he felt low, Lisa flattered and comforted him until he was refreshed. He told her, "You're the only person I've met who didn't want something from me. Many people drop my name to add luster to their own."

Yet Lisa *was* using Oscar, to help her acquire social status. He partied with the Old Money and the New Money whose homes he designed. He did not decorate the homes of the Peasantry, the third and unmoneyed class.

Lisa had started striving for social status even before she'd left Charleston. She wrote introductory letters for Miss Lisa Dunning and signed them with the names of Charleston gentry. These testimonials were sent on to the women whose well-dressed photos appeared in *Women's Wear Daily*. As soon as her bags arrived on East Sixty-first Street, she awaited the engraved invitations to dinner, dress showings, charity fund meetings. She received exactly two invitations, both to luncheon. It was a start. Lisa wondered if she'd have to stoop so low as to hire a publicist or an impoverished social secretary with blue blood.

Oscar discovered Lisa at the Russian Tea Room in November 1975, while she was with one of the two ladies who'd written back. His body, as big as an easy chair, was stuffed into one of the lipstick-red banquettes across from a client. "This restaurant's rainbow chaos of colors offends my sensibilities," he told his patron. The walls were green, the tablecloth pink, the flowers were loud, and the waiters and busboys wore red and green tunics. Lavish Christmas decorations hung on the chandeliers twelve months of the year. Oscar scarcely heard his client's reply, for he was looking over the sea of diners. He loved to observe people. He swore that studying people at restaurants told him more about their personalities than watching them in bed would ever reveal.

He stared at a blond girl of exceptional, imperturbable beauty seated at a banquette with an older woman. The face had the perfection and chill of a diamond, which was in marked contrast to her warm, feminine movements. As she sat there artlessly, her body telegraphed a strong sensuality. She picked up her wineglass, tilted her head, then poured the wine into her mouth with deft grace. The gesture exposed her long white throat and invited anyone to study the tops of her breasts, which pushed against her satin blouse. Her bearing said it all: Here is a sensational woman; here is the woman you want to sleep with; here is the embodiment of the American dream.

Regarding her from across the restaurant, Oscar thought, *There's one girl who could hold a moistened finger to the air and detect which direction the men were coming from.* He sent a glass of pink champagne and a card to her table. The card said, "What are your *unseen* charms, pretty young thing? O.M.T." Lisa's eyes streaked from the card to Oscar. He thought triumphantly, *From the moment she walked into the RTR, she knew where I sat.* Shamelessly,

Lisa left the matron's table and table-hopped straight to Oscar's.

Lisa knew if she played Oscar right, he could be her ladder to the top. She proceeded to make friends with him. Within weeks the ungainly pair was making the rounds of Manhattan clubs where similarly Andy Warhol and Edie Sedgwick had once journeyed. Though they claimed that Lisa was employed as his "personal assistant" for his design studio, she was nothing more than his escort, his "perma-date" and pilot fish.

Lisa became as much a fixture of the nighttime scene as Oscar Moore Travis. She made friends with paparazzi and gossip columnists who covered the brand-new disco scene that was bubbling up. She was photographed in perpetual motion as Oscar and she went from party to dance floor to party again. Lisa thrived on the constant stimulation of New York. Her skin acquired a luminous patina, glowing with all the limelight she was soaking up. Even her body was changing, developing rounder curves to fit into sexier dresses that Oscar Moore Travis was only glad to pick out for her.

Lisa's sensual allure drew men to her, just as Oscar Moore Travis had planned. Tactfully he'd take over their three-way conversation and serenade the boys with his barbed-wire wit. He'd tell them, "Oh, stop bragging about catching the latest venereal disease." Oscar's parley made the boy feel bright and witty. They'd make each other laugh, and then Oscar would invite his prey to another nightclub. They'd leave together, putting Lisa in a separate cab. Lisa didn't catch on till the summer of 1976 that she was the "beard" for Oscar Moore Travis and the straight or bisexual men they'd encounter. By then she was tiring of going out at night with a man she couldn't dominate, and she was tired of the incisive quips that issued from Oscar's moist, thick mouth. In July she told him honestly, "If I keep hanging around you like a fag hag, people will think I'm fruity. You know, queer."

Oscar Moore Travis replied slyly, "I think you've found the man of your dreams. *That's* who you want to go around with now."

There was no use for hypocrisy around O.M.T. "Yes, Oscar. Charles Herbert Stratham is my dream—a young man with a trust fund."

Oscar shot his cuffs. "I just don't know about him... Does he have any lead in his pencil?"

"Forget about pencil lead! Charlie's got a face like a Bentley. That's sufficient for me." Lisa and the interior decorator parted on good terms. Charles Stratham was an auto parts heir with money on his mother's side, money so old and so vast that the family was one of the private rich, the people who pay to keep their names *out* of the paper.

He dressed in the prim, somber style of a city gentleman, but there was nothing masculine about him. He was sweetly androgynous, slender in build, and he gestured adroitly as he talked. His face was like a cat's, with thin lips, a little pointy nose that looked as though it should have whiskers, and big eyes. Charles's hair was so pale his eyebrows were almost invisible, and the skin on his forehead was furrowed, making him look sorry for himself all the time.

He had no profession. He spent half of every year traveling around the world with effete friends, and he seemed to have no interest in girls or settling down. Mr. and Mrs. Stratham despaired of Charles's ever marrying and begetting a male heir. When Lisa Dunning began aggressively chasing him in the fall of 1976, they saw her as a possible solution to the problem. At her request, Charles took Lisa into a refined, protected world of afternoon teas and glittering evenings with international society. She learned more about social status and breeding, and what family was behind which conglomerate.

At every gathering of the privileged, Lisa's sharp blue eyes darted like a heat-seeking missile to beneficiaries of a family wad. Her ambition to win an awesomely rich husband was getting more grandiose. Charles Stratham was coming into Babylonian money, but Lisa didn't want to marry him. He was a wimp, a sweating wimp, and to touch his hand was to touch sticky perspiration. She was looking for a man with Vanderziel-size holdings, but he had to be tolerable. Martin Vanderziel was out of the question. At night he descended into the substrata of expensive vice. And Lisa would bet anything that his genes would produce mutant children. Children who would grow up to be Charlie Manson.

Charles had a light, trembling voice. The only interesting subject he could discuss was foreign travel. Sometimes he'd tentatively bring up the subject of marriage to Lisa, but she pretended that she hadn't heard him: "Lisa, have you ever considered the future?" "That tie is smashing, Charles!" By late November, Charles had worked up enough courage to give Lisa good-night kisses when he took her home to Sixty-first Street. Once inside the foyer, Lisa would wipe her mouth to rid herself of those cat-lipped kisses.

The party of the year was the December dinner dance at the Metropolitan Museum to benefit its Costume Institute. As Charles swept Lisa over the dance floor, she asked, "Who is that man? I've seen him more and more often as the season's worn on." She was referring to a man in evening clothes who leaned elegantly against a wall, decorating it, actually.

"You don't know?" Charles's face was transformed with surprise. "That's one of the greatest catches in the country, of the world, even. That's Deverell Wharton."

"So that's Deverell Wharton." Of Woodhill-Gannon Bank, shipping, aerospace and other international concerns. Lisa sighed, wondering why she hadn't seen him before. "Does he work?"

"He's in the business of breaking young ladies' hearts," Charles said warningly. He hoped that Deverell would be a pal to him and act as though Lisa didn't exist. "Deverell's

technique is to romance a girl till she's infatuated; then as
soon as she goes to bed with him, he turns on her and acts
as though he despises her."

"Is that right?" Lisa said. She kept studying Deverell
under slackened eyelids. She prayed he would break into
the dance. Deverell looked to be in his late twenties. His
bearing was that of a man of sophistication, reserve and
assurance. Those qualities all added up to a double treat:
old wealth and real society.

Charles was afraid of having a sexual rival, and to stomp
out that threat, he decided it was time to be a man with
Lisa. His only sexual experiences had been furtive, infre-
quent encounters with street hookers. He'd heard it was
good to act aggressive and demand favors from the person
you wanted to impress in bed. For years he'd tried to determine his sexuality, And under Lisa's influence he'd become indisputably masculine, he was sure.

A few nights later, Charles escorted Lisa to a Saturday
evening dinner party held in honor of some foreign poobah
at the United Nations. Lisa wore a long jersey dress whose
warm nutmeg color emphasized her height and drew attention to her crown of silvery blond hair. The other guests
looked admiringly at her as they sat down to dinner.

Each table was weighted by a heavy cloth and gleaming
silver service, with a center bouquet of tiger lilies and fragrant tiny white flowers. As guests found their chairs, their
eyes surreptitiously checked the room to see who was
worth talking to. Lisa saw the man alleged to be the most
amusing in town, an art dealer, a real estate tycoon, another self-made millionaire, a television newscaster, someone who'd just been acquitted after a sensational murder
trial, and a clotheshorse whose garments always seemed to
have been created for her slender body, no matter who the
designer was.

Charles pulled Lisa's chair out, and she sat down,
smugly congratulating herself on being at the right place
with the right people. Charles sat down at her left. She

asked him some questions as a man sat down on her right. She turned slightly, recognized the face and gasped sharply, as if someone had stabbed her.

"Are you all right?" Charles asked solicitously.

"Yes, yes I'm fine." Lisa breathed deeply, staring at the centerpiece, fighting for composure. When casting characters for a spicy table talk at a glittering gathering, it was always good to throw in someone who'd just been appointed to a post in Washington. Like former Congressman Andy Smith.

He pivoted in his seat and dropped the right arm. "Hi, I'm Andy Smith. And this is my honeypie, Ann." He shook Lisa's ice-cold hand, then reached for Charles's hand. Lisa burped out her name like an automaton, and she blinked at the woman sitting to the right of Andy, smiling like a simpleton. Ann Smith was a busty lady in an orange taffeta dress, and, Lisa could swear, there was a white mink stole dangling over her shoulders. Her eyes were empty over the crimson gash of her mouth, and her hair was formed into a concrete beehive. It was hard to believe Honeypie was on the Leukemia Society's board of directors. The charity was run by distinguished socialites, not by Stepford hicks.

Lisa stared at her plate as if it could be an escape route. She'd forgotten all about that night of eavesdropping on Andy and that foreign guy, but his physical presence made the Trojan Horse credible and threatening. She had read that he'd lost his House seat, and was to begin serving in a paper-pusher position, as controller of a subcommittee in the Federal Reserve Board. She knew nothing about the Federal Reserve Board except it was really big and established monetary policy for the United States. The possible ramifications were unsettling.

They were sitting so close that Lisa felt warmth radiating from Andy's arm. She supposed that she should tell him she'd been a Senate page, but her tongue seemed paralyzed. Lisa assured herself that this weak-chinned Republican with a creaky voice and receding hairline couldn't be involved in a plan any more difficult than screwing in a lightbulb.

"What do *you* think, Lisa?" asked a voice that was like the caw of a crow. It was Honeypie Ann Smith, who'd reached a plump arm around her husband to tag Lisa's arm.

"About what?"

"Don't you agree, since all the best men are married and the best women aren't, it would be a good idea to annul all marriage ties and let everyone start over?"

Lisa murmured, "What . . . ?" as the six others at the table broke out in a chorus of laughter. Seated across from her was the wife of a Swedish industrialist. In a heavy accent she said possessively, "Oh, I'd never annul! I luff Jens, ahnd we have the seven children to proooove it!"

"I love my cigar, too," Andy said, "but I take it out every once in a while." He fell into a spasm of vulgar hoots that would do a hillbilly proud.

Without discretion, Lisa asked Charles if they could leave. At the cloak room, Charles muttered indignantly, "He stole that line from Groucho Marx." Bundling into their coats, Charles and Lisa left the duplex. Usually Lisa, being more forceful than Charles, would hail their cab, but this time Charles walked to Madison Avenue and summoned a taxi. He helped Lisa into the back seat, climbed in and said, "You're feeling better, aren't you, Lise?"

She nodded, and in the dimness of the cab Charles's pale eyes met hers unsurely. This woman is for me, he asserted to himself, and his gaze grew steady and intent. He found himself aroused by the frozen solemnity of her face. He liked her stillness. Bravely he asked, "Would you like to come back to my house?"

The face didn't alter. "I don't mind."

Lisa yawned as Charles opened the door to his bachelor flat on Park Avenue. The place was obviously designer-decorated, and the gewgaws he'd lugged back from his forays abroad were at odds with the hypermodern furniture. Charles hit the switches that worked the dramatic spotlights pointed at his shelving. Lisa leaned past him to hit the switches for all the lights, which threw everything in the room under a raw revealing glare. It made Charles nervous.

As he headed for the bar to pour their drinks, Lisa pulled off her huge enveloping coat and tossed it onto a butter-soft leather couch. "Why do you have a bar, Charlie? I thought living room bars went out of style in the early sixties."

"Not for me. I'm a rugged individualist, ha ha." Decent repartee, he thought. "Double scotch for you?"

"Whatever."

Charles busied himself behind the bar, increasingly disturbed by Lisa's indifferent behavior. *Her neutral tone is the way she shows her acceptance*, he told himself. *I've got to follow up appropriately on her signals*. His tension was exhibiting itself in adrenaline-charged movements, and a whiskey tumbler smashed between his fingers. "Anything wrong?" Lisa asked, standing before the black marble fireplace.

"No, uh, no." Charles held up a bleeding finger and grinned. Lisa turned her back to him, and something crumpled inside his chest. Just as he started to rinse the blood off, he saw her hand reach to her dress zipper. She opened it straight to the small of her back, proferring a satin-textured back. He held his breath. Who was seducing whom?

The jersey dress whispered as it eased over her hips to her ankles. Lisa had on an exquisitely lacy bra and underpants, and she popped them off like snaps. Charles thought he was going to crash through the bar. Naked, Lisa was a deity. Her curves made soft mauve peaks and valleys all around her exquisite bones. He was certain that, if he bit her, milk and honey would flow from her body. He'd never seen a woman fully nude before, with the round breasts, the rose-colored nipples, the shadowed blond triangle of hair, the thighs so smooth and silky—all just for him.

The responsibility of taking on that divine body created a

statue out of fear-shocked Charles. He was unable to
move. He couldn't possibly live up to that magnificent
body. Lisa began walking toward him, her face set in a
cool mask. "Come on, Charles. Whaddaya wanna do?" He
realized that Lisa was agreeable to anything he proposed,
but there was nothing he could dream of. "Oh, God," he
squeaked. Lisa stepped around the bar and pulled off his tie
and unbuttoned his shirt as efficiently as if she were un-
dressing a store mannequin. Charles inhaled the musky
scent of her body combined with a floral perfume as she
started to slide his trousers down. It was intimidating. He
involuntarily compared the time in Kenya when he'd come
face to face with a tiger, because he was more scared of
Lisa than he'd been of the tiger.

He got hold of enough gumption to shuffle out of his
shoes and take Lisa's hand, and make the pretense that *he*
was leading *her* into the bedroom.

Lisa flopped down onto the satin-topped king-size bed,
and face up, stretched her body out like a starfish under the
rosy lights of the bedroom. Charles stood at the bedside,
cowed by the pillowy succulence offered him.

She was used to men being awestruck by her body, but
Charles was acting positively brain-damaged. "Come on,
Charles, yes or no? Any other man would have jumped me
by now."

Charles's little cat face puckered with despair at her lack
of romance. "I'm not just 'any other man,'" he said
bravely.

"Well, I can see that." Lisa's blue eyes dropped below
Charles's concave chest to his groin. "You've got a big
peter, but it's not working. It's just hanging there like a
dead fish." Charles barely groaned. She looked at his face.
"Do you want me to do all the foreplay stuff?" Lisa raised
her torso up on her elbows, and regarded Charles analytic-
ally. "You don't have any idea of what I'm talking about,
do you?"

Charles's eyes grew watery as his head shook. Fueled by

the unpleasantness of running into Andy Smith, Lisa began to take out her tension on Charles. No man had ever dare be impotent with her. She sat up on her knees. "Did you think I came over here for a *cuddle?* Do you want a maternal tit? Your castration-queen mother has kept you a little girl so you're only comfortable around other faggots, the kind of perverts who meet in subway latrines. That's the only way you know how to get off. *Isn't it?"*

Disdainfully Lisa walked out of the bedroom, fully naked, to retrieve her dress. "You're no man at all, just as I expected. The whole world knows it, too. Your type *makes me sick."*

Charles flopped down on the edge of the bed, exhausted by emotional fatigue. He heard the main entrance door close. His tear-filled eyes gazed unseeingly at the window, which looked out at blackness. "There goes my only chance for happiness," he said aloud. If Lisa couldn't arouse him, what woman ever would?

By the time she made it inside her little apartment, Lisa's rage at Andy was boiling in her head. She locked her door and went straight to the liquor cabinet for whiskey. Only after she'd had a shot did she remove her coat and her shoes. She turned on the television, sat on a velvet loveseat, and put the whiskey at a short reach. There was no better entertainment than the "Carol Carole Show" late at night when you were drunk. It provided lots of laughs. It was a syndicated televangelism show that starred luminous Carol Carole, a woman of indeterminate age who wore a white robe like an angel or a holy ghost. Her guests and co-hosts viewed religion as their own private Las Vegas, and turned faith into a tawdry, cheap game show.

The combination of the "Carol Carole Show" and liquor was relaxing. Lisa started to wonder if she'd been too harsh with Charles. She couldn't have helped herself, though. She was still upset by seeing Andy Smith, the liv-

ing reminder of some cockeyed world-domination project
she thought she'd erased from her memory. She'd battled
with the desire to pull Andy into a corner and tell him the
jig was up, just to watch his reaction. But whatever the
Trojan Horse was, it was valuable enough to be kept secret, and Lisa was sure there was a way she could profit
from the whole thing.

Her eyelids grew heavy. First thing on her agenda in the
morning was to call Charles and ask him to an apology
lunch.

The telephone rang, waking Lisa. She blinked drowsily
at her lovely sunlit room, and saw that the clock said it was
one P.M. She bolted upright and answered the phone. The
person on the other end was Trevor Bassden, a cousin of
Charles whom she had met at several parties. Trevor didn't
greet her; he just began telling her how hard it had been to
track her down. Lisa interrupted, "What is it? Why are you
calling?"

"It's about Charles. He's dead, Lisa."

"What?"

"Sometime last night he hanged himself in his bedroom.
No one knows why."

In school, Lisa had read when a person hits the end of
the hangman's rope, he goes on living for 15 to 20 minutes. The body continues gasping for air, struggling, bat-
tling for life as long as it can. She dimly heard Trevor.

"Lisa, are you there?"

"Yes," she whispered.

"I said I'll call you back as soon as we know where the
wake will be."

After Trevor had hung up, Lisa listened to the dial tone.
She tried to feel remorse. She reviewed the mean things
she'd snapped at Charles that might have affected him. If

he couldn't handle some meaningless taunts, well, jeez! How was he ever going to cope with *real* life!

I wasn't the cause of his suicide. I was merely a symptom of his inability to cope. Lisa gently set the telephone on its cradle.

• *Fourteen* •

Laurel wondered what it would be like to have someone like Sam Ross love you. Pensively she watched Viola Bierwalt move slowly from the back of the chapel to the altar. Sam came to her side. Viola turned and raised her beautiful eyes. He responded by taking her arm and sliding his fingers over her wrist. Together they turned to look up at the priest.

Laurel didn't know much about Viola, except that she was supposed to be the most wholesome girl in the world. She held the same conservative views about marriage as Sam. Her face was the picture of silver sweetness, with beguilingly rosy cheeks and fetchingly curled lips and gentle, big, blue eyes. The white wedding gown underlined the translucence of her face and neck. Her features were delicate, her wrists small where they emerged from the sleeves of her wedding dress. Tiny curling tendrils of shiny strawberry blonde hair escaped from her pulled-back coiffure to frame her face. She looked tender, untroubled, and dependently feminine, Laurel decided.

Femininity wasn't a characteristic Laurel could afford right now. It was January of 1977, and she was thinking about kicking off her campaign for a House seat back in

Nebraska. The election wouldn't take place till November of 1978, yet good, solid campaigns started a year before voting. When Laurel was out in the field glad-handing constituents, she had to be careful not to be so feminine that people would think she'd make a sissy congresswoman. She had to be careful not to come on so strong that her future constituents would think she was a lesbian. And she had to be careful to act like an unthreatening, basically friendly campaigner whom voters of either gender would look up to.

Laurel's current job was chief of staff for the Kansas lieutenant governor, who knew she'd leave at campaign time. She had just passed the Nebraska bar exam after getting her law degree at Georgetown University in Washington, D.C.

"Dearly beloved, we are gathered here today. . ."

The nave was nearly empty of wedding guests. Sam's dignified lawyer father was there, as were a group of his college buddies, and Viola's parents stood with a few of her cousins; then there were just Lisa and her beau, Meritt and her boyfriend Jeremy, and her roommate Heloise, and Laurel . . . alone. No one had even pretended to love her since she and Hal had broken up and his wife had moved back into his house.

Meritt's amber eyes followed the priest's hands intently as he blessed the radiant young couple. Sam was such a good friend, a man who could lift her spirits whenever she was down, a trustworthy person for when she needed trust. Meritt was happy Sam and Viola were moving to New York this fall after Sam finished his master's degree in business. Meritt hoped Viola wouldn't mind if she occasionally cried on Sam's shoulder.

Sam knew that Meritt's ongoing affair with Jeremy had become frustrating. They'd been together nearly five years, and he refused to commit himself, or even introduce Meritt to his parents in Flushing. Perhaps he thought it wasn't trendy to get married. Meritt didn't want to live with him, because she uncompromisingly wanted marriage. It definitely wasn't cool to discuss the issue of a serious future: he refused to.

Jeremy's career in stage-directing was keeping pace with Meritt's: completely stalled. Right now he was working as an assistant stage manager for an actual Broadway production—*Streamers*, a play about racial, sexual and other tensions at an army camp during the Vietnam War. Its superstar director was Mike Nichols, for whom Jeremy admitted grudging respect.

After her agent, Carrie, had jettisoned her, Meritt went knocking at other agents' doors. She thought she had an advantage because she'd worked almost steadily for three years, when she'd had an agent. Experience didn't help one bit. The ten-percenters would look her over, at the generously curved lips and arresting Creole face, framed by thick, waving black hair cascading to her shoulders. "I love your type—but there's no work for your type." She'd heard it all before.

As her savings account dwindled, Meritt signed up with a temporary office employment agency to add to her restaurant earnings. It paid only minimum wage. She was desperate to get a part-time job that would allow her to audition at odd hours. Throwing all caution to the wind, she looked at the "help wanted" ads in the *Village Voice*, and found an ad for "adult telephone consultants," a job that guaranteed "good pay at home in your spare time."

"This is a sex talk service," she was told when she called. "The job is as comfortable as you'd like to make it. We're completely discreet. No client calls you—everything is handled through our service. Neither our operator nor your caller will know anything about you. And you can refuse any call for any reason."

Armilla, the owner, went on to explain that "telephone consultants" were paid by the call, which usually lasted from two to thirty minutes. The caller paid thirty-five dollars, which would be charged to a major credit card. From her cut, Meritt figured she could easily earn a hundred a night.

That night when Meritt's phone rang, she began her career as "Stephanie." "How are you, Joe?" was the first thing she said when her caller gave her his first name.

"Fine, Stephanie. What are you wearing?"

Merritt looked down. She was in jeans and a T-shirt, and sitting in the kitchen-bathroom-living room of her apartment. "I'm wearing a black camisole. It's see-through." She continued to tell Joe that she was a busty blond coed from Texas, that she loved candlelit dinners and evenings spent in front of the fireplace, and that she lived in a luxury penthouse. She squeezed her eyes shut and tried to pretend she was talking to her movie star crush Christopher Colacello. The call lasted about fifteen minutes, and it consisted of "Stephanie" talking all about herself. The experience was innocuous enough that Meritt decided to keep working the phone whenever she felt like it.

In time two or three callers insisted that they'd fallen in love with her. "It's not me you love, it's my voice," Meritt would reply with her husky laugh. Many men spent hundreds of dollars just so they could talk with understanding, blond, busty Stephanie.

After Meritt had been working the phone for six months, Armilla had another job suggestion for her: photographic modeling.

"Not a chance in hell," Meritt said.

Armilla reassured her it wasn't what she thought. She knew a man who published a string of detective and "true crime" magazines, and he was always looking for fresh faces to exploit for the articles' illustrations. Meritt was willing to be photographed half-clad, so she soon was posing in scanty slips and wigs as "The Redhead with the Loose Lips" or "The Mystery of the Girl from the Wrong Side of the Tracks."

Jeremy knew about Meritt's modeling, and approved of it as high camp. He even bought the magazines to show the photos to his friends. It embarrassed Meritt, but she came to believe it meant Jeremy was proud to have a model for a girlfriend.

He knew nothing of her lip service for lonely men. He did wonder how Meritt could get by on her modeling and restaurant money alone. Since they'd been together so long without a commitment, she felt justified in lying and saying she was still pulling in residuals from old commercials.

Right now she felt herself getting burned out from servicing the intense phone calls. She'd been doing it for ten months and yearned to go back to acting; yet no producer in New York seemed to need someone like her. She wondered if she was getting burned out on Jeremy.

At the moment that thought coursed through Meritt's raven head, Jeremy reached his hand over and laced it with her left hand, right as Sam and Viola were saying their "I do's." She was astounded—he was making a P.D.A., a rare treat, a public display of affection! God, was there hope left for their relationship? In partial shock, she looked down at their entwined hands, and he gave hers a fond squeeze.

Lisa fiercely hoped that she'd be standing before a preacher soon. She hoped so intensely that her hands balled into fists, and she hid them in her lap. Deverell Wharton was her target. What a coup it had been to lure the jaded young roué to a wedding. Daintily clad in an understated cream silk tunic and puffy skirt, her head tilted prayerfully downward, she sat next to him. So strange to be attending a wedding with him when they'd met at a funeral, Charles Stratham's funeral. Charles's family asked Lisa to stand with them at the wake, where she'd been formally introduced to Deverell Wharton. Though he'd been properly somber, she saw his narrowed brown eyes sizing up her breasts, revealed by the tightness of her dove-gray mourning dress.

After a discreet couple of weeks had lapsed, Deverell called and asked Lisa if she would like to have lunch at La Côte Basque in two days. She panicked after she put down the phone. How could she package herself within two short days? Though they'd just met, she was planning on marrying into the glittering Wharton fortune. Every detail of her project had to go just right.

As one of the world's most eligible bachelors Deverell was hungrily pursued by women, or so Lisa read in the New York *Post*, but he did his share of the pursuing, too. He was rumored to have dated actresses Faye Dunaway and Jacqueline Bisset. He liked his women glamorous; he preferred them stunning. Branded onto Lisa's memory were the girls he'd brought to dinners and dances, women with heavily made-up eyes and long blond hair and garish outfits. The poor boy didn't know what he really wanted. She was just going to have to show him. She reached for the phone to schedule a day at Elizabeth Arden's Red Door.

In the sauna she had scrubbed until her soft skin glowed like a lustrous apricot pearl. Her fingernails were chopped off, and what was left was buffed and lacquered with clear polish. After a treatment of paraffin mittens, Lisa's hands were the hands of a nun. Her silken hair was shaped into a conservative crown, smoothed from the top in a front roll. A makeup artist showed her how to apply cosmetics so her face didn't look at all made-up, and he slipped her a tiny jar of fluorescent foundation that would make her face extra radiant.

The day of beauty paid off. Deverell appeared stunned by the visitation of an earthly angel, whose every unlipsticked smile was hopeful and vulnerable. The drink she ordered was Perrier. He stared at her, enraptured, through their vichyssoise and grilled sole. Admiring Deverell's languid brown eyes and wavy chestnut hair, Lisa made earnest noises and sat up very straight without letting her back touch the chair. Again and again she murmured, "Yes? You know? Really?," the three magic phrases that can convince any man he's the most fascinating being on earth. She kept her large blue eyes innocent and open wide so that Deverell could fall right into them.

Tactfully she avoided asking Deverell about his vocation in life, because his daily living consisted of being a spoiled brat who seduced any woman available, drove fast in the latest sports cars by Lancia and Ferrari, and took great pleasure in smashing them. He traveled the Western World with his polo ponies in search of the ultimate game. Lisa had heard that his passion for polo cost over $110,000 a year. His lust for gambling cost far more. Deverell loved skydiving and speedboats and freestyle skiing, almost as if his career was to speed. Though he brought an impassioned quality to each of his pursuits, indoors Deverell was relaxed, a picture of high sophistication. Lisa knew also that, like Martin Vanderziel, he'd been tutored till adulthood, but he'd never entered a college. His IQ was unthreatening.

After their lunch at La Côte Basque, Deverell asked Lisa if he could drive her home. Standing outside on the curb was a Rolls-Royce Silver Shadow. He always had one waiting, with one of three chauffeurs working an eight-hour shift. Once inside the car, Deverell shut the window opening to the driver and threw his arms around Lisa. He put his lips on hers and tried to insert his tongue into her mouth. She pushed him away gently. "No, Deverell, I don't know you well enough."

His brown eyes widened with surprise. "You can't be serious." Nearly every girl he knew would willingly accept his advances. Lisa's tactic was to present a challenge. Deverell put his lips against Lisa's ear and murmured sexily, "Come back to my house, honey. We can have a matinee."

Lisa couldn't believe he'd managed to proposition her even before the car had moved. "No, I don't do that," she whispered in a baby voice.

Three different expressions of disbelief played over Deverell's handsome visage. "You don't mean to say you're a virgin?" Lisa didn't answer, but gazed seriously through her lashes at Deverell in a way that said proudly, "I am indeed a virgin."

"But I need you," he said faintly. "You would love to love me. I'll be gentle. I'm a perfect lover. I want you."

"You don't want me. You want a woman you haven't slept with."

Deverell fell back against his corner of the wide seat and sulked, arms crossed. Lisa gazed straight ahead. When the limousine pulled up to her curb on Sixty-first Street, she laid her fingers on Deverell's forearm. "Deverell—you have to know me better."

"Fat chance of that happening."

The chauffeur opened her door and she stepped out gracefully. She laid odds that Deverell would call her within forty-eight hours, and he called that same night and asked her to a black-tie dinner aboard the Wharton yacht, anchored on the East River. It was November, but a party in any weather would be fabulous aboard the 325-foot yacht, with its own movie theater, ballroom, helicopter pad, hospital—and surface-to-air missiles. One never knew when terrorists might strike.

Lisa's mouth slid into a triumphant grin. She didn't reply.

"Please . . . it's on Saturday night. There will be other people there."

Forcing Deverell Wharton to plead made Lisa heady with victory. "I can't go," was all she said, giving no clue as to why. "I must say good-bye now."

The following morning saw the arrival of a huge spray

of white orchids. When Deverell called, he asked, "Did you get my flowers?"

"Yes," Lisa answered. "I'm wearing one right now."

She agreed to attend the dinner, which was sumptuous as expected, and she enjoyed the guests, all people with social talent. The table talk was charming and witty, and Deverell made Lisa feel comfortable and important. She was certain that after his other yacht dinners, the playboy enticed his female guests into one of the ten VIP suites, each one named after a distinguished Wharton ancestor. Yet Deverell conveyed her home with the most gentlemanly of manners.

He had experienced something he'd never known before this dinner: respect for his date. He was proud to be seen with such a principled girl, and his friends seemed to have approved of her.

As they dated throughout December, Deverell remained solicitous. He refrained from pouncing on Lisa, and kissed her only on the cheek and on her shining oval fingertips. When he spoke, Lisa never interrupted him, speaking only to agree with him. When he talked about his wildly extravagant life-style, Lisa was enthusiastic.

And now, at her friend's wedding, Deverell himself was beset by ideas of marriage. Though he was twenty-eight, he'd never considered getting married, especially since he'd never deemed his dates to be good enough for wife material. He was aroused by Lisa's virginity, and he often fantasized about her rapturous surrender to him. He was convinced that she'd turn into a grateful but insatiable animal once he'd introduced her to his sex techniques.

He looked down at Lisa's hand, which rested in his palm. It was almost a child's hand, it was so pure and unsoiled. He couldn't wait to feel those hands on his bare body.

At his side, Lisa closely watched the new Mrs. Ross as the ceremony came to a close. Viola's tiny voice and her dainty gestures were so modest, so humble, and so attentive that she could be some girl who had just come from

the convent. The way Lisa *acted* for Deverell, Viola *was*.
It made Lisa uncomfortable and angry . . . and jealous.

After the ceremony, Sam's friends clambered into a
Wharton limousine with Deverell, Lisa, and Laurel on the
backseat, Meritt and Jeremy on the jump seats, and Heloise
sitting up front with the driver. Laurel thought wealthy
Wharton was uncouth, because it went without saying that
the host should sit on the jump seat.

"Why wasn't Martin Vanderziel here?" Deverell asked.
"Wasn't he one of your page buddies?"

There was a moment of awkward silence before Meritt
said, "Uh, he's living in California right now. Couldn't
make it."

The reception was inside a dark banquet room at the
Hesslet Hotel on Park Avenue. The damask walls set off
the tapestry-trimmed velvet loveseats and chairs, opulent
but with restraint. The wedding party sat down at a long
gilt table and feasted on grilled chicken breasts stuffed with
garlic and basil, grilled zucchini, and warm compote.

The toasts to the bride and groom occurred after the slic-
ing of a small wedding cake. Then Sam's pals from Harvard stood up to say embarrassing things about him and
offer toasts.

Sam sat in the middle of the long, linen-covered table,
and grinned slyly as his friends made fun of him. His hand
covered one of Viola's, whose usual gentle poise wavered
as she laughed at his pals' jokes: "By marrying him, Viola
is exploiting Sam's personality disorders." "When Viola
said that marriage would give him respectability, Sam said,
'Respectability? What's that?' "

Viola glanced at Sam. Her small smile brought back the
kisses of their nights, and a reminder of the wonders that
had been unfolded between the sheets. Sam was sure his
friends and family thought that Viola, being a pious Catho-

lic girl, was a maiden, when most definitely she was not. After six months of courtship they'd given in to temptation in Sam's narrow bed. There, Viola had shown Sam secret parts of himself that he never knew existed. Sam had long imagined that the perfect lover would be the one who allowed him to drown himself in her, yet each time they made love, he began to know himself better. He and this marvelous girl had dissolved their boundaries and together formed one entity.

Viola was the first woman with whom Sam could envision having children. Appropriately, they'd met at church in the fall of 1975, on a Sunday when each was attending Mass alone. Viola caught Sam's eye as she strolled down the aisle after taking communion. After the service he waited at the main entrance for her, and she accepted his invitation to have coffee with him.

Before they knew it, they were talking about everything —even their earliest childhood memories. Over orange juice Sam told Viola that, as a boy, he'd played priest instead of cowboy. "I'd put on Dad's bathrobe, and build an altar out of an end table. I'd lay velvet scraps over some books, and light candles. We had a silver cup I used as a chalice. My friends came to the house to kneel as I administered Kool-Aid and torn bread crumbs, intoning 'Body of Christ, Body of Christ. . . .'"

Viola laughed delightedly. "When I was that age, I opened my own museum in the garage, and charged kids a penny to look at my junk. I displayed my best schoolwork, and a bloody used bandage, and a Barbie doll head without a body, school pictures of me that were a couple years old . . . I taped little informative labels under each exhibit."

Viola Bierwalt was twenty-five, three years older than Sam. She came from Long Island and was a registered nurse working at a Cambridge old-folks' home.

Sam found it easy to tell her about his problems and ambitions: that he'd been born with a harelip, how his mother's deathbed wishes for plastic surgery for him had been answered, that he was in his first year at Harvard "B" School, and that he intended to work on Wall Street when he'd earned his M.B.A.

The long, talky brunch extended till 3:00 P.M. After their good-byes Sam watched Viola walk away from him, looking at the way her rose-print dress was cinched around her small, perfect waist. What a beauty!

He'd never shared more than six weeks with any girl at Northwestern University. His friends marveled at his magical ability to recognize at what point he could cut off his romance with a girl so that it didn't hurt—much. This girl seemed like a "keeper." Viola had a serenity he'd never encountered before. In these past four hours he'd gathered intuitively that she viewed life as uncompromisingly as he did. She knew what was absolutely right and absolutely wrong.

Their companionability was deep. As their courtship developed, Viola became the first person besides Sam's father that he'd ever been able to talk to honestly in his life. He could say whatever was on his mind, and she would understand. Yet he couldn't confide to her the secret that he shared with Martin, Lisa, Meritt and Laurel.

It was decided that Viola would move to Manhattan to set up a home for them. That way, when Sam moved to the city after graduation, he could hit his job and not worry about starting a household from scratch. In November 1976 Viola moved into an apartment in the Upper East Eighties, then took a nursing job at Cumberland Hospital in Brooklyn Heights. Since she was a city resident, and since New York was convenient for most of the wedding guests, Sam and Viola had decided on a midtown wedding.

After the bridal couple made a lingering exit, Lisa, Deverell, Meritt, Heloise, Jeremy, and Laurel began walking down the great staircase of the Hesslet Hotel. The four "starving artist" members of the group tried to not stare at Deverell. It wasn't his money that had them in awe, it was his celebrity. Deverell Wharton had announced in a gossip columnist's presence that he planned never to do one useful thing during his lifetime. The entire world was his playground, to be used in whatever way he liked. Many times, he'd harmed people mentally or emotionally, then trotted off, apathetic and unaffected, to another field of play.

Lisa's friends were puzzled by her strangely reserved behavior. During the wedding and reception, she'd kept smiling bemusedly, laughing quietly, and speaking very little. When she looked at Deverell, her mouth was open just the smallest bit, as if she had had one kiss and was waiting for another. It seemed as though she'd given up her personal power and thrown it upon Deverell, letting him decide what to do with it.

The silver Rolls was ready for them at the curb. Deverell opened the rear door. "Would you like to come back to my place for coffee or drinks?" he asked deferentially. He was going out of his way to accommodate Lisa's middle-class friends, in hopes of impressing her.

"Sorry, I'm due at a play rehearsal," Jeremy said.

"Thanks, but I've got to go work at Charolais," Meritt begged off.

"I've got to return to the editing table," Heloise said.

"I've got to catch a plane to Kansas City," Laurel explained.

"Would you like us to take you to the airport?" Deverell asked. Laurel looked at Lisa, who nodded enthusiastically.

"All right." Laurel picked up her coat hem as she stepped into the car. "We have to stop at Meritt's place. My luggage is waiting in the lobby for me." They hugged each other good-bye, then Jeremy, Meritt and Heloise began walking west.

A block ahead in the twilight darkness they saw a lump of clothes piled on the sidewalk. As they came closer, they saw it was the crumpled body of a woman in heavy clothes and a floppy hat. Two Bloomingdale's bags sat by her. She looked like a bag lady, but she had a large purse and a new radio lying next to her. Naturally, the New York pedestrians walked by and around her without stopping to help.

Meritt bent over her. "Are you all right?" No response. Heloise wondered, "Is she dead?" Jeremy reached to turn her around, but as he put his hand on her arm, they heard a gruff, "Don't do that!" The three Samaritans nearly jumped back. "I'm a cop," the "lady" growled, not unkindly.

His would-be rescuers soberly complimented him on his disguise and burst into laughter at the next corner. "And, speaking of disguises," Laurel observed, "who do you suppose our friend Lisa is pretending to be?"

No one had the answer.

• *Fifteen* •

Martin slicked back his white, wet hair and pressed his palms into his temples, trying to keep a headache at bay. He looked out at the rolling Pacific and thought about sending a gift to Sam and his new wife; that was the tradition most people followed, wasn't it? Would they care if the gift was a month late? Lisa said that the bridal couple hadn't been able to afford a honeymoon. That's what he'd give Sam and Viola—a honeymoon. He decided to give them tickets for a long Caribbean cruise, because one of his brothers had given another pair of newlyweds the same gift. Martin found himself nearly incapable of original thought.

From his vantage on the beach, Martin glanced up at the large outside deck of *Manana*, the Vanderziel residence in

Acapulco, high up on a dramatic cliff. The silhouette of José blocked the sun. He was standing there with a small towel around his waist, lurking, waiting for Martin to return from his swim. There was a swimming pool outside the house, of course, but Martin had chosen to go all the way down to the beach to escape José's demanding entreaties for a while.

The newly rich T. Wayne Vanderziel had bought *Manana* in the thirties, and the house had been redecorated once every decade to keep it from getting dowdy. *Manana* had always been orderly and cleanly cold, like Martin. There were no curves to the house; everything was sharp and angular. The walls were covered with coconut matting and aluminum strips.

As the transparent ocean water wrapped around Martin's feet in the crystal sand, he took great gulps of sea air to rid himself of the stench in his nostrils. He smelled the odors of rotting food, overcrowded living quarters, and heavily oppressive damp heat. At night, he was possessed by bad dreams, and the dreams lingered all day. Hallucinations of green and black shapes vibrated before his eyes. Words were whispered into his ears, an effect as annoying as a mosquito's intimate buzzing. Frequently his ears would start to ring, loudly and piercingly.

At times like this, when Martin's head was bothering him, he'd wrap his arms over his head and sink it into a pillow. A fast cure for his headaches was to hurt another person. Transferring his pain into another human could satiate him for two whole weeks. But that form of relief wasn't acceptable behavior, he knew. The tiny speck of judgment left in him told him it was wrong to wreak the violence he craved, so Martin struggled to put off harming others as long as he could.

There had been times when the noise in his ears had reached such a high pitch that he was pressed beyond endurance and ripped into violence like a jet smashing through the speed of sound. The last time it had occurred was in December, when he'd attended a party at a stock-broker's duplex. At 2:00 A.M. in the morning, Martin re-treated to the bedroom where the coats lay so he could leave before his headache and accompanying hallucinations took him outside himself.

Only one light was on in the bedroom, spotlighting a young woman who lay across the pile of coats, dead drunk, passed out from overindulgence. The rest of the room wavered in black and green colors. A seizure came over Martin, and his limits of control and thought were obliterated. He was hard. Panting with haste, he brutally raped the unconscious girl. Afterward, his goal accomplished, he zipped his pants, gathered his coat and left, completely calm.

He might as well have left New York City right then. Two months after the incident one of his father's executive secretaries called him. It seemed that one Ivy Griswold was requesting funds for an abortion, and that Martin Vander-ziel was the originator of her pregnancy. "Your father would like to see if you could move to Los Angeles for a while, where you can be the West Coast trustee of the Van-derziel Foundation," the secretary said with professional coolness. "If you could leave as soon as you can, it would be greatly appreciated by your father and brothers."

Now Martin occupied a Vanderziel home in Bel-Air, where the weather was the same year-round. The weather was the major difference Martin noted between the East Coast and California. He often couldn't judge what was unpleasant or favorable to him. There was no yes or no in Martin's psychology, there simply *was*. In California he continued working every day at the Vanderziel Foundation. He had no other interests. Martin could stare at a wall all day and sometimes did.

People were drawn to Martin for his money, his looks, and his emotional remoteness. His slick gloss of decadence and aura of chic danger drew acquaintances to him, but he felt he had only four genuine friends. He spoke often to Lisa, and though he seldom communicated with Laurel, Meritt, and Sam, knowing they were there gave him a feeling of stability, durability, and concern.

This was the first time Martin had brought someone to the Acapulco house. His guest, José, was a beautiful boy from East Los Angeles, a friend of the man who came to clean his pool. Three weeks earlier, Martin had entered into a sexual relationship with José. Gender didn't matter to Martin. His efficient equipment worked with either sex. He didn't even have to think about it. Oftentimes he climaxed without even feeling it. His body did what people asked it to do. To Martin, no sexual practice was strange.

Martin had tried to give José gifts of money, but he had sulked and said he didn't want his presents; he wanted Martin to be his friend, and spend time with him. To shut up José he asked him to come to Acapulco with him. Perhaps that would get rid of the obligation José was thrusting on him.

Martin's pale, soot-surrounded, squinted eyes reflected the limitless blue horizon to the west. "Mar-teen!" he heard José yell over the sound of the ocean waves. "I need to talk to you!" Martin began climbing the long stairway that wound up the cliff to the vast deck. José was waiting at the top of the stairs, his black eyes unreadable. He'd splashed too much of an expensive men's cologne on his pale olive skin. "What is it?" Martin growled.

"Let's go inside."

Martin wore only a strip of man's underwear. He'd dropped a polo shirt in the living room earlier, and he pulled that on now. He sat in a chair and gazed up at José, who tightened his towel nervously around his wasp waist. "I must tell you," José started softly, "that I've misrepresented myself to you from the beginning. I work with an association that I don't know very much about, except they've got contacts around the world. One of the things they do is try to blackmail people with a lot of money."

Martin's perpetual mask revealed no reaction. "I didn't know you were a hustler. Arc you going to blackmail me?"

"Do you remember all the mirrors in my apartment . . . ?"

A frightening blizzard of sound swept from Martin's mouth. It was a tinny, crazy laugh. "Are you saying that someone has made movies of you attending to me?"

Startled by Martin's strange laughter, José still managed to reply, "Yes, we were filmed through two-way mirrors. I genuinely regret what's happened, because you've been very good to me."

"What's there to regret?" Martin stopped laughing. "It's impossible for anyone to blackmail me!"

José's voice squeaked. "But your name—your family's reputation—"

"The Vanderziels *have* no reputation. My father ruined the family name forty years ago!"

Martin started laughing again, making that strange, metallic noise. Suddenly he jumped over some scuba equipment dumped sloppily on the carpet and with a hummingbird speed choked José from behind by crushing his left arm around his throat. In his right hand was a diver's knife, which he pushed into José's side under his bottom right rib. José cried out as he was cut. The blade pressed on his taut skin. The slightest pressure would slip the knife up through José's ribcage to his heart.

You are to kill that which you love most.

Laughing some more, Martin stepped away. The knife fell to the floor, and José wanted to kiss him with relief.

Martin didn't ask him to leave or throw him out, but José made a quick exit. He was frightened, yet still captivated by Martin Vanderziel's strange, mysterious magnetism. He could make his own way home, where someone from the international vice underground would give him a new task and target.

• Sixteen •

Laurel withdrew the safety deposit box from the wall. She nodded at the bank guard and he left, shutting the day gate behind him. She needed her birth certificate to file for public office. Mavis had given her the key to the family safety deposit box, and here she was, standing in a gleaming bank vault that echoed her every sound. She placed the long steel box atop a high table.

Inside the box were some tiny loose diamonds that Mavis owned and had never had mounted, a couple of insurance policies, and, neatly bound together, the birth certificates for her sister, Barbara, her brother, Jon, and herself. Laurel's vivid blue eyes scanned the information on her certificate, because she'd never seen it before. It read the same as her siblings' certificates, except for the name of the newborn. Laurel expected to see, WILLIAMS, LAUREL JOY. She blinked twice; three times. Her name wasn't there! The typed-in name was BABY GIRL. Her birth name had been "Baby Girl." With a panic-stricken expression, she looked to the father's slot: UNKNOWN. The mother: UNKNOWN.

"Oh, God," Laurel whispered, digging quickly through the other papers in the box. The framework of her life was imploding, collapsing in on itself like a building wired for demolition. Her knees were watery. She found a certificate-of-adoption form that transferred "Baby Girl" to Herbert and Mavis Williams of Omaha, Nebraska.

Laurel's head spun, and she gripped the table for support. She was not the offspring of Mavis and Herbert, that man she saw about once every two years. She'd been born illegitimate and healthy, so she'd been given to a couple whose two biological children were born with handicaps. "So they'd get it right the third time..." she whispered. Mavis had needed a lively, perfectly formed newborn to continue in her political footsteps. She'd been preoccupied with dynasty, not motherhood.

Much later, Laurel walked outside to a changed world. She drove home, stumbled into the apartment and flipped on the TV. She didn't care what was on, she only wanted something to deaden her distress. She flopped on the couch and gazed at the stucco ceiling. Then her ears recognized the TV's noises—the bridge on the *U.S.S. Enterprise*. "Star Trek"—always there when you needed it. She sat up and let the best episode, "The City on the Edge of Forever," act as a balm to subdue the pain of losing her identity and the security of her mother's love.

The first full-blown meeting for Laurel's congressional campaign was scheduled several days after Laurel's discovery. Mavis Williams flew in from Washington especially to bless the campaign kick-off. Laurel picked her up in Omaha and headed back to Lincoln, the home base of Laurel's congressional district. They discussed the scandal-provoking resignation of Bert Lance, who was in President Jimmy Carter's cabinet, for nearly all the trip.

Mavis held her booze better than any of her male colleagues or members of the press. "Don't you think it'll be wonderful when Nebraska has three congressional seats, and two of them are Representative Williamses?" Mavis chortled as she carried her gin-and-tonic into Laurel's living room. Chairs were set up in a circle for the core committee, and ashtrays and scrap paper had been laid out. Mavis was wearing relaxed jeans with a sweater, while

Laurel dressed in an irreproachable wool skirt and a man-tailored shirt. She was only twenty-four, so she had to muster maturity every time she met supporters.

Mavis sat down and took a deep swallow of her drink. Laurel remained standing. "Mother, why haven't you ever told me I'm adopted?" Mavis choked and coughed. She turned amazed eyes on her daughter. "Did you send me to get my birth certificate on purpose so I'd finally find out I was a bastard? Or was it a Freudian slip?"

"No! I forgot all about those documents! I'm so used to thinking of you as my daughter—you've been my daughter so long that I'd kind of forgotten I didn't bear you—and that your birth certificate would say that." Her Barry Goldwater–like face took on a prissy expression. "And that's how it should remain. Neither of us should remember that you are not my natural child. Nor should our constituents know." Mavis's hands gathered solidly on her bosom, as if she were trying to draw a cloak of protection around herself.

Questions burst from Laurel's lips. "Why didn't you tell me when I was little? Why did you keep that knowledge from me? When was I supposed to learn about these things?"

"Many reasons. Back in the fifties we were advised against telling children they were adopted. There was a stigma about being born out of wedlock, even then." Mavis spoke with the straightforward candor that voters and the press loved her for. *"My* primary fear was that you'd try to find your biological mother and come to consider her as your mom. I wanted you *selfishly."* Mavis's iron-willed voice turned nearly pathetic. "What would you have done if you were in my place? Haven't I done a good job of raising you? I've tried to give you the best. Admit it, Laurel—the world is yours. I've helped give it to you."

Laurel looked at that tough, wrinkled, gray face framed in gray hair. She saw a middle-aged woman who had always assumed that whatever she wanted, Laurel would

want, too. Ever since she could remember, her mother had
been calling all the shots for her, dismissing the possibility
that Laurel might have a different choice or opinion. Would
her biological mother have respected her, allowed her a
will of her own? Laurel wondered. The goals that Mavis
had determined for her were now achieved: Her handraised
daughter was adding luster to Mavis's legend, and they
could make history as mother-daughter representatives.

"Are you going to try to find your mother now?"
Mavis's voice quavered.

"No, but it's an idea."

The intercom on the wall buzzed rudely, indicating that
Laurel's gung-ho campaign workers were arriving. Laurel
consigned her frustrations to a closed compartment in her
head.

The following week she registered with three nonprofit
adoption search-and-support organizations, called Search
Trinity, the United Birthparents of America, and Adoptive
Network. She felt almost guilty for wanting to find her
natural parents, but Mavis assured Laurel that her feelings
weren't hurt by the search for her past, as long as Laurel
recognized her as her *true* mother. The personnel at the
three registries warned Laurel that it would be a long time
before she'd hear news about her biological parents and
that the search might turn up nothing. Laurel could wait.
Since the day she found her birth certificate, she was convinced that somewhere out there was a wonderful second
family for her, and she'd find them.

When election time rolls around every two years for
U.S. House Representatives, it becomes necessary for candidates to prepare their campaign literature. The brochures
are a trying nuisance for everyone who works on them,
because that one slender pamphlet is supposed to make the
candidate look like God on a good day. Each paragraph on
the issues is written to make the reader think that the can-

didate's views duplicate his own. Every folder has black and white photos of the candidate posing with his nuclear family, bending down to listen to a nonagenarian, and shaking hands with common laborers.

If the candidate is running for the U.S. House or Senate, the main photo on the front of the flyer shows the political hopeful standing on the magnificent portico steps of the Capitol facing the Mall. If the aspirant is already in the office as an incumbent, his Capitol-steps photo demonstrates how damn good he looks there, as if he really should be allowed to stay. When the opponent is going up against the incumbent, as Laurel was, the Capitol-steps photo is supposed to scream out that she really belongs there.

That's where Laurel was, on a September morn when the sun made the Mall look autumn-golden and innocent, as though no protest demonstrators had ever trampled through its grass. In her rich suede jacket and wool tweed skirt, she seemed to have stepped out of a Ralph Lauren fantasy, though the outfit was a Gianni Versace she'd bought at a consignment shop. Her dark mink-colored hair fell to her shoulders in a schoolgirl-proper, off-the-face blunt cut. Laurel never photographed well, and she was edgy about posing for Jean Lombardi, the woman who'd photographed Mavis Williams for years. Hunched over a Hasselblad sitting on a tripod, Jean ordered, Drop the cigarette and refrain from nervous little gestures, please.

"I've never seen a photo that didn't make me look like I was on hard drugs," Laurel complained. Jean snapped, "Don't make me laugh." Laurel struck an exaggerated pose. "How's this, Jean—'the hot young congresswoman striding forward into the future'?"

Harland Mandower, a reporter from *People* magazine, had tagged along for the staging of the photograph. He cried, "Look, Laurel, a defenseless baby! Go kiss it!" Laurel laughed, and Jean snapped away. Harland had been assigned by *People* to write a small article on Mavis and

Laurel Williams, potentially the first mother-daughter team in Congress. Coincidentally, Harland and Laurel had been journalism majors together at the University of Nebraska in Lincoln.

Harland opened his reporter's notebook. With pen in hand he asked, "Miss Williams, what are your goals for office, once elected?"

Laurel said, "As my hero Conan the Barbarian put it, 'I want to crush my enemies, drive them before me and hear the lamentations of their women.'"

"What are your qualifications for this office?"

"I have the ability to list which presidents of the United States wore beards while they were in office."

"Are you in touch with your mother much?"

"I talk to Mom every day. Gotta keep that yenta guilt flowing."

"Watch it!" Walter, Laurel's campaign manager, whined like a toddler. "What if someone actually hears what you're saying, Laurel? Most voters don't have a sense of humor." Walter meant that. Then he looked back at Harland and cynically said, "I value keeping up appearances over all else. That's what's most important in this campaign."

Jean Lombardi quickly snapped photos while the two young men out of camera range kept Laurel smiling. "You know why I like to give other people advice?" Walter continued. "Because I can never take any of my own."

"Then you're in the right profession." Harland looked beyond Walter. "Here's my lunch date. George, how are you? Feel like going to Chinatown?"

Laurel turned, and her eyes locked with the sharp brown eyes of a man just a little older than she. He held her gaze and smiled slowly. Laurel's heart lurched. It was a smile with which she could have an intimate affair. He had an abundance of shining, shaggy bronze and copper hair, and he was dressed in an old black leather jacket over a sweat-shirt and faded jeans. For Laurel, it was love at first sight.

Walter Toodey called at Laurel, "Just a few more fashion magazine poses, and we'll be through. Keep going, Jean."

"So this is the baby congresswoman you're doing your piece for *Peephole* on," the young man said to Harland. Laurel answered for him, "Yes I am."

"Laurel, this is George St. Clark," Harland said. "George, this is Laurel Williams." To Laurel he explained, "George covers the congressional beat for the Washington *Tribune*. We wind up covering the same press conferences together."

That's why George looked like he'd been around—he was a reporter. Laurel kept looking straight at the camera. "It's good to meet you."

"I'm impressed. Really impressed," George returned. He was staring at her. She turned her head and looked back at him. Slowly her eyes moved over his face. The macho cool she saw in his hard eyes and straight nose was offset by the sensuality of his mouth. He had a charismatic-electromagnetic pull.

Harland asked George, "What's so impressive?"

"You didn't tell me that your baby congresswoman was so good-looking. My, my, look at those legs!"

Laurel blushed and giggled; she didn't know how to cast back flirtatious repartee. "You're distracting me, you guys. Jean, I've had just about all I can take of myself. Surely you've got all the shots you need."

Jean said, "Okay," and started to dismantle her equipment. Laurel found herself embarrassingly unnerved by George St. Clark. His steady eye contact tugged at her. She sent a telepathic command to the two reporters: *Ask me to lunch. Ask me to lunch.*

She couldn't think of a thing to say. "Did you listen to President Carter on the radio last night?" Cripes, she thought, is that the best I can do? She was referring to the unprecedented broadcast that had Jimmy Carter talking to forty-two random callers, to keep his campaign promise to stay in touch with his voters.

"Harland has heard me pontificate on Jimmy Carter before," George said. He had an East Coast accent. "In 1974 the president of our country was forced from office, and nothing happened. No power coups, no civil war, no revolutionary war. His handpicked successor does Chevy Chase pratfalls all over the globe, and nothing happens. So in 1976, when we're done with the Nixon era, whom do we elect? An unknown, a holy-rolling mushmouthed farmer! When is this country ever going to get an administration that they won't laugh at?"

"It could have been worse," Laurel said, pushing up the soft sleeves of her suede jacket. "We could have reelected Ford."

"*Re*elected? No, 1976 was his first time. Ford never was elected."

"Not as president. . . ." Laurel's voice trailed off.

Then she saw the girl.

Bottle-blond orange hair in a perfect Farrah Fawcett wind-tunnel shag. Body of mistress dimensions poured into army fatigues, army boots and a white, cotton-ribbed undershirt that showed the color of her nipples. She strode up to George and threw an arm around his shoulder, leaning against him as though they were army buddies. The girl needed only a bandelero of bullets and a red beret to turn her into Che Guevara. She was a rich girl, Laurel was sure. Those who came from the creamiest families leaned toward *companero* clothes, just to make sure people didn't mistake them for someone who loved dad's money.

"Where are we going to lunch?" the girl asked disinterestedly in lockjaw.

This isn't happening, Laurel told herself. This terrific guy can't really be with this—this type.

"Harland wants to go to Chinatown."

"Again?" the rich girl whimpered.

Laurel looked around for assistance. Her campaign manager! "Come on, Walter J. We've got business downtown.

Jeanie, we'll walk you to the Mayflower." She'd nearly forgotten they were with her.

"It was nice to meet you," George said.

"Laurel—I'll get in touch with you later," Harland said. Laurel gave them a tight smile, then turned away.

Though she'd spent all morning having flattering pictures made, Laurel was not feeling attractive. She felt lonely, and she knew it was from meeting George—and seeing his girlfriend. Why couldn't she attract a good man for herself? Did she overpower men, intimidate them?

As Laurel, Walter and Jean walked east, they saw groups of young black men handing around downtown corners, looking unemployed and bored. From a half block away, someone started yelling at Laurel: "Yo baby, yo baby, yo sure is lookin' good today, baby, I mean, really, truly *fahn!*" Disgusting smooching sounds were directed at Laurel as she walked right by. "Where you goin'? Don't you want to finish the conversation?" Laurel's walk slowed. She turned around and looked at three young men. The one who was hounding her wore a yellow cap turned backwards. "Oh, baby, come right over here. I gots to be selective nowadays, and I can tell that you is a professional woman, in the best sense of the word! Y'see, I can tell on the real side that you come from a good Christian home that makes you real special. You is special, baby, you is unique, you is beautiful, and I don't say this to every girl—"

His rap stopped because Laurel was walking straight for him. His brashness drained away and he apprehensively stood still while she kissed him on the cheek and said, "Thanks, cousin. That's the nicest thing anyone has ever said to me."

· *Seventeen* ·

Jeremy insisted on accompanying Meritt to JFK Airport, and on a cold March day, they huddled closely in the back of a yellow cab. As it came off the Triborough Bridge, Jeremy said, "Better look back and catch a glimpse of Manhattan, because it might be a while till you see it again."

Meritt giggled nervously and squeezed his hand. "I wish I were as confident as you."

For the first time in her uneven, temperamental career, Meritt was being flown to and lodged in Hollywood, all at the expense of a television producer. "They started running that cookie commercial again, and Hiram Stanwood tracked me down," Carrie Enright, Meritt's ex-agent had explained two days ago. "He wants you to audition for a principal role on a prime-time drama called 'Satin and Steel.' The network saw the pilot and bought the show, so it's definitely going on the air. As soon as it's cast, they're going to start shooting the fall premiere episode." Meritt was being considered for the part of "Melissa," the daughter of a marauding captain of industry.

Meritt looked back at the city, and saw a line of gray and brown buildings whose tops disappeared in the clouds because it was a foggy day. She fervently hoped that she'd be returning to New York only to collect all her belongings. Her spirit was suffused with confidence because this trip to Hollywood felt so right. Never before had she been so certain of success. Her face glowed with fearlessness, and she

looked gorgeous in a long cream wool coat that contrasted
strikingly with the black hair tumbling thickly to her
shoulders. Impulsively, she threw her arms around Jeremy's neck and kissed him on the cheek. Under his dark
Ray-Bans his eyes crinkled, but he gently pulled her arms
away.

"It's too bad you're moving into television," he said.
"There's no time to get things right. People shove you
around and say, 'Do this, do that. Even if it stinks we'll use
it.' How can anyone get acting done under those circumstances?"

I can, Meritt said silently. She knew what Jeremy's attitude toward television was, and she felt that his carping
had a smidgen of jealousy in it. She changed the subject.
"If . . . no, *when* I move west, what will happen to you and
me?" Meritt asked guilelessly. If she got this "Satin and
Steel" part and the future looked promising, she'd ask him
to marry her.

"As in 'us'? We can handle that later." Currently, Jeremy
was directing a play off-off-Broadway. For five years,
Meritt had been so proud to have a boyfriend who actually
lived on his theater income, since 90 percent of Manhattan
theater used cast and crew volunteers, or a wage like five
dollars a night. A couple of times he'd been employed in
Broadway productions.

Jeremy always got good reviews for the plays that he
directed at community theaters, actors' showcases, and
"little" theaters so little they were practically nonexistent.
Jeremy had won good reviews before he met Meritt, too. If
she looked objectively at his situation, he was a mouse
running in a wheel without making progress, so Meritt
tried *not* to look at his situation. Jeremy and she were destined to be a perfectly successful, golden, envied couple.
She'd invested so much time in him. It was going to happen; it was going to come true.

After fighting rush-hour traffic on the Long Island Ex-
pressway, the taxi made it to Kennedy Airport. The Pan

Am terminal was in sight, but a congested mass of taxis, buses, limousines, and other vehicles sat and honked, keeping Meritt's taxi a half-mile from the door. "Maybe I should just get out here and walk it," she muttered.

"Would it be all right if I saw you off here?" Jeremy asked. "It'd be so much simpler if I took this cab back to the city."

Though she was hurt, Meritt nodded her assent. The cab drew a little closer to the building, and Meritt decided to make a break for it. "Good-bye, Jeremy. I'll call you from the hotel." They shared a chaste, almost religious kiss on the lips. Jeremy clasped her forearm in a warm grip. With the other hand he slipped her a letter-size envelope. "This is from me." Intensely he said, "Good-bye, Meritt. I wish you the best of luck in everything you do. I wish the very best for you, always."

Meritt was faintly puzzled by Jeremy's ardent farewell. It put a dent in her excitement. She slid out of the back seat and began walking toward the terminal. She zig-zagged between the blocked cars and made it to the side-walk, where tourists and travelers and executives milled, waiting for transportation. A skycap swooped down on her with a cart. "Skycap, miss?" Meritt declined. If she'd made it a half-mile with her suitcase, she could make it to check-in. After her luggage was checked through, Meritt had a half hour before boarding. Slowly she started sauntering down the ramp, then went through security check. Something made her look at the people coming up the ramp. Her eyes lit on a figure from her past—Oliver Remick.

Meritt nearly screamed. She recognized him immediately, though six years had passed since she'd hidden in Smitty's room and looked down upon him. That middle Eastern face and that trim, elegant body were emblazoned on her mind.

Her hand came up to her throat. She stared at him horrified, as though he were all her bad dreams come to reality.

He wore a double-breasted suit and carried a briefcase made of eelskin. He looked neither to the right nor the left as he came up the ramp. Meritt was stopped in her tracks, ridiculously paralyzed, yet she didn't catch Remick's eye.

"Hey, lady, wake up!"

Blinking, Meritt turned her head and looked at the teen-ager who'd just crashed into her. Propped on his shoulder was a sidewalk stereo the size of a shady siding salesman's sample case. "Sorry, I, uh . . ."

Her gaze whipped back to Oliver Remick, but he had already disappeared into the terminal. Meritt hurried to her departure gate, sat down and tried to analyze her fear. She and her page friends had been perfectly happy to forget Remick's existence and his plans. The sight of him today, solid and real, reinforced her feeling: that the Trojan Horse Project was real, and still in the works. Suddenly, all her excitement about the future vanished.

Dully Meritt boarded the flight to Los Angeles, and found a first-class seat. She threw her head back against the headrest and tried to calm herself. It was futile. Soon a loud, steady roar wiped out all sound as the Pan Am jet lifted itself off the ground and hurtled into space, where the sky was black.

Meritt removed her coat and began to ball it up for stuffing in the overhead compartment. There was something stiff inside it, the envelope Jeremy had left for her. Meritt opened it, drew out a sheet of yellow legal paper and sat down to read Jeremy's fat, loopy handwriting.

Dear Meritt,
I think this is the best way to tell you that the lease is up on my apartment, so I'm going to move in with Katie Winward. This letter is concrete proof that I mean what I say. You and I had a very good time together, but we're getting older and it's time for me to think about marriage.

Please don't be bitter. You will always be special
to me. Nothing can ever change that.

Jeremy

Meritt's face contorted as though she'd witnessed a horrible accident, like a car running over an infant. How could
this be? Jeremy had maintained status quo behavior over
the past few months. He'd done nothing that would make a
girl suspicious—no rendezvous, no bad excuses, no crab-
biness, and most of all, their sex life hadn't altered one bit.
When had he started seeing Katie? Why? How long had he
been out of love with Meritt? How could he do this to her
when she was getting on a plane? She knew Katie Winward—a very pretty, near-albino babe so blonde her eyelashes and eyebrows were nearly white. What was she
giving Jeremy that Meritt had not?

Even as she drooped in her seat, her senses were darting
around, her thoughts going every which way, like a trapped
butterfly beating its wings against a jar. Meritt crushed the
note in one palm and rested her forehead on the other hand.
She was thankful that there were so few people in first
class and that the lights were turned down. She had to
remain calm. She had to moderate her thoughts before they
got ridiculous and she blew things way out of proportion.
There was no way that Jeremy could really mean he
wanted Katie Winward. He couldn't possibly mean, deep
down in his heart, that he wanted to split from Meritt. All
those years they had together, they'd never broken up for
even one night.

Nothing can ever change 'our special time' together!
he'd written. Shit, she wished the entire five years had
never even happened. She felt contaminated and wished
she could delete herself from Jeremy's "special" memories.
How banal his wording was. No wonder he'd never tried to
be a playwright.

Meritt—control yourself, she told herself. She tried to

look at the situation through a friend's eyes. Nothing like this would ever happen to Sam or Lisa—the sun always smiled on their charmed lives, and right now, Meritt was damned envious of them. Ill-starred Laurel, however, would tell her, "This is the most important trip of your life, and you're going to blow it. If you've ever acted in your life, act now, act as though Jeremy had never given you that kiss-off note."

But her body was taken over by a grief too overwhelming to stop. Her determination to remain cool-headed burned up like a paper in a gas flame.

The rest of the flight was an agony no one deserved. Every inch of Meritt's skin itched painfully. She kept twisting and untwisting her legs and shifted in her seat every few minutes. She couldn't blame the people across the aisle for staring. The in-flight movie was *Nevada*, which she'd already seen because Christopher Colacello starred in it.

His face was made for closeups that showed off his smoky blue eyes, thick, short-cropped hair, and strong chin. He'd been called both "Bogart-tough" and a heartthrob. Meritt had read that he was a "clean-cut American with a mystery, a dark side." Meritt glanced up at the screen every once in a while as if she could find support from the movie. She remembered telling Jeremy she'd never date an actor, because they were so unstable. Here she'd spent five years with a director, and look how well she'd fared!

The plane taxied to a stop, and she was up and trotting to the exit to climb through the door even before it was fully open. When she emerged from the tunnel ramp, she immediately spotted a uniformed man holding a placard that read MERITT DU NORD. It was the driver sent by the studio. She gave him a desultory greeting. "Would you mind if I made a phone call while we're waiting for my luggage?"

"Well, sure, but can't you wait till we're in the car? You can use the car phone."

Meritt's smile trembled. "Unh-uh."

They searched for a free phone, but each public telephone was occupied or broken. When she climbed into the rear of a long black Cadillac Fleetwood, she instantly reached for the phone, then stopped herself. If she got into an argument with Jeremy, what would her driver think? What if he told someone at the studio? She gave up and fell back into the overstuffed velvet seat. This outing had started out to be the poshest, the most thrilling, the most fun trip of her life, and now the ease of Meritt's surroundings only emphasized her misery. She could enjoy none of it.

She checked into the lavish Beverly Wilshire, whose magnificence and grandeur stopped just short of the garish. The aristocrat of L.A. hotels had a single room waiting for her. The driver told her to expect a call from the studio the next morning. The more dough Meritt saw paid out in her name, the surer she became that the part was going to be hers.

With shaking fingers, Meritt dialed an operator who put her through to Jeremy's number. She chewed a thumbnail while she listened to the whispers of the long distance lines, as though there were ghosts sitting on the wires. Then came a recording: "The number that you've dialed has been disconnected. Calls are being taken by. . . ."

Meritt copied down the number on a parchment Beverly Wilshire notepad. Then she had the operator dial that number.

The long distance hum again . . . the click of a phone being answered: "Hello?"

A shock ripped through Meritt like a lightning bolt, and she slammed the receiver down. Indeed, that was Katie Winward's voice. He'd certainly acted fast.

Meritt fell over into a snaillike ball on the luxurious bedcover. She wanted to die. Wait, no—there were a lot of things she wanted to do, and dying wasn't one of them.

She sat up straight and looked at her reflection in the mirror. She *had* to chill out by morning. The entire time she'd lived in New York, she'd considered her acting top priority; Jeremy came second. Which was the way she should think now. How could she care about a traitorous boyfriend when her dream was about to come true! She couldn't allow Jeremy's actions to affect her when she had the most important meeting of her life tomorrow. Hell, Jeremy didn't deserve one more thought from her.

In all her confusion and distress, Meritt had lost her appetite, yet she knew it would help if she had some nourishment in her body. She had to eat something. She had to sleep, too. She unpacked her bag, hung up her audition dress, and took a scalding shower. She went to bed, and discovered she'd lost her ability to sleep, so at 3:00 A.M. she ordered a light breakfast from room service.

Stay calm. Stay calm, Meritt told herself, as though she were confronting a mad dog with rabies. Okay, so she wasn't going to sleep the night before her audition. No problem. It happened to nervous people everywhere who had a lot on the line.

There was nothing passable to see on TV except for a "Carol Carole" show, so Meritt kept it on for laughs. The main speaker was Carol Carole, one of those rare, ageless women who could have been anywhere between twenty-five and fifty years old. Her flowing white gown covered all of her body except her breasts. The bodice left her generous white bosom generously exposed to display a huge diamond-studded cross pendant.

Carol Carole was presiding in an arena, where thousands of people were seated rapt under her evangelical spell. In the first few rows people in wheelchairs sat waiting. "Come closer to the magic of God," she called out in a liquid hillbilly English. Her right hand, as bejeweled as Liberace's, clutched a large microphone. Her left hand covered her forehead, under which her blue-shadowed eyes were shut with concentration.

"Someone in the auditorium—his name is Lyndon Whytteborg, and he's sixty years old—he fears diabetes.

Oh yes, Lyndon Whytteborg, of South Street in Rockwell City, Iowa, is afraid of the same diabetes that cut down his father and his brother—"

"That's me! I'm Lyndon Whytteborg!" A man in a green leisure suit and glasses leaped up in the tenth row. The camera swooped right down to focus on him as if it had been scripted.

Carol Carole glided down the aisle like Morticia on "The Addams Family" while people gasped, thrilled to be so close to her. She reached Lyndon Whytteborg and laid her left hand on his forehead. "Oh, this is terrible, obscene— there are devils trying to torment you with fear. You feel weak and dizzy so much of the time . . . you even have a hard time doing your chores! But I can see the angels of God all around your house on South Street. God is going to give you complete deliverance. You're gonna rejoice, you're gonna feel the power of God!" Carol Carole slapped the man's forehead so hard that he staggered back into two ushers.

"You're wonderful! Thank you, Carol! You're like Jesus!" the astounded crowd called to her.

She lowered her lashes modestly. "I do only what the Holy Spirit tells me to do. Praise Jesus." Carol Carole started to call out another person who was getting special abuse from Satan. Meritt couldn't take anymore, and shut off the TV.

To her, Carol Carole's gimmick was transparent—and dangerous. Before they'd enter the auditorium, people were requested to write their names, addresses and special concerns on a survey form. Carol Carole wore a tiny earpiece so some guy backstage could read off the surveys and tell her which suckers were ripe.

Coming from the South, Meritt thought faith-healing ministries were invented by the devil. Thinking they were healed, worshippers would stop seeing their doctors and get into serious trouble.

Before Meritt's father Philip turned bad, he had shown

her the magic tricks his grandpa used to sell snake oil. "Here comes your cancer a-poppin' out!" he'd say, then reach behind Meritt's ear to pull out a hunk of liver, which he'd wiggle as if it were alive.

Meritt curled up on top of the bed again in her bathrobe and stared at the ceiling. Watching Carol Carole hadn't distracted her at all from the hurt fresh inside her. She lifted her hands and saw how they vibrated from tension. She could use some of that belief that kept Carol Carole's congregation growing. How was she ever going to get through tomorrow?

Her phone rang at 9:00 A.M. It was Hiram Stanwood's secretary. "Miss du Nord? Would it be okay for you to meet with Mr. Stanwood at eleven?" When Meritt assented, she added, "Tim will be around with the car for you."

Meritt showered again, then put on her flattering audition dress and makeup and arranged her hair. The dress was of white stretch fabric that followed her body like a shoreline. She confronted herself in the full-length mirror. Recently she'd started to wear her black hair teased into a go-to-hell explosion swirling past her shoulders. Her smoky, tilted, amber eyes and full, ripe mouth, combined with the full-blown sexuality of her body, made her look as though she were fully prepared to undress and tumble into bed. Yet under the top layer of her skin was an ashy gray, pinched unhappiness at odds with the message of her body.

Two hours later, she was on a sound stage making a screen test. In New York she'd memorized thoroughly her part of the test script, but today there were gaps in her memory. The disturbing part of the audition was that her character was supposed to break up with her boyfriend. "I—I'm nervous," she told the director the third time she fluffed a line.

"That's okay," he said kindly.

They started again.

Meritt had been drained of energy. She knew how to

warm up a room simply by walking into it, but she couldn't call up that star quality today. Normally she could convey emotion by letting her face move as subtly as a breeze stirring a pond, but today she was trying so hard that her facial expressions were as subtle as Howdy Doody's.

As she left the studio, stepping between the cables, Meritt wanted to go to each cast and crew member and say, "I'm sorry . . . I'm really a lot better than this . . . I'm really sorry I wasted your time."

Tim drove Meritt back to the Beverly Wilshire and told her what time he'd return to drive her to LAX, where she'd catch the "Redeye Special" back to New York. The desk had a message for her from Carrie Enright. As soon as she heard her former agent's voice, she burst into exhausted tears and told her about Jeremy and about blowing the audition and that she'd been reminded of a scandal in her past. She rambled on so long that it took a few moments for her to realize that Carrie was trying to interrupt.

"Honey! I'm trying to tell you good news!" Carrie yelled. " 'Gold Coast' is having a cattle call tomorrow for a minor role, and you'd be perfect for it!"

A cattle call for a soap opera is supposed to make me happy? Meritt thought maliciously. Kindly she said, "Carrie, if I ever get a part. . . . will you take me back as a client?"

"I already have."

Back in New York the following afternoon, Meritt— who'd finally caught some sleep—put on her audition dress, and added a coat and boots for the frosty March weather. She took the subway to West Seventy-second Street, and as she was walking up the station's stairs, she came face to face with Mickey Bernsteiner, the sparkplug of a redhead who was Jeremy's best friend. Meritt nodded, then tried to push past him, but he took her arm to lead her into a tiled corner. "I know what Jeremy did to you," he said seriously. "And I think it stinks. He really did you wrong. I don't even know if I wanna be friends with such an asshole."

Meritt's throat thickened. "I'd just like to know what I did wrong, Mickey. There must be a reason he dropped me." A tear spilled out of her eye.

"You really don't know?" Uneasily Mickey related, "He always told me that his parents couldn't accept a 'negress' for a daughter-in-law."

"Huh?" Meritt's self-pity made a screeching halt. "What did he mean? I'm not a 'negress.'"

"Well, as Jeremy put it, 'just one drop of black blood makes the whitest person a tar-black spook.'"

"My God, Jeremy never told me any bigoted shit like that. He gave forty bucks to the Black Panthers once."

"Yeah, so he could tell everyone he had. He's a closet racist."

Her anger rose, flooding her with energetic fury. The hell with Jeremy, she needed an acting job! She whipped a kiss on his cheek. "Thanks, Mickey. I needed that."

Meritt came up onto Seventy-second Street with brisk strides, and headed west to the television network's New York studio building. She gave her name to the security guard. When she was given a script, she went to sit with twelve other women in a waiting room. Typical cattle call —each woman there saw a dozen of herself, with black hair and dark eyes and various levels of sultriness, because that "type" was what the script supervisor had asked for. Meritt knew her only chance to get the role was to be instantly perfect; there'd be no kindly director here who'd say "That's okay, take your time."

After an hour of waiting, Meritt was called into a drab office not unlike a police interrogation room, where three baggy-eyed men were waiting to listen to her reading. No screen tests in soap operas. Meritt made a unique entrance, sauntering in on black high-heeled boots. Without being aware of it she gyrated in a dress that hid her skin while revealing her body. Gold hoop earrings flashed from within midnight black hair that she'd pushed into high, wild masses. Her intense amber eyes were darkly rimmed in charcoal eye shadow and her lashes were drenched in mascara. Never in her entire life had she been so beautifully and wantonly alluring.

The casting director, named Brett, fed her lines in a lackluster voice, and she responded without looking at the script. She delivered back her lines as haughtily as if she were half Cleopatra and half Bette Davis. When they were finished, the three men looked at each other flatly, and nodded. Brett asked if she'd stick around while they finished with the others, yet Meritt knew better than to assume she had the role.

The last audition was at seven. Usually at this time of night Meritt was hostessing at Charolais, she thought with melancholy as she waited. When was she ever going to be able to quit that restaurant where she'd been a fixture for five years? And she *had* to quit the "phone rap" job. She had to!

After the last actress left, the three men came out. They all wore golfing clothes, with Arnold Palmer cardigan sweaters. "We don't want you for the role," Brett said. Meritt sat tensely expectant.

"No, you'd be wasted in that small part," said the man who wore two stopwatches around his neck.

The third, peppermint-breathed man said, "We've got another part, a principal role. We had a Shakespearean actress lined up for it, but you'd be better."

"What is the role?" Meritt squeaked impatiently.

Brett said, "You'd be playing the main tramp. A bitch." *My god, that's right up my alley!* Meritt thought. Her stunned expression must have looked like apprehension, because he quickly added, "Would a hundred thousand the first year be all right?"

It took Meritt a moment to realize he was talking

$100,000. No more hostessing at Charolais. No more posing in slips and wigs. Magisterially she said, "You'll have to talk to my agent."

When Meritt said goodnight to the security guard and walked out the building into the cold, exhilarating night, she had gotten over Jeremy Serkin, completely.

• *Eighteen* •

Lisa was afraid that Deverell would detect the smug triumph in her voice if she spoke, so she refrained from talking all the way to his parents' house. In the back of a Wharton limousine, she gazed out of the corner of her eye at her engagement ring, the symbol of her success in landing Deverell. It was an eight-carat chunk of ice, rated IF—internally flawless, for clarity, and its emerald shape, cut by a master, who brought sparkle and fire to the stone. Trying not to gloat, she lifted her ring finger a little so she could witness the bright rock glimmer. Her right hand was wrapped around Deverell's upper arm with a don't-leave-me-to-fend-for-myself hold.

"Pop's going to love you," Deverell promised for the tenth time that day.

"Do you really think so?" Lisa cooed. Actually, she was nervous, because she feared Winthrop Wharton would recognize her as a gold-digging adventuress. "I just know I'm going to love him." Lisa would not be meeting Mrs. Wharton tonight; the Whartons had separated because Mrs. Wharton was in love with the Brazilian plastic surgeon who'd done her last eye lift, and she was living with the doctor in Rio de Janiero.

Lisa wasn't going to relax her façade until after the wedding, when Deverell would be bound to her legally, giving her unlimited access to his wealth. For their wedding night she'd planned a superbly agonized defloration, so she'd have Deverell's guilt right where she wanted it. When she gave him an heir, she'd have even more power, more emotional blackmail.

When she'd called Sam in Cambridge to announce her engagement, he'd asked in a reporter-like way, "What makes you want to have lots of money, Lisa? Beside the benefits of social climbing. I don't understand—you already know that money doesn't bring happiness."

Sam and Martin Vanderziel were the only people with whom she was candid. "Sam," she said, "money is freedom. The more money you have, the more freedom. Freedom from having to work, freedom from house cleaning, freedom from bills. Money sets you free to ignore the clock or even what country you're in. Bribes allow you to dictate your own brand of law, no matter where you are. If you choose to tour the Antarctic, you do it in *total* comfort. Money allows you to hunt endangered species. With money you can murder someone and get away with it. Money gives you freedom of choice that's unlimited."

"So you think money is your shield," Sam postulated. "Money makes you invulnerable."

"There's only one thing money can't buy," Lisa said. "Money can't buy off death."

Lisa smiled as the car slowed along Fifth Avenue. It was silly for her to ride to the Wharton house since she lived four or five blocks away. Deverell squeezed her hand. "What are you laughing about, honey?"

"I'm thinking of the conversation I had with Sam Ross a couple of weeks ago. I told him *everything* about you. He thinks you're a pretty neat guy."

"Braggart."

They climbed the gray marble front steps in their nearly matching full-cut sweeping alpaca topcoats. There were pearl gray curtains visible through glass doors fortified with heavy iron grilles. Deverell rang the bell, and they were welcomed by a somber man in a somber suit, introduced as Orton. The huge entrance hall was lit by a heavy cut-glass chandelier. Though the ceiling was two stories high, the room was suffocating, with its engulfing tapestries and eight-foot-high El Greco on one wall, portraying a ghastly, elongated St. Sebastian shot through with arrows. The place reeked of flowers though there were none on display. After they gave their coats to Orton, Deverell showed Lisa to an exquisite little elevator fashioned of wrought iron to resemble a bird cage. They got out on a third floor and entered what Deverell called the upstairs living room. Everything in the forbidding room was enshrouded with gloomy, dark maroon velvet. The matching burgundy furniture all stood on legs covered in gold leaf. The windows were made of stained glass, but because it was night it was impossible to see their design clearly. On each expanse of wall a dim spotlight illuminated a Renaissance painting. Lisa identified a Raphael, a Giorgione, a Botticelli Madonna, and a Hans Holbein the Younger.

"What do you think of my boyhood home?"

Lisa couldn't take her eyes away from a large painting of Salome carrying St. John the Baptist's head. It was very gory, with St. John's decapitated head draining blood into a pool at Salome's bare feet. "I think it needs the woman's touch."

"I agree with you exactly," came Winthrop Wharton's voice from behind.

The first impression Lisa had of the elder Wharton strolling into the room was his age, his height, his looks. Then she felt the presence of strength of personality so immense that it nearly knocked her off guard. He was an alive, electric man of total charm.

"Pop, this is Lisa Dunning," Deverell said proudly.

"So pleased to meet you." Winthrop Wharton's smile was warm and so was his handshake.

Lisa half-curtsied and met his smile. She wondered if he'd notice she wore neither eye shadow nor perfume. Her dress was made of pale pink silk crepe with a circle skirt cut to fall in a column. Her blond hair had been simply sculptured. On her ears were modest pearls on posts. She looked like a model in an Estée Lauder perfume ad.

"Isn't she beautiful?" Deverell asked excitedly.

"Yes, indeed. I think you've finally met the girl who's going to end your days as an eligible bachelor." He looked to Lisa. "I'm sorry I couldn't meet you earlier, Lisa, but some petty negotiation in Brussels took longer than I expected."

She smiled and nodded forgivingly. She'd been tracking his "petty negotiation" every day in the financial papers, and knew that this week's overseas purchase of a small shipping company had turned Winthrop Wharton's reputation from white knight—an amicable takeover artist—into black knight, a hostile bandit. Lisa's opinion was that Deverell's father needn't care about his reputation, because ordinary people were just jealous.

Winthrop was short, squat, and pale, with a lidless stare and a bald bullet head. He was short-legged and thick-shouldered. Lisa wondered if Deverell would look like him as he got older. God knows, Deverell would never have enough smarts to run a lemonade stand, much less a multi-national conglomerate. Winthrop had been heir to the Wharton jackpot, but he hadn't nibbled away at it for fun, as did his sons. He had transformed the international shipping division of Woodhill-Gannon into a leading aerospace and electronics concern. Because of Winthrop's unaesthetic appearance, Lisa didn't like to look straight at him for long periods, but she genuinely admired Winthrop for his talent and dynamic personality.

It was April 21, and the day before, President Jimmy Carter had unveiled a new energy plan to ward off a "na-

tional catastrophe." Over dinner Winthrop spoke respectfully of Carter's courage in facing a national problem but
criticized specific elements of his plan. He clearly described the effects that the president's plan would have on
his business. He also criticized Carter's shortening of Watergate defender G. Gordon Liddy's prison sentence. Then
he began speaking of one of his passions, walking through
museums' period rooms. Art in general was his one dominating passion.

"At the Victoria and Albert Museum in London, you
begin walking through rooms of the Renaissance, from
1400 to 1600. Then you're walking into the Baroque
rooms, and Elizabethan, and before you know it you're
looking into Regency rooms. Isn't that exciting, Miss
Dunning? Walking through time like that? Passing into one
century and leaving another behind?"

From the time Deverell had picked Lisa up tonight, she
had been the ingenue, all pink and artlessness, ordinary
and nice. She hoped that Winthrop wouldn't think she was
too bold if she opened her mouth. Pushing her shoulders up
submissively, she whispered, "I like to look into antique
mirrors, because it's like sharing the experience with people who looked into the same mirror many years before."

Winthrop's lidless eyes squinted with delight. "I can envision you sharing the experience with many other beautiful women of the past—perhaps a king's mistress, a
courtesan, or a princess studied her image in that mirror."

"Mmmmm . . . I never thought of it that way before."

His round face radiating happiness, the elder Wharton
continued to discuss his love of art, the old masters in
particular. He told Lisa his dining room was a copy of the
banqueting hall inside King George IV's Royal Pavilion in
Brighton, England. His ceiling was a dome twenty-five
feet high, and at the top of it a huge green dragon clutched
a massive chandelier apearing to have been made of price-
less gems. The walls were festooned with wall panels that
pictured groups of Chinese royalty. Suspended from the

ceiling were six gilt gold dragons, and underfoot the design
of the ornate carpet included a huge golden circle that copied the dome's size. The cutlery was solid gold, and the
plates bore elaborate handmade porcelain paintings of
Diana the Huntress resting alongside a buck deer and a
fawn, a situation similar to Lisa's tonight.

Discreetly, she flicked her eyes around the room at the
antiques, checking credit references. The George II table,
$28,000. The oval basin on it, $65,000. A pair of floral
vases, $12,500. A pair of Russian chairs, $20,000, and an
Italian armchair, $17,500. In one corner there was a Louis
XVI upright secretary with painted porcelain insets, the
one thing in the room Lisa couldn't begin to put a price on.
The cash register in her mind skipped the secretary, then
kept ringing and making chah-kunnggg noises as she continued her appraisal of the dining room.

Finally her eyes came to rest on Winthrop Wharton. She
wondered what *his* price was. Her fiancé was immensely
rich, but Winthrop Wharton was one of the richest men in
the world.

As Deverell and she stepped out of the elevator, prepared to leave the house, Orton rushed down the magnificent staircase after them. He had a small box that he
slipped into Lisa's gloved hands, saying Mr. Wharton
wanted her to have this.

Inside the car Lisa's fingers longed to rip open the box,
yet she primly crossed her hands over it in her lap. "Well,
aren't you going to open it?" Deverell asked, almost huff-
ing. "My father isn't known for his generosity, but you,
apparently, have made a very favorable impression on
him." He snapped on one of the backseat lights.

With ladylike patience Lisa opened the horizontal box.
Nestled inside was a small pen-and-ink etching under
glass. Deverell drew in his breath. "It's a Rembrandt!"

"No. It's a da Vinci," Lisa corrected quietly. The drawing was of an elegant lady's head. She wondered if it had
served as a study for the Mona Lisa, or of St. Anne, for the

"Madonna with St. Anne." She decided to tell people it had.

The following day Lisa called Orton and asked where Mr. Wharton was today. "No, I don't need his phone number, just the address of his office." A tastefully dainty bouquet of rosebuds was delivered to the Woodhill-Gannon Bank's top floor. The next day a vast, all-out bouquet of dark red roses arrived at Lisa's apartment, so dark they were almost black, like Winthrop's funereal house. Attached was a card signed simply, "Charmed." Attached to the card were diamond drop earrings. They were a statement to her, Lisa decided as she held them up to sunlight. They dazzled like success.

Deverell called that evening to say he'd gotten hold of tickets for a dinner-dance fundraiser for a newly fashionable disease. Lisa said she had a cold and begged off.

Winthrop started sending roses to Lisa's apartment regularly in bouquets so lavish and ghastly she knew that he was choosing them himself, instead of having some underling do the task. At the end of May, Winthrop started calling her from whatever part of the globe he was visiting. He was such an enthralling monologist that Lisa actually found herself listening to the great man hold forth on culture, global politics, and the celebrities of high finance who were his close friends. He traveled so much that he seldom stayed at his New York City home more than a week each month.

One night in early June, Deverell came to Lisa's apartment and dolorously told her that his father was pressing for a divorce from his mother, on the charge of adultery. The news made Lisa strangely strong and energetic. With sympathetic murmurings, she made Deverell lie on her velvet couch, and she began stroking his chestnut hair. When others were weak, she could afford to be strong. Assertively she told him she wanted to break the engage-

ment. He started to sit up with the shock, and with firm
hands she kept him in a supine position. "I'm doing the
honorable thing," she insisted. "Isn't it better that you
know now instead of later?"

"No! If you'd waited, I would have more time to live
with the dream that you love me."

"I waited long enough. It's better this way. Would you
have wanted us to divorce later, just like your parents?"

"Why are you doing this? Have I tried to force myself on
you too much?"

"Certainly not. Though I'm aware of your past woman-
izing, my parents just learned about the kind of person you
used to be. They can't welcome such a man into our family." Lisa sought another tangible grievance. "Besides, you
want to be a farmer when you're older. I don't want to be a
farmer's wife!"

"How can you do this to me—the day my pop puts the
screws on Mother?"

"You can go running to your brothers and sister for sympathy," Lisa answered softly. "Your father was pretty humiliated by your mother's carrying-on with some wetback
quack. Everyone knew about it. The longer he waited to
dump her, the more people laughed at him."

Deverell sat up straight, then stood up and stared into
her face, his hair disarrayed and his eyes wild. "You know,
the bad side of me always suspected that under your milk-
maid appearance, there had to be something wrong. By
logic, how long could anyone manage to be so sweet all
the time? Now I've seen a sample of your bad side, and
I'm damn glad I'm not marrying it." Deverell's jaw tightened. "And here my father actually wanted you as a daughter-in-law."

"How can you say that!" Lisa's guileless blue gaze
rested innocently on her ex-fiancé. "Don't say things you
don't mean, Deverell. You're just a little upset." She
searched for words that wouldn't sound so hollow. "You
can't be mad at me, Dev. You know we'll continue to run

into each other at parties, you know, benefits. And you'll always be very special to me. In a way I will always love you . . . that will never change." She started to pull off the eight-karat ring.

"Keep it!" Deverell snarled. Lisa kept the delight off her face. "As a remembrance of me and how 'special' I am. Thank God I'm getting away so cheaply."

As he started pacing west on Sixty-first, a heavy ball of acrimony weighed down Deverell's stomach. He knew he could untangle it with some distraction—drinking, carousing, sport, sex. He could run out to the Southampton house, but the ocean there was still chilly. A trip to Martinique would provide diversion. From previous trips he knew the next plane heading that direction wouldn't depart for almost twenty hours. He might as well use up the meantime at Madam Anatola's. At a posh whorehouse you got what you wanted for merely laying down a G-note. So clean and honest. So unhypocritical. Everything straight out on the table. He headed south on Madison Avenue.

• *Nineteen* •

A week later Lisa was awakened by the floral delivery person. The bouquet was nearly the size of one draped over a winning horse. Only its design—lush orchids and white irises out of season—saved it from vulgarity. There was no card attached, but the identity of the sender bellowed his name.

Lisa sat in the middle of her inexpensively decorated apartment and gazed at the flowers. Their meaning only deepened her dragging despair. Winthrop Wharton had come to town, and he wanted to take Lisa out tonight to "comfort" her over the broken engagement. Her acceptance had significant ramifications, none of which she wanted to think about right now.

She went to the front door, tying a satin gown around her naked body. The New York *Post* lay on top of her daily delivery of fashion and antique connoisseur's magazines. The headline read in bold black print: VANDERZIEL SON RAPED MY DAUGHTER. Lisa quickly pulled it in, then collapsed on the carpet to read the story.

Apparently, Martin had been arrested two nights earlier and charged with the rape of an eighteen-year-old woman. He and another man allegedly lured the girl into a bedroom at a Bel Air party, then both raped her. His family's attorneys had sprung Martin out on bail.

Lisa recognized a chance to give herself a respite from emotional turmoil. She phoned one of Winthrop Wharton's secretaries and cancelled this evening's date, saying she was needed by a friend in California, then phoned her travel agent. Before noon she was on a jet. Martin welcomed her phlegmatically to the Vanderziel house in Bel-Air.

She sat opposite Martin in an airy, light-filled room that looked baronial in traditional English/Continental decor— so much more light and pleasing than the Wharton tomb. "What's the story, Martin? What is all this 'rape' shit?" Lisa asked after fixing herself a gin and tonic. She was wearing stiff new blue jeans with a T-shirt, an ensemble she'd never wear in Manhattan.

"It's true. This guy and I took a girl into a bedroom and had her. We thought she wanted to do it, but after we were done she started to freak out." Martin sat in wet swimming trunks on a white silk chair, which, along with his tan, accentuated the bizarre white of his hair.

"You idiot. What if she'd been under sixteen? It would have been statutory rape."

"She didn't act like a teenager," Martin replied unexcitably. "She made it clear that she wanted to . . . what do people say . . . 'get it on.'"

"Then she thought it over and decided she could perhaps extract some money from your family? And then you wouldn't play."

"That's about the size of it."

"What are you going to do?" Lisa had never met a criminal before, except for one white-collar criminal friend of her dad's, and one or two coke pushers, but they'd never been arrested. Come to think of it, maybe Dad was a white-collar criminal, too.

"My attorney is going to plead no contest to a sexual battery, which is a lesser charge. Sexual battery is defined as the touching of an intimate part of a restrained victim for sexual gratification. I could be sentenced to ninety days in jail, but the judge will suspend the sentence. I'll probably be put on three years probation, but that will be suspended, too. If I don't violate probation my record will be wiped clean and the case will be dismissed."

Lisa, her fingers propping up her chin, said, "Martin, you're graphic proof of something I told your old roommate Sam Ross—that wealthy people make their own law."

"Depending on how rich they are." He looked directly at his friend, and his eyes were disconcertingly glazed over. "You'll be a Wharton soon, won't you?"

"Yes, but not like you think." Lisa hesitated. "I mean, I think Winthrop Wharton wants to marry me. I dumped his son Deverell so I could be open to his offer."

The news animated Martin slightly. "You're going to marry a man thirty years older than you?"

"I . . . I don't know if I can, Martin. He's such a nice man, such an interesting man! He'd make a great dinner guest. But marry him? I want to marry his bucks, but I have to marry the man."

"Winthrop Wharton? He looks kind of like an ogre, doesn't he?"

"He's a little troll, shorter than me, even. Just . . . just think, Martin, if I marry him I'll have to kuh . . . kiss him. And he smells just like a hairy ape at the zoo."

"I'm sure you're imagining that," Martin said. "And you know you're going to be doing more than *kissing* him."

Lisa's face crumpled with revulsion. "Don't remind me! Oh Martin, I've worked so long for this—I've trained myself to be the wife of a very wealthy man. And now that I've gotten what I want, I'm afraid."

"No, you're not. You've never been afraid of anything. Think logically. He won't be home much, will he? And if worst came to worst, you could always kill him. You'd probably be caught, though."

Lisa discounted the sincerity in Martin's voice. She laughed gaily. "Oh Martin, you're so weird, sometimes. Are you still suffering from those bad headaches?"

Lisa was the only person to whom Martin had mentioned the great pains in his skull. "I felt like my head was coming apart until I did it to that girl. That helped."

Again Lisa laughed, amused by Martin's exaggerations. But he was telling the truth: his head had been killing him until, at that party, he'd abruptly grabbed the girl who'd been flirtatiously teasing him all night. Some other scum had followed them upstairs, wanting to get in on the action. Yet the bit of violence had not really relieved him.

Martin didn't want his confidante to know that his torment was no longer confined to his skull. His entire body, his limbs, his extremities felt as if acid were dripping onto the surface of his skin. Even as Martin spoke dispassionately to Lisa, a headache flamed right in the middle of his mind, a ball of fire that grew fatter and fiercer with every hour. His ears were tormented nearly all the time by those incoherent whisperings. No painkilling device or drug ever diminished his pain, not even Demerol or liquid cocaine.

He was no longer fighting the pain, but accepting it as a part of him. He was becoming an instrument of pain.

"You know what you could do," Martin said. "You could marry Wharton, and start a drug habit. You could certainly afford to. Then you could almost forget you married an old man."

"Don't patronize me!" Lisa snarled in Martin's impassive face. "You're a dirty toad degenerate. You've got too much money." She got up to pour another drink, and it took her a minute to realize he'd been serious. Logically, heroin *would* allow her to tolerate Wharton's caresses, just like the drug had helped American "grunts" get through the Vietnam war. But then, she wouldn't enjoy all the pleasure of having the world at her disposal.

Feeling resolved and decisive, Lisa soon returned to Manhattan and began packing her possessions into moving boxes. Winthrop Wharton's discreet courtship of Lisa Dunning lasted two weeks. He asked her to marry him when his divorce was final. She whispered acceptance with dainty down-cast eyes and a pawnbroker's heart. Thank Christ, he'd finally burped out the proposal, she thought. Her apartment was just about packed away.

After the wedding, Mr. and Mrs. Winthrop Wharton helicoptered from midtown Manhattan to LaGuardia airport, where a plane was fueled and waiting. The first "room" one entered when boarding was a salon stocked with masculine nineteenth-century Neo-Classical pieces, inspired by ancient Egyptian designs, yet shaped for an airplane fuselage. Winthrop explained to Lisa, "This is where the passengers sit. During most flights I'm usually in here." He opened the leather-padded door to a sumptuous suede-lined office equipped with telex, copying machine, telephone and LED-readout stock ticker. "Beyond that is the bathroom and a bed." Discreetly he didn't show her to the stateroom. "And behind the cockpit there's a small galley."

As soon as the tower gave clearance, the plane headed for a runway. Soon it was off the ground, heading into the night. Winthrop sank into the black cushions next to Lisa and patted her left hand, which now wore a wedding band over a twelve-carat engagement diamond encircled by gaudy Colombian emeralds. Her wedding ring matched her faceted emerald-and-diamond collar and earrings by Harry Winston. She'd changed from her white wedding dress to a hunter-green suit, which, with the emeralds, made her blue eyes look green, too.

Lisa wondered how long it would take for Winthrop's jewelry gifts to total to a million dollars. Then she thought about the divorce settlement he'd made on his wife, a figure which was not made public but was rumored to be around twenty-five million dollars. She wondered if that amount would make any dent in his fortune, and if he'd economize if that was the case. She wondered how long he'd owned this plane, and if he'd paint her name on the nose cone. Squinting her eyes at a porthole, Lisa assessed the plane at almost two million dollars.

Winthrop broke into her thinking. "In case you're wondering, it costs a thousand dollars an hour to run this plane. Whenever it's cheaper to fly commercial, we usually fly commercial. It's not so bad, because we can go straight to the plane instead of going through the terminal." *Away from all the grubby hoi-polloi,* Lisa silently added. "And this plane takes us anywhere commercial flights can't."

It was humbling to see the humbling effect she had on one of the world's most successful men. As the head of an old family and a great international conglomerate, he threw his weight around every day, making and breaking fortunes and reputations. Yet he seemed happiest when he tried to please his new wife, thirty-one years his junior.

The plane touched down in some rural airstrip in Canada, where a man with a car was waiting to drive the newlyweds to Murray Bay. The Whartons had spent their summers there since 1870. But it wasn't summer, it was

Thanksgiving and it was freezing! Lisa huddled miserably inside her silver fox in the back of the car while Winthrop glanced through the New York *Times*. The paper had been waiting for him inside the car along with a fresh bourbon. One of the headlines on the page read, WHARTON TO WED SOCIALITE, 24. It was safe to say that Lisa and Winthrop were the best-known newlyweds in the world, but it gave her no particular pleasure. Other publications had nicknamed him the obvious "Daddy Warbucks."

When they stepped out of the car, she saw a big white Victorian house that overlooked the bay. A wind scraped right off the water and right inside Lisa. She took Winthrop's arm and let him lead her inside a drafty entrance hall. She saw that he was a very happy man. His bald head reflected the overhead lighting, and nausea lunged through Lisa's chest.

"This house is one of my most favorite places in the world," Winthrop said as a chilled-looking butler took their coats. "I come here when I'm in need of recharging." He ushered her into a drawing room where huge logs burned in an open fireplace. The room didn't take any of the fire's warmth, and their breaths frosted in the air. "I only had this part of the house opened," Winthrop explained. "It should be warmer upstairs." Wherever Lisa looked she saw ghostly shapes made by the white cotton druggets over the furniture. Heavy bars criss-crossed every window. She couldn't see any of the quaintness she'd been led to expect in this house. There was a sense of dreariness here that money should have fixed long ago.

Another fire blazed away in the master bedroom suite, which was as cold as a cemetery at Halloween. Winthrop excused himself, then headed for his bathroom. Carelessly Lisa yanked off her clothes and threw them on the nineteenth-century Ushak rug. She had to use a little stand to climb into a rather narrow bed.

Her teeth chattered as she dived under the covers, but not from the cold. She was nearly terrified that she couldn't pretend to be a virgin successfully. Lisa just wanted this over with. She didn't know how long she could keep up her I-love-Winthrop act before he fell asleep.

Winthrop emerged from his dressing rooms and turned out the lights, so the only illumination was provided by the fire. He wore dark satin pajamas. He slid into the right side of the bed and lay without touching Lisa, but he was so close she could feel the sticky warmth of his body and the ape-man scent of his skin. *Close your eyes and think of England,* Lisa commanded herself. Boldly she moved her right hand to meet Winthrop's satin-sheathed arm. He nearly jumped.

He was almost paralyzed as she leaned over him to deliver a passionate kiss on his dry, chapped lips. Her breasts slid over what felt like hairy breasts. When he extended his arm over Lisa's back and realized she was completely nude, he turned into a madman with good manners. He rolled over and started kissing her everywhere. Lisa's eyes were squeezed tighter than a zip-locked plastic bag, and she wished she could block her nose to keep out Winthrop's smell. He scooched down and kissed her on top of her pubic hair, and it came to her that this was very daring for him to try sexually. He was as little educated about marital relations as a Cub Scout! Lisa had assumed that all men of wealth had some mistress stashed away who'd instruct them in ancient Oriental technique that made them rapt love slaves.

Winthrop mounted her, and Lisa tensed her vaginal walls. She yelped and bucked with cries of pain, and it was all over within a minute. He collapsed, gasping with pleasure, and rolled over so as not to rest his weight on his wife. Thank God that was over, Lisa sighed.

Winthrop was grateful. "Darling, I have so much to teach you. I promise you, pain will lead to pleasure. There's so much delight in intercourse, and I want you to know it all." For the umpteenth time that day, he shyly laid a hand over hers. "I love you. You make me so happy."

Not really knowing what to say, Lisa repeated the same phrases.

The next morning Lisa awoke as Winthrop was climbing out of bed. She kept her eyelids shut while he walked to his dressing room, then quickly leaped out. She tiptoed to her purse and withdrew a tiny jar. She used her finger to dig out a little Hershey's syrup and rushed back to the bed. Then she dabbed it on the bottom sheet, and rubbed it with her saliva to dilute some of the stain.

Lisa put on the handstitched satin gown that had been laid out for her. When Winthrop came back into the bedroom, he noticed that she had flung aside the linen so that the bottom sheet was fully exposed. There were traces of blood right in the middle of the bed, proof that Lisa was the virgin she had seemed to be—proof that his wife was indeed the pure, innocent maiden he'd courted He'd made no mistake in marrying her.

• *Twenty* •

There is no one as beautiful as a confident, happy woman, Sam decided as Meritt loped out of Il Cortile and into its large, skylit atrium where he was sitting at a table. She was feisty, fiery and flagrantly lovely, and her glamour quotient had doubled since she'd become a soap star. People in the restaurant stared at her not only because she was enchanting but because she appeared vaguely familiar. It was October 1978, and she'd been acting on the daytime soap opera "The Gold Coast" for a year and a half. In the time since her character, Tracy Robertson, had been introduced, Tracy had had one marriage and one divorce, one abortion, several affairs with men, and one hinted-at lesbian relationship.

"Sorry I'm late," she said as she came tableside, "but I've been trying to park my new Volkswagen."

"Did you hear that New Yorkers spend their time looking for three things: an apartment, a parking space, and a witness."

Meritt laughed. Since she'd begun making money, she had been able to afford the clothes she wanted to wear. She'd inherited her ex-roommate's fondness for black, so she was slightly punk in a tight black jersey tube dress, and her black hair was ratted into a pinnacle of tendrils. Sam helped her off with her striking motorcyclist's jacket, which fairly smoked with rebel spirit.

Sitting on top of the table was Barolo 1961 Paladino, and Sam filled her glass, then refilled his. "You look so contented. It looks great on you."

Meritt responded, "Did you know that at Lisa's wedding, I asked Winthrop Wharton for his secret of happiness? 'Do the one thing you can do better than anybody else in the world. Stick with that and you'll be happy.'" Meritt paused. "Did you know that he calls himself and Lisa 'the beauty and the beast'? What a guy, huh? Sam! You're putting away the last drops of Paladino as if it came with a screw-on top! Sam?"

The waiter came over to take their orders from the untranslated Italian menu that emphasized they were dining on Mulberry Street, in the heart of Little Italy. They asked for the penne, the gnocchi in rich cream, and something called io-scalciann, a green thing in a crust. When the waiter vanished, Meritt demanded, "Is there something wrong? Is it your job?"

He shook his head. After completing his M.B.A. last June, he'd moved to New York to work as a commodities clerk, which surprised friends, because working in the New York Cotton Exchange was one of the riskiest jobs in the city. Sam provided a pillar of security for his friends, because his life had been so well planned and orderly. He always handled things in the safest, stablest way. In minutes, Sam could lose and win ten times what his attorney father had made in a year. In December, he'd purchased a seat on the Cotton Exchange for thirty-eight hundred dollars and begun trading for others and himself.

"No, it's not my job. I'm pretty cheerful at work." Sam's lips compressed into a straight line. He looked sheepishly at Meritt. "I hate to sound like a soap opera character, but my marriage is in bad shape."

"Why?"

"Well, maybe it's not the marriage. Maybe it's just Viola."

Indignant, Meritt demanded protectively, "What's her problem? Is she giving you trouble, Sam?"

"It's embarrassing. For a year we tried to have kids, right? Watching the calendar and all that. About a month ago Viola was told she has a misshapen uterus because her mother used DES." Sam's voice had dropped to a whisper, and he couldn't look Meritt in the eye. "On top of that, she doesn't have many eggs, and out of what she's got, only a few are, uh, mature, it's called, and it's harder to fertilize immature eggs. So it looks like she can't get pregnant."

Sam couldn't convey the misery of his home life. Viola had stopped working as a nurse to be a homemaker. She'd been crying steadily since she'd heard the bad news. Viola would insist on being alone, then she'd beg Sam not to leave her alone. "What have I done wrong? Why am I being punished? Why can't I be a complete woman like my friends?" she'd moan. She claimed that she'd accepted his offer of marriage just to become a mother. "Why am I such a *failure?*" Sometimes she carried on so hysterically that she'd bring on minor seizures that left her weak and bewildered. It was impossible to match this miserable wraith with the restful, composed, breathtakingly lovely woman he'd married.

Meritt's eyes narrowed. "She doesn't give a tinker's dam how you're feeling, does she?" His silence said yes. He'd always been an open, uncomplicated person, more eager to help others than a Peace Corps volunteer. He was so handsome with those straight features, his dark honey hair and well-built body—and it was all being wasted on an undeserving woman. "At your wedding I looked at Viola's mother and decided she was a wicked pig. That's probably what Viola will grow into, if she hasn't already."

"Meritt! You're talking about my wife."

"Who is messing with my friend. Have you considered adoption?"

Sam confessed, "Viola says she could never raise a baby who wasn't hers." At Meritt's disgusted expression he quickly said, "Now don't get started on her."

Their food arrived. Both of them were in rotten moods as they attacked the incomparable Italian fare. When they were halfway through, Sam said, "Where is a witch doctor when you need one?"

Meritt said, "If worst comes to worst, would Viola ever consider allowing a surrogate mother to bear your children?"

"What?"

"You can make a babe in a Petri dish! Haven't you read about that attorney in Michigan who pays women to bear children by artificial insemination? It's a brand-new process."

Sam's eyes widened with the kind of delighted surprise any man feels when someone has told him there's still one possible solution to a problem that had doomed him forever. He reached across the table to squeeze Meritt's hand. "Meritt, will you always be the Wally to my Beaver?"

Sam spent the rest of the day researching the possibility of renting a womb. It was extremely expensive, but the money part was superfluous to Sam. The only obstacle to the plan was Viola, who'd said she didn't want adopted children. Yet a surrogate mother's child would be half his biologically, in effect a stepson to Viola.

That evening Sam walked to his new home in the Upper West Side. It was a row house, a decrepit, decaying monster he'd snapped up for forty thousand dollars. Sam and Viola lived on the first floor while the rest of the brownstone was being renovated. He unlocked the door and looked around at his apartment, a once wrecked, ready-to-be renovated hovel which Viola had magically transformed into a contemporary space that never failed to calm him. The floor was covered with wall-to-wall woven sisal rugs, and the chairs had lots of big-scale cushions that invited one to drop in. The colors were smoky and delicate, with lots of neutral pinks and grays.

The big TV in their bedroom was screaming like a banshee. When Sam went to turn it off, he saw it had been turned to one of the stations that seemed to run Carol Carole broadcasts all day and all night. Sam had been raised in the Bible Belt, hospitable to that kind of drooling hellfire ranting and wild-eyed, fundamentalist bigotry. It gave him the creeps. He wondered why Viola, as soundly Catholic as he, would have a Carol Carole station on.

Viola's absence probably meant that she was up on their roof, so Sam headed up there. It wasn't unusual for either of them to sit on the roof. Up there you could see the upthrusting Manhattan skyline in all its awesome, jeweled glory, and sometimes you could see stars. The noises of the street seemed farther away, and on the roof you had the dearest kind of real estate in all of New York—a vast, uncrowded space where you had total privacy. They planned to create a small plaza there, where Viola could catch a tan up on "tar beach."

As he came out the door, Viola turned to greet him, wearing a winter coat against the October air. Her reddish hair reflected the sunset, and the last rays of sunlight revealed the tears in her eyes and the crying-induced chapped skin over her delicate cheekbones. Sam stood with her hands in his while he gravely asked her opinion of surrogate motherhood. Instantly she agreed to the plan, surprising Sam all the way down to his toe knuckles. Her answer almost made him fall in love with her all over again.

The following week Sam and Viola flew to Detroit to meet with the attorney renowned for openly negotiating surrogate parenthood. They paid him ten thousand dollars. The surrogate mother, who signed a contract to gestate the fetus, would also get ten thousand. She preferred not to meet the Rosses. Gamely Sam handed in a sperm sample for the artificial insemination, which was frozen and delivered to a clinic.

Two months went by before the attorney gave the expectant parents the bad news: after several tries, the surrogate mother still wasn't pregnant. "But there's another woman available, if you want to try again." Sam and Viola consented.

Sam had made himself a well-to-do man very soon after he'd bought his seat on the Cotton Exchange. He gambled all his money, and some of his father's, on the cotton market at a time the cost per pound was making steep rises. He didn't have to pay a broker's commission, which saved him thousands of dollars. His abilities did not go unnoticed on Wall Street, which always looked for the next powerhouse trader. Yet Sam was as conservative with others' money as he had been aggressive with his own.

On a January morning Sam descended the red-carpeted steps of the cotton trading ring, and went to stand at a wood rail. He'd been in the dealing room at 7:00 A.M., taking care of paperwork and keeping track of premarket trading. Other men and women wore the uniform of brokers everywhere, trousers, tie, and shirtsleeves that would soon be perspiration-drenched. The twenty-thousand-square-foot hall they stood in was at 4 World Trade

Center, where other commodities were traded. At 10:30 A.M. the opening bell sounded, and all hell broke loose. The brokers were buying and selling contracts for the future delivery of fifty-thousand-pound lots of cotton. Along with the others, Sam was shouting at the dealers in the center of the ring, gesturing wildly. If he wanted to sell, he flashed his hand with the palm out, and if he was buying, he waved with the palm in. His clerk manned a telephone, taking orders from their broker in Memphis.

Yesterday morning at the opening of trading, Sam had bid for chunks of 250 contracts, then turned around and sold them. The price of cotton plunged. Other brokers started unloading them, and Sam was there to buy. The price soared. In this business, the bottom line at the end of the day was all that mattered.

Sometimes Sam had made so many maneuvers that he'd have to stay till midnight sorting through his trading tickets. Some days he was reluctant to head in to work because he was losing money. In a single morning one could lose $4 million—and make $6 million in the afternoon. He was in a business where milliseconds counted between brain and voice. Trading took one's emotions on a roller-coaster ride, and explosions of temper were common. Sam kept a poker face whether he was winning or losing.

This morning he was losing, but only by twelve thousand dollars so far. He stood in the ring and watched the others for a minute, their arms waving and voices hoarse with shouting. He loved this lunatic asylum. The atmosphere crackled with the electricity of people straining for a big score in a split second. The trading had been going on for an hour, and the air reeked of cigarettes, noise, sweat, worry. Sam knew that many of his cohorts were afflicted with ulcers and nerve strain. In Chicago, a man had died of a heart attack in the trading ring, and no one noticed till the close of trading.

And yet Sam worried about something no one else in the

room knew about. His job permitted him to monitor the economy closely. He could never forget that there was the possibility of an economic tailspin, constructed and implemented by a Trojan Horse Project. Like a big cat, sensitive to all the subtle movements around him, Sam was waiting for the first sign of a real doomsday. Then he'd go to the authorities to reveal the cause of an inexorable plunge in the U.S. financial systems. Sam gritted his teeth as he drove himself to depression. He should have gone to the authorities when he was a page. He should go *now*—there was nothing keeping him! Nothing but the fear of sounding ridiculous. As a page, Sam had seen the mail congressmen received, and many letters rabidly warned of plots to assassinate President Nixon, to destroy the United States, or to deliver it into Soviet hands. They were written by people seemingly sane, but their credibility was zero to the world at large. Sometimes the fanatics were wiretapped by the FBI, who kept files on conspiracy paranoids.

Sam was guilty and his wife was barren. What a swell couple, he thought.

Sam's clerk, a skinny young woman as fast as a whippet, rushed to him. "Got time for a call from your wife?"

"What is it, honey?" Sam said when he reached the phone.

"Are you sitting down?"

Sam's voice climbed. "What is it? Did she take? Is she pregnant!"

"Both of them are."

Time stood still for Sam as he pondered the meaning of her statement. "You mean . . . the first woman we tried is pregnant as well as the second?" Viola giggled affirmatively. Sam's personal Dow Jones soared off the board.

Where before he'd been resigned to childlessness, he was now about to become a father . . . a father of *twins!*

A father of *twins!*

• *Twenty-one* •

Standing before a politely interested crowd at the Student Union, Laurel hoped that she didn't look too young in her jeans and "Big Red" sweatshirt. *Should I try to come across as youthful or mature today?* she debated. She'd just turned twenty-five (the lowest legal age for U.S. House candidates), but since most students were twenty-two and under, the University of Nebraska audience probably viewed her as an old lady. It was noontime, and there were about five hundred people in the union, looking up at Laurel on a little stage. On a curtain behind her were two posters with her face and the slogan, TIME FOR A CHANGE. The motto was a twit at her opposition, a man who'd held the seat for nearly sixteen years. In speeches Laurel often said, "I represent change. I *am* change."

In her raspy voice Laurel began, "The sixties had protest. The seventies have narcissism. I believe the eighties are going to have attitude. Your attitude is what's going to count." The buzzword-craving crowd clapped their approval. Laurel couldn't prevent herself from glancing over at George St. Clark. The flashing smile he gave her lifted her confidence higher.

"You know what burns me? The fact that you save all your life for a higher education, you earn it, and when you graduate—no one hires you. Because you have no contacts, no sponsors, no mentors. When you move to Washington or Los Angeles or Chicago, you find out that the jobs are going to so-and-so's second cousin or what's-his-face's niece—"

The students had shown up en masse because by now, October of 1978, Laurel Williams was known as an entertaining speaker. She had the youth vote in her congressional district sewn up already because she addressed young adults' concerns in a way no one had before. This U of N campus in Lincoln was her alma mater, and for all the times she'd spoken there, Harold Means, her first lover, had never shown up. She wondered if, in this crowd, there was another girl who was being roped in willingly by her first love and learning that forever usually meant six months.

The most difficult issue of the campaign for Laurel had come recently, in the person of George St. Clark. George's employer, the Washington *Tribune,* had assigned Clark to collaborate on a lengthy series about Laurel's candidacy. It was his idea. Laurel's campaign was interesting to the *Tribune* because she was young, pretty, and quotable, because it was a good human interest story, and most of all, because the legendary Representative Mavis Williams was her mother. George had come to Nebraska at the middle of September, and a *Tribune* photographer flew in every couple of weeks to follow her around for a day, shooting candids.

The middle of October, Laurel's campaign manager Walter J. Toodey told her what an invaluable asset it was to have George on the bandwagon. When Laurel guilelessly asked why, pup-tent-pudgy Walter said, "Because whenever he's around, you act less neurotic, you smile more, your thinking is more clear and direct, and you come across as a real winner."

Laurel's face went sick with misgiving. "Oh no! Are you the only one on this campaign who can tell I'm in love with him?"

"I can only hope so."

Toodey was right. Whenever George St. Clark was in

the room, taking notes in his long, narrow reporter's note-book, her usual nervous habits (pushing her long brown hair back, fidgeting, darting glances) ceased. She'd also trained herself to maintain steady eye contact with strangers, and she'd stopped smoking in public places.

Already he'd written a couple of flattering articles for the Washington *Tribune*. His stories had been picked up and run in the Omaha daily *Chronicle,* and if his articles were good enough, he said he might repackage them for a magazine "like the pictorial essays *Life* magazine used to run." "Your stories make me sound like Mother Theresa," Laurel complained. "No, my stories show you exactly as you are," George insisted.

Toodey had observed, "It's not unrequited love. I think that reporter's in love with you."

Laurel didn't think so, because George didn't act particularly besotted by her. She could feel nothing from him but the same charisma she'd sensed when she first met him on the steps of the Capitol, an indiscriminating charisma that affected everyone in the same way.

During the days, he kept an undistracting distance from her as she shook hands and dealt with her campaign workers and volunteers, party officials and voters. But there were the wonderful times when they sat up talking late into the night in some anonymous hotel room, a rural bar, or a Country Kitchen. The velvet black summer night outside, loud with insects, created an intimate golden circle inside as they debated current events and teased each other, and discussed their childhoods and Laurel's search for her biological parents.

With campaign manager Walter J. Toodey in tow, Laurel spoke at political rallies and fund-raising dinners all over her congressional district, which stretched over one-third of Nebraska's population. She attended senior citizen programs, AFDC workshops and county fairs, and she'd milked at least twenty head of dairy cattle. Laurel was quoted in the press more often than incumbent congressman Chester Holtzman, and most of the media implied support of her, making it seem that, indeed, it was time for a change from Holtzman.

In her raspy voice, Laurel spoke to the University students without making a speech. She kept her tone friendly but not coaxing, warm but not demanding. In closing, she joked, "When I started running for office, I was told to go for the jugular. I am, but I hope it's not my own." The crowd applauded and dispersed, but about fifteen students lingered to talk to Laurel.

When Walter J. Toodey led her to his car he told her, "Y'know, you talk like an orchestra plays, but I think you've got a problem. You use long words that people don't understand. Sometimes they don't know what you're talking about."

"But that's me. I don't know how to sound any simpler." Laurel slid into the passenger seat of Toodey's four-door rustbucket. As Claire Sklenar, a campaign volunteer, scooted into the back seat, she said, "Stop jumping down her throat, Walter. You know Laurel's a shoo-in."

"A shoo-in doesn't always get in."

"But the newspaper poll shows that she's far ahead of Chester Holtzman."

Walter turned around in the driver's seat. "Listen. The margin is tighter in the party's secret polls. We've got to make Laurel seem more accessible to voters."

Claire asked, "What *if* . . . let's just say what if you lost, Laurel? I'm curious. What kind of work would you like to do? Would you go back to work as a political aide?"

"She's not going to lose!" Toodey snapped.

What if I lost? Laurel wondered. What kind of work *would* I get? Her wistful gaze went across the street to the sight of George climbing into his rented Mustang. She thought of the envy she'd felt at the happy-go-lucky camaraderie of the reporters she met on the road. *I'd like to go into journalism*, she answered herself.

When Laurel had formally announced her candidacy last

February, Lisa's husband Winthrop Wharton had contributed the maximum donation allowed for an individual. She was impressed; she'd met him at Christmastime and was very taken with the global tycoon. Later in the month Martin Vanderziel sent her the same amount, and Laurel was touched, since she hadn't been in touch with him since he'd come back to the States as a POW hero. From years ago she remembered him as fascinating, but deplorable; slackly affable, and at the same time morbid, smelling of fever, madness and scorn.

Summer had brought the carnival of hard-core campaigning, then September brought George St. Clark. He'd come to write an objective story, and he turned into a biased, very close friend Laurel wished was even closer.

Laurel had asked petulantly, "What happened to that bimbo you had when we were introduced in Washington?"

"Oh, that wasn't my bimbo. I was just minding her for a friend."

George, a Baltimore-reared city boy, was captivated by Nebraska's prairie landscape. "I think Baltimore exists in a whole different country from Nebraska."

At the close of a barbecue in Wilber, Nebraska, George and Laurel walked onto a small wooden footbridge crossing a tributary of the Platte River. There was a stunning orange-and-lavender sunset that burned half the sky with its flame. A rosy pink touched their faces as they leaned over the bridge to stare at the black water rushing underneath. He asked, "Do you ever think about the pioneers who had the guts to journey west in a covered wagon? Do you realize how daring your forefathers were? Mine lost enthusiasm and stayed on the East Coast."

"I haven't really thought about my antecedents and the risks they took," Laurel replied, looking straight into his eyes. "And now—who can even name someone who's really taken a risk?"

"You," George said seriously. His dark eyes were the color of brandy. "You took a huge risk to run for office. I admire you for it, because you're young and female, up against an old male incumbent with money to spare. You're a female in a man's world and a single in a couples' world."

Laurel was so pleasurably embarrassed she could feel her ears turn hot. "But what a boost I've got with my good name identification. . . ."

"No, I'd say there's little nepotism involved in your campaign. Your mother has her own campaign to run. She's wise to stay away from you." George stretched, and Laurel was acutely aware of the dark hair at the vee of his oxford-cloth shirt, darker than the shiny copper hair that fell over his forehead, making him look vulnerably mussed up. He added, "You should have seen the congressional campaigns in Michigan for Andy Smith!" Laurel stiffened in surprise. "His brochures barely mentioned the candidate, but they sure talked about his father and his grandfather. There aren't too many people who've been able to take a family name and turn it into a career."

A career as a traitor, Laurel thought viciously. This Nebraska sunset suddenly didn't feel so mellow. She trusted George, and she felt compelled to confide in him, but could not. "Uh, what post does Andy Smith hold now?" she asked conversationally, though she knew the answer.

"He held a Federal Reserve Board position a couple of years. And just a few months ago he was appointed as an assistant secretary to the office of Inter-American Affairs in the State Department. A crony of his dad's got him in there. I guess he can do little harm there, out of the way."

George stood up straight and jammed his fists deep into his jeans pockets, almost shyly. From out of nowhere he said, "Laurel, I really like you. You're so adept at the basic business of campaigning, yet so different from any politician I've known."

I don't want to be liked by you. I want you to love me. Laurel turned to face him, supporting her elbows on the rail behind her lackadaisically. "What do you mean?"

"You're so complex. Complicated. As if you don't know which door to walk through when you wake up in the morning."

"That's me!" Laurel saw a small smile flitter around the corner of George's mouth. "Let me guess . . . when you were in college, you were fascinated by moody, miserable girls with will-o-the-wisp-hair and haunted eyes."

"Were you one of them?" George sounded almost hopeful.

"Would you like me to be?"

There was a twilight stillness, broken by the evening call of the whippoorwill. George answered her question with his own. "What's wrong, Laurel? In front of people you're the glowing young idealist. The world is yours. But in private I see you drink too much and smoke too much, and your hands tremble. Do you *really* want that congressional seat?" George rested his hands on her shoulders so their impassioned faces were barely two feet apart. "You can't convince me of your sincerity. Can you convince *yourself?*"

The warm nearness of him caused a heat that started at Laurel's shoulders and swept down to her mound of Venus. She stood up straight to face him. "A House seat has been my fate since childhood. My entire life has served as the road to this campaign. I'm doing my duty."

From a distance she heard Walter J. Toodey calling. It was time to drive back to Lincoln. "You hear that? My campaign manager *thinks* I need him, but it's the other way around. I've got to do my best for all the people who've entrusted me with their money and time. My party deserves my effort." George looked doubtful, and she added, "I wouldn't have run unless I truly believed I'd make a great congresswoman."

She broke from his arms. "Let's head back to Lincoln."

* * *

By the end of October, Laurel had knocked on nearly every door in her House district. As the last week of campaigning wore on, energy and vitality drained from Laurel and increasingly she operated on automatic pilot. A forced quality entered her laughter.

Walter J. Toodey was proud of his work because Laurel was showing a strong lead in the newspaper polls, even though opponent Chester Holtzman spent four times as much on advertising than the Williams campaign. On the Sunday before Election Day, the Omaha *Chronicle* said she was eleven points ahead of incumbent Holtzman. It looked as though Laurel was about to become Nebraska's next great congresswoman.

"Will you be disappointed if I don't win?" she asked George.

"I'd be disappointed *for* you. I want you to have everything you really want, Laurel."

Come election night, Laurel instantly won the metropolitan areas of her congressional district. With 40 percent of the returns in, and rapid victory for the Republican governor and a Republican senator, Laurel's victory was assured. Her stomach bunched up with dread and fear even as she socialized election night at the main ballroom of the Lincoln Holiday Inn.

Exhausted, Laurel left the returns-watchers and went to her hotel room to get a little sleep. She was wakened at dawn by her mother, who brandished an early edition of the newspaper. Its headline read: WILLIAMS JR. DEFEATS HOLTZMAN. The accompanying story said, ". . . Williams consistently maintained a healthy lead over Holtzman last night, with results tabulated from 55 percent of all precincts reporting."

And yet . . . as the morning got rolling and more ballots were tabulated, Holtzman, who had heavy rural support, caught up to Laurel. The newspaper had printed the DEWEY

DEFEATS TRUMAN–like headline when it put the edition to bed because it appeared then that Laurel's lead couldn't be overcome. The results were final at 10:00 A.M. In the closest race Nebraska had ever seen, the incumbent defeated Laurel by a margin of just under two percent.

Gathering her courage, Laurel went down to the ballroom to make her speech conceding the election.

After a number of staffers and journalists had shaken her hand, she stepped to the stage microphone. She met her mother's eyes. The indomitable Representative Mavis stood in the rear of the room, her Barry Goldwater face sour. Then, very slowly, a grin split her face. Laurel was absolved. "I've greatly enjoyed my campaign, and I leave it contentedly. My life has been enriched immeasurably by those talented, honorable Nebraskans I've been privileged to meet.

"I lost a lot this morning, but I've won a lot, too."

The sky, when Laurel reached the street, was a better-than-life Technicolor blue. She looked a horrible mess; her hair was greasy, her fingers shook like tuning forks, and her cream suit looked as if it'd been run over by a tractor. She was headed for the residential hotel where George St. Clark had been staying and prayed he'd be there.

Her high heels tapped and echoed on the old tile stairway. As she approached door number 13, it opened and George looked into the hallway, as if he'd been expecting her. The meeting of their eyes was like an electrical charge straight to the heart. He smelled as though he'd just come from the shower, and his hair was a little wet. All he had on was a pair of black jeans. Laurel stood opposite him, dirty and disheveled.

Breathlessly she said, "I've got a journalism degree and clips, I'm a congressional brat, and I know where all the bodies in Washington are buried. I've got the lowdown on the big town! Do you think one of the newspapers would take me on as a reporter?"

"Politician to reporter? That's a unique switch." George's eyes flickered over Laurel's face perfunctorily, as if he didn't know her. He took two steps forward and placed one hand at her waist, the other hand at her hemline. The door banged shut behind her as her entire body was pushed against it. A flood of hungry desire abruptly seized Laurel, and she began to breathe faster. George shoved her skirt up and yanked at her pantyhose till they were off. Then he pulled open her silk blouse and pulled down her lacy bra. With sharp teeth he sucked hard at her taut nipples, while his left hand curved around her buttocks and roughly explored her from the back to the front. Laurel's breath started to come in long, shuddering moans.

George lifted her right leg higher as she unzipped his jeans. He wasn't wearing underwear, so she guided his manhood to the tender flesh that lay high between her legs.

It didn't work, and they fell down onto the carpet. No laughing; they were too taken with the madness of passion. They were dead serious on raw consummation. They'd waited so long for this realization that this urgent sexual act served as the act of final possession. Half-dressed, George lifted his pelvis as if poised to attack, then bore down. They rode fiercely and savagely, without making a sound.

Laurel had never made a man crazy like this before. Her heat was unbearable, and she started to beg. Very slowly George withdrew from her, only to drive in harder. The climax came suddenly, erupting and leaving them gasping in each other's arms.

George pushed some of Laurel's hair off her face, which was damp with perspiration, just like his. He lifted his watch hand. "That took about . . . three minutes, tops."

"What do you call that?" Laurel said, breathing as though she'd completed a race. "A quickie?"

"Nope," George said smugly. "That was the seal of our pact."

Laurel was mystified. "What pact?"

"Our pact to get married, of course."

"But George—I've never even kissed you!"

He didn't rectify the situation. "Well, honey—we've got to save *something* for our wedding night."

• *Twenty-two* •

"The Gold Coast," the soap opera set in Chicago and taped in New York, was watched by seven million faithful viewers, most of them women under fifty. In the five years that it had been on the air, its characters had continuously committed adultery, divorced and remarried, faked dozens of suicides, suffered through countless cases of amnesia and spent many months in pregnancies, real and false, all packed into twenty-two-minute-per-day segments.

The cast was allowed only one rehearsal before that day's taping. Meritt, playing the sexually glamorous town slut Tracy Robertson, ran through the lines she'd memorized. Tense as a panther, she stood and addressed a woman in a chair, "You may be his wife, Nikki, and you may have been carrying his child for five months, but it just so happens I have been carrying his child for *two* months."

The actress playing Nikki huffily responded, "Everyone told me that you were a lying bitch, and now I finally believe it."

"Stop." A production assistant clicked his stopwatch. "You're over two minutes on this scene. Speed it up. And don't forget, Nikki—the network always wants 'witch' in place of 'bitch.'"

"Yeah, like Glenda the good witch," Meritt joked. They played the same scene, this time with the cameras taping.

"Meritt, your mail is in your dressing room, about two hundred letters this week," a script assistant told her after her scenes were taped. In her cramped dressing cubicle, she found a sack of fan mail that she had no time to read. Most letters were sent to Tracy Robertson, not Meritt du Nord, and they often castigated her for wickedness or warned her that another character was "not all she seems." Tracy was nearly the most popular character on "The Gold Coast." After she washed her face of the thick TV makeup, she applied mascara and lipstick, then headed out of the building. It was 8:00 P.M. She wore high leather boots with her jeans tucked in, and a navy pea coat. Briskly she walked northward. The December wind made her hair furl as if it were weightless.

After she'd walked fourteen blocks, she turned into Sam's street, ascended the front steps, and touched his doorbell with a gloved hand. She had a long wait before Viola's voice issued from the intercom, demanding identification.

"Call off your guards, it's only me, Meritt du Nord."

As she entered the front door, she heard the babies crying loudly. The sound disturbed her, because it wasn't the complaining wail of soiled diapers, hunger or a cry for attention: it was the feverish cry of babies who aren't loved. Meritt entered the living room, taking off her coat as she walked. She heard the sound of the TV in the master bedroom, and ignored it as she rushed to the second-floor babies' room.

Kevin and Darrel were on their backs in their separate cribs, with red faces chapped as if they'd been crying for hours. Their diapers were dirty. Meritt efficiently changed them, giving them sponge baths, and put clean sleepers on them. They'd been born within a week of each other in August, and they both resembled Sam, rather than their surrogate mothers. Meritt sat down in a rocking chair in the babies' room, and with one infant in each arm, she rocked them until they stopped crying and became the happy, irresistible little boys she'd met in August. They both lay heavy on her chest, as if drawing sustenance from human contact. She hugged them and kissed them.

"So this is where you are!" Viola said from the door. "You didn't have to get the twins out of bed." They were not "twins," Sam said when he named them; they were brothers, two distinct children with their own identities. "I didn't rush out to you because I was on the phone."

Meritt asked coldly, "When's the last time you came up here today?"

"Oh I don't know, a couple of hours ago. They do pretty well on their own."

"When do they eat? Where are their bottles?"

"Oh, I guess it is that time." Viola was speaking from underwater.

At first Meritt had thought Sam's wife was drunk, but she wasn't: she was in a different reality. Her delicate beauty was still there, but it was dulled by the housecoat she wore. "Where is Sam, godammit?"

"He was supposed to be here an hour ago. You don't have to swear in my house, Meritt. God's last name isn't 'dammit.' "

Meritt wondered what would be the best tack to take with this deranged woman who was her best friend's wife. "Let's go downstairs and feed the kids, all right? Here, you take Kevin."

The two women returned to the first floor to feed the babies. There was a Christmas tree in the living room, but no other Christmas decorations, though religious materials were scattered everywhere—tracts, mailings, cassette tapes, devotionals, a Carol Carole calendar, a book titled

The Bible as Seen by Carol Carole. When they were finished feeding, Viola took a deep breath as if about to launch into a sermon, and Meritt hurried to deflect her: "The kids are ready for bed. Let's put them down and talk about Carol Carole and our souls later."

• *Twenty-three* •

Lisa woke up in a stranger's bed. She groaned as her eyes opened to the daylight glare. She was alone in a room the size of an arena, but this room was not in her house on Avenue Foch.

She sat up quickly, trying to recall where she was. The other side of the huge bed was empty. There were traces of a man scattered through the room—heavy brogues, parts to a suit, cigarette ashes everywhere. The room smelled of cigars and Old Spice—why did American men persist in using that scent? Rushing to the window, she looked out on an outstanding view of rue François-ler, then noticed the window was bullet-proof glass. The memory of the place came to her then; she was at the Nova-Park Élysées, in the Royal Suite. It was designed for the comfort of royalty and heads of state.

Her Bulgari watch read 10:00 A.M. Lisa caught a quick glimpse of herself in a mirror. Last night she'd been wearing a chenille sweater and a metallic-sparked chiffon skirt. She hoped her padded raw silk coat, the color of celery, looked daytime enough for the street. The bedroom's furniture was gilded Régence pieces. By the door was a desk with bronze-doré embellishment. Spread across the leather top were five American one-hundred-dollar bills. There was a note in the thick cream parchment of the Nova-Park Elysées that read: "You're one classy lady. Thank you very much."

"Wait a minute here," Lisa said out loud. He'd mistaken her for a prostitute. Or else he'd known who she was, and had left the money to deliberately gall her. *I'll show him.* She took five American hundred-dollar bills and added them alongside his money, and left a note that read: "For services rendered."

The doorman summoned her a taxi, and Lisa collapsed on the back seat after muttering her address. How shocking that the lady of the manor was actually traveling by taxi, she thought blearily. Her mouth felt as if a tar-covered cotton ball had been forced into it, and she had a champagne hangover. Outside the window the chestnut-lined boulevards sped by. Lisa was oblivious.

The Wharton apartment was on the second floor of an eighteenth-century building. Lisa didn't want a maid to let her in, so she disengaged the security system with a special key. She walked into a black-and-white Art Nouveau foyer with a glass-and-wood banister leading to the upper level and through a flower-fragrant house dominated by French old-world style. Some of the ceilings were covered in lacy rococo designs, and the walls were decorated with gilt pilasters. Excellent reproductions of Louis *Quatorze* and *Quinze* furniture, mixed with genuine pieces, were everywhere. On the living room floor was a flowery eighteenth-century Aubusson rug. When pear-shaped interior decorator Oscar Moore Travis, Lisa's one-time employer, first saw the rug, he fell to his knees in awe of its rare blue background. He had transformed their large dining room from a gloomy cave into a sunny entertaining space merely by ordering lemon yellow silk chairs for Lisa—the *right* lemon yellow.

Lisa's bedroom was carpeted with fake leopard skin. Her bed was covered with a lynx throw. Two sets of tapestry draperies kept out the light. She hit a switch and twenty tiny bulbs went on inside a dazzling miniature chandelier overhead.

Shedding her clothes where she stood, Lisa tried to recall what was scheduled for this week. She entered her shower, a large round space with a stained glass ceiling, artificially illuminated. Six water jets of brushed steel spurted water that hit her body like six infuriated wasps. Finally she remembered that Winthrop was coming in today, and the house had to be ready for guests at tomorrow's lunch. Thank God, the maisonette came with its own *patronne*, a "female boss" whose entire life was a celebration of aristocratic entertaining.

Without bothering to dry off, Lisa walked to one of her three dressing rooms, split into sportwear, formal wardrobes and travel wardrobes—necessary since Lisa frequently jumped between the five different Wharton houses. The racks of clothes were concealed by huge mirrors, in which she surveyed her body, still glistening with water. As always, it was in splendid condition, the form slender and firm, the breasts high, lush, creamy globes, the pubic fuzz pale. She had been so afraid the private hair would turn dark after she had the baby. She took notice of a bite mark on her inner thigh, and grinned. Too bad she couldn't remember how it got there.

Lisa had been married for two years to Winthrop Wharton, and boredom had settled in much earlier than she'd anticipated. When she'd first set her cap for the magnate, she'd expected the occasional stuffy evening with him, and all the tedious events she'd have to attend with him—no big deal. She hadn't bargained on the emptiness she felt, having attained all her dreams by the age of twenty-six. All the gloating was gone.

After the wedding two years ago, Winthrop had taken Lisa into his society, proudly introducing his blond beauty to every acquaintance. Hostesses who were friends with Winthrop's ex-wife received her frostily, but she never let drop the exterior of a shy, winsome, golden-haired maiden who loved her husband.

- For several months into the marriage, Winthrop had been rejuvenated. He stopped smoking, swore off cholesterol-laden food, and daringly had his tailor make him a couple of suits that were one or two tones lighter than the dark ones he'd been wearing all his years. For the first time in decades he glowed with an "Aren't I lucky to be me?" happiness. Lisa was slightly taken aback by the effect she had on this incredibly distinguished man.

Since he had a desirable property to show off, Winthrop accepted all invitations to cocktail parties and balls, dinner parties and receptions. He patronized the ballet and theater. Once Winthrop became reckless and asked his young wife to take him to a movie, since he'd never been in a movie theater. Afterward Lisa had taken him to McDonald's, and stifled her laughter when Winthrop asked the pimply order-taker for a medium rare hamburger.

Lisa became pregnant just three months after the wedding. The news left Winthrop delirious with joy. For a man nervously waiting for his sixties to roll over him like an avalanche, nothing would make him feel so young as having a child. With a child.

Old dogs can't learn new tricks, and will revert to habit. Neither Lisa nor her pregnancy could overpower the lure of important negotiations, and Winthrop gradually turned back into a workaholic and world traveler, and his sex drive leveled off. Lisa had gambled that Winthrop would return to his pre-Lisa behavior. She was free to revel in the lifestyle financed by an unlimited allowance. She teased her parents for being mere paper *millionaires,* while her husband was said to be a billionaire. She was happy.

It wasn't a charmed gestation; Lisa became irritatedly uncomfortable at the fourth month. Her gynecologist wanted her confined to the house most of the time.

That's when the world's longest cocktail party began. Lisa invited in any friend she'd made since her move to

New York. Oscar Moore Travis loved to enter the Fifth
Avenue mausoleum, slander it, and tell Lisa how he'd decorate it if he had the chance. (Lisa knew better than to ask
Winthrop if she could redecorate; the crypt was the ances-
tral home and an art museum.) Lisa followed "The Gold
Coast" on daytime TV. Meritt was very flattered. Sam Ross
visited, and so did Laurel, when she came in on an assign-
ment from Washington. Martin Vanderziel called her once
a month from California or whatever country he'd wan-
dered into. His father, T. Wayne Vanderziel, had never
slowed down his business piracy though he was in his late
seventies. Martin had seen him only once after he'd returned from Vietnam.

Winthrop's servants were among the best-paid in the
city, and they were very discreet. Some of her friends came
to the house dressed like punks, and others came in drunk
or high on drugs, but Orton and his fellow employees were
either apathetic or pretended not to notice Lisa's less con-
ventional guests.

In October of 1978 Lisa went into labor while Winthrop
was in town. She was conveyed to a maternity hospital
where a room had been specially prepared and decorated
for her. Too frightened of the pain, Lisa had herself put to
sleep. When the baby emerged and was found to be a boy,
word was relayed to Winthrop, who was working at his
New York office. The news filled him with incredulous
delight; and though he already had sons, this boy was
going to be Winthrop Junior. Lisa refused to breast-feed
him, since nourishing him might wreck her fine breasts.
The baby was turned over to a nurse. Winthrop embarked
on a world tour of his various subsidiaries.

Despite having attended finishing school in Switzerland,
Lisa had forgotten the art of running a household. The
pleasure she had in shopping had peaked a while ago. She
definitely didn't want to fill up her time by volunteering for
good causes or charity work. Except for the plentitude of
money, her needs weren't being met.

She sat now bare naked on the lush white carpet, staring at her beauty. In every mirror she saw or held, she devoured her own physical perfection. Yet the value of Lisa's beauty depended on others. No mirror could duplicate the dark desire in a man's eyes as he looked upon her. She needed to be paid attention to, to be desired and wanted. Which was why she had begun having affairs after her first anniversary, one-night stands when Winthrop was out of town.

Lisa felt much better than when she'd stepped into the shower. She stood up and hunted for a trouser suit made of azure shantung, then worked on her makeup till she looked as if she had bred-in composure. When Winthrop arrived late that afternoon, she threw up her arms, a gesture copied from the poster for *Evita*. "Winnie! You're here!" As she hugged her husband and pecked him on the cheek, Lisa thought that she and Eva Peron had one trait in common: they both believed in marrying up.

• *Twenty-four* •

"I think I may have found my mother," Laurel said breathlessly into the phone. At the other end of the line her husband, George, congratulated her and asked how soon she'd know and if she planned to visit the woman. He was in the Washington *Tribune* city room, a shirt-sleeved reporter sitting in the long rows of black desks with other shirtsleeved reporters. Laurel sat several blocks away inside the sole room which was the Washington bureau of the Boise, Idaho, *Herald*. Her building housed many Washington bureaus for daily newspapers around the country. Most of the impressively titled "bureaus" were staffed by one reporter.

"So what happens if your mystery mother is a convict?" George warned. He spoke over the din of the block-long city room, filled with the tapping of typewriters, the chattering wire service machines, and the steady murmur of voices. "Or if she's had a sex change. What if she's some lowlife you can't get rid of, who starts pestering you for money?"

"I don't care what situation she's in, I just want to know who she is," Laurel said as she gazed absently at her view of the Washington Monument. The birth registry might provide the name and address as soon as tomorrow.

"I'll certainly be interested in meeting your biological mother, to see how she compares with your adoptive one."

After Laurel had hung up, she started going through her mail, throwing away press releases and outdated material. The Boise *Herald* job was so easygoing it was humdrum. She'd been to Boise only once, for the job interview. Her bosses didn't expect her to be an investigative reporter, anyhow. They picked up most of their national affairs stories from the wire service. Laurel was there to cover the state's senators and its two congressmen, and government doings that affected Idaho. The job didn't pay that much, but it allowed her to work in the same city as her husband. It also paid her while she learned the trade.

Laurel's life had changed drastically after she lost the race for Congress. She refused to run for elective office ever again, and advised her mother to adopt another protégé. "There are plenty of bright, ambitious young kids out there who need a mentor," she'd told Mavis, "and too many politicians wasting their time trying to get their children to enter politics. You've helped me enough, Mom—help some people who *deserve* your aid."

On January 1, 1979, George and Laurel had been married in Maryland. That's a bad pun," Meritt had told Laurel a month later. "You didn't know George very long. Weren't you taking a big risk?"

"No. The emotion we felt toward one another was intense. It was clear that if we were going to be together at all, we should be married. We both were ready to make that commitment." After a pause Laurel asked, "What would 'Tracy Robertson' have done?"

"She would have blackmailed George into marriage with a false pregnancy, of course."

Laurel knew little about George's past or his former relationships with women, and she wanted to keep it that way. The happy comfort of her marriage felt so long delayed and deserved that she didn't want to rock the boat by finding out George's early peccadillos. If, for example, George had had some girlfriend who'd needed an abortion, Laurel would have been poisonously jealous, merely because someone on this earth had actually been impregnated by and could have had a child with the man she loved. She knew her fear of George's past was crazy and distasteful. Some year, when Laurel would be mature and fully confident, she would be able to hear such things.

As she flipped through the stack of press releases on her lap, Laurel lifted her feet up on her desk. The sun caught her brown hair and scattered it into glistening shades of auburn and goldenrod. Suddenly she came upon a press release from the Inter-American Affairs office of the State Department. A little bubble of nausea rose within her. Ex-congressman Andy Smith was still assistant to the assistant secretary, the last she knew. Inter-American meant South America, a continental land mass swarming with non-aligned nations. The question she'd been carrying around since 1971 came up in her again. When is something going to happen with the Trojan Horse Project, if ever? Who else besides Oliver Remick was building the Trojan Horse? Who else was running it? Were any trusted heads of state involved in the conspiracy?

Feeling frustrated, she tossed the rest of the paper on her

desk and gazed out her window at the shining Washington Monument, a shining shaft that put all ancient Egyptian obelisks to shame. Ever since that strange, inexplicably dooming night at Smitty's ghost house, she lived with an undercurrent of fear, a sense that suddenly the conspiracy she had learned about might suddenly erupt into horrible reality.

Even if the Trojan Horse Project was an elaborate joke, or if it was real and the plan was never implemented, Laurel and her friends had failed themselves and their country. Unless the ex-pages wanted to ruin their professional success at this time in their lives, it was too late to report now.

Laurel brought her legs down and put her head on her desk. She had never told George the secret she shared with four other people. The guilt, on top of guilt, plagued her at odd moments. She wondered if she'd ever be free of it.

The birth registry came through and supplied Laurel with a name the following day. Her mother was Eunice Cykauzski, and she lived in Algona, Iowa. The agency man asked, "Do you want to have us to attempt to reach her and determine if it would be good for you to see her?"

"No!" Laurel had waited too long. She wanted to see her mother, and in person, as soon as possible.

Early in the morning, George drove her to Dulles Airport, where she caught the next plane bound for Minneapolis, Minnesota, the nearest major airport to Algona. At the airport she dialed 712-555-1212 to get the number of the Cykauzski residence in Algona. When she tried her mother's number, there was no answer. She waited impatiently and redialed in fifteen minutes. No answer. Laurel gave up and walked to a rent-a-car counter carrying a small bag. Algona was a town of six thousand: it had to have a motel. She'd stay there and see if her mother was gone for the afternoon or for longer. If the woman was on vacation

or any other lengthy absence, Laurel would have to give up
and continue her wait in Washington.

Laurel loathed every second of her car trip to Iowa. Of
all the places she wanted to be in the world that afternoon,
she wanted to be in her natural mother's presence, and not
in this blasted car or an airplane. She drove seventy-five
miles per hour on Interstate 35W; and four hours after
leaving the airport she reached Algona. She drove at a
crawl through the town, looking for Maple Street.

The rural town was so quiet that the silence rang in her
ears, so accustomed to urban clamor. The trees were the
deep green of summer. In the dry heat children were playing at a municipal wading pool. The three billboards in
town all advertised seed and grain and insecticides. At last
she came to 279 Maple Street. Her hands started to shake
so violently she could hardly turn off the ignition. The
butterflies in her stomach were bigger than ravens. Laurel
looked down at her white jeans. She was wearing a turquoise men's shirt and long silver earrings. Was this an
appropriate outfit to meet your mother in? Laurel wondered. Her clothes were wrinkled from the long hot drive
south.

She willed herself to get out of the car, and walked the
dirt path to the house. It had Comet green siding with rust
coming through, and the white window frames needed to
be painted. Someone must be home, because the storm
door was open, exposing the screen door. The roof needed
shingles.

There was the sound of television inside, and Laurel
thought crazily it might be tuned to "The Gold Coast." She
knocked on the frame of the screen door, and her knees
wobbled as if they were rubber. "Just a minute," a woman
said inside.

Laurel's face flushed with heat when the woman came to
the other side of the screen. "Yes?" Was this her mother?
Her lapis blue eyes were identical to Laurel's, with long,
spikey lashes. Any further resemblance ended there. The

lady was in her fifties, and her hair sat gray and flat on her head. She looked like a kind, pleasant person.

Laurel took in the loud polyester muumuu and thought, *This is the mystery woman? This drab woman is my blood mother? It must be.* "Are you Eunice Cykauzski?"

"No, I'm her sister Bernice. Eunice doesn't live in these parts anymore, but they keep sending her junk mail here."

"Where does she live?"

The woman's guard came up then. *"You* know where she lives."

"Where?" The woman folded her arms, and with some desperation Laurel said, "I'm not a bill collector or anything. I'm searching for my mother, and a birth registry tracked my records back to here. Please tell me . . . is there any reason why I shouldn't know where Eunice Cykauzski is?"

"It's private. Only Eunice Cykauzski and I know who she is now. And you're a stranger." Bernice started to close the storm door.

"Who is she?" Laurel wasn't coming all this way to get a door in her face. She opened the screen door and pushed past the woman. "I'm your niece! Look, here are the copies of the documents saying I'm Eunice Cykauzski's daughter." She started to fish in her purse, but suddenly regarded the living room. Everywhere she looked there was a portrait of Carol Carole. On tabletops and shelves, on every wall. There were Bible-sized books on her religion, the Assembly of the True Jesus. There were coffee table-sized books on the mission of Carol Carole, and tiny prayer guides for "Steeple People." There were a couple of Carol Carole dolls wearing handkerchief-sized robes. There was even a plaster bust of Carol Carole, the face slanted at a heaven-gazing angle.

In every portrait the televangelist's hair was a dark brown, with auburn highlights. Her radiant gaze came from phosphorous blue eyes. Carol Carole's face was similar in shape and form to Laurel's.

A bile of disbelief came up Laurel's throat, and she swallowed hard. Her teeth started to chatter. "Is this r-r-r-ight? Is your suh-suh-sister . . . Carol Carole?"

Bernice nodded in resignation. She'd hoped to break the news to the young woman in a less direct way.

"Yes, that's right. And Carol Carole is your mother."

• *Twenty-five* •

Sam Ross sat at the computer terminal at 2:00 A.M. on a June night, staring blearily into the bluish light emitted by the IBM monitor. He rubbed his unshaven face unconsciously. Drops of sweat trickled down his broad forehead. He had to divorce his wife soon, and take custody of his boys. That was all there was to it.

Unable to sleep, Sam sat in his home office and listlessly looked at the electronic "bulletin boards" rolling down the screen, sent careening around the country by manic computer tinkerers. He felt like Dr. Frankenstein, running experiments alone in his Transylvanian lab. Upstairs slept his wife, the live-in *au pair,* and his children, who'd just turned one year old. For nine months, Sam had been sleeping in the guest room, because sleeping with Viola was like sleeping with a stranger. Despite all the people in the house, despite the millions of people in the city around him, Sam was plagued by loneliness edged by desperation, the loneliness of one forced to make a choice he'd never wanted.

Sam had avoided the issue for too long. He'd put it off by hiring Debbie Kersten, a part-time student at Columbia

University, to live in as a housekeeper, a quasi-mom. Debbie's stable presence in the house meant that Viola could run out to meet with fellow Steeple People anytime she wanted.

Viola had changed so much that her parents were worried about her. Her complexion had turned muddy and her blue eyes had acquired the wild gleam of a fanatic. The strawberry blond hair was cut close to her head, like Joan of Arc's. She'd thrown out all her trousers and wore the most conservative old-lady dresses. She'd become totally apathetic about Kevin and Darrel and forgot them for long periods. Studying and worshiping with the Assembly of the True Jesus wasn't her top priority; it was her only priority, and her obsession.

Fortunately Sam's work had become *his* priority, his passion, and he could forget about Viola once he sat down to a computer terminal. In February he'd left the commodities field to join Forster, Dunn, a powerful and prestigious Wall Street institution, as the chief of their equity trading desk. Sam had played with computers since college, and on his own time he designed a sophisticated computerized trading system. It supplied detailed information on securities trading through his self-designed analytical computer network.

Then he developed software that gave personal computer users up-to-the-minute stock quotes, interest rates, foreign exchange rates, and futures prices, even company histories. His programs even allowed a computer-user to execute a trade without calling a broker. His firm recognized that he had taken their creaky, white-elephant computers and turned them into state-of-the-art technology, the best on the Street. Quickly Forster, Dunn rewarded him with a vice-presidency. The firm let him work at his home terminal as much as he pleased. Sam could still work from "dark to dark," but now he could do it at home.

Computers were moving into households all across the country, spawning the shadowy subculture of "hackers."

Using the modem—a device that lets computers communicate over phone lines—any hacker could break into secret corporate and government files. All that was required for access was the password.

As a hacker, Sam had broken into a good number of complex computers at institutions throughout the United States. His ethics forbade him from breaking into data bases at other Wall Street firms, and he'd locked up Forster, Dunn's mainframe with the tightest security on the Street. Most of Sam's hacking was for practice, in preparation for that day, that time when all of Washington, D.C., was hooked into computers. All of Washington, D.C., included Andy Smith.

He raked his hand though his dark gold hair that stood up on end. He accepted that Viola was never going to return to her old self. An *au-pair* girl was a shoddy substitute for a mother. Sam had to make a better life for his children. It didn't matter how much alimony he'd have to cough up for the spurned Viola. His sons' lives would improve so much in her absence that it didn't matter what the cost would be.

Looking up at the ceiling, Sam ran his hands through his hair again. How strange it was that, as you grew older, life presented bizarre tragedies and conflicts that you'd never have imagined existed. "The world is yours," he muttered unconsciously. The world would be his again, as soon as he established an environment in which his kids could grow up properly.

• *Twenty-six* •

"Get those reporters out of here!" George yelled.

"How?" Laurel trembled in the face of his uncharacteristic anger.

"I don't care how you do it, just get rid of them!"

"Don't yell at me, help me!"

Outside their Arlington townhouse swarmed representatives from the Washington dailies and the three New York City dailies, crews from local stations plus the networks, wire service reporters, photographers, and stringers. The *National Enquirer* alone had sent five reporters. They all stood patiently in the suffocating humidity of a hot July night, waiting for Laurel to appear on her doorstep and give them juicy quotes about her bizarre biological mother.

For years Laurel had found the image of Carol Carole distasteful. She'd perceived the woman to be an extra shrewd con artist who fleeced guileless citizens of their hard-earned money, and she'd always viewed televangelism as a form of corrupt fascist mind control. Laurel had left Algona, Iowa, one minute after learning that Eunice was actually Carol Carole, the TV angel whose past had been kept a padlocked mystery. As Laurel climbed back into her rental car, Bernice had reached Carol Carole and informed her that her daughter had come looking for her.

The canny televangelist recognized this as an opportunity to whip up the fresh drama that her church had needed for some time. Three days after she learned about Laurel, she called a press conference. The subject was going to be the revelation of her illegitimate daughter. Carol Carole had long been something of a colorful novelty to the media because of her hillbilly weirdness. And because she was the nation's most charismatic female preacher, she'd always been a newsmaker. Jokes about her were a staple on "Saturday Night Live" and in comedians' acts.

The news conference in Salvation City was heavily attended. Carol Carole wore a white satin gown with a rough wooden cross (a piece of the "true cross") dangling from her neck. The room was specially lit to enhance her beauty, including tiny "key lights" that would make her eyes gleam. She wore contact lens that made her eyes bluer than they already were. Her dark brown hair flowed in waves past her shoulders. She was resplendent.

"As you know, I was a worthless sinner during my worldly life," Carol Carole began. She'd always discounted her past with her statement, and had given no more information on her origins except that she legally changed her name to Carol Carole, "because I sang carols when I accepted Jesus."

To the press she revealed that when she was very young, she'd borne a child without marrying the father. The media representatives gasped. "I gave my cherub up for adoption, for I knew I would have destroyed her life as I was destroying my own. My little baby was lost to me.

"After many years of searching, I have found my baby. She is twenty-six years old and a lovely, God-fearing person. Her name is Laurel Williams St. Clark. Her adoptive mother is Representative Mavis Williams of Nebraska. Laurel works in Washington, D.C., and her husband is a newspaper reporter. I so wish she were here today, but she preferred that I meet with you first.

"On Sunday I will tell my congregation here in Salvation City my unsavory life story, the dark times before Jesus rescued me and chose me as his own. My flock is my family, and I always considered my fellowship to be my children . . . until now."

Laurel and George had watched the press conference, broadcast live on Cable News Network. It left Laurel aghast at the woman's lies. She hadn't searched for her daughter; it was the other way around! Carol Carole had pounced on the discovery as an exploitable treasure, and she didn't care what her biological daughter thought. The church hadn't tried to reach Laurel before the preacher's news conference. Now the phone was off the hook and reporters swarmed around their house as if there was a free strip show on the front step. The Boise *Herald* had instructed Laurel to take some time off.

"What am I supposed to tell those people?" she asked George. "That I've never met Carol Carole and I never will? That would blow up the story half a dozen times over."

"Why won't you go see her?" George asked irritably. "What's keeping you?"

"If *your* mother was Carol Carole, would *you* like to meet *her?*" Laurel said bitterly.

"That's irrelevant!" George stalked to the kitchen. "I'm calling Mississippi and getting this thing settled."

Laurel's face was haggard. "This is none of your business."

"I'm doing what's best for you. If you don't meet Carol Carole at least once, this will hang over you for the rest of your life. The sooner you're rid of her, the better."

Laurel leaned on the kitchen doorway and glumly watched her husband get the main number for Salvation City, Mississippi. He was shuttled through a hierarchy of Steeple People. After he'd been transferred five times, he reached Karen, Carol Carole's Most Exalted Disciple. Carol Carole was meditating and couldn't be disturbed.

George hung up, then set the phone back on the counter. "She said she'd have Carol Carole get in touch with you." He snarled the words at her.

Laurel was puzzled by his threatening voice. To appease him, she said, "I guess I'm ready to go out and give a statement to the ladies and gentlemen of the press. Would

you like to come with me? Playing the role of the suppor-
tive spouse?"

Laurel and George put on somber clothing—George in a
tie and jacket and Laurel in a Wedgwood blue linen dress.
The avid horde of reporters at her door looked eerie under
the videocameras' white spotlights. A drove of cameras
began clicking. "Have you met your mother face-to-face
yet, Laurel? Have you talked on the phone? What was your
reaction to learning your mother was Carol Carole? What's
it like to be the daughter of a national religious figure?
What does Mavis Williams say about all this?"

I told you so is what she'd say, Laurel thought. "My
mother supports me in all I do. I'm happy I've found my
biological mother and I'll meet her soon," was what she
said. A uniformed messenger girl darted through the mob
scene and put a telegram in Laurel's hands. With his arm
around her George smiled to the cameras and led his wife
back into the house. Once inside Laurel sighed heavily.
"How do you think I did, honey?"

In answer George's right arm shot out and slammed into
her stomach. The pain didn't hurt as much as the surprise.
Doubled over, Laura sank full-length on a couch while
clutching her stomach. "What was that for?" she gasped.

"This whole damn thing is making me look like a fool in
front of the world!" George retreated to a den, where he
began calling friends to explain his situation. Laurel lay on
the couch letting the pain go away. *Hitting me was probably his way of losing tension,* she told herself. *He's going
through a lot right now. This is just a one-time thing.*

Laurel's eyes spotted the telegram on the floor where it
had dropped. She opened it and read:

ADOPTION DOCUMENTS VERIFIED STOP CAROL CAROLE
ASKS TO SEE LAUREL WILLIAMS MEET SATURDAY STOP
SPECIAL PLANE AT DULLES FIELD SATURDAY 6 PM
GATE 39 STOP

Cripes, how fast do those Steeple People operate? Laurel wondered. Karen, the Most Exalted Disciple, must have made arrangements as soon as she'd hung up on George.

George. Laurel lay on the couch, waiting for an apology. She listened intently for footfalls on the stairway. They never came.

When growing up in Iowa, Eunice Cykauzski was labeled "The School Pump." In senior high she graduated to "The Town Pump." It wasn't long before she became "The County Pump." Eunice never went without a date. She liked men, whether they were crude farmhands who grunted, "Let's go screw," or church-bred Future Farmers of America whose sexual proposition was, "May I kiss you?" Her sister Bernice was almost as promiscuous. Eunice's looks and body were splendid, almost remarkable. She thought a body like hers deserved bigger and better things than Algona, so she dropped out of school, dyed her hair carrot orange, and hightailed it to the big city of Des Moines. There she wrote a blizzard of bad checks that were accepted everywhere because Des Moines was a small town at heart. The shop people were so trusting that Eunice practiced shoplifting there.

Her last purchase by rubber check was a 1939 Chevrolet sedan with which she could skip town. She rolled into Las Vegas with a pompadoured tough who wanted to marry her. On her wedding night Eunice's tough got into a territorial fist fight at the Lucky Lady Casino downtown. When her hoodlum husband shoved the other guy outside, his head hit a fire hydrant, killing him instantly. Eunice's new husband was tried in Clark County, and convicted of manslaughter. Eunice went to work as a call girl, and became the favorite of a minor mafioso who taught her flim-flam scams to bilk out-of-towners.

When she was twenty, Eunice found out she was pregnant. The baby was given up for adoption to the Clark County Welfare Department. The pregnancy hadn't cramped Eunice's style one bit.

Her boyfriends took Eunice all over the country till there was hardly a major city in the States where she hadn't forged or bounced a check.

The gestation had matured Eunice in a way. It made her wonder what she was doing with her life. She couldn't keep turning tricks much after she'd hit forty. Every man who'd ever supported her was under some indictment, and a man couldn't keep you from inside the big house. She wanted big money, too. There had to be a legal way to get big money fast.

Eunice chanced upon a magazine article that detailed the reemergence of old-time religion and the surprising amount of revenue accumulated through pledges. It seemed to her that a business person, using a specific plan, could quickly build up a lucrative financial organization.

She began to investigate the business. She traveled along the Bible Belt of the deep South, the nation's cauldron of steamy sin and steamy repentance, the only place in the world whose roads are decorated with red neon crosses proclaiming JESUS SAVES.

Eunice patronized the backroad tent shows to reach the roots of a fundamentalist operation. She witnessed dramatic "healings," and saw that they occurred mostly in people who wanted a moment of glory under the tent's lightbulb limelight. Even the people who came up to declare themselves saved and born again (often for the thirtieth time) could get some time on the stage. She saw how collective plates would start empty and brim with bucks just a few minutes later. The ranting, raving minister of the word always yelled, "Hey, none of the that change that you're clankin' in the bucket! We want *paper* money!" Open displays of naked greed were commonplace.

It was all show business. It was Las Vegas. The word of

God would be mentioned during the services, but not interpreted. Those country folk wanted a floor show. Preaching credentials like divinity school or ordainment didn't matter. Long-term spiritual benefit didn't matter. The more charisma a Bible-thumper had, the more star quality, the bigger the take.

Eunice decided she'd give it a go. With bad checks she bought a used one-ring circus tent, a wheezy organ, and a kettle drum. She went to a hardware store and bought a huge sheet of aluminum that sounded like thunder when it was shaken.

There was another matter she had to take care of before she started rehearsing. She called her sister Bernice, the only family with whom Eunice had kept in contact. Their parents were dead, but Eunice hadn't bothered to return to Algona for their funerals. "Bernice, I'm changing my name to Carol Carole. That's right, an 'e' on the second Carole. And if you let anyone—anyone—know that Carol Carole was Eunice Cykauzski, I'm going to have someone come mess up your face."

Carol Carole's camp meetings appealed to repressed people who needed release. She encouraged orgiastic weeping and uninhibited shrieks of joy. She hired "disciples" to expand the show and a special effects technician who designed a portable light-and-sound apparatus for her. She made up a name for her church.

Within time The Assembly of the True Jesus was well-heeled enough to produce a Sunday hour for television syndication. In 1978 the church started a cable-TV network called the Steeple People Network, or SPN. By 1980 annual donations were $58 million. In 1979 she opened "Salvation City," her home base, near Vicksburg, Mississippi. Her domain included a "family worship center" and television studios.

A year later, Carol Carole was looking for a fresh twist for her ministry, a new direction, a novelty to jazz up TV ratings and the Steeple People gospel. When her sister called to tell her Laurel Williams had tracked her down, Carol Carole would have fallen to her knees to thank God if she had believed in him. She'd been granted the gimmick that would rock the cutthroat, competitive TV preaching world.

On Saturday, after she'd boarded the private plane that had been waiting for her at Dulles Gate 39, Laurel wondered if Carol Carole felt the need to impress her daughter. The single-engine plane was a Cessna Turbo Stationair 6, its innards quietly plush, with oversized seats, doeskin walls . . . and a bar. Strange. Carol Carole preached that liquor was "of the devil." The nose cone of the plane bore the Steeple People logo, but there was nothing inside the fuselage that implied the plane belonged to a church, not even a Bible or a cross.

At the airstrip in Vicksburg, Laurel stepped out into the burning hot evening, and into the back of a Bentley, a Mulsanne Turbo. Carol Carole had taste in large goods, she observed. Her driver wore a seersucker suit with white shoes. His teeth flashed under a straggly black mustache. "Hi, I'm Irwin. I feel so lucky that Jesus chose me to be the first to meet Carol's daughter."

He was so sincere, so Laurel was extra-nice in return. "Thank you, Irwin. That's a lovely thing to say."

She closed her eyes and sat back into the leather seat. Laurel had not wanted to meet this flamboyant, pay-for-pray preacher, but George had insisted. She begged him to come along on the flight, but he said he'd been embarrassed enough already.

The Bentley passed Vicksburg's outskirts, highways dotted with mediocre motels. After fifteen minutes more, Irwin stopped at an eight-foot-high chain link gate, and unlocked a massive padlock. He got back in the car and said, "Welcome to Salvation City, Miss Williams. I'm taking you in on one of the service roads. If we came in the main gate, which is really pretty, I'm afraid too many curious people would see you're in this car. We wanna keep your arrival as kinda a secret."

"How big is Salvation City?"

"Twenty-three hundred acres, all of it surrounded by eight-foot walls. Kinda like the Great Wall of China, I say." The car continued on a dirt road leading through a forest. At a clearing in the trees, Irwin pointed out in his southern drawl, "That's where the Carol Carole Bible College is gonna be." A mile farther, construction was under way for a large group of buildings. "That's gonna be the Salvation City medical center."

The forest ended and turned into a wide, flat space resembling a college campus. Predominating was an aqua glass-walled edifice topped with five peaks, known nationwide as The Steeples, from which Carol Carole preached about the power of faith. There were a couple of banners and signs that read, JESUS FOR AMERICA.

Irwin stopped at the delivery dock behind an anonymous building without windows. Another entrance from the rear. This arrival was making Laurel feel like a black person sitting in the rear of a 1950s segregated bus. Just as she started to get out, a woman in mint green robes emerged from a door and came running toward her. The woman embraced her, then stood back. She was about forty, and her plain face shone with tranquillity. "Hi, I'm Karen, the Most Exalted Disciple. Your mother asked me to bring you to her."

"Couldn't she come herself?" So far, Laurel hadn't even spoken with Carol Carole.

"No, she wants you brought before her."

As if I'm begging for forgiveness!

Laurel followed Karen into the building, down narrow gray halls. She smoothed her white linen skirt, worn with an emerald blouse tightly belted by a multicolored sash. She wished that she'd given in to temptation and worn something vaguely defiant, like a PLO headdress over her Moscow University T-shirt.

Karen glanced at her stainless steel nurse's watch, then picked up her pace. "Hurry, we must hurry."

Laurel had given up being mystified by these people. Resignedly she followed her into a large room cluttered by television equipment, and realized she was in Carol Carole's broadcast studio. Karen went to a set of industrial double doors and motioned Laurel to come to her. She placed her left hand on Laurel's back while opening the right door. When the gap was wide enough, the left hand forcefully shoved Laurel into the next room.

Twenty feet from her, Carol Carole stopped preaching. A millisecond later two television cameras swung toward Laurel as technicians blinded her with klieglights. The crowd gasped loudly. Laurel gasped and fumbled for the door, but Carol Carole reached her and wrapped her in the white wings of her robe. Laurel smelled her heavy television makeup. The red lights of the camera meant the show was being broadcast live. She'd been led straight into the Steeple People's Saturday evening worship show.

"You see?" Carol Carole said to the vast audience beyond the lights. "Here she is, just like I promised—my lost lamb, Laurel Williams! Isn't she beautiful?"

The audience clapped and shouted as if their team was winning in the World Series. "Hallelujah!" "Amen!" "Praise Jesus!" were some of the calls Laurel heard within the din.

"Come along, Laurel. Come meet your family." Stunned, Laurel allowed Carol Carole to lead her by the hand to the Plexiglas altar toward the front of the soundstage. She threw outstretched arms at the audience. "Laurel, *this* is your family! The Assembly of the True Jesus! And we're mighty glad to have you."

Laurel nodded slightly. As her senses gradually started coming back to her, she realized how she'd been tricked into this live TV spectacle. After she'd waited for years to find out who her mother was, her mother was using her as a prop, in theatrics aimed at raising money.

When the crowd quieted a little, Carol Carole kept a hand firmly on Laurel's forearm as she announced, "Yes, this is my child of sin, returned to me by Jesus' grace. Laurel was born when I was a rank sinner, fleeing from the eyes of God, a lamb who had lost her way."

Her voice was mellifluous, her tones pear-shaped. "Yes, Steeple People, I concealed my past because I was so ashamed of the time I lived in the world. But Jesus told me it was all right to stop covering up! He said that you'd still love me, but only if I confessed everything.

"For the two decades before I was saved, I was a professional shoplifter and forger." The crowd gasped. "Yes, I was a thief. I sold myself to men. I consorted with hoodlums and gangsters. In fact, I committed so much sin that the only way to repent was to detail it to you fully, week after week."

A signal light came on, and the crowd started "spontaneously" yelling, "We love you, Carol Carole! We love you!"

For the rest of the service Laurel made some calculations. Since the show ended just before the newspapers' Sunday deadline, Carol Carole's revelations would make it into tomorrow's headlines. By inviting criticism and censure, she was deflecting it. By throwing her sins out at her congregation, she was daring them not to forgive her. The test of faith would make the woman a martyr before the media. The publicity of her transgressions would prompt people to check out the Steeple People TV network, resulting in more money and viewers. *I wish I'd inherited her brains,* Laurel thought. She was admiring her mother for her savvy even as she bitterly resented her.

A crowd of disciples and sycophants tried to surround Carol Carole and her daughter when the director cued the end credits. "I must be alone with her!" the older woman piously announced behind the soundstage. She opened a door and pushed Laurel inside a lavish dressing room.

Laurel stood, watching the evangelist warily, as Carol pulled a thick hair fall from her head and let it drop to the floor. The large room was strewn with half-empty coffee cups, dirty ashtrays, satin gowns and underwear, scripts and Bible studies pamphlets. The mirror of the dressing table glared with lights that would cruelly show up any flaws in one's looks. The top was covered by bottles, jars, and spills.

Framed and signed photographs of celebrities were scattered over the walls. Laurel recognized a shot of Andy Smith's wife, Ann, or Honeypie. "You've changed my life. Thanks for encouraging me to push for my place on the Leukemia Society board," she'd written. There were four theology degrees, each granted by Bible colleges that existed as real estate tax write-offs, Laurel bet.

Carol pulled off her high heels, fell onto a white damask chaise longue and hitched up her robe. For the first time she looked at her daughter personally. "Want a drink?" she asked, waving a hand toward a table set with bottles. Laurel didn't answer, and Carol said, "Suit yourself." She picked up a joint from an ashtray and lazily lit up.

"I take it no one else is allowed in the room," Laurel said.

"That's right. I've got to have *some*place where I can cool it."

"So no one else knows how much of a hypocrite you are."

"Well, if I can't relax in front of my own blood daughter, who then?" Carol inhaled deeply on the marijuana. She looked like an older sister of Laurel. She was better looking than her daughter, her features more refined and delicate. "Besides, I know you're smart. I knew you wouldn't buy my act. Good as it is."

"Who is my father?"

"Some guy looking to get his rocks off."

Laurel shuddered with distaste. "Why did you ask me

back here for this private interview? You must have figured I wouldn't like you."

"To get a good look atcha, I guess."

Belligerently Laurel asked, "What's to keep me from writing an exposé of your operation?"

"How much more can you expose than what I'm going to expose by my own little self? I know I'm a sinner, kid. And if you try to tell the world what a queen rat I am, you'll look bad, not me." Carol put down the joint and plucked out her blue-tinted contact lens, and put them into a tiny case. Without them, her eyes looked washed-out.

Genuine bewilderment strained Laurel's voice. "If you have to practice such an elaborate deception all the time, doesn't it wear you down? What's in this charade for you?"

"Money. And adoration. Those were two things I never was well acquainted with till I set up shop." Carol picked up a fresh joint and lit it. "Those hicks out there have more money than brains."

"I can't believe you're so immoral. What about all the elderly poor who send you their rent money?"

Carol's eyebrows arched upward, and she emitted a harsh laugh. "Salvation feels a lot more pleasin' than a roof over your head does." Laurel stood up. Carol's laugh, the laugh of a victorious barbarian, filled the room. "Had enough, kiddo? I bet myself you couldn't stand Salvation City for even overnight. Irwin's waitin' down the hall. He'll take you right back to the airstrip."

As Laurel walked out the door, she heard the preacher lady cackle. "Got any more questions, *reporter?*"

Laurel's neatly formed, happy life as a young go-getter in Washington quickly crumbled. The Boise *Herald* suspended her, without pay, for an indefinite period. George seldom spoke to her and walked around the house as if she didn't exist. The man who supposedly never asked favors for himself and never turned his back on a friend. Laurel questioned if she'd married a fake—a fake "good guy." With fake unpretentious charm. Fake wide-open honesty.

When Carol Carole released the first "chapter" of her lurid past, his employer, the Washington *Tribune*, ran the story on the front page. George came home in the afternoon and threw a rolled-up copy of the newspaper at Laurel. He growled just like a dog. "Look at what an ass you've turned me into." She read the story; it mentioned her name once, and George's not at all.

With one hand George grabbed her long hair and pulled Laurel off the couch. His fist smashed into her face, splintering her reading glasses. The shards bit into her eye area before falling to the carpet, and Laurel instinctively squeezed her eyelids shut. Blindly she tried to reach out at him. She kicked at him with her powerful legs, but it didn't prevent him from beating upon her face. Finally, as if he were too tired to continue, he let Laurel drop to the floor. "You'd better find a damned good way to make up for all the mortification you caused me."

When Laurel heard the front door shut, she slowly opened her eyes. Her vision was fine. She thanked a God her biological mother had never known. Like an old, old woman she lifted herself from the carpet, with a cracked rib stabbing her side.

In the bathroom mirror Laurel saw small cuts and scrapes around her eyes. Purple, puffy flesh was swelling around the right eye even as she watched. Her left ear was ringing. Her face looked like a raw red slab of meat, and she knew it would soon turn purple. Laurel had seen photographs of abused women, taken when they arrived at the police station; and in comparison, her face was the worst mess she'd seen. It was entirely numb. She picked up a brush and smoothed it through her hair, and handfuls of ripped strands came out.

Using a phone number Meritt had given her long ago, Laurel dialed the set of "The Gold Coast," and prayed she'd be there. Meritt had spoken of her wish to leave the soap a while back.

Meritt was in the dressing room. "What's going on, baby?"

"Meritt, I have to get out of this town. George has just beaten the living daylights out of me."

Her friend's tone was unsurprised. "Take it from me. If he hits you once, he'll keep doing it. Why don't you stay at my place here? It's big. How bad are you hurt? I can come get you."

"Don't bother. I'm taking the shuttle and I'll call your house from the airport . . . But my face! I'm going to have to wear a blanket over it, like the Elephant Man."

"Why don't I take you to a photographer friend of mine tonight?"

"What for?"

"To take your picture, of course!" Laurel was baffled. Meritt said, "You need evidence. For the court."

"What?"

"You're going to divorce him, aren't you?"

• *Twenty-seven* •

The same day Laurel left her husband, Sam Ross asked Viola for a divorce. She took the news with surprising aplomb.

"Will you give me enough money to move to Salvation City?" she asked hopefully.

"Sure," Sam said, relieved that her demand was so reasonable. He'd been prepared to give her any amount of money to leave his house. "But just one thing . . . I want full custody of the boys."

"Sure," Viola said blithely. "They never really were mine, anyhow." She widened her big blue eyes and Sam almost recalled what it had been like to be dazzled by them. She'd been so fresh and young and innocently beautiful. Now all the personality was gone from her face. It was unmarked. Forgettable. "You know, I've been ready to separate, Sam. I was just waiting for you to say when." Viola looked around the living room and sighed. "Just let me stay here till I put my things together, okay?"

"Take your time."

Viola picked up a copy of the New York *Post*. Carol Carole's face beamed beatifically from the cover. She looked up at Sam. "I just don't fathom your friend. How could she resist moving in with her mother? She must not understand Carol Carole and the Steeple People."

Two days later, the front cover of the New York *Post* showed a picture of Sam and Viola's townhouse. An artist had drawn in a segmented arrow that arced from the rooftop down onto the street. The adjoining headline said TWO WESTSIDE TOTS IN DEATH PLUNGE.

The story inside reported the deaths of Kevin and Darrel Ross, each one year old, in a five-story fall. The facts were murky. Their mother, Viola Ross, had told her *au pair* she was taking the children to the flat roof where the Rosses had a small terrace. Viola explained to the investigating authorities that the three of them had been sunning. The boys were growing faster than she realized, for they quickly crawled away from her to the cornice. Before she could reach them, Darrel fell off. Just as she about had Kevin within her grasp, he followed.

"They went over just like lemmings. One, then the other," was the comment of the meter maid who saw the children fall. A moment later she saw their mother looking down and screaming incoherently at the sight of the bodies lying next to each other on the hot tar street. There were no other witnesses. There were no particulars that incriminated Viola, except for her husband's remark that the children had never been on the roof before.

No one would ever know for sure whether it had been a dire accident, or whether Viola, under all her crazy piety, had wanted to get back at the man who'd rejected her.

Andrew "Smitty" Smith's death was reported the same day as the Ross babies'. He had died of natural causes at age ninety-four at a Michigan nursing home. The news stories reported that FDR's challenger had been hopelessly senile for at least a decade.

Meritt's eyes were red from weeping. "She murdered those babies. You know she did. Pushed 'em right off the roof."

Laurel's stomach was cramped with guilt. "My *mother* is responsible for making Viola what she is."

Meritt erupted. "Shut up, I'm sick of hearing you say that! When Sam married Viola, we both thought there was something a little strange about her. If it hadn't been Carol Carole, she'd have found Reverend Moon. Or the Life Science Church. Or Reverend Ike. Bhagwan Shree Rajneesh. The Movement of Spiritual Inner Aware—"

"You've made your point." Laurel gave her a wan smile. She was sitting in a loveseat opposite Meritt in her high-rise Roosevelt Island apartment. The orange disc of the sun was just about to turn red and dip behind the Manhattan skyline. Its low rays covered both women with amber light.

"We've got to stop dwelling on this. It's been two weeks

since the world stood still. We've got to move—" The phone rang, and Meritt picked it up off the parquet floor. "Hello? George? Stop calling. She's here, but you're supposed to communicate through your lawyers, remember?" Meritt glanced over at Laurel's face, which was still puffy and bruised. "Oh, just piss off!" She hung up.

The events of the past three weeks had wrought changes so dramatic they were nearly reversals. Meritt had given notice to the producers of "The Gold Coast" because she'd been given the ingenue lead in an off-Broadway musical version of *The Importance of Being Earnest*. Laurel had found a reassuring divorce lawyer through a D.C. friend, and resigned from the Boise *Herald*. "Now I face a major career decision . . . do I pump gas at Amoco, or Exxon?"

Neither of them had gotten too close to Sam during the events following his son's deaths, because his male friends had surrounded him like a flying wedge. He was stoic, absolutely granite-faced throughout the police inquiry, the wake, the funeral, the burial. Now he was taking it easy at his father's house in Lubbock, Texas. His rowhouse was put up for sale.

Laurel had been staying at Meritt's two-bedroom apartment since leaving Washington. "This furniture," she said to Meritt, gesturing with a hand. "Did it all come from Workbench, the Door Store, Conran's?"

"From all those places." Puzzled, Meritt looked around at her economical, practical, and functional furniture. "Why do you ask?"

Laurel pulled a knee under her chin. "George and I bought all our things at those kinds of stores. I was just looking at it now, seeing how light and clean every chair and table is. Easily assembled and easily knocked down. Just the right fixtures for people who keep moving around. As if you'll never stop moving around . . . Unless you're very lucky."

* * *

"Mrs. Wharton, you have knocked my socks off. Let's get out of here and make tonight special. I'll do anything you want. Everything and more."

Lisa's lovely face was animated as the ongoing flattery poured nectar from Jock Harvey's lips into her shell-like ear. They stood in a Florence palazzo, transformed into a Xanadu with ribbons, sprays of flowers, silk banners, and tiny, brilliant lights. It was 3:00 A.M. and people were starting to leave the party, which had been thrown by some *principessa* who'd married into a weak Medici bloodline.

All night long Lisa had been amused by Jock, an American descended from a robber baron oil monopolist. Jock had no profession. He lived off three trust funds, cagily established in the favorable tax climates of Hong Kong, the Bahamas, and Liechtenstein. He was richer than Martin Vanderziel; he was richer than her own son would be. He wasn't very good-looking, though. He had tiny eyes, nose and mouth, which got lost on a big face. He hadn't been showered with every blessing.

Lisa gently pushed Jock away, and pulled up the satin bodice of her strapless gown, the shade of caramel. It underscored the glittering wealth of uncut topaz stones that were strung around her neck. "I can't go with you, Jock. I'm here with Gerthe. She's my guest."

"Doesn't she play with the San Francisco Giants?"

"Cut that out. You know damn well she's German."

"She's a Valkyrie. I keep expecting to see her carry in her spear and shield."

Gerthe was six feet tall, with yellow hair worn in Princess Grace of Monaco hemp braids. Her face even had the same Grace Kelly purity of features, but on an Amazon scale. Lisa found herself fascinated with Gerthe's larger-than-life proportions. She was currently married to the Indian ambassador to Italy. He was a minor maharajah, and he was a good foot shorter than Gerthe. She wasn't really Lisa's guest; they coincidentally both had suites on the top floor of the Excelsior Hotel, and they'd both come alone to

Florence to shop and attend the *principessa*'s dinner and dance party.

Jock's rabbity eyes flickered across the terrace to Gerthe, who was engaged in conversation with two South American men who kept stealing glances at her overflowing décolletage. "Do you think either one of those old farts used to be a Nazi? Reminiscing about good times like the Beer Hall Putsch with a fellow countrywoman?" His mouth came closer to Lisa's ear again. "Would you come with me if Gerthe came with?"

"What are you saying?"

"You haven't heard? Gerthe is a sister of the sorority of Sappho." Lisa froze, not knowing how to react. "Don't give me those big blue eyes as if you don't understand. You've been looking at her all night." Jock ran his finger horizontally across Lisa's bare back. The touch unleashed an obscure desire in her. She trembled for a second. Jock continued, "So let's bring her along. Just the three of us. I'm broadminded."

Lisa continued staring at the other woman. Her mouth was dry. "You go ask her."

Two days later, Jock Harvey left for the States. Lisa remained in Florence with Gerthe.

During the first week she could have sworn she was in love with the German woman. Under the astonishing glamor of her looks was a pretty ordinary, nice, and straightforward country girl, and Lisa was roped in by her artless conversation. She was enthralled by Gerthe's body, as large and tan as any *Playboy* centerfold's charms. Yet having sex with the woman was a narcissistic act—Lisa was playing with a human being whose body parts were essentially the same as hers.

With the energetic enthusiasm of a ten-year-old, Gerthe insisted that Lisa tour the capital of the Renaissance with her. Lisa hated it. The town was hot and overrun by tourists. People gawked at the double blast of blond beauty anywhere Lisa and Gerthe went. All the restaurants served microwaved food, and the *avante-vogue* boutiques carried cheap knockoffs. When Gerthe wanted to see all forty-four rooms of the Uffizi, Lisa put her foot down. Winthrop's homes were jammed to the rafters with great paintings and antiques, and she had little interest in looking at more of the same.

As the second week wore on, Lisa remained infatuated by what Gerthe could do for her in bed. However, she was tiring of Gerthe's simple pleasures. Every new sight, whether it was the Boboli Gardens or a tomcat, provoked a big squeal from big Gerthe. Lisa had thought the sound was cute when she'd met her lover; now she thought it was like a half-slaughtered hog's.

By the middle of August Lisa felt like Gerthe's prisoner. Gerthe always wanted to be in the same room with Lisa, to the point of coming into the bathroom with her. It was a sticky situation. Gerthe was a born victim, the kind of hysteric who'd create a messy scene if she felt she was being rejected. Worst of all, Gerthe could tell the entire world that she'd turned Lisa Wharton into a dyke. All of Florence suspected it right now. Winthrop Wharton would not remain married to a woman who'd overindulged in Sapphic bliss.

What had been forbidden and carnal and novel was now wearisome. She'd used Gerthe. Now she wanted to leave her.

Lisa was rescued by a long distance phone call from Martin Vanderziel, who'd stopped in at the Whartons' Paris home. "Lisa, did you hear?" he asked in a curiously uninflected voice. "Sam's wife killed those two kids that he fathered."

Her gay idyll had kept Lisa out of touch. Across the suite's sun room Gerthe watched balefully as Lisa turned white with disbelief. "How long ago? Where is his wife? What is he doing now? What are you doing in Paris? I'll join you there tomorrow."

Lisa put down the phone. Suddenly her life was full of

purpose. Gerthe's face started to twist, and her mouth opened to hurl the first onslaught of jealousy. Lisa beat her to the punch.

"I don't have time for a possessive tantrum! A dear friend of mine has just lost his children. Don't you understand? I must go to him, alone!" Lisa picked up the phone again, to get a chambermaid to pack her clothes.

Gerthe was as sad as a punished dog as Lisa prepared to leave. Her eyes brimmed gratifyingly with tears as Lisa's mountain of luggage, made of water buffalo hide, disappeared within a van at the Hotel Excelsior's entrance. Lisa hugged her quickly and said she'd had a marvelous time. "Go see your husband or something. I'll contact you when I reach New York."

Martin paid the compliment of waiting for Lisa when she disembarked at Orly. "Martin, I love you!" she yelled impulsively, and hugged him very tightly. "You got me out of the *trickiest* situation. . . ." In a lower voice she muttered, "I was having sex with my own sex and it wasn't turning out to be a fairy tale."

"It never does."

Lisa hadn't seen Martin for two years. She was shocked by the ravages worn into his features. At the age of twenty-eight his face was weathered, like the side of a barn, yet fish-belly pale. His chin line sagged, and his countenance was criss-crossed with a network of wrinkles. In the midst of the elegant and eroded face, his pale blue eyes were limpid as a mountain lake.

He was eerie. He was disturbing. He was Martin—her friend.

· *Twenty-eight* ·

Sam had moved into a drab midtown hotel because he never wanted to set foot again in the house where his children had lived and died. Lisa surveyed his hotel room, whose disorder reflected the chaos of the guest's mental state. The counters and tables were piled with old newspapers, stacked with books and several room service trays of half-eaten food. There were many folders of documents from work, and computer printouts covered the extra double bed. Half-full coffee cups sat amongst overflowing ashtrays.

"I didn't know you smoked," Lisa said.

Sam shrugged. "I just started. It's never too late to start a bad habit."

Lisa was there because, after they'd shared a steak dinner at Sparks, she had demanded that Sam show her his living quarters, to check if he was living in total squalor. He was.

This was Lisa's first time alone with Sam Ross since she'd returned from Europe. When she looked upon his gray face, shaggy hair, and red-rimmed eyes, she felt sympathy. Sympathy felt good. It let you know how much a friend you were being.

She heard a ticking sound and looked down; a cockroach the size of a Studebaker was walking over the Formica counter top. Lisa picked up a coffee cup and brought it down on the bug. "That does it. You're coming with me."

"Where?"

"To that gray cave Winthrop calls his house. We've got plenty of room. The place is so big that my husband and I can be in the place at the same time, and not find out for days."

"Which is the way you like it."

"Yes. And you can stay there as long as you please. The staff will be at your disposal."

Sam started to demur, but Lisa wouldn't hear his objections. He gave up, and reached for a suitcase. He wished he had some of her aggressiveness. She was so unabashed. She always did what she set out to do.

An hour later they were met at the door by Orton, the major-domo. Lisa hoped Orton hadn't caught the funky smell of Sam's breath, though she felt a man deserved to be as drunk as a skid-row, fully-juiced stumbling bum when his babies had been murdered just six weeks ago. Orton suggested that Sam stay in the room that had been Winthrop's as a boy. It didn't look like a boy's room, though, with its dull-colored, masculine furnishings. Sam was more pleased than he expected, and asked if he could set up a computer terminal on the black-and-gold lacquer desk. "Sure, but if you put any cigarette burns on it, Winthrop will have you wasted," Lisa said. She wanted to talk to Sam some more, but tactfully withdrew. "If you'd like to visit with the Big Man himself, Winthrop is going to have breakfast at seven A.M., before he leaves for Tokyo."

The charity she'd just doled out to Sam left Lisa feeling high-hearted and magnanimous. She looked for Winthrop and found him in his library. She gave him oral sex. Then she went to wake up their baby (as his nanny fumed silently) and brought him to daddy, to reinforce the maternal tie. Lisa's timid, coy sexuality was probably the attribute that kept Winthrop most in love with her, followed by the birth of Winthrop, Jr., then by her skill at playing a demure aristocrat. Publicly, Winthrop, Sr. said that Winthrop, Jr.

"is the most successful of my many successful enterprises, and by far the most attractive."

While the rest of the house slept, Lisa remained awake, staring at the all-black ensemble she'd laid over her bed's embroidered silk counterpane. There was a very short leather skirt, an oversize motorcyclist's jacket with little chains and zippers all over it; black nylons, short high-heeled boots, and a Harley-Davidson T-shirt, with a large silver skull on a choker necklace. The outfit would turn any punker's mohawk sour-apple green with envy. Lisa had bought the garments knowing she could never wear them. She loathed keeping herself restrained in a royal role.

Safe. She had to play it safe all the time, when her nature was defiant.

Nowadays she was seeing more of Laurel and Meritt than she had during the entire decade after they'd left Washington. Laughingly, they fought over who could do what favor for Sam. Yet Meritt's and Laurel's good deeds were more valuable than Lisa's, because they were so short of time. They were always running up and down Manhattan Island, frantically trying to keep up with the busy schedules that impelled their lives forward.

Caught in a reverie, Lisa's blue eyes glazed over. She couldn't understand the strange mood that had taken her over, or what had inspired it.

Like a sleepwalker, she walked the corridors till she reached Sam's room. She snapped on the green banker's lamp next to the bed. The scotch he'd had tonight insured he wouldn't wake up. Sam worked at Forster, Dunn by day and drank at night. His friends knew he'd stop drinking eventually because the swinishness would bore him. He was sad, but he wasn't touched by self-pity.

She thought of the first day she'd met him, in the U.S. Capitol, of all places. Vaguely she remembered vowing she'd get him into bed sometime. He really is handsome, Lisa thought as she looked down at Sam's sleeping face. Yet Sam obviously set no store by his looks. His lack of ego was charming. She patted his springy dark blond hair, and leaned down to smell smoke, shampoo and sweat in it. His torso was bare under the sheets, revealing strong, square shoulders and a light mat of brown chest hair, which Lisa desperately longed to touch. Her fists were clenched at her sides, her back was ramrod straight, her eyes glittered like a demon's as she stood paralyzed, staring at him with fascination.

Sam woke, and saw that a light was on. Maybe it'd been turned on by one of the staff, looking for his shoes to polish, he thought. In this old-fashioned kind of household they probably did that. Maybe. Sam closed his eyes. He hated being awake.

The following night, Sam and Lisa had dinner in. She overmixed his drinks to get him drunk. When he was malleable, she led him upstairs, where he fell upon her bed in a stupor. He chuckled as she strained to get all his clothes off without his help. Naked, she climbed on top of him and bent over, and as she kissed him his arms came up around her smooth, bare neck. After a clumsy bout of sex, Sam passed out.

Lisa lay beside him, her body transported, her face illuminated by the twin stars of her eyes. An honest, true emotion was filtering into her; she loved Sam! It was Sam Ross she'd been waiting for all these empty, meaningless years. It was Sam who was worthy of her. She didn't need the money of a Winthrop Wharton—she only needed her old friend, who was now and forever, her love.

Restless, she got up to turn on a light and regard herself in the mirror, and saw a beauty she'd never known before. Lisa rejoiced at the appearance of her hair, which stood on end where Sam had pulled at it. She ran her hands up her thighs, which Sam had caressed, and they tingled agreeably. Lisa's entire being had come to life, as if ecstasy was something she'd breathed into every pore. This emotion, so alien to her, made her feel free and joyous, brimming with self-respect.

For the rest of the night she lay next to Sam, enraptured, studying all the mysteries of his face. In the morning he opened bloodshot eyes and looked around Lisa's room in confusion. His eyebrows shot up when he saw Lisa right beside him.

"Take it easy," she said in a low, silken voice, pressing a hand against Sam's chest. "It's Saturday morning, you don't have to be at work." The heavy curtains were shut against the morning light.

"But there are things I needed to get done—Lisa, what am I doing in your bed? What did I do to you last night? God, I'm sorry..."

Lisa made a seductive smirk. "I'm not sorry. You were wonderful."

"I was?" Sam was floundering. What was a tactful way to tell a generous friend that they couldn't do this again?

Lisa extended her naked left leg over Sam's legs, and half-rolled on top of him. He already had an erection. "Prove to me that you can be just as wonderful this morning."

Even as he despised himself for passivity and lack of control, Sam pulled her to him.

That day he stopped drinking hard liquor, because he never wanted to make an alcohol-influenced mistake again.

Still shellshocked by his personal tragedy, Sam robotically continued to accept Lisa's *largesse*. Her personality was a blend of seductiveness and iron, and he knew better than to oppose her. When he made love to her, the emotions that inspired him were gratitude and affection.

Lisa realized how destiny had put them together so conveniently, at the right time. Without knowing, they'd been waiting for each other for almost a decade. Everything Sam said, Lisa interpreted as love, love with a future. When he'd say, "I'd like to see Springsteen again sometime soon," Lisa took it to mean, "I'd like to see Springsteen *with you* soon." A couple of days after his remark, she asked Sam, "Would you like to invite Bruce Springsteen to dinner?" She wanted him to know she could lay the world at his feet. Sam laughed and said, "He's a pretty busy guy. . . ."

Where her life had been a drab continuum enlivened only by shopping, suddenly every day was magic and exhilarating. Sam would go to work early in the morning and return late in the evening when a fire had been built up in Lisa's drawing room. Sitting before the fireplace, they'd drink from Winthrop's wine cellar and dine on York ham, lobster, rosy prawns, and strawberries and cream.

Lisa was enthralled by Sam's conversation; she adored every opinion that issued from his lips. She was charmed by his slightest gesture; she was enchanted even by the way he brushed his teeth. He looked so handsome lighting a cigarette it took her breath away. Every night her hungry body ate and tasted of Sam's, and could never get enough of it. Love was the best aphrodisiac, she'd read, and certainly, none of her orgasms were faked with Sam.

For the first time she saw paradise. No wonder people made such a big deal about love and romance. During the day Lisa listened to the top forty radio, because she finally identified with all those dopey teenybopper songs: "Do That to Me One More Time," "Love You Inside Out," "You Light Up My Life." The world re-created anew to her, the skies bluer, the flowers sweeter, food tastier. Winthrop's wine came from bursting grapes grown specially for Lisa and Sam.

Lisa showed him how to have fun in ways only the very wealthy can afford to indulge. When he offhandedly remarked, "I'd like to visit the Grand Canyon," she hired a private plane for them the next day; and they made an overnight pilgrimage to Colorado. She took him to Christie's to watch an auction and to stores that were open by appointment only.

Lisa learned the thrill of seeing through a lover's eyes when Sam pointed out funny little sights on the street and indicated odd details on buildings that escaped normal notice. He showed her New York sites that had been used in *Kramer vs. Kramer, Manhattan, Taxi Driver* and *Midnight Cowboy.* No man had ever delighted her so totally. Sam often bought Lisa ratty little bunches of daisies sold on the corner; they were much more precious to her than any bouquet from florist Kenneth Turner. Over-eager, Lisa took them as a proclamation of love. She read far too much into his kindness.

She was so sure that no one, not even her servants, knew she was infatuated with her houseguest, though her eyes were an open book to read. Reality rudely intruded when Laurel called her one day. "How would you like to go to lunch and hear me whine about unemployment?"

Christ, Laurel! If Laurel had any idea Sam was having sex with Lisa, she'd call it incest. Lisa made up an excuse, then Laurel asked how Sam was doing. "Just fine," Lisa snapped, and hung up in a foul mood. Wait till the day Laurel and Meritt found out Sam had chosen Lisa for his very own!

Three weeks after Sam had moved into the Wharton house, Winthrop came home, and Sam was relieved of sexual duty. When Winthrop left one week later, Lisa caught on that Sam wanted to pull away from her. They never discussed the affair openly, but Lisa stopped pressing him for sex and time. "He needs time to himself," she justified aloud, pacing in her bedroom. "When he's ready, he'll come back, and we can plan our future."

Late one evening Sam returned from work and told Lisa he'd bought a condominium on East Eighty-fifth Street. His belongings were going to be moved from the West Side to the East Side within the week. "I can't thank you and Winthrop enough for letting me stay in this wonderful house for such a long stay. In particular, I want to thank *you* for getting me through this tough time. I hope I wasn't too much of a burden." He was referring obliquely to their fling.

The smile Lisa had affected hurt at the cheeks. She knew if she had a fit or pressured him, he'd never come back. "Oh, it was nothing. Think no more of it."

Sam's guilt was monumental, as if he'd been on a month-long drunk and just returned to his senses. He would never stop regretting his sexual involvement with Lisa. He felt guilty for having slept with a married woman and guilty for perhaps leading her on. Since Lisa made no big deal of their affair, he assumed that she wanted to forget it as much as he did.

The day Sam left her house for good, she broke down in anguished hysterics. Since she'd never been in love before, she'd also never experienced the pain of loss.

She lay in her drawing room before the fireplace on the rug where she and her lover had dined and laughed and talked. The black, empty hole of the unlit hearth represented her insides. She wondered how to continue her life, or how she'd even have the strength to get up and leave this room.

Then Lisa's sensible side took over. She reassured herself that her future with Sam was merely temporarily delayed. After all, he'd bought a place on the East Side only twenty blocks from her. That meant he wanted to remain relatively close by. Tomorrow she should begin investigating the terms of a divorce from Winthrop Wharton. She'd grant him full custody of their baby; that should make Daddy Warbucks happy.

She still felt the need for comfort from a person who

also knew Sam, a person who was the closest thing she knew of a soul mate. She called California and told Martin Vanderziel, "Martin, I need you." Without questions he booked a flight on the next plane flying to New York.

• *Twenty-nine* •

Feeling almost mischievous, Laurel called George St. Clark's managing editor of the Washington *Tribune*, a man she'd come to know over the course of many D.C. parties. "Hey Manny, is there room enough for both me and my soon-to-be ex on your paper?"

After talking some more, the editor said, "What kind of position were you looking for?"

Laurel gibed, "Something that gives me wealth, power and fame."

"You want to be Wayne Newton, huh?" Then Manny discreetly asked, "You don't really want to work in the same place as George, do you?" From the disbelief in his tone, Laurel knew he'd heard the brutal way her marriage had ended.

"No, I've decided to stay in the Big Onion. So I'm calling to see if you need any stringers up here."

"I'll tell you what we could use—a body on the Street. It's not enough anymore to get all the Wall Street stats via the wires. I'd really like to have somebody who can chart the effect of the Big Board on federal policy, and vice versa. Especially if Reagan wins the election and tries supply-side economics. Do you know anything about high finance?"

"Me? Are you kidding? When I ran for Congress, my

strongest area of expertise was in U.S. economic indicators and domestic business circles. I'm no Maynard Keynes, but I'm on par with David Stockman."

"Really? Listen, I'll kick this around with the guys and see if we've got enough money in the budget to put you on the Street. Send your résumé in, too. I'll call you in a couple of days to tell you how it's going." Manny added, "Have you voted yet?" It was the first Tuesday of November—Election Day, the Superbowl that would determine who was going to be the most powerful man in the world: Carter or Reagan.

"No, but I'm registered locally and I'm just about to go pull the lever."

Laurel hung up and threw her arms into the air, shouting "Yeah!" She knew it would rankle George eternally if she were hired by his *Tribune*, but she didn't care. He was history. Out of all the job prospects she'd considered, the *Tribune* position sounded most likely. Then her face clouded over, for she had lied to Manny. She didn't know a damn thing about government expenditure and trade deficits and budget projections! Sam Ross did. Her face brightened. He had the rare talent of turning inflation figures and interest rates into layman's terms. She could tap into Sam.

She looked around Meritt's austere living room, which caught the morning sun so brightly it hurt her eyes. She had never liked living on her friend's charity. Meritt had babysat her for nearly four months. Quickly Laurel covered her camisole with a thick chocolate turtleneck and pulled on jeans. She threw on a leather jacket, grabbed her shoulder bag and left for the tram.

Her hair billowing behind her, she ran for it and leapt on. As the ugly little car shimmied along its cable over the East River, she thought of *Nighthawks*, the Sylvester Stallone movie in which a terrorist stopped the car mid-way over the river and started killing passenger after passenger until his demands were met. Just a typical day in the big city. The car traveled over York, First, Second, and swung into Fifty-ninth Street, letting Laurel off in the heart of the city.

The presidential vote was a hard decision, since Laurel knew reporters who knew the candidates all too well. With her own eyes she'd seen Jimmy Carter lash out viciously at an aide, then display his big toothed-smile for the camera. Reagan would be a great guy to ask over for a barbecue, but she didn't think she wanted his finger on the Button.

After she voted, Laurel caught the subway to the East Village. Reaching St. Mark's Place, she felt as if she were taking a walk into Meritt's past. This was the tough turf where Meritt had lived as a teenager, in the days of Jeremy Serkin and Heloise Kiedrowski, who was now a baby mogul in Hollywood. Jeremy was reduced to directing puppets on a kiddies TV show. Laurel walked beside the ever-present black-clad punks, past cafés where night-crawling trendies were finishing breakfast in their party-going duds. She tried the door of a large, domed Moorish-type building and found it open. This was the theater where the musical version of Oscar Wilde's *The Importance of Being Earnest* would open.

Laurel entered the auditorium and plunked down in a rear row. On the stage six dancers were running through an elaborately choreographed number. The small orchestra under the stage played a prelude, and Meritt assumed center stage wearing street clothes. Laurel was in luck: Meritt, in the role of Gwendolyn Fairfax, was about to do her big solo number.

Meritt had never considered singing as one of her assets, but the theater company wanted her voice anyway. She sang a sincere, shuddering vibrato that ached with loneliness. As Laurel listened, Meritt's voice slid down the back of Laurel's spine like an ice cube.

The song was well-written, too. It was a catchy pop tune, with hooks in all the right places. Laurel sat up attentively, like a dog who's just heard a whistle no one else could. Was it imaginable that this version of *The Impor-tance of Being Ernest* was going to be a hit? After the play had become a cliché in the English-speaking world, since it had been staged everywhere and filmed several times? Laurel had long worried about Meritt's vocation, even when she was a hit on "The Gold Coast." Unless you got to the top and became a star, your life was wasted. After Meritt had spent nine years in show business, was it possi-ble she would finally become a star?

Meritt would never be the same again.

The best-read critics all showed up on opening night, eager to chew apart some pretentious upstarts for their vul-garization of Oscar Wilde's wit. They left charmed, and wrote that the musical version brought a hip eighties sensi-bility to *The Importance of Being Earnest*.

Singled out for special mention was exotically lovely Meritt du Nord, who added a unique twist to each of her lines, squeezing out the maximum possible humor. As soon as she appeared on the stage the audience stirred in-stinctively with expectation. There was a special cachet even to her least significant gestures. It seemed that until this show, Meritt had kept her talent in eclipse, saving her very best for the role of Gwendolyn Fairfax.

During rehearsals, Meritt's weekly pay had been thirty-five dollars. Her agent, Carrie Enright, got her top salary, a private dressing room, and her name on the marquee. Mer-itt's performance and the accompanying excitement over her "overnight discovery" was partly attributable to the move of *The Importance of Being Earnest* to a Broadway theater, where the show continued playing to sold-out audiences. The show also drew a lot of unwarranted attention to Oscar Moore Travis, the fortunately named interior decorator often compared to Wilde.

* * *

"What was it like living in Winthrop Wharton's house?" Laurel asked Sam as she faced him over his glass desk. "Tell me what it's like to have the best things in life available at the touch of a button."

Sam leaned back in his upholstered swivel chair and laced his fingers atop his faded Harvard sweatshirt. "It was fun to try that life-style once. I absolutely loved it that Lisa could summon a plane to zip us out to the Grand Canyon and back within a day. But when the luxury goes to the point of glut—it's just not that great. Would *you* like to dine on caviar and champagne every day?"

Laurel had been given a job at the New York desk of the Washington *Tribune*. Today was Saturday, and Sam was conducting his special class in economics at his Forster, Dunn office. It was inside a gleaming chrome and glass tower, and Sam's office was furnished in gleaming chrome and glass as well. His window afforded him a view of the stately Brooklyn Bridge, blurred today by January snowflakes that filled the sky with spun sugar.

Sam started to say something, then stopped. Inhaling a deep breath, he said, "You know what I feel guilty about?" His mouth twisted down in absolute shame. "I—I had an affair with Lisa while I stayed with her." He looked out at the whirling snowflakes with an angry expression. "Damn! I was sleeping with the wife of a man *right in his own house*. A man I deeply admire! Fine way of showing it."

Laurel had suspected a fling between the two. After all, Lisa's hit list was longer than the Manhattan phone book. Yet Laurel was shocked, and queerly jealous. Her eyes flicked to platinum-framed photos of Kevin and Darrel. She cleared her throat. "Well, face it. You were in real rough shape when you accepted Lisa's offer."

"That's no excuse. I feel that I used her."

"Did you ever consider that *she* might have been using *you?*"

"What?" Sam struck her with the high beam of his coruscating green eyes. "What interest of Lisa's could I possibly serve?"

"You could provide her with something she's never allowed herself to feel—kindness. Respect."

Sam shifted uncomfortably in his chair. "I don't know about that. She had a lot of fun with me, even though I was pretty out of it back then."

"How did you two end it?"

"I bought my place on Eighty-fifth and left."

"So are you in touch now, or are things a little strained?"

"No. Since I'm rarely home, Lisa calls me here about once a day. To check on me."

Laurel said sarcastically, "Yeah, I'll bet. She doesn't call to 'check on' me or Meritt anymore, even though Meritt's the newest celebrity in town."

"I feel so dirty I'm not even fit to grow penicillin on." Sam shut off the IBM computer on his desk, and they took the elevator to the first floor. The building's cavernous lobby was dominated by angular, abstract silver sculpture, and a fountain that sent patterns of water sheeting over green marble. Today the fountain was shut off. Bundled against the cold, they walked from the deserted streets of the financial district to the Lion's Head, a writer's hangout on Christopher Street. Settled in a wooden booth, Sam ordered Bailey's and coffee for the two of them. Their cheeks were rosy from the cold.

He toyed with some matches after he'd lit a cigarette. Avoiding Laurel's eyes, he said, "You know, when my boys died, you were going through a real hard thing . . . but I wasn't around to help. There you were at the wake and all, your face swollen and bruised, but I didn't know what to say."

"You know how it is," Laurel said, shrugging. "What could you have done for me? Warned me not to go to Carol Carole? Could you have been on the spot to defend me from the pugilist I married?" She brought a coffee cup up to her lips, but detected that the ebony brew was hot enough to melt lead. "No, no one can help you in a disaster that's going to happen unless God stops it."

"I feel God is everywhere . . . but He wasn't there at my children's deaths."

Laurel's expression was soft and clouded. "In life people experience so many tragedies, and if they wish, they can share their troubles with others. But who would dream of the horror that hit you? No one can really empathize with you." Unconsciously, her hand crossed the table to lie on Sam's. Of its own volition his thumb lightly stroked her knuckles.

"I don't care what others say; you never get over a loss like death. You never accept it. You live with it. Your pain always travels alongside you." He added, "I'd grown up thinking that we are all capable of running our lives, and now I know how little control we have."

He released Laurel's hand, and she tried her coffee again. "Hey, I've always been too scared or tactful to ask this, but . . . are you divorced yet? What happened to Viola?"

"She moved to Salvation City and allowed me to divorce her, just like she said she wanted." Sam gave Laurel a rather sly look. "So she is now in the hands of your natural mother."

"And Carol Carole is welcome to her." Laurel ran both hands over the sides of her head, so that her hair fell in layers to her shoulders. "So, are you thinking of dating again?"

"No. After my involvement with Lisa I'm going to cool it for a long while, I think." Awkward with the subject, Sam raised his glass for a toast. "Here's to those who wish me well, and those who don't can go to hell."

When Laurel returned to the Roosevelt Island apartment late that afternoon, she found Meritt home between her Saturday matinee and evening performances, doing as little as possible; in other words, relaxing aggressively. She lay on the living room couch like Cleopatra on her royal barge, with newspapers, magazines, coffee cups and remains of snacks strewn all over the floor and end tables. Her glossy raven hair was pulled into a topknot like Pebbles Flintstone's. "Have you seen the papers today?" she asked Laurel.

"Of course not," Laurel answered flippantly. "Reporters never read the paper." The front section of the New York *Times* came flying at her.

"It's on page three. Andy Smith has been given an appointment in the new administration."

Laurel read that Ronald Reagan's director of internal affairs had asked Andy Smith to be his assistant director of internal affairs. "Ugh! That chicken sucker! This means he'll be working inside the White House."

Hearing the words spoken aloud, Meritt felt a shiver of dread. Her eyes met Laurel's, and they were pages again, worried, uncertain, and immobilized.

• *Thirty* •

The following month Sam called Laurel at her Washington *Tribune* bureau, an office she shared with two other *Tribune* correspondents. "Are you free after work?" he asked. "Now that you've learned your ABC's in economics, I want to burden you with a private project of mine."

"How private is it?" Laurel swiveled her chair around to look out at East Forty-first Street. She could see part of Grand Central Station's elaborate *beaux arts* façade.

"It's so private that only five of us know about it."

Laurel's jaw dropped. "You mean the . . . Trojan Horse Project?"

"The same."

At 8:30 Sam was waiting for Laurel in the lobby of his building at East Eighty-fifth Street. She unzipped her leather bomber jacket to reveal the cartons of Cantonese delights staying warm inside. The elevator whisked them to the twelfth floor. When he opened his door, Laurel started at the cigar store Indian who loomed in the entrance, intimidating and powerful. "Like it?" Sam asked. "It was in the window of an antique store on Madison. It said, 'Take me home.'"

"I'm more partial to giant fire-breathing statues of Ramses, myself."

Sam's home was almost vacant. The rooms looked onto Central Park, four blocks away . . . and the dull apartment building across Eighty-fifth Street. There were two balconies, and three and a half bathrooms, only one of which offered toilet paper. The dining room boasted a card table with two chairs. Unpacked boxes were scattered in every room. In the guest room a group of high school sports trophies stood on the floor by a television set. Sam's room had a large comforter-covered futon mattress lying on the floor next to a reading lamp and an alarm clock. "Did you decorate this place yourself?" Laurel teased. "Or did Oscar Moore Travis help you?"

His living room had some furniture, but the room was so large all the pieces looked marooned. He had a long white couch which he urged Laurel to put her shoes on. "If I can't soil a piece of furniture, I don't want it," he said. A majestic George III mirror hung on the wall over it, and in front of it, a large Parsons table lacquered onyx black was covered with computer equipment and wires. From a distance, two large armchairs covered in leopard-spotted calfskin faced the Parsons table and couch. Track lighting created a soft golden glow over the room. "There's very little here from my house on the Upper West Side," Sam commented. "It's not due to bad memories. It's 'cause I'm in an income bracket to afford some better furnishings."

They ate out of the food cartons in the dining room, then Sam brought a coffee jug with two cups into the living room.

He sat down at the main terminal, which was hooked into Forster, Dunn's mainframe system. Still wearing his banker's suit, he turned on the computer and logged on. His fingers deftly flew over the keyboard to request a program. Laurel didn't feel comfortable sitting right next to him, so she folded her lanky body in sections and sat on the soft gray carpeting next to Sam's legs. They immediately got down to business.

"Laurel," Sam asked, "over the years, have you thought much about that bogus 'Trojan Horse' conspiracy? Everything we overheard at Smitty's house?"

Very gravely she answered, "It's almost become an obsession for me. We all said, 'Let's just forget this; let's pretend it never happened; let's not talk about it.' But whatever we've done, wherever we've gone, there's been this *thing* around us, this feeling that something horrible is going to happen." She looked up at Sam's pensive face. "And nothing's happened."

"It will happen. Soon. I've studied the economic indicators, and they show that the country is vulnerable to a Trojan Horse scenario." Sam opened a file to show Laurel a list of megabillion-buck banks. "These banks have lent over two hundred billion dollars to foreign countries. If several of those countries—Argentina, Poland, Mexico, Brazil—defaulted, these American banks would tumble into insolvency.

"My guess is that the Trojan Horse list includes people in those countries with the power to declare default."

He scrolled to another list of financial institutions. "These are more of the largest banks in the country. Each of their portfolios is filled with loans to corporations that recently have either filed for bankruptcy or are in very sad shape.

"Again, I'll guess that the Trojan Horse list includes people in those debtor companies who would be blackmailed into bankruptcy."

Sam paused to light a cigarette. Laurel was puzzled. "You're way beyond me."

"I have no idea what I'm saying, but I can't stop," said Sam deprecatingly. "From what I've read, top honchos at the Federal Reserve Board are demanding that interest rates go up, which could possibly trigger deep plunges in stock and bond prices. The Fed Chairman, Paul Volcker, wants lower interest rates, but his advisers are fighting him."

Laurel asked, "Do you think some of those underlings at the Federal Reserve Board are *already* being blackmailed by Oliver Remick's operatives?"

"Who knows?" Sam gazed down at Laurel. His face was lit by a faint green glow from the screen. "So, what do you think? Doesn't it seem that the scene is set for trouble?"

"These are scarcy circumstances," Laurel answered. "Meritt ought to know about this. I'll tell her when I get back to the apartment. We've got to figure out what to do here. Doesn't our government have built-in safeguards against total collapse now? Some front line of security?"

"If the situation wasn't so serious, the mutual interest of all sectors responsible for the U.S. economy could pull together to keep the overall system from falling apart. But the strain *this* time would be too strong. There'd be no way to stimulate our economy. The banks couldn't help faltering corporations because they wouldn't have any cash flow. Any crisis of confidence in the banking system could give us another depression more disastrous than the big one of the thirties.

"If the Trojan Horse does exist, everything could come crashing down tomorrow—or anytime in the next couple of years. It depends on when Remick's operatives decide to put the squeeze on potential blackmail victims."

Laurel shivered. "What's the next step we can take? Can we find out any more through the computer?"

"We can break into Andy's computer with this modem." Sam pointed at the telephone hookup that enabled one computer to talk to another.

"How do you know he's got a computer?"

"Because IBM installed personal desk computers at the White House just this month. And round-the-clock typists have already put a lot of files on disc. Watch." Sam punched 202-456-1414 on the keyboard.

"That's the main phone number at the White House," Laurel recalled. Just as she spoke, the green wording on Sam's monitor read:

THIS IS THE WHITE HOUSE MAIN DATANET. PLEASE LOG ON WITH USER PASSWORD.

Sam typed in eight letters: WHITEHSE. "Not very clever, is it? It took me about nine tries to guess the right password. Every computer hacker in the country is going to be messing with the White House system until they come up with an uncrackable security system."

"It's typical of the way the country's run—bad security on stuff that should be the most guarded," Laurel commented.

"Too bad you didn't get into Congress." Sam sighed as the monitor displayed a Jackson Pollock chaos of data. "They need someone with the sense to change basic things." The screen went blank a moment, then presented a lengthy list of White House subsystems to choose from. Each heading listed the fourteen Administration departments, followed by dozens of bureaus and offices.

Sam moved the cursor to Office of Internal Affairs. When he hit the enter key, the message read: "LOG ON PLEASE." Sam typed in the phone number of the Assistant Director to the Director of Internal Affairs, Andy's White House office number: 202-456-9970. Again the screen read: "LOG ON PLEASE."

"This is how far I got last night," Sam said. "I can't figure out the password."

"Ask the computer to help you out. Isn't it true that the more complex the security system, the more it helps you?"

Sam typed in, "HELP LOG ON." The monitor replied, "HELP NOT AVAILABLE. LOG ON."

"Try 'Help Andrew Smith III,'" Laurel urged. When Sam typed that in, the computer responded, "HELP ANDREW SMITH III NOT AVAILABLE. LOG ON." Sam typed in, "HELP ANDY SMITH."

The monitor displayed, "ANDY SMITH, ASSISTANT DIRECTOR TO DIRECTOR OF OFFICE OF INTERNAL AFFAIRS." Laurel cheered. Under the title was the list of files in Andy's White House office: insurance, correspondence, office management, personal. At the bottom of the list was the heading: "TROJAN HORSE LISTS." Stunned, they both gaped at the screen for a full minute.

"Holy mackerel, Batman," Laurel whispered. "We've been right all along."

Sam placed the cursor on "TROJAN HORSE," then hit the enter key. Again the screen displayed the request: "LOG ON." He typed in eight numbers, and the screen read, "IDENTIFICATION NOT RECOGNIZED BY SYSTEM. YOU HAVE BEEN DISCONNECTED."

The screen went blank. Sam took off his jacket and sat back. "All that's keeping us from opening the Trojan Horse is the password. It's got to be an eight-letter or number password. If could be anything." His dark blond hair fell over his face, but he was too troubled to notice.

Laurel suggested, "Program your computer to try different combinations of letters and numbers."

"Do you know how many millions of combinations of the twenty-six letters and/or the ten numbers there can be in eight spaces?"

"No matter how many there are, we've got to try!" Laurel looked at Sam steadily and gravely.

He tilted his head with a resigned expression, sat forward and reached for a box of floppy discs, all the size of 45 rpm records. He inserted a disc into a disc drive, then punched in "00000000." The number combination appeared in the upper left corner of his monitor. After punching a combination of commands, the number was automatically followed by a "00000001," then "00000011," then "00000111."

Sam explained, "As fast as you see those numbers appear, each of them is tried as a password. If it hits the right number . . . it'll be 'open sesame' to the Trojan Horse."

"Sam, even if we gain entry to the file, there's a possibility there's nothing in it."

He appeared not to have heard. "Can you imagine the arrogance and stupidity of Andy's using the Trojan Horse as a file name?" He put his palms together and raised them to the ceiling. "I thank the Lord for cretins in high places. Still, it's going to take weeks to run through all those combinations. Time is on Andy's side."

It was late. "Excuse me," Laurel said, and went to use the bathroom. Before entering the living room again she paused in the hallway where it led into the kitchen. She spied on Sam there, watching him clean up, rinsing their coffee cups and utensils, throwing out the empty food cartons, prudently saving the ones with food left in them. The future of the world might depend on this quiet, careful man—this man who'd lost everything, but still kept going. She felt a sudden, terrible surge of love for him.

Two weeks later Meritt called Sam at his office. "Sam, have you figured out the password yet? Laurel and I have been chewing our nails off worrying, but we didn't want to bother you. Now I have to go to the Coast. My plane leaves at midnight and I can't take off without knowing."

"Well then, let's meet in my lobby tonight at eight, and I'll show you what I've got so far, then I'll take you to the airport."

When Sam took Meritt up to his apartment, she went right to his computer setup. Her mouth dropped. The monitor was filled solidly with eight-digit number combinations. They scrolled up in steady horizontal lines, like rows of infantrymen marching en masse, as the computer continued attempting to log on to Andy's Trojan Horse file.

"This is nuts!" she exclaimed, and she looked up at Sam

with a face that said, *"You're* nuts." "Has this system been trying passwords for the past two weeks?"

Sam nodded. "It's been trying for twelve days straight, twenty-four hours a day. And it hasn't even started on alphabet letters yet."

"I'll bet your system is going to find every existing eight-digit password *except* Andy's. There's got to be a simpler way to figure out the password into the file."

"I'm sure there's a simpler way, but then, when have any of us done anything the simple way?" Sam shoved his hands into his coat pockets. "What are you going to the airport for? You're supposed to be appearing every night on Broadway."

Meritt's eyebrows quirked upward. "You'll get a charge out of this. We've got a hiatus this week. I'm running out to California to see friends, and appear in . . . the new *Star Trek* movie!"

Excitedly Sam rushed to her and whirled her around. "My God! That's wonderful! One of us Trekkies is finally getting a chance to serve on the Starship *Enterprise!*"

Meritt sighed a bit regretfully. "I won't get to serve on the *Enterprise,* exactly. I'm going to be a crew member on an enemy ship. I don't get any lines, but I get to die in the background, behind Ricardo Montalban. My costume, or my uniform, actually, is a fur bikini. I got the part when my agent sent the casting director a picture of me in a *real* bikini." Meritt gave a little grin. "Carrie doesn't like me taking such a small credit. She got the role as a favor to me." Keyed up, she bounced on her feet. Her amber eyes sparkled with happiness. "Oh, Sam, everything's come full circle for me. But now that I've got what I really want, the awful *thing* that we kept buried so long . . . is it really coming true? Is everything going to fall apart?"

"We've got to keep trying to prevent it, Meritt," Sam answered. "Come on, get your coat. You've got a date in space, and it's time to beam you up."

· *Thirty-one* ·

Sam was running around the Central Park reservoir at dawn. His legs moved automatically while his mind tried out password ideas and discarded them. When he got into his apartment, the phone was ringing. Meritt was on the other end, sounding very far away. "Meritt, what are you doing? It's three A.M. where you are."

"I just figured it out. Remember you told Laurel and me that passwords usually have something to do with the person who chose the password? 'Honeypie.' Andy's wife. The password to the Trojan Horse file is 'Honeypie'!"

"'Honey...' That's eight letters. Huh. Let me try that on the computer." Sam carried the phone to his couch. While cradling the receiver between his neck and his right ear, he punched in a return to the Andy Smith system, then put the cursor on "Trojan Horse" and hit the enter key.

"Log on," he read to Meritt. "Let's see—H-O-N-E-Y-P-I-E."

The screen went blank, and the computer whirred. Meritt heard Sam gasp long distance. "My god, you *are* right! There's this huge list coming up on the screen."

The structure rolling before his eyes was as complicated and layered as *War and Peace* and *Crime and Punishment* put together. "Here are names of guys at major banks... corporations... insurance companies... the Federal Reserve Board... the Pentagon!" Sam started hooting as loudly and vigorously as if he were watching a grand slam at a World Series baseball game. "Men and women from the entire spectrum of the military industrial complex, Meritt! It must have taken the Trojan Horse organization years to get the goods on these guys."

"It did," Meritt said dryly. "Over ten years, Sam, I've got to go to bed now."

"How can you sleep when you've given us the key to evidence that could hang a hundred men for treason?"

"Because I've stayed up all night, and now I'm tired. And I'm too frightened to let myself think anymore."

Sleepily Laurel answered her phone on the tenth ring. "Grab the tram and get over here!" Sam told her.

When she entered his building lobby, Sam was waiting. His arms went over her shoulders and scooped her toward the elevator. Zipping skyward, he told her everything that had happened since Meritt's phone call. "The operation has its own communication network and bank accounts. Wait till you see all the people accumulated on the Trojan Horse list, all the people the nonaligned nations' organization has power over."

"The ones who can be blackmailed into submission?"

"Yes. The names look like missiles ready for launching." Sam was full of the triumph of discovery. "It's amazing how just a couple of hundred people, employed in the right organizations, working singly, unaware that they're acting in unison, could bring down the economy."

Laurel sat down in front of the monitor and looked at the lists illuminated there. On the left side, alphabetically, was a long roster of businesses, financial institutions, and influence groups: the Business Council, the Council of Foreign Relations, the Committee for Economic Development, the Trilateral Commission. In the middle was a column of names, followed by job titles like investment group manager and director of the board. None of the names were familiar.

The right side of the screen held a letter or letters of the alphabet for each name. "Is this a code?" Laurel asked Sam, who was banging cupboard doors in the kitchen.

"Yes, a very simple one. I've figured out that the letters stand for the crime or indiscretion each man or woman can be exploited for. 'D' for drug dealing, 'E' for embezzlement or extortion, 'H' for homosexual..."

"'I' for infidelity?"

"That's my guess. Would you like a bowl of cereal?"

"No, thanks, I'm too wrought up to eat." Laurel kept hitting the return key, and the names rolled up the screen from the bottom. "Judging from these folks' jobs, I'd say 'B' stands for unethical business deals," she guessed. "'T' for tax dodging... Then it looks like 'LM' for, uh, legal malpractice."

Sam came into the room holding a bowl of cereal in one hand. He sat next to Laurel on the couch. "Of course, there's a lot more detail to some of the codes, but I think we've got the basics. The more comprehensive list of extortion situations and behaviors must be with the heads of the Trojan Horse. The perpetrators, wherever they are."

"Should we take this to the FBI?" Sam shook his head no, and Laurel added, "I'm still afraid of coming across like a conspiracy paranoid."

Sam set down the cereal bowl. "We have to talk to the whole bunch first. When we take our information to the authorities, we'll have to explain that we heard about the conspiracy when we were pages, which means all five of us will be implicated. Even Lisa and Martin deserve the chance to make suggestions about how we proceed from there."

"You're right," Laurel agreed. "We should get together as soon as possible."

"I guess there's nothing left to do except... start the printout."

While the printer was running, Sam stood in front of his window. He gazed without seeing as the morning sun cast saffron rays over Central Park's treetops and tinted the eastern faces of the tall buildings of the Upper West Side. Laurel regarded him from across the room. Something about the way the light glowed around his silhouette revealed a beauty in him that she felt deeply.

"Sam," she said, "I can't ever see you alone again. Let's do any further work over the phone . . ."

"*Why?*"

"You're not my friend anymore. I think of you differently now . . . and it hurts to be around you." Her voice trembled.

"What are you saying?"

"Over the past month we've been dealing with issues that are, without exaggeration, earth-shaking. Living on the edge of global disaster teaches you what's basic and important— what really matters. I've . . . I've fallen in love with you. And I can't be with you so much, knowing I can't have you."

Behind her, Sam cleared his throat. "Don't go away, please." He paused. "After all that's happened to me, I've been afraid to even think of loving again, afraid of the risk. But I can't keep pushing down my feelings anymore, Laurel, and pretending we're just friends. I love you, too."

Laurel turned to face him, and a hot tear fell from her cheek to his hand. "Are you telling me the truth? Is this real?"

Sam linked his arms behind her back, and she had had her answer. His face shone with affection, desire, and rejoicing. "I'm for you," he declared, and she knew it was for certain.

Suddenly awkward, they drew together in a clumsy kiss. They tried again, and their lips met crookedly. Swept up with bliss, Laurel gave out a gravelly, gurgling laugh. "I don't know what it's like to kiss a friend!"

Sam directed, "You kiss him like a lover." He pulled her to him, and this time when they kissed, clear, clean light danced through their bodies. They'd yearned to *really hug* during all those years of friendly half-embraces. Now, clasping her close to him, Sam could feel where all of Laurel's pain was, and Laurel felt everything Sam had been through, as if they were inside each other.

"My God," Laurel sighed as Sam besieged her face with

kisses, "if this is what it's like to hug you, then what is it like to make love with you?"

"That's the best part," he whispered. He cupped his hands to bring her face to him roughly, and possessed her with his mouth, kissing her passionately. She parted her lips and pushed her tongue in his mouth, sliding up and over his tongue, savoring the taste of him. Rapture unraveled through her like a ribbon. Sam pulled out the pins restraining her hair, and it cascaded silkily over her shoulders as he ran his hands through it. Then he gathered her up into his arms and carried her into the bedroom.

"I want you inside me so badly." Laurel drew Sam down against her, and as he entered her the heat within him, so fierce it hurt, raced from his loins through his heart and into his mind. She moved with him, their perfect rhythm immediately found. Simultaneously they went out of control, and the violence of the release left them both drained. It was everything they hoped for, and more.

"I love you, Sam," Laurel whispered against his moist throat as they lay entwined.

"And I love you, too, sweetheart." Sam's arms tightened around Laurel. "Oh God, how I love you."

They lay together on the warm mattress while the evening slipped into night. Sam was a passionate and artful lover, and all his sadness evaporated as Laurel welcomed every caress. Again and again he took her to the edge of the cliff, and they fell off together, floating out over the sparkling lights of the city.

At midnight they rose, disheveled and dazed from the narcotic of discovery, and looked in the refrigerator. There was a six-pack of beer and half a pizza, frosty with freezer burn. "Don't they have room service in this dump?" Laurel looped her arm around Sam's neck from behind and leaned against him. "I want some bread and wine, as well as thou. I've got to keep up my strength."

Sam dialed a place that made California pizzas. After he

hung up the phone, Laurel wrapped herself around his naked body and whispered, "More."

When the pizza arrived, they took it into the room where all of Sam's trophies and unpacked boxes were stored. He turned on a small TV and they sat on the floor to eat.

"This is the best pizza I've ever had," Laurel exclaimed.

Sam grinned knowingly. "You're imagining that. It tastes great because this is the best night we've ever had."

• *Thirty-two* •

Lisa wanted the small group to meet at her house. "Come on over tomorrow night," she told Laurel. "We'll make a dinner party of it." When Laurel asked if it wasn't awfully short notice for a party, Lisa bragged, "Look, if I wanted Peking duck served at a harem in Tangiers in a half hour, my staff could take care of it." Lisa was hoping that when Sam was reminded of what a great hostess she was, he'd want her back sooner.

"Meritt's in L.A. right now," Laurel reminded her. "How about Thursday? That's when she's due back."

The following Thursday, three of Lisa's four guests sat in Winthrop's living room. Its austere art gallery atmosphere was softened by the presence of champagne and a silver tray of hors d'oeuvres so picturesquely arranged they would have pleased Diana Vreeland. Tall, white, jasmine-scented candles flickered in candelabra set on most of the tables, washing everyone with ghostly light. There was an undercurrent of tension in the room.

"What's it like to be a star on Broadway, Meritt?" Lisa

asked. She sipped at the Cristal bubbling inside a fluted champagne glass, and savored its slight burning sensation on her tongue.

Meritt had been watching Martin, who stood in the doorway with his hands shoved deep into his jeans pockets. His forehead was tense, as though he was plagued with a migraine. The candlelight over his haunted, haunting visage made him seem as if he were half in this world and half out of it. She shuddered, and turned to Lisa. "Acting on Broadway is like having your dreams come true."

"Cut out the false modesty, Meritt," Laurel said. "Lisa wants to know what it's like to appear in national magazines, making television appearances, attending important parties, being nominated for a Tony . . . all that boring stuff." She looked at Lisa. "Did you know Meritt's already won her first award? The New York Drama Critics named her 'Best Supporting Actress in a Musical.'"

Meritt said, "Let's put it this way, Lisa. No matter what happens in my career, no matter how much talent I have or how much money I earn, I can never have anything like— like this." Meritt moved her arms to indicate the cheerless splendor of the room.

"I bet this crypt hasn't been rearranged in fifty years," Lisa muttered. She was keyed up, waiting to see Sam again. She had dressed especially for him in a thin silk flare-shouldered top that clearly displayed her breasts. The matching inky navy skirt was slit high on her left thigh. When she crossed her legs the white net of her panties could be seen.

"You know what else?" Laurel went on. "The company of *The Importance of Being Earnest* has been asked to perform in Washington, for a presidential benefit, at Kennedy Center. *And* the musical has been sold to Hollywood."

The gold gypsy chains cascading from Meritt's neck clanked and jingled as she shook her head. "A sale does not a movie make. Who knows if our version of *Ernest* will ever go into production." Nervously she ran her hand up over her face and through her hair. "Oh, what does it matter? *Every-*

thing is going to be meaningless if the Trojan Horse is implemented."

This summit on the Trojan Horse had little importance to Lisa. All she could think of was Sam. He made his entrance, carrying sheafs of computer paper in one arm. "Sorry I'm late, I just picked these up from the copy shop." With the other arm he held out a rose spray to Lisa, his hostess, and gave her a kiss on the cheek.

Lisa's back arched for his kiss. Her entire being strained greedily for him. Roses! He *did* love her, he did! Joy invaded her with the thought, and she crushed the bouquet to her breasts.

Sam gave everyone a copy of the Trojan Horse lists, then retreated to the love seat to sit with Meritt. *Of course he's trying to conceal his feeling for me,* Lisa thought, just as I am for him. No one could know until the divorce was announced.

Without wasting a word or a gesture, Sam outlined his search for proof of a Trojan Horse, and how he'd broken into Andy Smith's White House computer. He tried to keep from glancing at Laurel too much. They had agreed to hide their relationship from Lisa for a while, because Sam was afraid she might have lingering feelings for him, and he didn't want to hurt her. He wished the evening would pass quickly. Sam hated being in Winthrop Wharton's house, because it reminded him of his adultery. One month around Lisa had caused him $10 million in guilt.

He concluded by saying, "Our ten years of worry weren't groundless at all. The evidence that Oliver Remick's scheme is a reality is overwhelming. And because we five were there at the start of it, *we're* as deeply involved as Oliver Remick. It's up to us to subvert the plot."

"Why?" Lisa demanded. "No one has to know we were there! We don't have to do anything."

Speaking slowly, as if to a child, Sam explained, "Whenever any impropriety occurs, all the people associated with it are inevitably flushed out. Look at Watergate—anyone with the slightest connection to the coverup has been run down like a trapped rat and caught and indicted."

"We'll be in deep mud no matter what we do now," Merritt said.

Laurel said, "That's what we're here to decide—what do we do now?"

"How about if we go to dinner?" Lisa suggested.

Winthrop's chef had prepared cold asparagus soup, grilled swordfish, and haricots verts. Simple meal though it was, it was served on baroque hand-painted plates, with solid gold cutlery. Each place setting featured wine and water glasses and a knife rest. The table was decorated with silver candelabra, a bust of a Renaissance boy, and urns holding lilacs and peonies.

The overriding purpose of the meeting muted the dinner's elegance. Martin, Meritt, Sam, Laurel and Lisa ate silently, speaking only to comment on the food.

Throughout the main course, Lisa's eyes fixed steadily on Sam. She couldn't help it any longer. Despite his sloppy Donegal sweater and chino pants, he was devastatingly attractive, and soon he was to be hers completely.

She watched as he picked up a sea horse ornament connecting two tiny dishes that held salt and pepper. "How beautiful," he murmured. Without thinking, he twirled it in his fingers, and the salt and pepper flew. Some of it hit Laurel, and, startled, she turned to look at Sam. They both started laughing, the fond, sharing laughter of love. Lisa's insides shriveled as if she'd swallowed a bottle of lye.

Suddenly Martin brought them back to the reason for their meeting. "Look, man, as soon as we turn this information over to the FBI or CIA or whatever, *we're* going to be under suspicion. Even if we're cleared of participating in the Trojan Horse plot, we'll be accessories to treason, because we've withheld information. And no matter what happens, good or bad, the press will enjoy making headlines of everything we've ever done wrong. Each one of us has a lot to hide."

Laurel was incensed. "So you're saying that to protect

our reputations, we should forget the Trojan Horse? And let our country go down the tubes? We're not frightened teenagers anymore. We're adults, and it's time to face the responsibility we've avoided for so long."

"Why don't we dump this whole thing into Andy Smith's lap?" Meritt suggested. "He's the kingpin in the whole conspiracy. Let him decide how to turn himself into the authorities and shoulder the burden of explaining the plot."

"When that disgusting worm turns himself in he'll accuse us of whatever he can think of," Lisa warned. "Why don't we just off him? Let's can the talk, and go for action."

"'Off him'?"

"Yeah, kill him. Since Andy's the player in the White House, we could stop the entire thing by getting rid of him."

With heavy sarcasm Meritt said, "*Sure!* Why don't we all run down to Little Italy right now to hire a Mafia hit man!"

"We don't need to hire a hit man," Lisa continued. "Martin would be glad to kill Andy. After all, he's killed for his country before, in Vietnam. Bumping off Andy would *really* be a service to this country."

Martin had scarcely seen action during his brief months as a soldier, but he took up Lisa's arguments. "I go practice-shooting every week at a rifle gallery in town. I'm an excellent marksman."

As if everything were decided, Lisa said, "We'll take care of it, then."

Taken aback, Laurel said, "Lisa, *no!* Andy Smith is the tip of the iceberg! He's just one figure in the plot—and our only connection to it. We've got to talk to him." She added, "If you killed Andy we'd never have a chance at cutting off the Trojan Horse before it started."

Martin said, "Okay, talk to him, get the information you need, and then I'll wipe him out before he can finger us."

In unison Meritt, Laurel, and Sam yelled, "No!"

Lisa was taking none of them seriously. She was watching Sam's eyes as they traveled from person to person,

Meritt, Martin, Laurel and herself. Sam's eyes. They always came back to Laurel, singling her out. Yes, he was looking more at Laurel. How close were they? She knew they'd spent some time together when Sam prepped Laurel for her financial reporting job.

Laurel was dressed in a slate blue blouse with billowing sleeves and asymmetric collar. It emphasized the bright blue of her vivid eyes. Her coffee-brown hair was set in tangled curls and ringlets. Lisa had always considered Laurel to be very ordinary, though she did wear clothes well; but tonight there was a sensuality, a voluptuousness in Laurel's loosened lips that had never been there before. A low, ominous alarm coursed into Lisa's veins. The serving girl came in to take away their plates. Lisa asked her to bring a bottle of Chivas.

With a tone of finality, Meritt said, "Okay, how about this: we order Andy to turn himself in, and give him a deadline. If he doesn't do what we say, we go to the authorities."

"And either way our reputations are shot," Lisa said.

"We'll have to accept that." Meritt looked around the table. "Is it agreed?" Martin glanced quickly at Lisa. With the tiniest turn of her head she indicated "no." To the others Martin and Lisa appeared to agree. "Then it's done."

They began discussing how to approach Andy Smith. Martin sat back in his chair and stopped listening. They were such fools: he'd have to protect them because they couldn't protect themselves. It was the only way he could express his gratitude for their acceptance of him.

Through a thickening fog of Chivas, Lisa observed Laurel, Meritt and Sam, the trio. The troika. The Triple Alliance. The Three Wise Guys. How effectively they'd managed to exclude her!

"We've got to approach Andy Smith cautiously," Meritt said. "We don't want to frighten him off. And remember, if we call him at home, it's likely his phone is bugged by the Trojan Horse; if we call him at the White House, that phone is automatically bugged."

"I think I should go to him," Laurel said. "He has a vague awareness of who I am because of my mother, I think."

"Use flattery as a lure," Sam suggested. "Say you're thinking of writing a biography of the Smith dynasty. He'd buy into that."

She laughed grimly. "If a biography of 'the Smith dynasty' were published, no one would read it. The only Smith of interest to the world was Andrew Smith the First, and like Howard Hughes, he's best remembered for his bizarre hermit act."

Sam flashed Laurel a ten-thousand-watt smile, a look that Lisa could not misinterpret. Something deep was going on between them! The bond between the two was utterly unmistakeable. It was time to stop deluding herself. The man she worshipped and loved was in love with another woman. He would never gentle her nights again. Consummate actress that she was, Lisa kept her face as unperturbed and serene as a sleeping infant's. The only outward manifestation of the despair roiling inside her was her knuckles, which were white from clenching her chair arms so tightly.

It was agreed that Laurel would contact Andy the next day. The business talk was over. When the table was cleared, Laurel asked Lisa, "Do we get to see your baby tonight? Winthrop, Junior?"

"What? No! You don't want to see my kid. He's boring! My God, all babies ever do is sit in their own urine."

Meritt exploded with anger. "How can you speak of your own child like that!"

"Because that's the way I feel about my offspring," Lisa responded flatly. "Unlike others in this room, I'm not a hypocrite pretending feelings I don't have." The venom in her tone poisoned the air. "You're hardly one to criticize my family relations. What about your own? The brightest, shiniest star on Broadway pretends to the world that she doesn't even have a family, as if she emerged like Venus on a half shell!"

Meritt's jaw slid out. "In all the years I've known you, my family has never once attempted to contact me."

Lisa stood up, and did a drunken little dance holding her glass of Chivas aloft. "And have you ever once attempted to contact them? No-o-o-o! Wait till the cops leak that fact to the press!"

"Rot in hell, honey."

"The same to you, girl. You want the whole world to think you're pure lily white. No one knows the reason you're dark and beautiful is because you're *black* and beautiful. You won't publicly admit that little bit of black blood that makes you look so hot 'n sexy."

"Lisa, you're drunk! Stop before you go any further," Meritt commanded.

"Yeah, I'm drunk. And Martin's a sexual deviant, but at least he knows it." Martin's head was slightly bowed. Lisa moved to stand behind Laurel. "Now here's a real degenerate! She screws a man even before she kisses him. Marries a man knowing nothing about him, except that he's a great lay."

Laurel was redfaced. What would Sam think? "I stand guilty of being retarded enough to confide in you."

"Oh, retarded! Picking up habits from that institutionalized brother you never visit." Lisa's eyes narrowed, and she leaned close to Laurel's head while Laurel sat up straight, looking ahead. "You don't like to acknowledge that you were adopted to fill in for two handicapped kids. You cringe at the fact that Carol Carole is your mother. You're a monster of *hypocrisy!*"

She screamed the word in Laurel's ear. *I have to forgive her,* Laurel told herself, *because Lisa's got nothing but money, and I have Sam.*

Lisa slowly walked behind Sam's chair. She emptied her glass and set it on the table. Her hands came down around his neck. "And Sam," she said in the softest voice, "my own little stud puppet. The Catholic so strict he even observed Forty Hours and All Souls' Day. His wife throws his test tube bastards off a roof, and all of a sudden Sam throws his faith away. Obviously you never feel anything very deep. Sam's not your ordinary asshole."

Sam's rigid expression was that of a stoic suppressing physical pain. He got out of his chair. "Lisa, calm down—"

He extended his arm, and Lisa backed away. "I saw you looking at Laurel as if she's the dessert. What's going on?" Her voice trembled with outrage.

Sam met her eyes levelly. "Nothing's going on. Laurel and I are in love. It's just that we haven't told the whole world yet. I should have let you know earlier."

"What about us?"

"What do you mean—me and you? What does that have to do with anything?"

"Get rid of her, Sam. We have to get back together. I'll divorce Winthrop, and I'll make you happier than you ever dreamed."

Sam stared at Lisa as though she'd lost her mind. There was no sense of reality to what she was saying. They'd never been "together." Sam had had no idea that their three-week affair had been enough to build such an elaborate, deep-seated fantasy. She'd taken what little attention he'd given her and turned it into a ripe, rich, legend-sized passion. She was acting as if they were the only two people in the room. He had to work around that premise. Thank God, he had no secrets from the other two women at the table.

"Lisa, you are in love with some image you've created. I couldn't possibly be the man you imagine." Lisa wasn't listening. Her eyes continued to puncture him. Weakly, Sam added, "What about this house? What about your feelings for Winthrop? Don't you love him?"

"No, I have never loved him! Haven't you ever heard of marrying for money? Now I'm going to marry for love."

"It's not like that. You're already married, with a child . . . and you have this life." Sam gestured helplessly at the opulent surroundings. "You couldn't really love me, Lisa.

You're too big a person for me. You always have been. You've always known more grandeur . . . this is the life you chose for yourself."

"No!" Lisa countered shrilly. "I took the life I got." She challenged, "You've known Laurel and me for the same stretch of time. What does Laurel have that I don't?"

Quietly Sam attempted to explain. "Our friendship grew into love. It just didn't work that way for you and me. I should have asked you for forgiveness—for leading you on. For using you. I should have explained myself fully a while ago. I did you wrong as a friend."

Lisa couldn't comprehend anything he said. She was staring into a black hole. Ever since she'd used her body to buy good grades, she'd shopped for the man who would give her social position and wealth. After she'd attained that goal, she'd found the man who was meant to redeem her. And here he was, turning her down!

She couldn't understand why Sam would prefer Laurel to her. "I'm prettier than she is, much prettier. Is it her personality that you like? Good Christ, Sam, you're supposed to marry substance! You don't throw your life away by marrying mere *personality!*"

Disbelievingly, Meritt said, "Here the entire country is on the verge of destruction and you're going on and on about yourself, Lisa! Only you could take a discussion this serious and center it on yourself."

Lisa blinked, as if she'd just realized Meritt was in the room. "Fuck your Hardy Boys detective work! FUCK THE TROJAN HORSE!" Laurel and Meritt began walking toward the door, and Lisa convulsed in a spasm of fury. "That's right, run away, you mediocre, middle-class morons! Who needs you?" Wild-eyed, she leaped at Sam and hit at his face with her fists. He caught her wrists. His expression was one of helplessness and pity. Lisa recognized the look. "How dare you treat me like this? After I took you in? Cared for you, saved you from yourself?"

Sam whispered, "Lisa, I'm so sorry. I'm so sorry for

everything." His words seemed to cover the events of the entire past decade. He released her hands, then walked out of the room.

Lisa trailed him. As he descended the stairs behind Meritt and Laurel, she leaned over the balustrade and shrieked, "I only fucked you because I felt sorry for you! You're not even good in bed!"

During the entire fight Martin had remained sitting at the table, as motionless as if he'd been nailed there. His head had been bothering him all night. Aural hallucinations rang in his ears.

Abruptly he dropped his head into his hands. Death was mocking him, he knew it. Something told him that relief would come when he vanquished "the thing" that he loved most. But he loved nothing, and he continued to suffer in silence.

• *Thirty-three* •

"Andy Smith here."

"This is Laurel Williams. Mavis Williams's daughter, remember?"

"Sure. You ran for the House once and got beat."

So much for tact. Into the phone Laurel said, "I'm a reporter for the Washington *Tribune* now, but I'm working on an independent project. A book, maybe. A book about Smitty, your father and you—the Smith dynasty."

Andy grunted. "You mean you're gonna write a book that I'm in without asking me for permission?"

"Permission isn't necessary for an unauthorized biography. If you cooperate, then it will be an authorized biography," Laurel said crisply. "I live in New York. How about I come down, whenever it's convenient, and get a few minutes with you?"

"Hmmm . . . I don't know," Andy stalled. Laurel knew he was drooling at the idea of a biography. She could almost hear the saliva dripping from his puckered mouth.

She proposed, "How about next Tuesday? In the afternoon?"

"I guess I could pencil that in." He couldn't resist.

Now came the tricky part. "If you don't mind, could we meet at your grandfather's place in Virginia?"

"That old wreck? Why?"

Laurel laid it on thick. "Since I'm writing about you and him, I'd like to get a sense of family continuity. You know, grandpa to grandson, full circle. I'd get a good start on the biography by symbolically connecting Smith One and Three. You'd be doing me a big favor, actually. Or we could meet elsewhere."

Andy hesitated, then said, "Sure, why not. I should check up on the old place more often, anyway. I'm going to hold onto it till the suburban developers are weepin' at my asking price. Do you know where the house is?"

"Oddly, I do. While I was a page in Congress some of us took an excursion there."

They agreed on a day and time to meet. Andy asked, "Have you interviewed anybody else for the book yet?" Laurel told him she'd spoken with several people. "Who are they?"

"I'll tell you on Tuesday."

Laurel didn't inform her congresswoman mother or her bosses at the *Tribune* about her quickie visit to Washington. Right off the air shuttle she rented a Plymouth TC3, and drove west.

Soon she was in Virginia, driving through crumbled

brick pillars to the weather-beaten house, which rose out of tangled thickets. In the near distance suburban houses encroached on forsaken farmland. Soon the developers' relentless march would overtake every acre.

Andy hadn't arrived yet. Laurel climbed out of the car and smelled the air, which promised rain. It was cool, and she was glad she had worn her leather bomber jacket with creamy corduroy pants tucked into ankle boots. The sky was an unearthly shade of tin grey, and was eerie with rain-filled thunderclouds. The weather could hardly be more ominous. Laurel's spine tingled with uneasiness, though she was not afraid of Andy Smith. Now that Sam loved her, she feared nothing.

Nature had taken over the house. Carrying a briefcase, Laurel stepped gingerly onto the veranda, wondering if it was safe to walk on its rotting floorboards. Her boots echoed on the wood. Apparently all the wild cats had decamped, for no felines were hanging around. The dining room was in the same condition it'd been when Oliver Remick and Andy had their talk. Wickedly fertile sycamore trees grew right into the windows where panes had been smashed by vandals.

Laurel stood in the middle of the dim room, thinking Old Smitty must have been removed from this house very shortly before the pages had discovered it. Perhaps only several months before. The cats had been there because they still expected to be fed by Smitty. Andy Smith had made his grandfather live in this haunted house, perhaps without heat or electricity, for God knew how long. The crazy wretch had once been a candidate for president. He'd shaken hands with FDR and Al Capone. And he'd spent his golden years in this house, letting cats crawl over him and befoul him.

"Miss Williams! Are you here?" Andy Smith's voice came from the doorway.

Laurel turned to meet him face to face.

"Hello, Laurel. I remember you well." Andy's round, muddy brown eyes scanned her body through the wire-rimmed circles of his glasses. "Quite the place, huh?"

Andy's hair had receded like a low tide, making him appear years older than he was. He looked no more prosperous in his synthetic brown suit. In addition to his weak chin, skinny neck and narrow, pursed mouth, he now had a big belly. "How is your mother these days? Good old Mavis."

Laurel stood motionless. She was thinking about the good old boys who'd given Andy administrative jobs after his congressional term: "Let's appoint Andy Smith; he's dumb, but the party still owes his grandpa a lot of favors."

Unnerved by Laurel's silence and her odd, probing stare, Andy laughed anxiously. He turned to look out the window, then back, and put his palms up in a supplicating gesture. "Here I am, in my grandpa's house, just like you wanted. So, ya gettin' inspired yet?"

Laurel peered out at Andy's Honda Civic, parked next to her TC3 in the deep grass. "Did anyone come with you?"

Andy chuckled. "I don't need a baby-sitter." He imitated a vaudeville leer. "I'd say you being here alone with me, you're the one who needs a baby-sitter, ha ha!"

"Who is Oliver Remick?"

Immediately a garish pink stain sprang from Andy's neck and spread to his forehead. The connection was so visible, and so dangerous to him, that it was impossible for him to hide it behind a lie. He tried. "I don't know any Oliver Remick."

"Why not? You met with a man who called himself Oliver Remick in this room in May of 1971. Don't you remember?"

Andy took an aggressive step closer to Laurel, and twisted his round face in anger. "Say, you're not working on any biography! You tricked me out here! Wait till I tell your boss at the *Tribune* about this!"

Laurel popped open the locks on her briefcase and withdrew a fat printout. She pushed it into Andy's hands. The briefcase fell with a clatter. She couldn't resist mimicking Andy's threat. "Wait till I tell your boss at the White House about this!"

He flipped through a couple of the accordion-folded pages, and the redness faded from his face till it was light yellow. His mouth worked silently. Deciding to act furious, he yelled. "What the hell is this?" He threw the printout on the floor. "What did you ask me here for? Really?" His trembling finger pointed at the paper he'd tossed on the floor. "Where did you get that from?"

"From your personal computer files at the office of internal affairs."

"Who busted into my office?"

Each question an answer. Laurel was amused by the way Andy incriminated himself while denying. "No one did. We gained entry with a computer modem in New York. Every personal computer can be accessed if it has a modem. Once we figured out your passward was 'Honeypie,' your system was ours."

"We? Who's we?"

"Remember when I told you that a group of pages came out here to look at the house? There were five of us, a whole posse. You and Remick met here in the dining room while we were upstairs. We listened, and we watched, and we witnessed everything—including your acceptance of cash. You agreed to be a stooge in a long-term terrorist plot to overthrow the American economy. That makes you a traitor."

As Laurel spoke, Andy's expression slowly collapsed in on itself like a ruined soufflé. Denial was useless. Laurel continued, "For the last ten years we tried to convince ourselves it was a hoax, but your computer files proved that a Trojan Horse does exist, and that it's ready for implementation."

Laurel shoved her hands into her jacket and began to circle around Andy. "We never could figure out which nonaligned nations were behind Remick and his organization. But we do know that the Trojan Horse handpicked you a dozen years ago to infiltrate at a level as high as your name could take you. They were right. You've slid on your last name all the way into the White House, right down into the basement. I'm sure you can create all kinds of mischief down there."

"If you really believe I'm involved in something, if you think there's a real dangerous deal going on—how come you didn't call the police?" Sweat and rapid breathing betrayed the depth of Andy's fear.

"We've discussed bringing our evidence to the Feds, but the Justice Department isn't known for swift action. Who knows when they'd come across with the first conspiracy indictment? We're afraid that by the time they'd finally move in on you and the other Trojan Horse kingpins, the plan will already have been set in motion."

"Why are you telling me this? What do you want?"

"Abort the entire plan. Sabotage it. Or we'll turn you in."

His eyebrows shot up and his voice went high with panic. "Abort the Trojan Horse! Do you realize the number of years and the incredible effort expended to build it! The Trojan Horse plan has taken ten times more preparation than the entire Allied invasion of Europe in World War Two!" He was admitting his participation! Laurel's pulse quickened at her success. "The plan is so beautiful that it's nearly a work of art." Andy started to break into tears. "And five pages want to stop it. *Kids*." His lower lip trembled, and he slipped into his bully guise. "Liquidating you would be no trouble, you know."

"Liquidate me and all the other pages from 1971? You know damn well if anything happens to me, you'll be exposed. I'm offering you a way to get out of trouble. You don't want to get rid of me." Andy looked away, and Laurel could tell he was considering her words. She added a threat. "Besides, I've got good reason to believe your life is in danger. We've got a couple of people who are high on the idea of wiping you out. Abort the Trojan Horse, and I'll protect you."

"Protect me? You dumb bitch hog, do you think my life is gonna be safe if I double-cross the Trojan Horse people?" Irrationally he shifted his attack. "Why are you so self-righteous? You're a fine one to talk about getting by on a name. You did the same thing when you ran for a House seat."

"I've had my showdown with the family name. Now it's time for yours. And if you want to protect your family honor, you'll stop the Trojan Horse in its tracks."

Andy pushed up his glasses and brushed away some tears with his knuckles. He sighed, then began to confess. "You could say Oliver Remick is the chief executive officer of the Trojan Horse. As his man in the White House, I'm entrusted with the general lists of extortion victims. They're at pressure points in the U.S. economy. There are about fifty of us at the top, but few possess files quite this detailed." Andy indicated the printouts. He sounded deeply proud that he'd been trusted with top secret information. "The individual names of people to be blackmailed have been parceled out in small numbers, so if one of us got caught and searched, the FBI or whoever wouldn't be able to draw any significant conclusions."

Tears clouded Andy's speech and he pleadingly asked Laurel, "Can't you see why I wanted to get in on something big? All my life I've wanted to be top dog at somethin' . . . but I could never live up to my grandpa—or my dad. People called Dad a saint. I've always wanted to be important. Do you blame me for switching to the other side, where I was needed? Where I'd be important?" Andy lurched toward a chair as if it could serve as a substitute for the foundations that had just been blasted out from under him.

Laurel leaned against a wall and commanded, "Tell me all about 'the other side,' Andy. Who's behind the Trojan Horse?"

In a voice punctuated with sobs, sighs, and gasps, he told her that the Trojan Horse Project had been devised in the late sixties by a number of nationalistic fanatics whose countries were members of the Nonaligned Movement. These men and women hated the United States, for its wealth, the CIA, its support of Israel, its nuclear weaponry, its purported imperialism. Specifically, they were from

Libya, Colombia, Argentina, El Salvador, Nicaragua, Paraguay, Angola, and Namibia. Totally without their countries' knowledge, they used their treasuries' funds to construct the Trojan Horse. They were acting on their own without sanction from their governments.

Oliver Remick was one of five key architects. His forebears hailed from a remote corner of Yemen, in the Middle East. They moved a continent away to Guyana, where Remick was born and had been given a Moslem name. He wanted to be the first member of the family to earn a college degree, and he enrolled at the University of Mali, on the African continent. After taking another degree, in diplomacy and protocol at Georgetown University, Remick Americanized his name and took a position in Mali's foreign affairs department. His brother had attended the University of Michigan, where he became acquainted with Andrew Smith III. It was Mohammed who had suggested Andy would be perfect as a lieutenant for Oliver Remick.

It had been relatively easy to find pigeons in decision-making nerve points of the American economy. Some of the citizens in key positions in the plan were recruited with simple bribery. Those who didn't succumb to the classic lure of money were pressured with blackmail. If those two methods failed, then they were seduced into an illegal incident the group threatened to reveal.

Laurel drawled, "I'm curious about Oliver Remick, the mystery man. Where does he live?"

"In hotels." Andy shuddered. "He carries a stiletto knife on him at all times."

"It won't do him much good once you ruin his scheme." As she'd taken in Andy's explanation, Laurel became certain that never, during the past ten years, had Andy considered interfering with the foreigners' Trojan Horse. Her voice went hard as nails. "How do you plan to stop the Trojan Horse?"

"I don't know, I don't know!"

"Does Oliver Remick have a data base?"

"Yuh-yes. The comprehensive strategy is kept on his system."

"That's the weak underbelly of the Trojan Horse!" Laurel crowed triumphantly. "Give me the access codes and we'll wreck it."

"Omigod. I'm gonna be killed. I'm gonna die." Andy took out his notepad and tearfully wrote down the information. "Like I said, I don't know where he lives, but this computer's in Houston." Laurel memorized the bit of paper before tucking it in her jacket. He repeated, "Omigod. The crucial files will disappear. All those years of work, all that money, down the drain."

"So what." Laurel picked up the briefcase and files. "The original Trojan Horse took a lot of work, too, and it was turned into firewood."

"You've got to give me time to work out an escape plan!"

"Don't worry. The Trojan Horse jerks won't know it was you who let us into Oliver Remick's computer."

"Yes, they will. They know everything. These are dangerous people. They're the most sophisticated terrorists on the planet. They're going to come gunning for me *and you* once they learn what I've done."

"If you let any of your partners in crime learn my name, you'll have another reason to live in fear." What an empty threat, Laurel said to herself. She had to phone the news to Sam as soon as she could, so he could invade that computer system in Houston. *Then* the Trojan Horse people could kill her.

Andy's plump hand slapped over his mouth, and he cried to himself, "My God, I can't run away now. There's that big Leukemia Society Gala next month. I have to be there —my wife helped organize it!"

Laurel had just about been ready to walk out, but she froze. "Are you talking about the benefit at Kennedy Center? Where's there's going to be a presidential command performance of *The Importance of Being Earnest?*"

Andy nodded, then said, "Wait until that's over, then I'll pull a Robert Vesco and go into exile."

"What'll happen to your wife?"

"Nothing. Who'd think the chief do-gooder of the Leukemia Society was involved in this? From the way she acts, you'd think it was her dad who died of leukemia, not mine." A certain strength came into Andy's face. "Listen . . . go ahead and tap into the mainframe in Houston. Just give me time . . . I wanna keep my White House files till I've got an escape plan. As long as I have a file titled 'Trojan Horse,' the nonaligned nations people won't get wise. They won't have to know that I'll be erasing it each day, bit by bit."

At the doorway she said, "Why don't you just be a man and face up to what's happening? If I were you, I'd turn myself into the FBI, and have them make you a new identity."

"They'd send me up the river."

"No. Talk to them. If you can prove that you saved this country from a disaster it didn't even know about . . . you might wind up as the biggest hero of the Smith family."

• *Thirty-four* •

Meritt called around looking for Martin Vanderziel the following week. She reached him at the New York office of the Vanderziel Foundation. "Martin, it's all over. The main data base for the Trojan Horse project has been destroyed." After a silence, she asked, "Martin, do you hear me?"

"What's this about, Meritt?"

"It means if you have any bedrock-crazy plans about killing Andy Smith, can them. It's all over."

"All right." His voice sounded blurred. Meritt made a face as she hung up the phone in her Roosevelt Island apartment, wondering if she'd gotten through to him.

Martin replaced the phone and looked up at Lisa, who'd arrived to take him to lunch. She was sitting on the edge of his desk, wearing a white suit and matching sailor hat. "That was Meritt," Martin intoned. "She says the Trojan Horse lists are gone."

"So what," Lisa said in a bored voice. "The conspiracy may be over, but the human element remains." She began rummaging through her purse, looking for the tiny amber bottle holding her pharmaceutical-quality cocaine. "As long as Andy Smith is running around, he can denounce Laurel." She snapped her finger, "That means he can finger us."

By April Laurel and Sam knew they wanted to get married. The first time each had married someone who seemed perfect. This time around each was marrying someone whose faults and foibles were known and understood. It was almost as though they were attracted as much by each other's battle scars as by strengths.

Laurel wanted to tell Lisa about the impending marriage and break it to her gently, but Lisa wouldn't accept Laurel's calls. Lisa's resentment scared Laurel, because she felt hate was just as passionate an emotion as love, if not more so. She wished to God Lisa would hurry up and grow indifferent to Sam.

That's why she was amazed when Lisa called her. "Laurel, you're going to Washington for the command performance of *The Importance of Being Earnest*, aren't you?" It was formally known as the Presidential Command Performance for the Benefit of the Leukemia Society.

"You bet. I wouldn't miss Meritt's appearance at a Reagan ritual! Sam and I both are going."

"So are Martin and I. Would you like to fly down with us in the jet I've leased?" Laurel was so eager to make up with Lisa that she accepted the offer. Then Lisa said, "You realize that Andy Smith and his wife are going to be social lions there that night. The Leukemia Society is Ann's big thing. Their participation is the way they can pretend they're high society."

Laurel couldn't resist saying, "You'd know all about that, wouldn't you?" She added seriously, "It's been a couple weeks since Sam sabotaged the Trojan Horse computers, and no one's gone gunning for Andy. His fears were unfounded."

"No one's gone gunning for him *yet*." At her end of the line Lisa smiled. She was offering transportation to people she despised, to guarantee their presence at the assassination of Andy Smith, a man who had the power to end the world Lisa had strived for so long.

Inside the bathroom stall, Martin slammed his head against the wall tiles. There was a fire in his head, with flames that blazed around his brain, inside his skull. Two centimeters above Martin's internal carotid artery, an occiptial artery was swelling. A tiny bubble had began to form on the arterial wall.

His body was going crazy, as if he were a robot that had short-circuited. All of the anatomical protective devices were working at once. Tears leaked from his eyes, and mucus formed high in his throat. Thin liquid dripped from his nostrils, and his ears rang. His arms and legs twitched as if strung to a marionette's jiggled wires. He knew that this pain had its origins somewhere in Southeast Asia, and he felt himself returning to the jungle. Drops of sweat rolled down his face as if here in the humidity of a rain forest.

The violence to his head allowed Martin to calm himself slightly, and he sank onto the toilet stool like a rag doll, his Savile Row suit crumpling around him. The half-baked scenario he and Lisa had concocted for Andy Smith's death rotated in his mind like numbers on a roulette wheel. His head rolled back and forth against the wall. He mouthed the words, "Lisa's crazy. She's crazier than I am." This was the first moral judgment Martin had made in years, and it frightened him more than the pain.

As Laurel walked to the dress circle, her heather pleated georgette dress swayed fluidly around her slender hips. Behind her, Sam was still chuckling about the people who'd descended on them outside, thinking they were important because they'd climbed out of a stretch limousine. Lisa had arranged for the car to pick them up at the jetstrip.

President Reagan had had to cancel at the last minute because he needed a gall bladder operation. Since his wife also declined, there were no Secret Service members talking into lapel microphones and packing submachine guns in their specially tailored suits and no metal detectors.

Some of Reagan's Hollywood cronies, such as Claudette Colbert and Bob Hope, were expected to attend. When Sam and Laurel reached their row Sam exclaimed, "Look over there, it's Moses."

Laurel turned around to see Charlton Heston, the star of *The Ten Commandments* and *Ben Hur*. As Sam and she scooted past several people to take their seats, she remarked, "There's one actor who's trusty, brave, clean, and *reverent*." She glanced toward the back of the theater, where Martin and Lisa sat in a box in the first tier above the crowd. "What did you think of Martin on the flight down?"

"He looks like he should check into a hospital. Let's talk to him about it."

Laurel shifted in her chair. Even before they'd left New York, she'd been agitated for no reason. She was getting more uneasy by the moment. She said, "There's something not quite right in this place."

"Yeah, there *is* something weird going on. I'm no Nostradamus, but I can feel it coming in the air."

Laurel opened her program for the gala. "Oh-oh. Look at this." She pointed to the blurb in the program notes. Under the title "Closing Remarks," a note said: *President Reagan has asked Andrew Smith III of the Internal Affairs Department to speak in his stead. Mr. Smith and Mrs. Ann Smith serve on the board of the Leukemia Society.*

Sam's mouth compressed. "If there'd be any time to bump off Andy, tonight would be perfect. Without the Reagans, they'll have called off the Secret Service. A huge crowd can trample over the evidence. When Andy makes his speech he'll be a sitting duck."

"How far has he progressed on cleaning out his Trojan Horse files?"

"I haven't looked for the past couple of days," Sam admitted. "Do you think Lisa and Martin are still hot on the idea of taking out Andy themselves?"

"Who knows, Sam? They're both missing a few dots off their dice." The theater's warning bells sounded, urging the audience to their seats. Laurel's natural instinct was acting as surveillance radar, feeling out danger in the auditorium. "What if a Trojan Horse assassin were coming for *us* tonight? All five of the former pages are here in the town where we all met originally. The situation is weird, and worrisome."

"Would you like to go?" Sam asked her solicitously. "I'd say we've got good cause to leave."

Laurel was frozen with indecision. Finally she made her tongue move. "What if I'm just antsy, imagining things that don't exist? Meritt would be angry if she knew we hadn't hung around for the performance." She shook her head.

The opera house's dramatic blossoming chandelier—a gift of Austria—started to dim. Lisa put her head down and tooted a line of cocaine from a purse-size mirror. When all the powder was inhaled, she held up the mirror for a last glimpse of herself before darkness overtook the theater. Her heavy drug use had no effect on her face. The skin was still so flawless and unlined that she never wore foundation.

The pink hue on her cheeks was always there, lustrous and pearlescent. Lisa's blue eyes sparkled with vivacity, not drugs. No wonder she'd won an important man like Winthrop Wharton—she was outstandingly beautiful!

She had to come up with a revenge against Sam, some form of outrage that would pay him back for dumping her and nearly ruining her life. When vengeance was hers, she'd be able to focus again on being a rich man's wife. Before too long, maybe she could go to Europe and visit Gerthe.

Reluctantly she put away the mirror, and the heavy bugle beads on her black silk dress rattled against each other. Martin opened the door behind her and took his seat. She snarled, "What have *you* been doing, tricking in the john?" The cocaine had released her inhibitions, and she was suddenly bitchy. "You look terrible. You look like something from a can that's stamped 'use before December 1981.'"

As he looked at her balefully, Martin's ice-blue eyes were like a timber wolf's, primitive and animated. The rest of his face was inert, full of death. "I want to die," he intoned.

Lisa placed a hand on his knee. "Don't be dramatic, Martin. Relax. Lighten up and enjoy the play. After tonight, all of our Trojan Horse problems will be gone."

As the room went dark, the hum of the crowd lifted like a sheet in the wind, then died. After the briefest silence the orchestra began the overture, and Laurel's vision adjusted to the dim. The gleam on the orchestra's brass instruments was like the shine of gun metal to her. As she scanned the sides of the auditorium, covered with deep red fabric, she took notice of the curtains around each box seat. There could be a rifle barrel sticking out of every fold of cloth. She could clearly see that Lisa and Martin made a handsome couple sitting attentively in their box.

The vast curtain lifted slowly from the stage, pouring gold light over the first rows of the applauding crowd. Like an overcurious child, Laurel turned fully in her seat to look at the back of the theater, as if expecting to spot a firearm aimed from the recesses of the audience. The actors onstage were talking, but she was only dimly aware of their voices because her ears were straining to hear the distinctive cock of a rifle. She couldn't help her paranoia. Determinedly she turned around and focused on the stage and the sumptuously Victorian drawing room that had been created up on it.

Emerging like a goddess from stage left, Meritt took command of the audience. She was a vision. Her elaborate costume was made of iridescent apricot-and-ivory watered silk, with a huge bustle bunched in the back and a tight bodice. The costume designers had thrown historical accuracy to the winds and scooped out the Victorian bodice to exhibit Meritt's fabulous, satiny cleavage. They'd also tamed her hair and pinned to it a huge hat laden with a stuffed parrot and ostrich plumes. It weighed twenty pounds and it limited Meritt's vision as effectively as a horse's blinders.

Martin studied Meritt, sauntering across the stage Mae West-style, checking out the men right under Lady Bracknell's nose. She was magnificent as Gwendolyn Fairfax, and she'd been magnificent as a struggling actress. He'd never known anyone who'd worked so hard and suffered so many indignities. Once when she'd been low on money, she'd even considered accepting a gig as a mud wrestler. A peculiar pride made its way through his pained mind and rose in him, an emotion akin to love.

Out of his suit jacket he drew an automatic pistol, a custom-modified Smith and Wesson M39. The black Teflon finish was smooth in his hand. He took a silencer out of his pocket and screwed it on over the barrel. Lisa didn't look to see what he was doing, but kept watching the show. Soon he'd take care of Andy. Once they got him, their problems would all be over.

Martin cocked a round into the gun's chamber. He looked over the crowd, and spotted the back of Sam's and Laurel's heads. The nicest people he'd ever known. Martin had never classified *himself* as people, exactly. He was a

Vanderziel slime, oozing his own special evil. Yet Sam and
Laurel had accepted him. He felt no pressure, no guilt
around them. They'd always given him the kind of acceptance his own siblings refused to give him.

He turned his head to the right, to look at Lisa. Blood
was rushing through his occipital artery, straining the weak
point on its muscle tissue. Martin thought of the times he'd
seen Lisa over all the years. Since he'd returned from
Vietnam she'd treated him as a human being. She'd been
the only person who wanted him around. She'd given him
thousands of times more consideration and attention than
his family ever had, more than any of his many lovers.
Lisa had been the only person who had *needed* him, ever.
The realization that he loved her came out and smote him
like a sword. His nausea became unbearable.

Martin spoke without lowering his voice. "I love you,
Lisa."

"Pipe down!" Lisa commanded, annoyed. In a whisper
she added, "Why are you telling me this? Are you trying to
be funny?"

He heard Dr. Ping Chung speak to him, with the heavy
accent, softly and clearly. In a hollow, mechanical voice,
Martin said, "You are the thing that I love the most."

Lisa responded with her practiced boarding school
laugh. "Martin, what in hell *are* you going on about?"

Wetness erupted from Martin's eyes as he gazed upon
her. His tears, which reflected the stage lights, were a terri-
fying sight. An incoherent rumble issued from his throat as
he raised his right hand, which clutched the small gun.
Slowly he rose, to assume a solid shooting stance. Lisa
exposed her velvety white neck as she looked up at him.
Her cocky, derisive smile showed how she trusted him. She
would never believe her pet could turn on her.

Music filled the auditorium as the orchestra played the
prologue for one of the show's numbers. Martin used his
left hand to steady the weapon, and his left forefinger

curled over the trigger guard. Before Lisa could realize what he was doing, he pressed the silencer against her left temple and squeezed the trigger.

No one heard, not even the man in the adjoining box. He was too absorbed to hear much. He was there to fulfill a contract, the only thing that mattered.

The man was a seasoned killer, an expert at the art of death. He came from Cambodia. When the Khmer Rouge Communists took over Phnom Penh in 1975, he'd executed hundreds of countrymen, using every method of killing imaginable; then he'd emigrated to the United States, masquerading as a naive refugee. Schooled in murder, he'd become a free-lance hit man. His pose as a humble, displaced alien was a perfect cover for his deadly work.

With professional patience he sat stiffly in a chair, waiting for the play to come to an end. His employers wanted the job done at a public place, so their revenge would be a particularly splashy one. His rifle was the Mauser .458 Winchester Magnum, sneaked in inside a cello case. A fat silencer covered the end of the barrel. The gun was usually employed by park rangers to kill rogue grizzly bears.

The organization that hired him said his target was their double agent working in the White House. Using his personal access code for the organization's main computer system, Andy Smith had destroyed a project that had taken over a decade to construct. His betrayal was revealed when the steady erasure of the confidential project information on his personal computer was noted. The organization's crucial White House player had chosen, in the end, to protect his country. The traitor had turned patriot.

The details mattered little to the Cambodian. When he accepted a contract, he did the job, efficiently and flawlessly.

* * *

The Presidential Command Performance had gone off without a hitch, and the applause was like a vast roll of thunder. As the cast took their bows, Laurel spotted Andy standing in the wings, the wire-rimmed glasses and round face distinctive. He wore a tuxedo whose sleeves and trousers were too short. Suddenly he tripped onto the stage, and raised his hand for silence. The audience's applause died quickly, indicating their confusion about his abrupt appearance. His face was as waxy as an embalmed corpse's. Sweat rolled from his forehead into his beady eyes. The *Ernest* actors looked at each other in puzzlement, and quickly exited, leaving Andy alone.

Trembling with a fear greater than stage fright, Andy began, "The President asked me to speak in his stead. He knows that the Leukemia Society is a cause that is near and dear to my heart, and also near and dear to my heart's heart, my wife Ann. The disease cut down my father in his youth, and we all know who *his* father was, ha ha . . ."

He rambled pointlessly. The audience shifted uncomfortably, whispering to each other. Blinking and twitching, he went on, "It is a great honor indeed for the Leukemia Society to bring a Broadway musical to our splendid Kennedy Center . . ."

There was something vaguely sacrificial about his determination to stay on that stage. By agreeing to join the Trojan Horse plot, he'd thrown himself among the lions, and now he stood exposed to their vengeance.

Again Laurel felt the compulsion to scan the theater. She glanced behind her at Martin and Lisa's box. It was empty. As she started to turn back to say something to Sam, the edge of her vision caught a glimpse of a marksman in the adjacent box, dead center, in a can't-miss position where he could fire down on anyone in the theater. She could see nothing more of him than a black silhouette, and the black line of his gun. Then he took aim at the stage. Laurel shot to her feet and yelled as loudly as she could, "Andy Smith, DUCK!"

He froze in a gawky position, his mouth agape. Again

Laurel screamed, "Duck!" In the moment between stillness and sound, there was a high-pitched whine of a shot muted by a silencer. Panic-stricken, the audience of twenty-three hundred stood up, swaying like the tentacles of a sea anemone, then fled in different directions, some to the exits, some diving under the seats.

Disbelief kept Laurel and Sam in their seats, watching Andy slowly crumple to the floor. Then, shocked into action, Sam vaulted out of his seat and sped for the stage. Simultaneously Laurel barrelled toward the back of the theater. The house lights finally went on.

She flew up a ramp leading to the boxes. The passage was choked with stampeding people, and as Laurel fought against them she heard her dress rip. The assassin's box, dead center middle opposite the stage, was abandoned. She couldn't think about the killer now. Next to it was Lisa and Martin's box. She flung open the door to see if they were all right.

The first thing she saw was Lisa's body stretched out on the floor. Blood congealed at the site of the bullet hole in her temple. Holy God. There was a pool of blood under her neck. She was dead! Martin sat limply in a chair, and his hands dangled in his lap. Sweat dripped from the ends of his white hair. His face was covered with the wetness of his tears.

"Oh, Martin," Laurel said helplessly. She knelt on the floor next to his discarded handgun, and looked up at him. His countenance had always been under the shadow of death. He gripped her forearms with heavy pressure, as if to maximize the human contact. "I never deserved to live, Laurel. Never. Never." A rivulet of blood seeped out his nostril.

"Don't say that."

The weak spot on Martin's occipital artery was bulging with his life's blood. His head lolled back on the chair rest. "I've gotten what I wanted. I'm not dying alone. That was my only fear, when that Chinese doctor was messing with my mind. I was afraid I was going to die in that jungle."

His eyes rolled back in his head, showing the whites of

his eyes. He was slipping away. "No one deserves to die alone," he said.

Inside his cranium the muscle fibers tried to hold against the pressure of the blood, till they were stretched to the membrane thinness of exactly one cell. The arterial wall held a second, then burst apart violently, shooting blood through Martin's cerebellum, filling the subdural space between the skull and the brain. His legs stiffened like broomsticks, and his head flew forward as if kicked. He sagged heavily in the chair, a dead animal.

An hour later a janitor let Meritt, Laurel and Sam into the Washington office of Forster, Dunn. Meritt's stage makeup still covered her face, and Laurel's ripped bodice hung open, exposing her midriff. As Sam logged into an IBM computer, Meritt and Laurel leaned over him, peering as intently into the monitor as if it were an oracle.

Sam's fingers flew as he logged onto the White House databank. "We won't be able to break in like this much longer, I bet. They've got to lock a tighter security system on this, and soon."

The subsystem of the Office of Internal Affairs rolled into view, then the files for Andy Smith, Assistant Director to Director of the Office of Internal Affairs. There were only four lists under his logon.

"The heading for 'Trojan Horse Lists' is gone," Meritt said in a tone of wonder as she stared into the screen. "He must have finally found a place to hide away."

"I wonder where he planned to go," Laurel said.

"Maybe he planned to be a hermit, somewhere, like his grandfather." Sam suggested. "He never had the chance to escape. I don't think he ever could."

• *Thirty-Five* •

It was morning on Roosevelt Island. Meritt switched the little TV in her apartment to "Star Trek," so she'd have friendly background noise for the task at hand. The table before her was covered with newspaper and magazine clippings about the assassination of Andy Smith. She'd been keeping a private file of all the media stories ever since her eventful Kennedy Center performance of *The Importance of Being Earnest*, back in May. It was now August and her apartment lease was up. Because she was thinking of moving, Meritt was throwing out household nonessentials. The task included a sifting through the clippings, trying to see if there were any she wanted to keep.

While the public murder of the Reagan administration official was not considered to be a major assassination or even a political one, its mystery titillated the public. Who had shot Andy Smith, and why would anyone want to?

For Meritt, Sam and Laurel there was no doubt that the Trojan Horse perpetrators had had Andy bumped off. Yet to come forward and accuse some phantom Trojan Horse was to offer themselves up as fruity conspiracy paranoids. Since there was no strong evidence, only the wackiest mole at the CIA would take seriously the concept of a group of renegade nonaligned nations who thought they could tip over the United States. Sam's printouts of Andy's file could be fake.

Meritt decided that if ever an investigative historian came forth with solid proof of the conspiracy, she would be glad to tell her story. But until that day, she—and Laurel and Sam—would let the sleeping dogs lie. If the Trojan Horse knew of them, they would have been killed before Andy. As things stood, they were safe.

Since she wasn't really listening to "Star Trek," she turned off the TV. Absentmindedly she rubbed her jaw as her gaze roamed onto a copy of the New York *Post,* published a month ago. DIPLOMAT DEAD IN SUBWAY PLUNGE was the headline on the tabloid newspaper. There was an arrowed photograph on the front page, with the standard segmented arrow arcing off a subway platform down to the rails. A photo of Oliver Remick's elegant face sat aside it. Last month Oliver Remick, a representative to the United Nations, had fallen off the subway platform under an oncoming train during rush hour, when the surging crowds had "accidentally jostled Remick too strongly." "If the train hadn't gotten him, the third rail would've fried him" was the comment of a subway conductor on the scene. The article mentioned that Remick had no family or permanent address, and his current profession was given as "international business executive."

Laurel had called Meritt when she first saw the headline. "Remick didn't fall; he was pushed," she said.

"It might have taken his Trojan Horse collaborators these three months after Andy's assassination to pin blame on Remick," Meritt speculated. Because Andy was Remick's protégé, Oliver Remick was ultimately responsible for screwing up their plans.

The following day Meritt had gone to the United Nations, where she confirmed that Mali, the large African country bordering Algeria, had dropped out of the General Assembly ten years ago. Its last ambassador had been the mysterious Oliver Remick. Mali currently had embassies in neither New York nor Washington. It was almost as if the country had dropped off the face of the earth, along with Remick.

The newspaper crumpled as Meritt's hands made fists around it. She started sliding all the clippings off the table into a wastebasket. The past was over, and she should think about more crucial matters, such as deciding where to live next, and the dental appointment she had scheduled at noon.

Meritt left her dentist's office on Central Park South and began walking eastward, happy that she could hardly feel the tiny bit of Novocaine left in her gums. The day was warm and welcoming, almost beautifully bright, with skies a stainless periwinkle blue. Across the street the sunlight danced over the deep emerald green of Central Park's trees.

It was a flawless, fresh-smelling day like today that kept her swearing she'd never move to the West Coast. She loved New York too much, partly because, as Frank Sinatra sang on every jukebox in town, she'd *made it* there." However, the juicy movie roles she was considering just about required her to head west.

In a preoccupied fog, Meritt walked squarely into the back of a young man waiting for the light at Central Park South and Seventh Avenue. "Oh, I'm terribly sorry!" Meritt said. She'd nearly knocked the poor guy over. "No problem," he replied. From the corner of her eye she saw he had his hands jammed into khaki army shorts, which he wore with an overwashed teal polo shirt. They proceeded to cross the street side by side.

In the middle of the next block a reptilian, crazy-eyed scag leaped in front of Meritt. "I know you! I know you!" he jabbered. Meritt tried to ignore him but he walked at her side burbling that they'd grown up together, that he was friends with her brother, but he couldn't recall her name.

The man Meritt had bumped into stopped suddenly and laid his hand heavily on the drunkard. "Just what exactly makes you think you know my wife?"

Meritt's admirer halted, and his tongue worked silently in his mouth as he peered up at her rescuer. "Sweetheart, do you know this guy?" the young man asked in a resigned voice. From the corner of her eyes she caught the impression of his well-formed face and ash-blond hair.

"Honey, I have never seen him before in my life."

The white knight then curled his arm around her and they walked on, leaving Meritt's suitor standing dumbfounded.

The fit of her "husband's" arm around Meritt's waist was smooth and perfect. After a minute she allowed her gaze to slide up at him. It was her turn to halt and stand flabbergasted. "You're Christopher Colacello!"

For the first time he looked upon her. "Meritt du Nord!"

"You know who I am?"

"Hey, you're my new idol. I've seen you in *The Importance of Being Earnest*. Four times."

She couldn't believe he'd paid to see her. Four times! "Then why didn't you come backstage to meet me?"

"I asked your agent, Carrie Enright, to introduce us, but she said you weren't particularly interested. You know she used to be my agent before I moved to the West Coast."

Meritt made a noise that meant she was exasperated at herself. "When Carrie asked if I wanted to meet you, I said no because I was too intimidated! I didn't want to trouble you, and I was afraid you were a snob."

"Not at all." With his arm steering her waist, they nimbly took a left onto Broadway. "How long are you going to stay in the play?"

"A couple more weeks. I have movie commitments after that." Meritt burst into tense giggles at the excitement of being with him. "I can't believe it's you! I'm worse than any teenager—I think I've even told my friends that you're 'dreamy'! I've been your most immature, zealous fan."

"Don't say that—your most devoted fanatics turn against you when they learn that, in reality, you're nothing like the god they've imagined you to be."

Colacello didn't have the in-person impact she had expected. His lack of star quality was refreshing. She thought, *There is a lot about him that I like.* "I told everyone you should have won the best acting Oscar last spring."

"When I watched you on stage I thought you were the hottest thing I've ever laid eyes on." As if hit by a bolt of inspiration, Colacello said, "What are you doing right now? I mean, could we go to some restaurant to discuss this mutual idolatry?"

Inside a dark, cool, anonymous little restaurant, Meritt and Colacello at first kept their chat safely neutral, discussing the acting business. Quickly the talk became intimate.

"Would you ever consider being a product spokesperson?" Colacello asked. "You know, making TV commercials? My friends think I'm insane for turning down endorsements, and missing out on all that money."

"I used to make commercials," she said, "but now that I've got a bit of a name, I can't flatly tell people that one ketchup is better than another. That's putting my trust on the line!"

"How about if you're a has-been at forty and the ketchup company offers you a million dollars for two hours' work?"

Meritt pondered the question. "Maybe. But let's put it this way—commercials have never enhanced anyone's career. For example, I can't take Orson Welles seriously as an artist because he's a shill for Perrier and wine companies."

"Oh, no, Meritt. There's nothing Orson Welles could do to diminish the genius of *Citizen Kane*." Unconsciously Colacello placed a hand over hers. His thick black eyelashes gave his full, smoky-blue eyes darkness and mystery and melancholy. "Do you remember the scene where Kane's elderly business manager reminisces about seeing the girl in the white dress on the Jersey ferry? He says, 'She didn't see me at all, but I'll bet not a month has gone by since that I haven't thought of that girl.'"

Meritt's heart started to beat a little faster. Christopher's voice rasped as he added, "And that's how I've thought of you, ever since I saw you on stage. The girl I could never forget."

There was a poignant shift in moods as they looked into one another's eyes. "Did you *really* think of me that way? Did you really?" Meritt asked helplessly. "How can I possibly live up to that image?"

Christopher regarded Meritt with the tenderest smile. She was not a woman who would disappoint.

Across town, in line at the Little Apple Supermarket, Laurel's eyes were caught by the screaming headline on the supermarket tabloid: BILLIONAIRE BOY'S LAST WORDS TO CAROL CAROLE'S DAUGHTER—EXCLUSIVE!" The lady in front of her grabbed a *TV Guide*, then reached for the tabloid. Making a resigned face, Laurel added a copy to her purchase of oranges and a chicken.

When she returned to Sam's apartment, she put the groceries away and read the "exclusive." The story had her claiming that Martin confessed: "I'm dying of a brain tumor, Laurel. I knew that Lisa couldn't get along without me, so I had to take her with me. We've been secret lovers for ten years!" The rest of the piece worked to justify the statement.

To the empty room she muttered, "I can't believe they're still dragging this one out!" Wasn't Prince Charles's honeymoon sufficient scandal for these rags?

She laid the tabloid down on the living room floor. It was the tenth lurid article she'd found detailing Martin Vanderziel's deathbed confession to Carol Carole's daughter. To the yellow press, she had no other identity. These papers could get away with the horrid lie, because they knew Laurel didn't have enough money to sue, and besides, how could she prove them wrong?

Laurel had never revealed Martin's last words, since they were inexplicable, pathetic, and private; but her status as sole witness to his death had made her infamous. Suddenly, Laurel's checkered past had become hot news once again. Sam and she had postponed marriage because they didn't want the inevitable publicity that would accompany it. They were skittish about adding even one more paragraph of hype to their names.

The lurid deaths of Martin and Lisa, occurring at the same time and place as Andy Smith's, had turned that night at Kennedy Center into a seamy bedlam that delighted gossips everywhere. Homicide detectives and coroners were baffled by the death of industrialist T. Wayne Vanderziel's ex-POW son, and his motiveless murder of Lisa Dunning Wharton, the gorgeous young wife of industrialist Winthrop Wharton. It hadn't been the standard tragic murder-suicide, because Martin had died of natural causes. Had Lisa's murder, or the reason for it, been so traumatic that the pressure had actually popped Martin's brain?

It was a mystery that upset Laurel, Sam, and Meritt because it involved them, and they wanted it solved. It was strange and so sad to suddenly have both of them gone. Laurel was positive the trouble had originated during the brief period Martin had been a POW. He had never been an upright ideal of manhood exactly, but something he'd encountered in Vietnam had turned him into a fetid zombie straight out of a Stephen King novel.

Laurel stopped staring at the carpet, and looked up to see that the sky was red with sunset over the city. She wondered what she could find out about American POWs if she went to Vietnam. Of course, it was a Communist country now, but she'd read that tourists were welcome. Tourists, not investigative reporters.

That was a problem for another time. Sam's key was in the front door. He slammed it shut behind him, yelling, "Hello, honey!" Smiling, Laurel stood, pushing back her dark brown hair. Sam walked toward her with purposive energy, dropping his briefcase on the floor. In one broad swooping motion he gathered Laurel into his arms, and kissed her passionately. He nibbled at the tip of her nose, then said, "What's got you looking so preoccupied?"

"Martin and Lisa. I'm thinking about writing a book about them. It wouldn't focus on their deaths—that would be the ending. I'd depict Martin as the poor little rich boy turned pathetic psychopath . . . and Lisa would be the gold digger so spoiled she brought on her own destruction."

"If you wrote it the right way, I think Lisa's and Martin's

stories would make a bestseller," Sam said. "The American public has an intense interest in how the rich and famous live, and especially in how they die."

"It'll be tough. I'm going to have to track down a lot of people. Like that hustler Martin befriended, and those debauched, sick, rich kids Lisa hung out with." The pensive cloudiness left her eyes as she looked sharply at Sam. "Would you be willing to tell about your time with Lisa?"

"Only if my story is handled with the utmost taste."

"It will be, believe me!" Laurel kissed Sam quickly.

"But before you get too much further into that project, there's another matter I'd like to get out of the way . . . marriage."

Laurel asked wistfully, "Can we have a big ceremony?"

"Let's make it big and ostentatious. Invite all the scandal rags."

"I'll check the *National Examiner* to see if we passed our blood tests." Laurel squeezed Sam closer and began a feathery rain of kisses along his hairline and temple. Then his lips were in her hair, and on her cheeks, a murmur of kisses. Laurel said his name, hardly conscious of doing so.

Effortlessly Sam picked up Laurel in his arms, and carried her into the bedroom, where his futon mattress now rested on a laminated bed platform. The room was filled with the strange, dreamy light of sunset. He pulled the white T-shirt off over her head and undid her jeans. Without taking his green eyes off Laurel, he dropped each piece of his banker's suit on the floor.

They knelt together on the bed and embraced. Her breasts were warm where they flattened against his scratchy chest hair. With her lips against Sam's strong, clean-smelling neck, Laurel whispered, "I'll settle for a little wedding."

"It'll be big no matter what," Sam declared, "because you'll be there with me."

319